# A Hero of Our Time

MIHAIL YURIEVICH LERMONTOV was born in Moscow in 1814. At sixteen he entered the University of Moscow but two years later switched to the School of Cavalry Cadets in St. Petersburg, and in 1834 received a commission in the Hussars of the Guard. In 1837 he was transferred to the Nizhegorodski Dragoons and sent to the Caucasus as punishment for the composition and circulation (in MS.) of a violent poem directed at the Court clique responsible for driving Pushkin into fighting his fatal duel (January 1837). He was back in the Guards by the end of the year. Between 1838 and 1841 he wrote his best verse and prose and was acclaimed by the reviewers as Pushkin's successor. An incident at a St. Petersburg ball in the spring of 1840 resulted in a duel with the son of the French Ambassador. Lieutenant Lermontov was transferred again, this time to an infantry regiment in the Caucasus, where he took part in dangerous expeditions against the natives. A trivial quarrel with a fellow officer, one Martinov, led to another duel. The meeting took place on July 15, 1841, near Pyatigorsk, and Lermontov was shot through the heart at the first fire.

# A Hero
# of Our Time

*A Novel by*

Mihail Lermontov

*Translated*
*from the Russian by*
Vladimir Nabokov
*in collaboration with*
Dmitri Nabokov

Doubleday Anchor Books
*Doubleday & Company, Inc.*
*Garden City, New York*

The cover by Edward Gorey is taken from
a portion of a painting by Lermontov, re-
produced in a collection of essays on Lermontov, in the series *Literaturnoe nasledstvo*, part 1 of issue 43–44, Moscow, 1941,
facing p. 752, Caucasian view with Mount
Elbruz, oil, 1837, *Institut literaturi*, Leningrad. Typography by Edward Gorey. Map
by Raphael Palacios adapted from an original by Dmitri Nabokov.

The Anchor Books edition is the first publication of this
translation of *A Hero of Our Time*.

Anchor Books edition: 1958

Library of Congress Catalog Card Number 58–6585

# Translator's Foreword

---

## 1

In 1841, a few months before his death (in a pistol duel with a fellow officer at the foot of Mount Mashuk in the Caucasus), Mihail Lermontov (1814-41) composed a prophetic poem:

In noon's heat, in a dale of Dagestan,
With lead inside my breast, stirless I lay;
The deep wound still smoked on; my blood
Kept trickling drop by drop away.

On the dale's sand alone I lay. The cliffs
Crowded around in ledges steep,
And the sun scorched their tawny tops
And scorched me—but I slept death's sleep.

And in a dream I saw an evening feast
That in my native land with bright lights shone;
Among young women crowned with flowers,
A merry talk concerning me went on.

But in the merry talk not joining,
One of them sat there lost in thought,
And in a melancholy dream
Her young soul was immersed—God knows by what.

And of a dale in Dagestan she dreamt;
In that dale lay the corpse of one she knew;
Within his breast a smoking wound showed black,
And blood ran in a stream that colder grew.

This remarkable composition (which, in the original, is in iambic pentameter throughout, with alternate feminine and masculine rhymes) might be entitled "The Triple Dream."

There is an initial dreamer (Lermontov, or more exactly, his poetical impersonator) who dreams that he lies dying in a valley of Eastern Caucasus. This is Dream One, dreamt by Dreamer One.

The fatally wounded man (Dreamer Two) dreams in his turn of a young woman sitting at a feast in St. Petersburg or Moscow. This is Dream Two within Dream One.

The young woman sitting at the feast sees in her mind Dreamer Two (who dies in the course of the poem) in the surroundings of remote Dagestan. This is Dream Three within Dream Two within Dream One—which describes a spiral by bringing us back to the first stanza.

The whorls of these five strophes have a certain structural affinity with the interlacings of the five stories that make up Lermontov's novel, *A Hero of Our Time* (*Geroy Nashego Vremeni*).

In the first two stories, "Bela" and "Maksim Maksimich," Lermontov or, more exactly, his fictional impersonator, an inquisitive traveler, relates a journey he made along the Military Georgian Road (*Voenno-gruzinskaya doroga*) in the Caucasus around 1837. This is Narrator One.

On the way north from Tiflis he meets an old campaigner, Maksim Maksimich. They travel together for a while and Maksim Maksimich tells

Narrator One about a certain Grigoriy Pechorin who, five years before, in the Chechnya Region, north of Dagestan, kidnapped a Circassian girl. Maksim Maksimich is Narrator Two, and the story is "Bela."

At a second meeting on the road (in "Maksim Maksimich"), Narrator One and Narrator Two come across Pechorin in the flesh. Henceforth, Pechorin, whose journal Narrator One publishes, becomes Narrator Three, for it is from his journal that the remaining three stories are posthumously drawn.

It will be marked by the good reader that the structural trick consists in bringing Pechorin gradually nearer and nearer until he takes over; but by the time he takes over he is dead. In the first story, Pechorin is twice removed from the reader since his personality is described through Maksim Maksimich, whose words are transmitted to us by Narrator One. In the second story the personality of Narrator Two no longer stands between Pechorin and Narrator One, who, at last, sees the hero for himself. Maksim Maksimich is, in fact, pathetically eager to produce the real Pechorin on top of the subject of his yarn. And, finally, in the last three stories, both Narrator One and Narrator Two step aside, and the reader meets Pechorin, Narrator Three, face to face.

This involute structure is responsible for blurring somewhat the time sequence of the novel. The five stories grow, revolve, reveal, and mask their contours, turn away and reappear in a new attitude or light like five mountain peaks attending a traveler along the meanders of a Caucasian canyon road. The traveler is Lermontov, not Pechorin. The five tales are placed in the novel according to the order in which the events become known to Narrator One;

but their chronological sequence is different, going something like this:

1. Around 1830 an officer, Grigoriy Pechorin (Narrator Three), on his way from St. Petersburg to the Caucasus, whither he is being sent on some military errand to a detachment on active duty, happens to be stranded at the village of Taman (a port facing the NE coast of the Crimea). An adventure he has there forms the subject of "Taman," the third story in the book.

2. After some time spent on active duty in skirmishes with the mountain tribes, Pechorin, on May 10, 1832, arrives for a rest at a Caucasian spa, Pyatigorsk. At Pyatigorsk and at Kislovodsk, a neighboring resort, he participates in a series of dramatic events that lead to his killing a fellow officer in a duel on June 17. These events are related by him in the fourth story, "Princess Mary."

3. On June 19, the military authorities have Pechorin dispatched to a fort in the Chechnya Region, Northeast Caucasus, where he arrives only in autumn (after an unexplained delay). There he meets the junior captain Maksim Maksimich. This is related to Narrator One by Narrator Two in the first story, "Bela."

4. In December of the same year (1832) Pechorin leaves the fort for a fortnight which he spends in a Cossack settlement north of the Terek River, and there has the adventure described by him in the fifth (last) story, "The Fatalist."

5. In the spring of 1833, he kidnaps a Circassian girl who is assassinated by a bandit four and a half months later. In December 1833, Pechorin leaves for Georgia and some time later goes home to St. Petersburg. This is related in "Bela."

6. Some four years later, in the autumn of 1837,

Narrator One and Narrator Two, on their way north, stop at the town of Vladikavkaz and there run into Pechorin who, in the meantime, has returned to the Caucasus, and is now on his way south, to Persia. This is related by Narrator One in "Maksim Maksimich," the second story in the book.

7. In 1838 or 1839, on his way back from Persia, Pechorin dies under circumstances possibly related to a prediction made to him that he would die in consequence of an unfortunate marriage. Narrator One now publishes the dead man's journal, obtained from Narrator Two. Pechorin's death is mentioned by Narrator One in his editorial Foreword (1841) to Pechorin's Journal containing "Taman," "Princess Mary," and "The Fatalist."

Thus the order of the five stories, in relation to Pechorin, is: "Taman," "Princess Mary," "The Fatalist," "Bela," and "Maksim Maksimich."

It is unlikely that Lermontov foresaw the plot of "Princess Mary" while he was writing "Bela." The details of Pechorin's arrival at the Kamennïy Brod Fort, as given in "Bela" by Maksim Maksimich, do not quite tally with the details given by Pechorin himself in "Princess Mary."

The inconsistencies in the five stories are numerous and glaring, but the narrative surges on with such speed and force; such manly and romantic beauty pervades it; and the general purpose of Lermontov breathes such fierce integrity, that the reader does not stop to wonder why the mermaid in *Taman* assumed that Pechorin could not swim, or why the Captain of Dragoons thought that Pechorin's seconds would not want to supervise the loading of the pistols. The plight of Pechorin, who is forced, after all, to face Grushnitski's pistol, would be rather ridiculous, had we not understood that our hero relied not on chance but on fate. This is made quite clear in the last and best story, "The Fatalist," where the crucial passage also turns on a pistol being or not being loaded, and where a kind of duel by proxy is fought between Pechorin and Vulich, with Fate, instead of the smirking dragoon, supervising the lethal arrangements.

A special feature of the structure of our book is the monstrous but perfectly organic part that eavesdropping plays in it. Now Eavesdropping is only one form of a more general device which can be classified under the heading of Coincidence, to which belongs, for instance, the Coincidental Meeting—another variety. It is pretty clear that when a novelist desires to combine the traditional tale of romantic adventure (amorous intrigue, jealousy, revenge, etc.) with a narrative in the first person, and has no desire to invent new techniques, he is somewhat limited in the choice of devices.

The eighteenth century epistolary form of novel (with the heroine writing to her girl friend, and the hero writing to his old schoolmate, followed by at least ten other combinations) was so stale by Lermontov's time that he could hardly have used it; and since, on the other hand, our author was more eager to have his story move than to vary, elaborate and conceal the methods of its propulsion, he employed the convenient device of having his Maksim Maksimich and Pechorin overhear, spy upon, and witness any such scene as was needed for the elucidation or the promotion of the plot. Indeed, the author's use of this device is so consistent throughout the book that it ceases to strike the reader as a marvelous vagary of chance and becomes, as it were, the barely noticeable routine of fate.

In "Bela," there are three cases of eavesdropping:

from behind a fence, Narrator Two overhears a boy
trying to coax a robber into selling him a horse (p.
15); and later on, the same Narrator overhears, first
from under a window, and then from behind a door,
two crucial conversations between Pechorin and
Bela (pp. 25–27).

In "Taman," from behind a jutting rock, Narrator
Three overhears a conversation between a girl and
and a blind lad, which informs everybody concerned, including the reader, of the smuggling
business (p. 69); and the same eavesdropper, from
another point of vantage, a cliff above the shore,
overhears the final conversation between the smugglers (pp. 78–79).

In "Princess Mary," Narrator Three eavesdrops as
many as eight times, in consequence of which he is
always in the know. From behind the corner of a
covered walk, he sees Mary retrieving the mug
dropped by disabled Grushnitski (p. 88); from behind a tall shrub, he overhears a sentimental dia-
logue between the two (p. 108); from behind a stout
lady, he overhears the talk that leads to an attempt,
on the part of the dragoon, to have Mary insulted
by a pre-Dostoevskian drunk (p. 112); from an
unspecified distance, he stealthily watches Mary
yawning at Grushnitski's jokes (p. 122); from the
midst of a ballroom crowd, he catches her ironic re-
torts to Grushnitski's romantic entreaties (pp. 133–
34); from outside "an improperly closed shutter," he
sees and hears the dragoon plotting with Grushnitski
to fake a duel with him, Pechorin (pp. 145–47);
through a window curtain which is "not completely
drawn," he observes Mary pensively sitting on her
bed (p. 151); in a restaurant, from behind a door
that leads to the corner room, where Grushnitski
and his friends are assembled, Pechorin hears him-

self accused of visiting Mary at night (pp. 153–54); and finally, and most conveniently, Dr. Werner, Pechorin's second, overhears a conversation between the dragoon and Grushnitski, which leads Werner and Pechorin to conclude that only one pistol will be loaded (p. 157). This accumulation of knowledge on the part of the hero causes the reader to await, with frantic interest, the inevitable scene when Pechorin will crush Grushnitski with the disclosure of this knowledge.

2

This is the first English translation of Lermontov's novel. The book has been paraphrased into English several times,[1] but never translated before. The experienced hack may find it quite easy to turn Lermontov's Russian into slick English clichés by means of judicious omission, amplification, and levigation; and he will tone down everything that might seem unfamiliar to the meek and imbecile reader visualized by his publisher. But the honest translator is faced with a different task.

In the first place, we must dismiss, once and for all the conventional notion that a translation "should read smoothly," and "should not sound like a translation" (to quote the would-be compliments, addressed to vague versions, by genteel reviewers who never have and never will read the original texts). In point of fact, any translation that does *not* sound like a translation is bound to be inexact upon inspection; while, on the other hand, the only virtue of a good translation is faithfulness and completeness. Whether it reads smoothly or not, depends on the model, not on the mimic.

In attempting to translate Lermontov, I have

gladly sacrificed to the requirements of exactness a number of important things—good taste, neat diction, and even grammar (when some characteristic solecism occurs in the Russian text). The English reader should be aware that Lermontov's prose style in Russian is inelegant; it is dry and drab; it is the tool of an energetic, incredibly gifted, bitterly honest, but definitely inexperienced young man. His Russian is, at times, almost as crude as Stendhal's French; his similes and metaphors are utterly commonplace; his hackneyed epithets are only redeemed by occasionally being incorrectly used. Repetition of words in descriptive sentences irritates the purist. And all this, the translator should faithfully render, no matter how much he may be tempted to fill out the lapse and delete the redundancy.

When Lermontov started to write, Russian prose had already evolved that predilection for certain terms that became typical of the Russian novel. Every translator becomes aware, in the course of his task, that, apart from idiomatic locutions, the "From" language has a certain number of constantly iterated words which, though readily translatable, occur in the "Into" language far less frequently and less colloquially. Through long use, these words have become mere pegs or signs, the meeting places of mental associations, the reunions of related notions. They are tokens of sense, rather than particularizations of sense. Of the hundred or so peg words familiar to any student of Russian literature, the following may be listed as being especial favorites with Lermontov:

| | |
|---|---|
| *zadúmat'sya* | To become pensive; to lapse into thought; to be lost in thought. |

| | |
|---|---|
| *podoytí* | To approach; to go up to. |
| *prinyát' vid* | To assume an air (serious, gay, etc.). Fr. *prendre un air.* |
| *molchát'* | To be silent. Fr. *se taire.* |
| *mel'kát'* | To flick; to flicker; to dart; to be glimpsed. |
| *neiz'yasnímïy* | Ineffable (a Gallicism). |
| *gíbkiy* | Supple; flexible. Too often said of human bodies. |
| *mráchnïy* | Gloomy. |
| *pristal'no* | Intently; fixedly; steadily; steadfastly (said of looking, gazing, peering, etc.). |
| *nevól'no* | Involuntarily. Fr. *malgré soi.* |
| *on nevól'no zadúmalsya* | He could not help growing thoughtful. |
| *vdrug* | Suddenly. |
| *uzhé* | Already; by now. |

It is the translator's duty to have, as far as possible, these words reoccur in English as often, and as irritatingly, as they do in the Russian text; I say, as far as possible, because in some cases the word has two or more shades of meaning depending on the context. "A slight pause," or "a moment of silence," for instance, may render the recurrent *minuta molchan'ya* better than "a minute of silence" would.

Another thing that has to be kept in mind is that in one language great care is taken by novelists to tabulate certain facial expressions, gestures, or motions that writers in another language will take

for granted and mention seldom, or not at all. The
nineteenth century Russian writer's indifference to
exact shades of visual color leads to an acceptance
of rather droll epithets condoned by literary usage
(a surprising thing in the case of Lermontov, who
was not only a painter in the literal sense, but saw
colors and was able to name them); thus in the
course of *A Hero* the faces of various people turn
purple, red, rosy, orange, yellow, green and blue.[2]
A romantic epithet of Gallic origin that occurs four
times in the course of the novel is *tusklaya blednost'*,
*paleur mate*, dull (or lusterless) pallor. In "Taman,"
the delinquent girl's face is covered with "a dull
pallor betraying inner agitation" (p. 76). In "Princess Mary," this phenomenon occurs three times: a
dull pallor is spread over Mary's face (p. 137) when
she accuses Pechorin of disrespect; a dull pallor is
spread over Pechorin's face revealing "the traces of
painful insomnia" (p. 160); and just before the duel,
a dull pallor is spread over Grushnitski's cheeks as
his conscience struggles with his pride (p. 163).

Besides such code sentences as "her lips grew
pale," "he flushed," "her hand trembled slightly,"
and so forth, emotions are signalled by certain
abrupt and violent gestures. In "Bela," Pechorin
hits the table with his fist to punctuate with a bang
his words "she won't belong to anybody but me"
(p. 24). Two pages further, it is his forehead he
strikes with his fist (a gesture deemed Oriental by
some commentators) upon realizing he has bungled
the seduction and driven Bela to tears (p. 26). In
his turn, Grushnitski strikes the table with his fist
(p. 102) when convinced by Pechorin's remarks
that Mary is merely a flirt. And the Captain of
Dragoons does the same when demanding attention
(p. 145). There is also a great deal of the "seizing

his arm," "taking him by the arm," and "pulling by the sleeve" business throughout the novel.

"Stamping on the ground" is another emotional signal much in favor with Lermontov, and, in Russian literature of the time, this was new. Maksim Maksimich, in "Bela" (p. 19), stamps his foot in self-accusation. Grushnitski, in "Princess Mary," stamps his in petulance (p. 134); and the Captain of Dragoons stamps his in disgust (p. 170).

### 3

It is unnecessary to discuss here Pechorin's character. The good reader will easily understand it by studying the book; but so much nonsense has been written about Pechorin, by those who adopt a sociological approach to literature, that a few warning words must be said.

We should not take, as seriously as most Russian commentators, Lermontov's statement in his Introduction (a stylized bit of make-believe in its own right) that Pechorin's portrait is "composed of all the vices of our generation." Actually, the bored and bizarre hero is a product of several generations, some of them non-Russian; he is the fictional descendant of a number of fictional self-analysts, beginning with Saint-Preux (the lover of Julie d'Etange in Rousseau's *Julie ou la nouvelle Héloïse*, 1761) and Werther (the admirer of Charlotte S—— in Goethe's *Die Leiden des jungen Werthers*, 1774, known to Russians mainly in French versions such as that by Sévelinges, 1804), going through Chateaubriand's *René* (1802), Constant's *Adolphe* (1815), and the heroes of Byron's long poems (especially *The Giaour*, 1813, and *The Corsair*, 1814, known to Russians in Pichot's French prose versions, from 1820 on), and ending with Pushkin's *Eugene Onegin* (1825–32) and with various more ephem eral products of the French novelists of the first half of the century (Nodier, Balzac, etc.). Pechorin's association with a given time and a given place tends to lend a new flavor to the transplanted fruit, but it is doubtful whether much is added to an appreciation of this flavor by generalizing about the exacerbation of thought produced in independent minds by the tyranny of Nicholas I's reign (1825–56).

The point to be marked in a study of *A Hero of Our Time* is that, though of tremendous and at times somewhat morbid interest to the sociologist, the "time" is of less interest to the student of literature than the "hero." In the latter, young Lermontov managed to create a fictional person whose romantic dash and cynicism, tigerlike suppleness and eagle eye, hot blood and cool head, tenderness and taciturnity, elegance and brutality, delicacy of perception and harsh passion to dominate, ruthlessness and awareness of it, are of lasting appeal to readers of all countries and centuries—especially to young readers; for it would seem that the veneration elderly critics have for *A Hero* is rather a glorified recollection of youthful readings in the summer twilight, and of ardent self-identification, than the direct result of a mature consciousness of art.

Of the other characters in the book there is, likewise, little to say. The most endearing one is obviously the old Captain Maksim Maksimich, stolid, gruff, naïvely poetical, matter-of-fact, simple-hearted, and completely neurotic. His hysterical behavior at the abortive meeting with his old friend Pechorin is one of the passages most dear to human-interest readers. Of the several villains in the book, Kazbich and his florid speech (as rendered by Maksim Maksimich) are an obvious product of literary orientalia, while the American reader may be excused for substituting the Indians of Fenimore Cooper for Lermontov's Circassians. In the worst story of the book, "Taman" (deemed by some Russian critics the greatest, for reasons incomprehensible to me), Yanko is saved from utter banality when we notice that the connection between him and the blind lad is a pleasing echo of the scene between hero and hero-worshipper in "Maksim Maksimich."

Another kind of interplay occurs in "Princess Mary." If Pechorin is a romantic shadow of Lermontov, Grushnitski, as Russian critics have already noted, is a grotesque shadow of Pechorin, and the lowest level of imitation is supplied by Pechorin's valet. Grushnitski's evil genius, the Captain of Dragoons, is little more than a stock character of comedy, and the continuous references to the hugger-mugger he indulges in are rather painful. No less painful is the skipping and singing of the wild girl in "Taman." Lermontov was singularly inept in his descriptions of women. Mary is the generalized young thing of novelettes, with no attempt at individualization except perhaps her "velvety" eyes, which however are forgotten in the course of the story. Vera is a mere phantom, with a phantom birthmark on her cheek; Bela, an Oriental beauty on the lid of a box of Turkish delight.

What, then, makes the everlasting charm of this book? Why is it so interesting to read and reread? Certainly not for its style—although, curiously enough, Russian schoolteachers used to see in it the perfection of Russian prose. This is a ridiculous opinion, voiced (according to a memoirist) by Chehov, and can only be held if and when a moral quality or a social virtue is confused with literary art, or when an ascetic critic regards the rich and ornate with such suspicion that, in contrast, the awkward and frequently commonplace style of Lermontov seems delightfully chaste and simple. But genuine art is neither chaste nor simple, and it is sufficient to glance at the prodigiously elaborate and magically artistic style of Tolstoy (who, by some, is considered to be a literary descendant of Lermontov) to realize the depressing flaws of Lermontov's prose.

But if we regard him as a storyteller, and if we remember that Russian prose was still in her teens, and the man still in his middle twenties when he wrote, then we do marvel indeed at the superb energy of the tale and at the remarkable rhythm into which the paragraphs, rather than the sentences, fall. It is the agglomeration of otherwise insignificant words that come to life. When we start to break the sentence or the verse line into its quantitative elements, the banalities we perceive are often shocking, the shortcomings not seldom comic; but, in the long run, it is the compound effect that counts, and this final effect can be traced down in Lermontov to the beautiful timing of all the parts and particles of the novel. Its author was careful to dissociate himself from his hero; but, for the emotional type of reader, much of the novel's poignancy and fascination resides in the fact that Lermontov's own tragic fate is somehow superimposed upon that of Pechorin, just as the Dagestan dream acquires an additional strain of pathos when the reader realizes that the poet's dream came true.

# Contents

# A Hero of Our Time[3]

LERMONTOV'S CAUCASUS

# The Author's Introduction

IN EVERY BOOK the preface is the first and also the last thing. It serves either to explain the purpose of the work or to justify it and answer criticism. But readers are generally not concerned with moral purposes or with attacks in reviews, and in result, they do not read prefaces. It is a pity that this should be so, particularly in our country. Our public is still so young and naïve that it fails to understand a fable unless it finds a lesson at its end. It misses a humorous point and does not feel irony; it simply is badly brought up. It has not yet learned that in decent company as in a decent book open abuse cannot occur; that modern education has evolved a much sharper weapon—which, though almost invisible, is nevertheless lethal and which, under the guise of flattery, deals an inescapable and accurate blow. Our public resembles a provincial who, upon overhearing the conversation of two diplomats belonging to two warring Courts, is convinced that each envoy is betraying his government in the interests of a most tender mutual friendship.

The present book has only recently suffered from the unfortunate faith that certain readers and even certain reviewers have in the literal meaning of words. Some were dreadfully offended, quite in

earnest, that such an immoral person as the Hero of
Our Time should be set as a model to them; others
very subtly remarked that the author had drawn
his own portrait and the portraits of his acquaintances . . . What an old and paltry jest! But apparently Russia is created in such a way that everything
in it changes for the better, except this sort of nonsense. With us the most fantastic of all fairy tales
would hardly escape the reproach of being meant as
some personal insult.

*A Hero of Our Time,* gentlemen, is indeed a portrait, but not of a single individual; it is a portrait
composed of all the vices of our generation in the
fullness of their development. You will tell me again
that a man cannot be as bad as all that; and I shall
tell you that since you have believed in the possibility of so many tragic and romantic villains having
existed, why can you not believe in the reality of
Pechorin? If you have admired fictions far more
frightful and hideous, why does this character, even
as fiction, find no quarter with you? Is it not, perchance, because there is more truth in this character
than you would desire there to be?

You will say that morality gains nothing from this.
I beg your pardon. People have been fed enough
sweetmeats; it has given them indigestion: they
need some bitter medicine, some caustic truths.
However, do not think after this that the author of
this book ever had the proud dream of becoming a
reformer of mankind's vices. The Lord preserve him
from such benightedness! He merely found it amusing to draw modern man such as he understood him,
such as he met him—too often, unfortunately, for
him and you. Suffice it that the disease has been
pointed out; goodness knows how to cure it.

# Bela

I WAS TRAVELING post from Tiflis.[4] All the luggage in
my small springless carriage[5] consisted of one valise
stuffed half-full of notes on my travels in Georgia.[6]
The greater part of them, luckily for you, has been
lost; while the valise with its other contents, luckily
for me, remains safe.

The sun had already begun to hide behind the
snowy range when I drove into the Koyshaur Valley.
My Ossetian driver urged the horses on unceasingly,
in order that we might get to the top of Mount Koyshaur before nightfall, and sang songs at the top of
his voice. What a delightful place, that valley! On
all sides rise inaccessible mountains, reddish cliffs,
hung over with green ivy and crowned with clumps
of plane trees; tawny precipices streaked with
washes, and, far above, the golden fringe of the
snows; below, Aragva River, infolding another,
nameless, river which noisily bursts forth from a
black gorge full of gloom, stretches out in a silver
thread and glistens like the scaling of a snake.

Having arrived at the foot of Mount Koyshaur, we
stopped near a native inn. Here a score or so of
Georgians and mountain tribesmen were crowding
noisily about; close by, a camel caravan had en-
camped for the night. I had to hire oxen to drag my

carriage up that confounded mountain, because it was already autumn and there was ice on the roads; and the ascent was nearly one mile and a half long.

There was nothing to do: I hired six oxen and several Ossetians. One of them heaved my valise up on his shoulders, the others began to help the oxen along, almost exclusively by means of cries.

Behind my carriage, a team of four oxen was pulling another carriage with perfect ease, despite its being loaded up to the top. This circumstance surprised me. Behind it walked its owner puffing at a small Kabardan pipe mounted with silver. He wore an officer's surtout, without epaulets, and a Circassian shaggy cap. He seemed about fifty years old; his tanned complexion indicated that his face had long been acquainted with the Trans-Caucasian sun, and his prematurely grayed mustache did not harmonize with his firm gait and his vigorous appearance. I walked over to him and made a bow. He silently acknowledged my bow and exhaled a huge puff of tobacco smoke.

"We seem to be fellow-travelers?"

In silence, he bowed again.

"I presume you are going to Stavropol?"

"Yes, sir, that's right. With government property."

"Tell me, please, why is it that four oxen draw your heavy carriage with ease while my empty one can barely be moved by means of six brutes with the help of these Ossetians?"

He smiled slyly and glanced significantly at me.

"You've probably not been long in the Caucasus?"

"About a year," I replied.

He smiled a second time.

"Well—why?"

"It's this way, sir: these Asiatics are terrible rascals! You think they are trying to help with that shouting? But the devil knows what it is they are shouting. The oxen—they understand; you may hitch a score of them but as soon as those drivers start to shout in their own way, the oxen will not budge . . . Dreadful rogues! But what can you do to them? They love to squeeze money out of travelers . . . They have been spoiled, the robbers! You'll see, they'll get you to tip them, too. I know them well, they can't take me in!"

"And have you been stationed here long?"

"I was already serving here in General Aleksey Ermolov's[7] time," he replied with a certain loftiness. "When he took over the Border Command, I was a second lieutenant," he added, "and, under him, was twice promoted for action against the mountain tribes."

"And now you are——?"

"Now I am attached to the third battalion of the line. And you, may I ask?"

I told him.

With this, the conversation ended, and we continued to walk side by side in silence. At the summit of the mountain, we found snow. The sun had set, and night followed day without any interval, as is usual in the south; however, owing to the sheen of the snows, we could easily make out the road, which still went uphill, although no longer so steeply. I ordered my valise to be put into the carriage, the oxen to be replaced by horses, and turned back for a last glance down at the valley; but a dense mist that had surged in waves from the gorges completely covered it, and not a single sound reached our hearing from there. The Ossetians clustered around me noisily, and clamored for tips, but the junior captain[8] berated them so sternly that they at once dispersed.

"What a crew!" he said. "They can't even say 'bread' in Russian, but they've managed to learn 'officer, give me a tip.' In my opinion, even the Tatars are better: at least, they don't drink."

We were still about a mile from the station. All was quiet around, so quiet that you could follow a mosquito's flight by its hum. On our left, a deep gorge yawned black; beyond it and in front of us the dark-blue mountain tops, furrowed with wrinkles, covered with layers of snow, were silhouetted against the pale horizon, which still retained the last reflection of the sunset. Stars were beginning to twinkle in the dark sky, and, strange to say, they seemed to me to be much higher than at home, in the north. On either side of the road, bare, black rocks jutted out; here and there, from beneath the snow there emerged shrubs; but not a single dry leaf stirred, and it was a joy to hear, amid the dead sleep of nature, the snorting of the three tired posters and the irregular jangling of the Russian shaft bell.

"It will be fine tomorrow!" I said. The junior captain did not answer a word, and pointed out to me with his finger a high mountain rising directly in front of us.

"What is it?" I asked.

"Mount Gud."[9]

"Well, what about it?"

"Look how it smokes."

And indeed, Mount Gud was smoking; along its flanks there crept light wisps of clouds, while on its summit there lay a black cloud, so black that it looked like a blot on the dark sky.

We could already distinguish the post station, as well as the roofs of the Caucasian huts surrounding it; and cheery lights flickered before us, when there

came a gust of damp cold wind, the gorge reverber-
ated, and a fine rain began to fall. I barely had time
to throw my felt cloak over my shoulders, when it
began to snow heavily. I looked with reverence at
the junior captain.

"We'll have to stop here for the night," he said
with vexation. "In a blizzard like this you can't drive
over the mountains. Tell me," he asked the coachman, "have there been any avalanches on *Krestovaya Gora* [Mountain of the Cross]?"

"There haven't, sir," answered the Ossetian
driver, "but there's lots and lots waiting to come
down."

In the absence of a room for travelers at the post
station, we were assigned night quarters in a smoky
native hut. I invited my companion to have a glass
of tea with me since I traveled with a cast iron tea
kettle—my sole comfort on my journeys through the
Caucasus.

The hut was built with one wall against a cliff;
three slippery wet steps led to its door. I groped my
way in and ran smack into a cow (with these people
a cattle shed replaces a vestibule). I did not know
which way to turn: here, sheep were bleating, there,
a dog was growling. Fortunately, a dim light
gleamed on one side and helped me to find another
opening in the guise of a doorway. There, a rather
entertaining picture was disclosed. The spacious hut
whose roof rested on two smoke-blackened posts,
was full of people. In the center, there crackled a
small fire built on the ground, and the smoke, forced
back by the wind from the hole in the roof, spread
all around in such a thick pall that, for a long time, I
could not see around me: by the fire sat two old
women, a multitude of children, and one lean Georgian, all of them in rags. There was nothing we could

do, except settle down by the fire and light our
pipes; and soon the tea kettle began to emit a
friendly simmer.

"What wretched people," I said to the junior captain, indicating our grimy hosts, who were silently
gazing at us in a sort of stupor.

"An extremely foolish people," he replied. "Can
you imagine, they don't know how to do anything
and are incapable of any education! Our Kabardans
or our Chechens, though they may be robbers and
paupers, are at least reckless daredevils; but these
people aren't even interested in weapons: you won't
see a decent dagger on a single one of them. These
are real Ossetians for you!"

"And have you been long in the Chechen region?"

"Yes, I was stationed there for about ten years
with my company in a fort near *Kamennïy Brod*
[Stone Ford].[10] Know the place?"

"I've heard of it."

"Well, my good sir, we did get tired of those cut-
throats. Nowadays, thank goodness, things have
quieted down, but the way it used to be—you just
walked a hundred paces beyond the rampart, and
there was bound to be some shaggy devil sitting and
watching you: one second off guard, and it would
happen: either a lariat would be around your neck
or there would be a bullet in the back of your head.
But what brave fellows! . . ."

"You've surely had a lot of adventures," I said,
prompted by curiosity.

"How could it be otherwise? Of course I
had. . . ."

At this point, he began to pull at the left end of
his mustache, hung his head, and was lost in thought.
I was dying to get some kind of yarn out of him—a
desire peculiar to all people who travel and take

notes. Meanwhile, tea was ready; I dug out of my valise, two small traveling glasses, filled them and set one of them in front of him. He took a gulp and said, as though to himself: "Yes, indeed!" This exclamation gave me great hopes. I knew that veterans of Caucasian wars like to have a talk and tell a tale; they so seldom have a chance to do so: the man might be stationed for some five years in a remote place with his company, and, during the whole five years, nobody would say "Hello" to him (because the sergeant says "Good morning, sir"). And there would be quite a number of things to chat about: around you there is a wild people, provoking one's curiosity, there is danger every day, extraordinary incidents happen; and no wonder there is occasion to regret that so few of us take notes.

"Would you not like to add some rum?" I said to my interlocutor. "I have white rum from Tiflis; it is a cold night."

"No, thanks a lot, but I do not drink."

"How come?"

"Well, it's like this. I made a vow to myself. When I was still a second lieutenant we all got a little high one time, and during the night there was an alarm; so we came out lit up in front of the soldiers, and did we get it from Aleksey Petrovich when he found out: goodness, how furious he was! He very nearly had us court-martialed. And, indeed, here, you go a whole year without seeing a soul, and if vodka is then added, you are a lost man!"

When I heard that, I almost lost hope!

"Take the Circassians, for instance," he went on. "As soon as they get drunk on buza,[11] at a wedding, or at a funeral, the knife-play begins. I barely escaped once with my life, and at the house of a neutral prince[12] at that."

"How did that happen?"

"Well . . ." (He filled his pipe, inhaled the smoke, and began his tale.)[13] "Well, you see, I was stationed then, with my company, in a fort beyond the Terek—it will soon be five years since that happened. One autumn day, a convoy came with supplies; with it there arrived an officer, a young fellow of twenty-five or so. He reported to me in full uniform and announced that he had orders to remain at my fort. He was so thin, with such fair skin, the uniform he wore was so new, that I guessed at once that he had been but a short time in the Caucasus with our forces. "You've probably been transferred here from Russia?"[14] I asked him. "That's right, sir," he answered. I clasped his hand and said: "Delighted, delighted. You will find it a little dull—but we'll get along on a friendly footing, the two of us. So please call me simply Maksim Maksimich, and please—there is no need for a full uniform. A cap will do whenever you come to see me." Quarters were given him, and he took up residence in the fort.

"And what was his name?" I asked Maksim Maksimich.

"He was named . . . Grigoriy Aleksandrovich Pechorin. A charming fellow he was, I can assure you, but a little odd. He might spend, for instance, the whole day hunting in the rain, in the cold; everybody would get chilled through and exhausted, but not he; and some other time he'd be sitting in his room, and just a gust of wind would come, and there he would be, insisting that he had caught cold; or if the shutter banged, he'd start and grow pale; yet I had seen him take on a wild boar all by himself; there were times when you could not get a word out of him for hours, but on the other hand when he happened to start telling stories you'd split your sides with laughter . . . Yes, sir, there were many odd things about him; must have been a rich fellow, too: how many different expensive trinkets he had!"

"Did he stay long with you?" I asked again.

"About a year. But a memorable year it was for me, indeed; he caused me no end of trouble, though this, certainly, is not what I remember him by. You know, there really exist certain people to whom it is assigned, at their birth, to have all sorts of extraordinary things happen to them."

"Extraordinary things?" I exclaimed with an air of curiosity, while I poured him some more tea.

"Well, let me tell you. About four miles from the fort, there lived a neutral prince. His young son, a boy of fifteen or so, took to riding over to our place: every day he would come for one thing or another. We had really spoiled him, Pechorin[15] and I. And what a daredevil he was, game for anything—picking up a cap at full gallop or shooting a rifle. There was one thing bad about him: he had an awful weakness for money. Once, in jest, Pechorin promised him a gold piece if he would steal for him the best goat from his father's herd. And what do you think? The very next night, there he came, dragging the goat by the horns. And sometimes, we would start teasing him, and then his eyes would get all bloodshot, and his hand would at once fly to his dagger. 'Hey, Azamat, you won't keep your head long on your shoulders,' I would say to him, '*yaman* [bad] it will be with your head!'

"One day the old prince himself came to invite us to a wedding: he was marrying off his eldest daughter, and we were *kunaks*[16] with him; there was, therefore, no way to refuse, even though he was a Tatar. So we went. At his village, a lot of dogs met us with loud barking. The women hid at the sight of us. Those whose faces we were able to make out were far from being beauties. 'I had a far better opinion of Circassian women,' said Pechorin to me. 'Just wait!' I replied with a smile. I had something up my sleeve.

"A lot of people had already gathered at the prince's house. With those Asiatics,[17] you know, it is the custom to invite one and all to their weddings. We were received with all possible honors and shown into the *kunak* room. However, I did not forget to note where they had put our horses—just in case, you know."

"How do they celebrate a wedding?" I asked the junior captain.

"Oh, the usual way. At first, the mullah reads them something out of the Koran; then, presents are given to the young couple and all their relatives; they eat, they drink buza; then the trick-riding begins, and there is always some ragamuffin, greasy with dirt, on a wretched lame pony, who fools and clowns, much to the amusement of the good company; and then after dark, what we would call a ball begins in the *kunak* room. Some miserable little old man twangs his three-stringed . . . I forget the local word for it . . .[18] anyway, something like our balalaika. The girls and the young men form two rows opposite each other, clap their hands and sing. Then one girl and one man step out into the middle and begin chanting verses to each other, anything they happen to think of, and the others pick up the refrain in chorus. Pechorin and I were sitting in the place of honor, and up to him came our host's younger daughter, a girl of about sixteen, and sang to him . . . how shall I say? . . . a kind of compliment."

"And what was it she sang to him, do you remember?"

"Yes, I believe it was like this: 'Svelte', it went, 'are our young warriors, and their caftans are trimmed with silver, but the young Russian officer is svelter than they, and his coat is braided with gold. He stands like a poplar among them, but it is not fated that he should grow and blossom in our garden.' Pechorin stood up, bowed to her, touched his hand to his forehead and then to his heart, and asked me to answer her. I know their language well, and translated his answer.

"When she had moved away from us, I whispered to Pechorin: 'Well, what do you think of her?'

"'Charming,' he answered. 'What is her name?' 'Her name is Bela,' I replied.

"And indeed, she was beautiful: tall, slender, with black eyes which resembled those of a mountain gazelle and practically peered into your soul. Lost in thought, Pechorin did not take his eyes off her, and quite often she would steal a glance at him from under her brows. But Pechorin was not the only one to admire the pretty young princess: from a corner of the room, there looked at her another pair of eyes, immobile and fiery. I looked closer, and recognized my old acquaintance, Kazbich. He was, do you know, neither exactly neutral, nor exactly hostile. He was suspected of many things, though he had never been involved in any mischief. At times, he would bring sheep[19] to our fort and sell them cheap, but he would never haggle: whatever his asking price was, you had to pay it—you could cut his throat and still he would not come down. It was rumored of him that he liked to prowl on the Russian side of the Kuban River[20] with *abreks*.[21] And to tell the truth, his countenance was that of a regular robber: he was small, wiry, broad-shouldered . . . And how nimble he was; it was the nimbleness of a devil! His *beshmet*[22] was always in tatters, all patched up, but his weapons were chased with silver. And his horse was the talk of the whole Kabardan region—indeed, you could not think of anything more handsome than that horse. No wonder, every horseman envied him; and there had been more than one attempt to steal it, but none succeeded. It is as if I were looking at that horse now: pitch black, legs like taut strings, and eyes no less beautiful than Bela's; and what strength!—you could ride him thirty miles; and how well he was trained—ran after his master like a dog; even knew his voice! As a matter of fact, Kazbich would never tie him. Just the right horse for a bandit!

"That night Kazbich was gloomier than ever, and I noticed that under his *beshmet* he wore a coat of mail. 'It is not without reason that he has that coat of mail on,' I reflected. 'He must be planning something.'[23]

"It got stuffy indoors, and I went outside to get a breath of fresh air. Night was already descending upon the mountains, and a mist had begun to float in the gorges. It occurred to me to look into the shelter where our horses stood, in order to check if they had any feed, and then again it never hurts to be careful; the more so as my horse was a fine one, and many a Kabardan had ogled it tenderly as he muttered to himself: 'yakshi tkhe, chek yakshi [good horse, very good]!'

"As I was picking my way along the fence, I suddenly heard voices; one voice I recognized immediately: it belonged to that scamp, Azamat, the son of our host; the other spoke more seldom and more softly. 'What can they be conferring about?' I thought. 'Might it be about my pony?' So I squatted

by the fence and began listening, trying not to miss
a single word. At times, the sounds of the songs and
the clamor of voices, carrying from the house, would
drown the conversation that interested me.

"'That's a fine horse you have,' Azamat was saying. 'If I were master in the house and had a herd of
three hundred mares, I'd give half of them for your
courser, Kazbich!'

"'Aha—Kazbich,' I said to myself, and recalled the
coat of mail.

"'Yes,' answered Kazbich after a pause. 'In the
whole of Kabarda you won't find one like it. One
time—this happened beyond the Terek—I rode with
the *abreks* to seize Russian horse herds; we had bad
luck, and scattered, each his own way. Four Cossacks were tearing after me; already I could hear the
cries of the Giaours behind me, and in front of me,
there was a dense forest. I leaned forward in the
saddle, entrusted myself to Allah, and for the first
time in my life insulted my horse with a blow of the
lash. Like a bird he dived among the branches;
sharp thorns tore my clothes, dry elm twigs struck
my face. My horse jumped over tree stumps, tore
the brush apart with his chest. It would have been
better for me to abandon him at the forest edge and
disappear in the woods on foot, but I could not bear
to part from him—and the prophet rewarded me.
Several bullets whined above my head; I could already hear the dismounted Cossacks running in pursuit . . . Suddenly, I saw a deep ravine before me;
my courser hesitated, and then jumped. His hind
hooves slipped back from the far edge, and he hung
by his front legs. I abandoned the reins and tumbled
into the ravine; this saved my steed and he scram-
bled up. The Cossacks saw all this, but not one of

them went down to look for me: they must have
thought that I had killed myself, and I heard them
rush off to capture my horse. My heart bled; I began
crawling through the thick grass along the ravine,
then took a look: the forest had come to an end;
several Cossacks rode out of it into a clearing, and
there came my Karagyoz[24] galloping right upon
them; they all took off after him, yelling; for a long,
long time[25] they pursued him, and one, in particular, very nearly got a lasso over his head a couple of
times; I trembled, lowered my eyes, and began to
pray. A few seconds later, I raised them again, and
saw my Karagyoz flying with streaming tail, as free
as the wind, and the Giaours strung out far behind
him in the steppe on their worn-out horses. By Allah! It is the truth, the truest truth. I stayed in my
ravine late into the night. Suddenly—imagine, Azamat!—in the dark I heard a horse running back and
forth, along the lip of the ravine, snorting, neighing,
and beating the ground with his hooves; I recognized the voice of my Karagyoz: it was he, my comrade! . . . Since then we have never parted.'

"And I could hear Kazbich patting the smooth
neck of his steed and calling him various pet names.

" 'If I had a herd of a *thousand* mares,' said Azamat, 'I'd give them all to you in exchange for your
Karagyoz.'

" '*Yok* [no], I'm not interested,' Kazbich answered
with indifference.

" 'Listen, Kazbich,' said Azamat coaxingly. 'You're
a good man, you're a brave warrior. Now, my father
is afraid of the Russians and won't let me join the
mountain bands; give me your horse, and I'll do anything you want, I'll steal for you my father's best
rifle or sword, anything you might desire—and his

sword is a real *Gurda* one; just apply its edge to your hand, and it will bite into the flesh of its own accord; even a coat of mail like yours won't help.'

"Kazbich was silent.

"'The first time I saw your horse,' Azamat went on, 'when he pranced under you, and jumped, dilating his nostrils, and flint sparks sprayed from under his hooves, something strange happened inside my soul, and since then everything became dull to me: I looked at my father's best coursers with contempt, I was ashamed to be seen on them, and heartache possessed me; and, with aching heart, I would spend whole days sitting on the top of a cliff, and every moment there would appear to me, in thought, that black steed of yours, with his graceful gait, and his smooth spine as straight as an arrow; his lively eyes looked into my eyes, as though he wanted to utter words. I'll die, Kazbich, if you don't sell him to me!' said Azamat in a trembling voice.

"I thought I heard him start crying: and you must know that Azamat was a most stubborn boy, and there was no way you could knock a tear out of him, even when he was younger.

"In reply to his tears there sounded something like laughter.

"'Listen,' said Azamat, in a firm voice. 'You will see I'm ready to dare anything. Do you want me to steal my sister for you? How she can dance! How she can sing! And the gold embroidery she does is a wonder! The Turkish padishah himself never had such a wife . . . Do you want me to do it? Wait for me tomorrow night, over there, in the gorge where the torrent runs; I'll walk by with her, on the way to the next village—and she is yours. Don't tell me that Bela is not worth your courser.'

"Kazbich was silent for a long, long time; finally,

instead of an answer, he intoned, in a low voice, an ancient song:[26]

"We have many beautiful girls in our villages,
Stars are ablaze in the dark of their eyes.
Sweet is to love them—an enviable lot;
Bold freedom, however, is merrier still.
Gold can purchase you a foursome of wives,
But a spirited steed is a priceless possession:
He will not be outstripped by the wind in the
    steppes,
He will never betray, he will never deceive.

"In vain did Azamat entreat him to agree, in vain did he weep, and fawn on him, and make oaths. At last, Kazbich interrupted him impatiently:

"'Go away, mad boy! *You* ride my steed? Before you've ridden three steps, he'll throw you and you'll crack the back of your head on the stones.'

"'Throw me?' screamed Azamat in a rage, and the iron of a child's dagger rang against chain-armor. A strong arm pushed him away, and he hit the fence so hard that it shook. 'Now we shall have some sport!' I thought, dashed into the stable, bridled our horses and led them out into the back yard. Two minutes later, there was a terrible uproar indoors. Here's what had happened: Azamat had burst in, his *beshmet* torn, saying that Kazbich had wanted to cut his throat. Everybody dashed out, grabbed their rifles—and the sport began! There was shouting, noise, rifle shots; but Kazbich was already on his horse and was wheeling in the midst of the crowd along the street, like a devil, swinging his sword in defense. 'It is no fun to pay with a hangover for the feasting of others,' said I to Pechorin, catching him by the arm. 'Hadn't we better clear out at once?'

"'Oh, wait a minute, let's see the end.'

"'You may be sure that the end will be bad: it is always so with these Asiatics. they got tight on buza, and the knife-play starts!' We mounted and galloped off home."

"And what about Kazbich?" I asked the junior captain eagerly.

"What would you expect to happen to that sort of fellow?" he answered, as he finished his glass of tea. "He gave them the slip, naturally!"

"Unhurt?" I asked.

"Goodness only knows! These bandits are indestructible. I've had occasion to see them in action, sir; for example, he may be as full of holes as a sieve, and still brandish his sword."

After a short silence, the junior captain stamped his foot on the ground and continued:

"There's one thing I'll never forgive myself: when we got back to the fort, the devil moved me to relate to Pechorin all I had overheard while crouching behind that fence; he chuckled—such a sly fellow!— he had thought up something."

"And what was it? Do tell me, please."[27]

"Well, there is nothing to be done! Since I have started this story, I'll have to go on with it.

"In about four days, Azamat rode over to our fort. As usual, he visited Pechorin, who always fed him sweetmeats. I was present. The conversation turned to horses, and Pechorin began to praise Kazbich's mount: it was so spirited, so handsome, a regular gazelle—well, to hear him, there was not another like it in the whole world.

"The little Moslem's eyes sparkled, but Pechorin seemed not to notice; I would start speaking of something else, but before you knew, he had switched the talk back to Kazbich's horse. This business would go on every time Azamat came over.

About three weeks later, I began to notice that Azamat was getting pale and pining away, as it happens from love in novels, sir. I marveled.

"Well, you see, I discovered the whole thing later: Pechorin had driven him to such a point with his teasing that he was close to jumping into the water. So once he said to him: 'I can see, Azamat, that you've taken a mighty liking to that horse; yet you've got no more chance of seeing it than your own nape! Well, tell me, what would you give the person who made you a present of it?'

" 'Anything he wanted,' answered Azamat.

" 'In that case I'll obtain it for you—but under one condition . . . Swear that you'll fulfill it. . . .'

" 'I swear . . . But you must swear too!'

" 'Good! I swear that you will own that steed; but in return you must give me your sister, Bela. Karagyoz will be the *kalïm* [bride money]. I hope that you find the bargain profitable.'

"Azamat was silent.

" 'You're not interested? Well, as you wish! I thought you were a man, but you're still a child; it is too early for you to ride a horse.'

"Azamat flushed. 'What about my father?' he said.

" 'Doesn't he ever go away?'

" 'True. . . .'

" 'Do you consent?'

" 'I consent,' whispered Azamat, as pale as death. 'When is it to be?'

" 'The very next time Kazbich comes here; he promised to drive ten rams over; the rest is my business. I count on you, Azamat!'

"And so they clinched the deal—a rotten one, to say the truth! I said so to Pechorin later, but he only answered that a wild Circassian girl should consider herself lucky to have such a nice husband as he, because, according to their way of thinking, he was, after all, a husband, while Kazbich was a bandit who deserved to be punished. Judge for yourself, what could I say against that? But at the time I knew nothing of their plot. Well, one day, Kazbich arrived and asked if we did not need sheep or honey. I told him to bring some next day. 'Azamat!' said Pechorin, 'Tomorrow, Karagyoz will be in my hands; if Bela is not here tonight, you'll never see that steed . . .'

" 'All right!' said Azamat, and galloped off to the village. In the evening, Pechorin armed himself and rode out of the fort. How they managed the business, I do not know; only they both got back at night, and the sentry saw that Azamat had a woman lying across his saddle, her hands and feet tied, and a yashmak wrapped around her head."

"What about the horse?" I asked the junior captain.

"Presently, presently. Early the next morning, Kazbich arrived, driving ten rams for sale. After tying his horse to the fence,[28] he came to see me; I treated him to some tea, since, robber though he was, he was still a *kunak* of mine.

"We began to chat about this and that . . . All at once, I saw Kazbich give a start, his face changed . . . and he made for the window; but the window, unfortunately, faced the back yard. 'What's the matter with you?' I asked.

" 'My horse! . . . my horse,' he said, trembling all over.

"Sure enough, I heard hoofbeats. 'Must be a Cossack riding by.'

" 'No! *Urus-yaman, yaman* [A bad, bad Russian]!' he roared, and dashed headlong out of the room, like a wild panther. In two bounds, he was in the courtyard; at the fortress gate, the sentry, with his rifle, barred Kazbich's path. He leapt over the rifle and dashed off down the road. . . . Dust was whirling in the distance—it was Azamat galloping on the gallant Karagyoz. Kazbich, as he ran, pulled his rifle out of its canvas case and fired. For a moment, he stood motionless, until he was certain that he had missed; then he uttered a shrill scream, struck his rifle against a stone, smashing the weapon to bits, fell on the ground and began to sob like a child . . . Presently people from the fort gathered around him, but he did not notice anyone; they stood around for awhile, exchanged views, and went back: I had the money for the sheep placed next to him; he never touched it, but remained lying on his face, as if he were dead. Would you believe it: he lay like that until late at night, and the whole night through.[29] Then next morning, he came to the fort and asked to be told who the thief was. The sentry, who had seen Azamat untie the horse and gallop away on it, did not deem it necessary to conceal the truth. At the mention of that name, Kazbich's eyes flashed, and he set off for the village where Azamat's father lived."

"And what did the father do?"

"Ah, that's just it, Kazbich did not find him, he was away somewhere, for six days or so; how else could Azamat have succeeded in carrying off his sister?

"When the father got back, there was neither son nor daughter. The slyboots! He realized perfectly well he would lose his life if he got caught. So he vanished, there and then; must have joined some gang of *abreks* and laid down his reckless head on the Russian side of the Terek[30] or of the Kuban; serves him right, too!

"I must confess that I also got my share of trouble.

As soon as I discovered that the Circassian girl was at Pechorin's quarters, I put on my epaulets and my sword, and went to him.

"He lay on his bed in the front room, with one hand under his head; in the other, he held a pipe that had gone out; the door leading to the second room was locked, and the key was not in the key-hole. All this I noticed, at once . . . I began to clear my throat and tap the threshold with my heel, but he pretended not to hear.

"'Ensign!'[31] I said, as sternly as I could, 'don't you see that I am here?'

"'Oh, hello, Maksim Maksimich! Want a pipe?' he answered, without getting up.

"'I beg your pardon, I am not Maksim Maksimich; I'm junior captain to you.'

"'Makes no difference. How about some tea? If you only knew what a worry torments me!'

"'I know everything,' I answered, walking up to the bed.

"'So much the better, I am not in a mood to relate.'

"'Ensign, you have committed an offense for which I, too, may be held responsible. . . .'

"'Oh, come! Where's the harm? We've long shared everything, haven't we?'

"'It's no time for joking. Your sword, if you please!'

"'Mitka,[32] my sword!'

"Mitka brought the sword. Having fulfilled my duty, I sat down beside him on the bed and said: 'Look here, Grigoriy Aleksandrovich, you must admit that it was not a nice thing to do.'

"'What wasn't?'

"'Why, your carrying off Bela . . . Ah, that blackguard Azamat! . . . Come on, own up,' I said to him.

"'Suppose I like her?'

"Well, what could one say to that? . . . I was nonplussed. However, after a silence, I told him that if the father demanded her back, it would be necessary to return her.

"'Not at all necessary.'

"'But if he finds out she is here?'

"'How will he find out?'

"I was again nonplussed. 'Look here, Maksim Maksimich,' said Pechorin, raising himself, 'you're a kind man, aren't you? Now, if we give his daughter back to that savage, he'll either slit her throat or sell her. What's done is done, let's not go out of our way to make things worse than they are; let me keep Bela, and you keep my sword . . .'

"'You can at least show her to me,' I said.

"'She's behind that door, but I myself have tried in vain to see her today; keeps sitting in a corner, wrapped up in her veil, neither speaks nor looks at one; shy as a wild gazelle. I've hired the wife of our innkeeper: she can speak Tatar and will take care of Bela and accustom her to the idea that she is mine, for she won't belong to anybody but me,' he added, hitting the table with his fist. I agreed to this too . . . What would you have me do? There are some people with whom you just must agree."

"And what happened?" I asked Maksim Maksimich. "Did he actually tame her, or did she pine away in captivity from homesickness?"

"Oh come, why should she be homesick? From the fort one could see the same mountains as from her village—and that's all these savages need. Besides, Pechorin would make her some present every day; during the first days, she would silently and proudly push away the gifts, which would then go to the innkeeper's wife and excite her eloquence. Ah, gifts! What won't a woman do for a bit of colored rag . . . Let's not digress, however . . . For a long time, Pechorin wasted his efforts on her; meanwhile, he was learning Tatar,[33] and she was beginning to understand Russian. Little by little she got used to looking at him, at first from under her brows, askance, and she would be sad, and softly hum her songs, so that at times I would get sad myself, as I listened to her from the adjoining room. Never shall I forget one scene: I was going past her window and glanced in; Bela was sitting on the stove ledge with her head bent low, and Pechorin was standing before her. 'Listen to me, my peri,' he was saying. 'You know very well that, sooner or later, you must be mine—why then do you keep tormenting me? You are not in love with some Chechen, are you? If you are, I'll let you go home immediately.' She gave a hardly perceptible start and shook her head. 'Or is it,' he went on, 'that I am completely hateful to you?' She sighed. 'Or does your faith forbid you to fall in love with me?' She grew pale and remained silent. 'Believe me, Allah is the same for all races, and if he allows me to love you, why should he forbid you to return my feelings?' She looked intently into his face, as if struck with this new idea; her eyes expressed distrust and the desire to make sure. What eyes they were! They simply glowed like two coals.

"'Listen, my dear and good Bela!' continued Pechorin. 'You see how I love you; I'm ready to give anything to cheer you up; I want you to be happy, and if you start brooding again, I shall die. Tell me, will you be more cheerful?' She lapsed into thought, never taking her black eyes off him, then she smiled sweetly and nodded her head in sign of assent. He took her hand and began persuading her to kiss him;

she weakly defended herself, and only repeated in broken Russian: 'Please, please, don't, don't.' He insisted, she started trembling and began to cry. 'I am your captive,' she said, 'your slave; of course, you can compel me,'—and there were more tears.

"Pechorin struck his forehead with his fist and rushed into the next room. I went there; he was gloomily pacing to and fro, with his arms folded on his chest. 'Well, old man?' I said to him. 'A demon, not a woman!' he answered. 'Only I give you my word of honor that she will be mine . . .' I shook my head. 'Would you like to bet?' he said. 'In a week's time!' 'Agreed!' We shook hands on it and parted.

"The first thing he did next day was to dispatch an express messenger to Kizlyar[34] to make various purchases; quantities of various Persian fabrics, too many to enumerate, were brought back.

" 'What do you think, Maksim Maksimich,' he said to me as he showed me the presents, 'could an Asiatic belle withstand such an array?' 'You don't know these Circassian girls,'[35] I replied. 'It is not at all the same thing as the Georgian girls or the Trans-Caucasian Tatar girls . . .[36] not at all the same thing. These have their own rules, they are brought up differently.' Pechorin smiled and began to whistle a march.

"And it turned out I was right; the presents produced only half the desired effect: she became sweeter, more trusting—but that was all, so he decided to try a final resource. One morning, he ordered his horse to be saddled, put on Circassian dress, armed himself and went to her. 'Bela!' he said, 'You know how I love you. I dared to carry you off, thinking that when you got to know me, you would love me; I have made a mistake; farewell! Remain in complete possession of everything I own; if you

like, go back to your father—you are free. I am guilty
before you, and must punish myself. Farewell, I am
going—where? How should I know? Perchance, I
shall not be long running after a bullet or a sword
blow: remember me then, and forgive me.' He
turned away and extended his hand in farewell. She
did not take his hand, she was silent. But as I stood
behind the door, I could distinguish her face
through the chink, and I felt sorry . . . such a
deathly pallor had spread over that sweet little face!
Hearing no answer, Pechorin took a few steps toward the door; he was trembling—and shall I tell
you? I think he was really capable of carrying out
what he had spoken of in jest. That was the kind of
man he was, the Lord knows! But barely had he
touched the door, than she jumped up, burst into
sobs and threw herself on his neck. Would you believe it? As I stood behind the door, I, too, began to
cry; I mean, you know, it was not really crying, it
was just—oh, silliness!"

The junior captain paused.

"Yes, I must admit," he said after a while, pulling
at his mustache. "It vexed me to think that no
woman ever loved me like that."

"And did their happiness last long?" I asked.

"Yes, she confessed to us that ever since the day
she first saw Pechorin, he often appeared to her in
dreams, and that no man had ever made such an
impression on her before. Yes, they were happy!"

"How dull!" I exclaimed involuntarily. Indeed, I
had expected a tragic denouement, and, all of a sudden, my hopes had been deceived so unexpectedly!
"Is it possible," I went on, "that the father did not
suspect you had her in the fortress?"

"As a matter of fact, he did suspect, I think. A few

days later we learned that the old man had been killed. Here is how it happened. . . ."

My attention was aroused again.

"I should tell you that Kazbich imagined that Azamat had stolen his horse with the father's consent—this is, at least, what I conjecture. Well, there he was one day, waiting by the road, a couple of miles beyond the village; the old man was riding home after a vain search for his daughter; his retainers had fallen behind—it was dusk—he was riding pensively at a walk, when suddenly Kazbich, like a cat, darted out of a bush, jumped onto his horse behind him, with a thrust of his dagger threw him to the ground, grabbed the reins, and was gone. Some of the retainers saw all this from a knoll; they dashed off after him, but could not catch up with him."

"He made up for the loss of his horse and avenged himself," I said, to elicit an opinion from my interlocutor.

"Of course, according to their standards," said the junior captain, "he was completely in the right."

I could not help being struck by the capacity of the Russian to adapt himself to the customs of that people among which he happens to be living. I do not know whether this trait of the mind deserves blame or praise, but it attests to his incredible flexibility and the presence of that lucid common sense that pardons evil wherever it recognizes its necessity or the impossibility of its abolishment.

Meanwhile, we had finished our tea; the horses, long since harnessed, had got chilled in the snow; the moon was paling in the west and was ready to immerse herself in her black clouds suspended on the distant peaks like the shreds of a torn curtain. We left the hut. Contrary to my fellow-traveler's prediction, the weather had cleared, and promised us a serene morning; the dances of stars[37] were interlinked in wondrous patterns above the distant horizon, and went out, one by one, while the palish reflection of dawn flooded the dark-violet vault, gradually illumining the steep slopes of the mountains, covered with virgin snow. Right and left, gloomy and mysterious abysses yawned black, and thither glided the mists, whirling and winding, like snakes, down the furrows of nearby cliffs, as if aware and afraid of the approach of day.

All was silent in heaven and on earth, as it is in the heart of man at the moment of his morning prayer; only once in a while, a cool wind would come rippling from the east, raising a little the rime-covered manes of the horses. We set out; five skinny nags dragged our carriages with difficulty along the road winding up Mount Gud. We followed on foot, chocking the wheels with stones whenever the horses became exhausted; the road seemed to lead up into the sky because, as far as the eye could see, it kept ascending and, finally, it lost itself in the cloud which, since the previous evening, had been resting on the summit of Mount Gud, like a vulture awaiting its prey; the snow crunched underfoot; the air was becoming so rare, that it was painful to breathe; the blood kept rushing to our heads every moment, but despite all this, a delightful kind of feeling spread along all my veins, and I felt somehow elated at being so far above the world—a childish feeling, no doubt, but, on getting away from social conventions and coming closer to nature, we cannot help becoming children: all the things that have been acquired are shed by the soul, and it becomes again as it was once, and as it is surely to be again some day. He who, like me, has had occasion to wander over wild mountains and scrutinize, for a

long time, their fantastic shapes, and avidly swallow
the vivifying air pervading their gorges, will certainly understand my desire to render, to relate, to
paint those magical images. Finally, we got to the
top of Mount Gud, stopped, and looked around us:
upon it hung the gray cloud whose cold breath
threatened us with a gathering storm; but everything was so limpid and golden-bright in the east
that we, that is to say the junior captain and I, completely forgot that cloud. Yes, the junior captain too:
in simple hearts, the sense of the beauty and gran-
deur of nature is a hundred times stronger and more
vivid than it is in us, enthusiastic tellers of tales,
oral or written.[38]

"You are accustomed, I suppose, to these mag-
nificent views?" I said to him.

"Yes, sir, one can become accustomed even to the
whistle of bullets, that is to say become accustomed
to concealing an involuntary throbbing of the heart."

"I have heard that, on the contrary, some old
warriors find that music even pleasant?"

"Of course, it is pleasant, if you like; but again,
only because one's heart beats faster. Look," he
added, pointing eastward, "what country!"

And indeed, I doubt if I shall ever see such a
panorama anywhere again: below us, lay the Koyshaur Valley, crossed by the Aragva and by another
river, as by two silver threads; a pale, bluish haze
glided over it, heading for the neighboring canyons,
away from the warm rays of morning; right and
left, the crests of mountains, each higher than the
next, intersected and stretched out, covered with
snow or shrubs; in the distance, more mountains, but
no two cliffs were alike; and all these snows burned
with a ruddy glow, so merrily so brightly, that it
made one wonder why one should not stay here for-

ever; the sun peeped from behind a dark-blue mountain which only a practiced eye could have distinguished from a storm-cloud; but above the sun there was a blood-red band, to which my companion paid particular attention. "I told you," he exclaimed, "that we'd have some nasty weather tonight; we've got to hurry, or else it may well catch us on the Mountain of the Cross. Get going!" he shouted to the drivers.

Chains were placed under the wheels as a substitute for brakes, so as to keep them from gathering momentum; the horses were held by the bridle, and we began to descend; on the right was the cliff, on the left, such a precipice that a whole hamlet of Ossetians dwelling at its bottom looked like a swallow's nest; I shuddered to think that often here, in the dead of night, along this road, where there is not room enough for two carriages to pass each other, some courier drives a dozen times a year, without getting out of his jolting vehicle. One of our coachmen was a Russian peasant from the Province of Yaroslavl', the other an Ossetian. The Ossetian led his shaft horse by the bridle with all possible precautions, having unhitched the outside horses beforehand; but our easygoing Russ did not even bother to get off his box seat! When I observed to him that he might, at least, take this trouble on account of my valise, which I had no desire whatever to retrieve from that abyss, he answered me: "Why, sir! With God's help, we'll make it no worse than they: after all, this isn't my first time." And he was right, we might well not have made it; but then again we did, and if all people reasoned more, they would be convinced that life is not worth worrying about so much. . . .

But perhaps you would like to know the ending of Bela's story? In the first place, it is not a novella

I am writing, but traveling notes; consequently, I
cannot make the junior captain tell the story before
he actually began telling it. Therefore, wait a while,
or, if you wish, turn several pages; however, I do not
advise you to do this since traversing Krestovaya-
Gora, Mountain of the Cross (or, as the scholarly
Gamba miscalls it, *le Mont St. Christophe*[39]) is something worth your curiosity. So there we were going
down Mount Gud into Chertova Valley . . . What a
romantic name! You derive Chertova from *chort*
[devil] and visualize, at once, the aerie of the Evil
Spirit among forbidding cliffs, but this is not the case
at all; the name of the valley comes from the word
*cherta* [border] and not *chort*, for here once lay the
boundary of Georgia. This valley was now packed
with snowdrifts which called to mind, rather vividly,
Saratov, Tambov, and other *good old places*[40] in our
fatherland.

"Here we are at the Mountain of the Cross!" said
the junior captain when we had driven down into
Border Valley, and he indicated a hill covered by a
shroud of snow; on its summit, a cross of stone
showed black, and past it there ran a barely perceptible road which is traveled only when the lower one,
running around the hill, is blocked by snow: our
drivers announced that there had not been any snow-
slides, as yet, and, to spare their horses, took us by
the lower road. At the turn, we met half a dozen Ossetians; they offered us their services and, taking
hold of the wheels, with much shouting, set about
dragging and supporting our carriages. And indeed,
the road was dangerous: on the right, there hung,
over our heads, masses of snow, ready, it seemed, at
the first gust of wind, to come tumbling into the
gorge; the narrow road was partly covered by snow
which, at some places, gave way underfoot, while in

others, it had turned into ice from the action of the sun's rays and night frosts, so that we had trouble making our way on foot; the horses kept falling: on our left, yawned a deep gulch, where a torrent rolled, now hiding under the icy crust, now leaping foamily over the black boulders. In two hours we could hardly get around Mt. Cross—a little more than a mile in two hours! Meanwhile, the clouds had settled, it began to hail and to snow heavily; the wind, bursting into the gorges, roared, whistled like Nightingale, the Robber,[41] and soon the stone cross disappeared in the mist, which was rolling in from the east, in billows each thicker and more compact than the one before. Incidentally, there exists a bizarre, but generally accepted, legend about that cross, of which it is said that it was set there by the Emperor Peter I, when he drove through the Caucasus.[42] But, in the first place, Peter went only as far as Dagestan, and in the second, an inscription on the cross, in large letters, says that it was set by order of General Ermolov, and namely, in 1824. But the legend, despite that inscription, has become so deeply rooted, that one really does not know what to believe, especially since we are not accustomed to believe inscriptions.

We had still to descend some three miles over icy rocks and treacherous snow in order to reach the Kobi station. The horses were exhausted; we were chilled; the blizzard hummed louder and louder, just like one of our own in the north, only its savage melody was more sorrowful, more plaintive. "You, too, are an exile," I reflected. "You wail for your wide spacious steppes! There you had room to unfurl your cold wings, while here you are stifled and cramped like an eagle that beats with cries against the bars of his iron cage."

"This is bad!" the junior captain was saying, "look, you can't see a thing around, only mist and snow; any moment, one can expect to fall into a chasm or get stuck in the brushwood, and further down, the Baydara River has swollen so much, I presume, that it cannot be crossed. That's Asia for you, be it people or rivers, there is absolutely no depending on them!"

The drivers were shouting and swearing as they beat the horses, which snorted and balked and refused to budge for anything in the world, despite the eloquence of the whips. "Your Excellency," said one of the coachmen at last, "we'll never make Kobi today: won't you have us turn off to the left while we still can? Over there, on the mountainside, there's a black blur, must be huts; travelers always stop there in bad weather, sir. He says he'll show the way, if you tip him," he added, pointing to one of the Ossetians.

"I know, my friend, I know without your telling me!" said the junior captain. "Ah, those rascals! They'll jump at any chance to extract a tip."

"Still, you must admit," said I, "that, without them, we would have been worse off."

"That's so, that's so," he muttered. "I'm fed up with those guides! They have a flair for lucre. As if you could not find the road without them!"

So we turned off to the left, and, somehow, after a good deal of fuss, reached a meager shelter, consisting of two huts put together out of slabs and boulders and surrounded by a wall of the same material. The ragged proprietors received us cordially. I learned afterwards that the government pays them and feeds them on condition that they receive travelers overtaken by the storm. "It is all for the better," I said settling down by the fire. "Now

you can finish telling me your story about Bela: I
am sure that that was not the end of it."

"And why are you so sure?" answered the junior
captain with a wink and a sly smile.

"Because that's not the way things happen: what
began in an unusual way must end likewise."

"Well, you have guessed. . . ."

"I'm very glad."

"It's all right for you to be glad, but it makes me
really sad to recall it. She was a nice little girl, that
Bela! Eventually I got so used to her, she might have
been my daughter; and she was fond of me, too. I
should tell you that I don't have a family; it's already been twelve years or so since I have had news
of my father and mother, and I never thought of
providing myself with a wife. And now, don't you
know, somehow it would not seem becoming; so I
was happy that I had found someone to spoil. She
used to sing songs for us, or dance the *lezginka* . . .
And how she danced! I have seen our young ladies
in provincial cities, and once, sir, I visited the Club
of the Nobility, in Moscow;[43] some twenty years ago
—only none of them would stand a chance against
her! It was a different thing altogether! Pechorin
would dress her up like a little doll, he would pam-
per her and dote on her, and her beauty improved
marvelously under our care! Her face and hands
lost their tan, color came into her cheeks . . . And
how gay she was! She would constantly make fun of
me, the saucy little thing, God forgive her!"

"And what happened when you told her about her
father's death?"

"We kept it from her for a long time, until she got
used to her situation; and when we did tell her, she
cried for a couple of days, and then forgot.

"For about four months, things could not have

gone better. Pechorin, as I think I've already told you, was passionately fond of hunting: at times he would feel an uncontrollable urge to go into the woods after boar or wild goats, but now he would not even step outside the rampart of the fort. Soon, however, I began to notice that he would become pensive again, would pace his room with his hands clasped behind his back. Then one day, without telling anybody, he was off to shoot, was gone the whole morning—this happened once, and it happened again, and became more and more frequent. 'That's bad,' I thought, 'no doubt, they must have had a tiff.'

"One morning, I went to see them—I can still visualize it vividly: Bela was sitting on the bed, in a black silk *beshmet*, and the little thing looked so pale and sad, that I was frightened!

" 'And where is Pechorin?' I asked.

" 'Out hunting.'

" 'Did he go today?'

She was silent, as though she found it difficult to articulate. 'No, he's been away since yesterday,' she said at last, with a heavy sigh.

" 'I hope nothing happened to him?'

" 'Yesterday, I thought and thought all day,' she answered through her tears, 'I imagined various accidents: it would now seem to me that he had been wounded by a wild boar, and now, that a Chechen had carried him off to the mountains. And today I'm beginning to think that he does not love me.'

" 'Really, my dear, you couldn't have thought up anything worse!'

"She started to cry, then proudly lifted her head, wiped her tears and went on:

" 'If he does not love me, who prevents him from

sending me home? I don't force him. But if things go on like this, I'll go away myself: I'm not his slave, I am the daughter of a prince!'

"I began to reason with her. 'Listen, Bela, after all, he can't be expected to stay here, as if sewn to your skirt; he is a young man, he likes to chase game; he'll roam for a while, and then come back, but if you are going to mope, you'll bore him all the sooner.'

"'You're right, you're right!' she answered. 'I'll be gay.' And with a peal of laughter, she seized her tambourine, and began to sing, dance, and skip around me; but this, too, did not last; she fell on the bed again and covered her face with her hands.

"What was I to do with her? After all, do you know, I've never had occasion to deal with women. I thought and thought how I could comfort her, and could not think of anything; for some time we both remained silent . . . A most unpleasant predicament, sir!

"Finally I said to her: 'How about a stroll on the rampart? The weather is fine!' This was in September.[44] And indeed, the day was wonderful, bright and not hot; you could see all the mountains as if served on a plate. We went and walked, back and forth, on the rampart, in silence; finally, she sat down on the turf, and I sat down beside her. Really, it makes me laugh to think about it: I kept running after her as if I were some kind of nurse.

"Our fort stood on high ground, and the view from the rampart was beautiful: on one side, an extensive meadow,[45] furrowed by several ravines, ended in a forest which stretched all the way up to the mountain ridge; here and there, native hamlets smoked upon it, and herds of horses ranged; on the other side, there ran a shallow river, margined by the dense brush, which covered the flinty heights, linked up with the main Caucasian range. We sat in a corner of the bastion, and thus could see everything in either direction. This is what I saw: somebody rode out of the forest on a gray horse, he came nearer and nearer, and finally, stopped on the far side of the river, some two hundred and fifty yards from us, and began wheeling his horse around like a madman. What could it mean? 'Take a look, Bela,' I said, 'you've got young eyes, who is that fancy horseman? Whom has he come to entertain?'

"She looked, and cried: 'It's Kazbich!'

"'Ah, the rascal! Has he come to make fun of us?' I looked more closely. Yes, it was Kazbich, with his swarthy face, his tatters, and dirty as usual. 'That is my father's horse,' said Bela, grasping me by the arm; she shook like a leaf, and her eyes flashed. 'Oho!' I thought to myself, 'in you, too, my dear girl, the robber blood is not silent!'

"'Come over here,' I said to the sentry. 'Check your rifle, and knock that fellow out of his saddle for me—you'll get a silver ruble.' 'Yes, sir, only he won't stay put . . .' 'Order him to,' I said, laughing. 'Hey, chum,' shouted the sentry waving to him, 'wait a bit; why do you spin like a top?'

"Kazbich actually did stop and listened; he thought, no doubt, that we were opening negotiations with him. Negotiations, indeed! My grenadier took aim . . . fired . . . and missed. The instant the powder flashed in the pan, Kazbich pushed his horse, and it leaped to one side.[46] He rose in the stirrups, cried something in his own tongue, made a threatening gesture with his riding whip—and disappeared.

"'You ought to be ashamed of yourself,' I said to the sentry.

"'He's gone off to die, sir,' he answered. 'You can't kill those damned people outright.'

"A quarter of an hour later, Pechorin returned from the hunt. Bela threw herself on his neck, and there was not a word of complaint, nor was there a single reproach for his long absence.

"By now, even I was cross with him. 'For goodness sake!' I said, 'just a moment ago, Kazbich was right over there, on the other side of the river, and we fired at him: nothing easier for you than to run into him. Those mountain folks are vengeful; do you think he has not guessed that you had a hand in helping Azamat? Moreover, I'll bet you anything that he recognized Bela today. I know that, a year ago, he was mightily attracted to her—he told me so himself—and if he could have hoped to get together a decent amount of bride money, he would certainly have asked her in marriage.' Pechorin looked thoughtful. 'Yes,' he answered, 'we have to be more careful . . . Bela, from now on, you must not go walking on the rampart any more.'

"That evening, I had a long talk with him. I was vexed that he had changed toward that poor little girl; besides spending half the day hunting, his treatment of her had become cold, he would seldom caress her, and she began to wilt noticeably; her little face became thinner, her big eyes lost their luster. You would ask her: 'What are you sighing about, Bela? Are you sad?' 'No.' 'Is there anything you'd like?' 'No.' 'Do you miss your family?' 'I have no family.' Sometimes, for days on end, you could not get anything but 'yes' or 'no' out of her.

"Well, this was what I started talking to him about. 'Now look here, Maksim Maksimich,' he answered, 'I have an unfortunate disposition: whether it is my upbringing that made me thus or whether

God created me so, I don't know: I only know that if I am a cause of unhappiness for others, I am no less unhappy myself. Naturally, that is poor comfort for them, nevertheless, this is a fact. In my early youth, from the minute I emerged from under my family's supervision, I began madly to enjoy every pleasure that money could buy, and, naturally, those pleasures became repulsive to me. Then I ventured out into the *grand monde*, and, soon, I became likewise fed up with society: I have been in love with fashionable belles, and have been loved, but their love only irritated my imagination and vanity, while my heart remained empty . . . I began to read, to study—I got just as sick of studies—I saw that neither fame nor happiness depended on them in the least, since the happiest people are dunces, while fame is a question of luck, and in order to obtain it, you only have to be nimble. Then I began to be bored . . . Soon after, I was transferred to the Caucasus: this was the happiest time of my life. I hoped that boredom did not exist amid Chechen bullets. In vain! After one month, I got so used to their buzzing and to the nearness of death, that, really, I paid more attention to the mosquitoes, and I was even more bored than before, because I had almost lost my last hope.[47] When I saw Bela in my home, when for the first time I held her in my lap and kissed her black curls, I—fool that I was—imagined she was an angel sent me by compassionate fate . . . I was wrong again. The love of a wild girl was little better than than that of a lady of rank; the ignorance and the naïveté of one pall on you as much as the coquetry of the other. I still like her, I suppose; I am grateful to her for several rather sweet moments; I am ready to die for her—only I find her company dull. Whether I am a fool or a villain, I don't know; but of

one thing I'm sure, that I also deserve pity, even
more perhaps than she. My soul has been impaired
by the fashionable world, I have a restless fancy, an
insatiable heart; whatever I get is not enough; I become used as easily to sorrow as to delight, and my
life becomes more empty day by day; there is only
one remedy left for me: to travel. As soon as I can,
I shall set out—but not for Europe, God preserve!
I shall go to America, to Arabia, to India—perchance
I may die somewhere, on the way! At least, I am
sure that this last consolation will not soon be exhausted with the help of storms and bad roads.' He
went on like this for a long time, and his words became engraved in my memory because it was the
first time that I had heard such things from a man of
twenty-five, and I hope to God it may also be the
last. . . ."

"What a strange thing! Would you be so kind as
to tell me," the junior captain continued, addressing
me, "you've lived, it seems, in the capital, haven't
you, and not too long ago: Is it true that all the
young men there are like that?"

I replied that there were many people who talked
like that; that probably there were some who were
telling the truth; that, on the other hand, disillusion-
ment, like all fashions, having begun in the upper
strata of society, had descended to the lower, which
were now wearing it out, and that nowadays those
people who were really bored the most tried to conceal this misfortune as though it were a vice. The
junior captain did not understand these subtle distinctions. He shook his head and smiled slyly.

"It was the French, was it, who introduced the
fashion of being bored?"

"No, the English."

"Ah, that's how it is!" he answered. "Well, they have always been inveterate drunkards!"

I could not help recalling one Moscow lady who maintained that Byron was nothing more than a drunkard. But then, the junior captain's remark was more pardonable: in order to abstain from liquor, he naturally tried to convince himself that all misfortunes in the world come from drinking.

Meanwhile he continued his narrative as follows:

"Kazbich did not show up again. But, somehow, I don't know why, I could not drive the thought out of my head that there had been some reason for his coming and that he was cooking up some trouble.

"Well, one day, Pechorin began persuading me to go boar-hunting with him; for a long time I kept refusing: after all, a wild boar was no novelty to me; nevertheless he did succeed in dragging me off with him. We took half a dozen soldiers with us and left early in the morning. Until ten o'clock we poked around in the rushes and in the woods, but found not one brute. 'Hey, how about turning back?' I said. 'What's the point in persisting? It is obviously our unlucky day!' But Pechorin, despite the heat and fatigue, did not want to return without a kill. That's the kind of man he was: whatever he set his heart on he had to have, you could see he had been spoiled by his mamma when he was young. At last, at noontime, we tracked down that damned boar. Bang, bang! went our guns, but it was not to be, the boar escaped into the rushes. It was that kind of unlucky day! Well, we rested for a little while and set out for home.

"We rode side by side, in silence, our reins slack, we were almost at the fort, only the brush was now hiding it from us. Suddenly a shot rang out. We glanced at each other, the same suspicion struck us

both. We galloped headlong in the direction of the
shot. We saw soldiers crowding on the rampart and
pointing toward the field, and there a horseman was
flying at full speed, holding something white across
his saddle. Pechorin let out a yell no worse than that
of any Chechen. His rifle came out of its case, and
off he went; I followed. Fortunately, because of our
unsuccessful hunt, our horses were not worn out,
they strained forward from under the saddles, and
with every moment we came closer and closer. And
at last I recognized Kazbich, only I could not distinguish what it was that he held in front of him. At
this point I came abreast of Pechorin and cried to
him 'It's Kazbich!' He glanced at me, nodded his
head and whipped his horse.

"Well, at last we got within rifle range of him;
whether Kazbich's horse was worn out or was worse
than our mounts, I don't know; only, in spite of all
his efforts, it was not making a great deal of progress. I think that at this moment he must have remembered his Karagyoz.

"I looked and saw Pechorin take aim at full gallop.
'Don't fire!' I cried to him. 'Save your shot, we'll
catch up with him anyway.' But those youngsters,
they always lose their heads at the wrong time. The
shot rang out and the bullet broke the hind leg of
Kazbich's horse: carried on by impetus, it took another ten bounds or so, then stumbled and fell to its
knees. Kazbich jumped off, and then we saw that he
was holding in his arms a woman wrapped up in a
yashmak. It was Bela, poor Bela! He shouted something at us in his own tongue, and raised his dagger
over her. No time could be lost; I fired in my turn,
at random; the bullet must have hit him in the shoulder because he suddenly lowered his arm. When the
smoke had cleared, the wounded horse lay on the

ground, and beside it lay Bela, while Kazbich, having abandoned his rifle, was scrambling like a cat up the scrub on the cliff. I would have liked to bring him down, but I had no charge ready. We jumped off our horses and rushed toward Bela. Poor little thing, she was lying motionless, and blood poured out of her wound in streams. What a villain! He could at least have hit her in the heart—then after all, it would have been over with one blow, but in the back, the most treacherous stab! She was unconscious. We tore up the veil and bound up the wound as tight as we could. In vain did Pechorin kiss her cold lips—nothing could restore her to consciousness.

"Pechorin mounted his horse; I lifted her off the ground and seated her on his saddle as best I could; he put his arm around her, and we rode back. After a few minutes of silence, Pechorin said to me: 'Look here, Maksim Maksimich, we'll never get her home alive this way.' 'That's true,' I said, and we set our horses going at full speed. A crowd of people was waiting for us at the gate of the fort. Carefully we carried the wounded girl to Pechorin's quarters and sent for the doctor. Although he was drunk, he came, examined the wound, and announced that she could not live more than one day; only he was wrong. . . ."

"She recovered?" I asked the junior captain, grasping him by the arm and involuntarily feeling glad.

"No," he answered, "the doctor's mistake was that she lingered two days."

"But explain to me how on earth Kazbich managed to carry her off?"

"Well, this is how it happened: despite Pechorin's prohibition, she had gone out of the fort to the river. It was, don't you know, a very hot day; she sat down on a stone and dipped her feet in the water. Here

Kazbich stealthly approached, scrabbled her up, clapped his hand over her mouth and dragged her off into the bushes. Once there, he jumped onto his horse, and off he went. Meanwhile, she had had time to scream, the sentries were alerted, they fired but missed, and at the next moment, we rode up."

"But why did Kazbich want to take her away?"

"Well, you see, it is a known fact that these Circassians are a bunch of thieves. They cannot help filching anything that is within reach; they may not need the thing, and yet they will steal it. They simply can't be held responsible for that! And besides, he had had a liking for her, for a long time."

"And Bela died?"

"She died; but she suffered for quite a while, and we suffered a good bit with her. Around ten at night she came to; we were sitting by her bed; as soon as she opened her eyes, she began calling for Pechorin. 'I'm right here beside you, my *janechka* (that is, as we would say, "darling"),' he answered, taking her by the hand. 'I'm going to die,' she said.

"We began trying to comfort her; we told her that the doctor had promised to cure her without fail. She shook her head and turned away to the wall; she did not want to die!

"In the night she became delirious; her forehead was burning; a shiver of fever ran now and then over her entire body. She spoke in incoherent accents about her father, about her brother; she wanted to go to the mountains, to her home. Then she would also talk of Pechorin, give him various pet names, or else reproach him for having stopped loving his *janechka*.

"He listened to her in silence, with his head in his hands; but not once did I notice a single tear on his eyelashes: whether he actually could not cry, or whether he was controlling himself, I don't know. As for me, I'd never seen anything more pitiful.

"Toward morning her delirium ceased; for an hour or so she lay motionless and pale, and in such a state of weakness that one could hardly notice if she were breathing or not; then she felt better, and began to speak, and what do you think she spoke about? An idea like that could only have occurred to a dying person! She began to grieve that she was not a Christian, and that in the next world her soul would not meet Pechorin's soul, and that some other woman would be his sweetheart in heaven. The thought occurred to me to have her baptized before her death; this I suggested to her. She looked at me hesitantly, and for a long time could not say a word; at last she replied that she would die in the same faith in which she was born. Thus passed a whole day. How she changed in the course of that day! Her pale cheeks sank in, her eyes became so very, very large, her lips burned. She felt an inner heat as if red-hot iron lay in her breast.

"Another night came; we never closed our eyes, nor moved from her bed. She suffered dreadfully, she moaned, and whenever the pain began to subside, she endeavored to convince Pechorin that she was better, tried to persuade him to get some sleep, kissed his hand and kept holding it in her hands. Toward morning she began to feel the restlessness before death, and started to toss; she dislodged the bandage, and the blood flowed again. When the wound was rebandaged, she quieted down for a minute and began asking Pechorin to kiss her. He knelt beside the bed, raised her head up a little from the pillow and pressed his lips to her lips which were growing cold; she firmly wound her trembling arms round his neck, as though in this kiss she had

wanted to transmit her soul to him . . . Ah, she did
well to die! What, indeed, would have become of
her if Pechorin abandoned her? And this is what
would have happened, sooner or later. . . .

"For half the next day, she was calm, silent and
submissive, no matter how much our army doctor
tormented her with poultices and potions. 'For goodness' sake,' I told him, 'haven't you said yourself
that she was sure to die, why then all those medica-
tions of yours?' 'Still it's better this way, Maksim
Maksimich,' he answered, 'so as to have a clear conscience.' A clear conscience, indeed!

"In the afternoon she began to be tortured by
thirst. We opened the windows, but outside it was
even hotter than in the room; we put ice by the bed,
but nothing helped. I knew that this unbearable
thirst was a sign that the end was near, and this I
told Pechorin.

"Water, water! . . ." she said hoarsely, raising herself on the bed.

"He turned as white as a sheet, grabbed a glass,
filled it and brought it to her. I covered my eyes with
my hands and began to say a prayer—I don't remember which one. Yes, sir, I've seen a lot of people die
in hospitals and on the battlefield, but it was not at
all like this, not at all! And another thing, I admit,
saddened me: before her death she did not remember me once, and yet, it seems, I had loved her like
a father. Well, God will forgive her! . . . And in
truth who am I to be remembered by anybody before death?

"Immediately after that draught of water, she felt
better, and three minutes later she expired. We held
a mirror up to her lips—it remained unclouded!
I led Pechorin out of the room and we went on to
the rampart; for a long while we walked up and

down, side by side, without saying a word, our hands behind our backs; his face did not express anything unusual, and this annoyed me; in his place, I would have died of grief. Finally he sat down on the ground in the shade and began to trace something in the sand with a bit of stick. I wanted to comfort him, mainly for the sake of propriety, don't you know, and started to speak; he lifted his head and laughed. A chill ran over my skin at this laughter. I went off to order the coffin.

"I must admit, I busied myself with this partly for the sake of distraction. I possessed a piece of heavy silk, and with this I lined the coffin and adorned it with Circassian silver braid which Pechorin had bought for her, anyway.

"Early the next day we buried her behind the fort, by the river, near the place where she had sat for the last time; around her little grave, bushes of white acacia and elder have spread since then. I wanted to set up a cross, but somehow, don't you know, it did not seem right; after all, she was not a Christian."

"And what happened to Pechorin?" I asked.

"Pechorin was ill for a long time, and he lost weight, poor fellow, but never again did we talk about Bela: I saw that it would have been unpleasant for him, so why talk about it? Some three months later, he was assigned to the E. regiment, and he left for Georgia. We have not met since then . . . Yes, now that I think of it, someone was telling me recently that he had returned to Russia, but there was nothing about it in divisional orders. But then news is late in reaching the likes of us."

Here he launched upon a long dissertation about how unpleasant it was to get news a year late—he was probably trying to drown sad memories.

I neither interrupted him, nor listened.

After an hour it became possible to continue our journey; the blizzard had subsided, the sky had cleared, and we set out. On the way I could not help starting to talk again about Pechorin and Bela.

"And have you heard what became of Kazbich?" I asked.

"Kazbich? Well, I really don't know . . . I've heard that on the right flank of the Shapsugs[48] there is a Kazbich, a daredevil who wears a red *beshmet* and rides back and forth at a walk under our gunfire, and bows most politely when a bullet buzzes near him; but it could hardly be the same man!"

At Kobi, Maksim Maksimich and I parted; I continued with post horses, while he, because of his heavy load, could not follow me. We did not expect ever to meet again, and yet we did meet, and if you like, I'll tell you about it; it's quite a story . . . You must admit, though, that Maksim Maksimich is a man worthy of respect, isn't he? If you admit that, I shall be fully rewarded for my story, which perhaps has been too long.

# Maksim Maksimich

AFTER PARTING with Maksim Maksimich, I drove swiftly through Terek Gorge[49] and Daryal Gorge, lunched at Kazbek, had tea at Lars, and reached Vladikavkaz in time for supper. I shall spare you a description of the mountains—exclamations that do not express anything, pictures that do not represent anything, especially for those who have not been there themselves, and statistical notes that decidedly nobody would want to read.

I stopped at an inn where all travelers stop, but where, nonetheless, you cannot find anybody to roast a pheasant or cook some cabbage soup, since the three war invalids, who have been put in charge of the place, are so stupid or so drunk that no good whatever can be got out of them.

I was informed that I would have to spend three more days there: the military detail, the *okaziya*, from Ekaterinograd had not yet arrived and, consequently, could not start back. What an aggravating detail! . . . But a bad pun is no consolation to a Russian. It occurred to me then that I might find some diversion in writing down Maksim Maksimich's tale about Bela. Little did I think that it would become the first link of a long chain of stories: you will observe how sometimes an insignificant event has dire consequences! . . . By the way, you may not know what an *okaziya* is. It means a protective detail consisting of half a company of infantry and a cannon with which convoys travel through the Kabarda region, from Vladikavkaz to Ekaterinograd.

The first day I spent most dully; on the next, early in the morning, a carriage drove into the yard. Why, Maksim Maksimich! We met like two old friends. I offered him the use of my room; he made no pretense of ceremony, he even clapped me on the shoulder and twisted his mouth into the semblance of a smile. Such a queer chap!

Maksim Maksimich was deeply versed in the culinary art; he made a wonderful job of roasting a pheasant, and had the happy thought of basting it with a cucumber marinade; I must admit that had it not been for him, I would have been confined to dry rations. A bottle of Kahetian wine helped us to forget the modest number of courses (there was but one of them) and, upon lighting our pipes, we settled down—I, by the window, he, by the burning stove, for the day was damp and cold. We were silent. What was there to talk about? He had already told me everything about himself that was entertaining, while I had nothing to tell. I sat looking out of the window. Through the trees a multitude of squat little houses showed here and there, scattered along the bank of the Terek River, which hereabouts keeps running wider and wider; further away blue mountains loomed like a crenulated wall, and from behind them peered forth Mount Kazbek in its white cardinalic mitre.[50] I was taking leave of them mentally; I had begun to feel sorry about it.

We sat like this for a long time. The sun had hidden behind the cold peaks, and a whitish mist had begun to spread in the valleys, when from without

came the jingle of a harness bell and the shouts of
coachmen. A few carts with grimy Armenians entered the yard of the inn, followed by an empty
traveling calash: there was a foreign touch about its
easy ride, comfortable arrangement and smart appearance. Behind it walked a man with a big mustache, clad in a Hungarian jacket, fairly well dressed
for a valet; his calling could not be mistaken once
you observed the swaggering way he shook the ashes
out of his pipe and shouted at the driver. He was
obviously the spoiled servant of an easygoing master
—a kind of Russian Figaro.[51] "Say, my good man," I
cried to him from the window, "has the convoy
arrived or what?" He looked at me in a rather insolent manner, adjusted his neckcloth, and turned
away; the Armenian who walked beside him answered for him, with a smile, that the convoy had,
indeed, arrived and would go back on the morrow.
"Thank goodness," said Maksim Maksimich, who by
that time had come up to the window. "What a
marvelous carriage!" he added. "Must be some func-
tionary going to an inquest in Tiflis. Seems he's not
yet acquainted with our little mountain roads! Well,
the joke is on you, friend, they're not the familiar
brand; they'll loosen the screws even in an English
carriage!" "But who might it be anyway? Let's go
and find out . . ." We stepped out into the passage.
At the end of the passage, a door stood open into a
side room. Into it, the valet and the driver were lug-
ging suitcases.

"I say, friend," the junior captain asked him,
"whose is this marvelous carriage, hey? A splendid
carriage!" The man, without turning, muttered
something under his breath, while he unfastened a
suitcase. Maksim Maksimich became angry; he

touched the uncivil fellow on the shoulder and said: "It's you I'm talking to, my good fellow. . . ."

"Whose carriage? My master's. . . ."

"And what's your master's name?"

"Pechorin."

"How's that? How's that? Pechorin? . . . Good Lord! . . . And might he have served in the Caucasus?" exclaimed Maksim Maksimich, jerking me by the sleeve. Joy sparkled in his eyes.

"He did, I believe. I have not been with him long."

"That's it! That's it! Grigoriy Aleksandrovich? Is that his first name and patronymic? Your master and I used to be pals," he added, dealing the valet a friendly blow on the shoulder which made the man totter.

"Beg pardon, sir, you are getting in my way," said the latter, with a frown.

"You've odd manners, my friend! . . . Do you realize that your master and I have been boon companions, that we roomed together? . . . But where is he himself?"

The servant declared that Pechorin had remained for supper and for the night at Colonel N——'s.

"And will he not drop in here tonight? Or else, my friend, will you not go to see him for something or other? If you do, then tell him that Maksim Maksimich is here—just that—he'll know. I'll tip you eighty kopeks."

The valet made a scornful grimace on hearing such a modest promise, but assured Maksim Maksimich that he would carry out his errand.

"And won't he come right away at a run!" said Maksim Maksimich to me with a triumphant look. "I'll go wait for him outside the gate . . . What a pity I am not acquainted with Colonel N——."

Maksim Maksimich seated himself on a bench

outside the gate, and I went to my room. I confess that I, too, looked forward rather eagerly for this Pechorin person to appear; and although the idea of him I made myself from the captain's narrative was not particularly flattering, still certain features of his character seemed to me remarkable. An hour later, one of the veterans brought in a simmering samovar and a teapot. "Maksim Maksimich," I called from the window, "won't you have some tea?"

"Thanks, I don't want any particularly."

"Oh do have some! Look, it's getting late and chilly."

"I'm all right, thanks."

"Well, please yourself!" I started to have tea by myself; ten minutes later, the old fellow came in.

"I say, you're right, it is better to have a spot of tea. You see, I kept waiting. His man went to him a long time ago, but evidently something has detained him."

Hurriedly he gulped down one cup, declined a second, and went out again to the gate looking somewhat worried. It was clear that the old man was hurt by Pechorin's neglect, the more so as he had been telling me recently about their friendship, and only an hour before, had been sure that Pechorin would come at a run the moment he heard Maksim Maksimich's name.

It was late and dark when I opened the window again and started to call Maksim Maksimich, saying that it was time to go to bed; he muttered something between his teeth; I repeated the invitation; he did not answer.

I lay down on the couch, wrapped myself in my military overcoat, left the candle burning on the stove ledge and soon dozed off. I would have had a quiet night, if, at a very late hour, Maksim Maksimich had not roused me by entering the room. He threw his pipe on the table, he began to walk about, he stirred the embers in the stove, finally he lay down, but for a long time he kept coughing, spitting, turning from side to side.

"Are bedbugs biting you?" I queried.

"Yes, bedbugs," he answered with a heavy sigh.

Next morning I woke up early, but Maksim Maksimich had forestalled me. I found him sitting on the bench outside the gate. "I must see the commandant," he said, "so please, if Pechorin comes, send for me."

I promised. He hurried away as if his limbs had regained their youthful strength and suppleness.

The morning was fresh, but fine. Golden clouds had accumulated on the mountains like an additional, airy range. A wide square spread before the gate; beyond it, a market-place was seething with people, it being Sunday; barefooted Ossetian lads, carrying on their shoulders sacks[52] of honey combs, swarmed around me; I chased them away. I could not be bothered by them. I was beginning to share the restlessness of my good captain.

Ten minutes had hardly elapsed when, at the other end of the square, there appeared the person we were expecting. He was accompanied by Colonel N—— who, after seeing him to the inn, took his leave and turned back in the direction of the fort. I immediately sent one of the veterans to fetch Maksim Maksimich.

Pechorin's valet came out to meet his master, reported that the horses were about to be harnessed, presented to him a box of cigars, and, upon receiving several instructions, went away to take care of things. His master, having lit a cigar, yawned once or twice, and sat down on the bench beyond the gate. I must now draw his portrait for you.

He was of medium height;[53] a slim waist and broad shoulders testified to a sturdy constitution which was suited to bear all the hardships of a roving life and the changes of climate, and was undefeated either by the dissolution of city life or by the tempests of the soul; his dusty velvet jacket was fastened only by the two lower buttons and allowed one to see the dazzlingly clean linen which bespeaks the habits of a gentleman; his soiled gloves appeared to be made to order, so well did they fit his small aristocratic hands, and when he took off one glove I was surprised to see how thin his pale fingers were. His gait was loose and indolent, but I observed that he did not swing his arms—a sure sign of a certain reticence of nature. However, these are but my private notes based on my own observations, and by no means do I expect you to believe in them blindly.

When he settled upon the bench, his straight figure flexed in such a way that you would think there was not a single bone in his spine; the attitude of his whole body expressed a kind of nervous debility; he sat there as a thirty-year-old coquette of Balzac's would sit after a fatiguing ball, in her armchair stuffed with down.[54] After a first glance at his face, I would not have given him more than twenty-three years, though later I was ready to give him thirty. There was something childish about his smile. His skin had a kind of feminine tenderness of texture; his fair hair, wavy by nature, framed, so picturesquely, his pale, noble brow, upon which only prolonged observation could make out the traces of intersecting wrinkles, which probably became much more clearly marked in moments of wrath or spiritual restlessness. In contrast to the light shade of his hair, his mustache and eyebrows were black—a sign of breeding in man, as are a black mane and a black tail in a white horse. To complete his portrait, let me say that he had a slightly bobbed nose, dazzlingly white teeth, and brown eyes—I must add a few words about those eyes of his.

In the first place, they never laughed when he was laughing! Have you observed this bizarre trait in some people? It is either the sign of a wicked nature or of a deep and constant melancholy. From behind half-lowered lashes, they shone with a kind of phosphorescent glitter, if I can put it thus. It was not the reflection of the soul's glow or of an effervescent imagination; this was a gleam akin to the gleam of smooth steel, dazzling but cold; his glance, while not lingering, was penetrating and oppressive, it left the disagreeable impression of an indiscreet question and might have appeared insolent had it not been indifferently serene. Perhaps all these observations came to my mind only because I knew some details of his life, and perhaps upon someone else his looks might have produced an entirely different impression; but since you will hear of him from no one but me, you must needs be satisfied with this portrayal. I shall say, in conclusion, that on the whole, he was rather handsome and had one of those original faces which especially appeal to women of fashion.

The horses had been already hitched; now and then, the shaftbow bell would tinkle, and twice already the valet had come to Pechorin to report that all was ready, but still Maksim Maksimich had not turned up. Fortunately, Pechorin was immersed in meditation as he looked at the blue crenulations of the Caucasian range, and apparently was in no haste to set out on his journey. I went up to him. "If you care to wait a little longer," I said, "you will have the pleasure of seeing an old comrade of yours."

"Oh, that's right!" he answered quickly. "They told me so last night; but where is he?" I turned toward the square and saw Maksim Maksimich running as fast as he could. A few moments later, he was near us; he could hardly breathe; sweat was trickling down his face; wet shags of gray hair, escaping from under his cap, had glued themselves to his forehead; his knees were shaking, he was about to fall on Pechorin's neck, but the latter, rather coolly, though with a friendly smile, stretched out his hand. For a second the captain stood transfixed, but then avidly seized that hand in both of his; he still was not able to speak.

"How glad I am, dear Maksim Maksimich! Well, how are you?" said Pechorin.

"And thou? . . .[55] And you?" stammered the old man with tears in his eyes. "All those years . . . all those days . . . but where are you off to?"

"I am going to Persia, and then further on. . . ."

"Not right now? . . . Oh, but wait, my dearest friend! . . . We aren't going to part right now, are we? We have not seen each other such a long time."

"I have to go right now, Maksim Maksimich," was the answer.

"Oh good Lord! What is all this hurry? I'd like to tell you so much, ask so much . . . Well, how are you? retired? how's everything? what have you been doing with yourself?"

"I have been bored!" answered Pechorin with a smile.

"Remember our days at the fort? Fine country for hunting! You used to be a passionate sportsman . . . And remember Bela?"[56]

Pechorin paled slightly and turned away.[57]

"Oh yes, I remember," he said, almost at once feigning to yawn.

Maksim Maksimich began to implore him to remain a couple of hours longer. "We'll have a capital dinner," he said, "I have a brace of pheasants, and the Kahetian wine is excellent here—naturally, not what they have in Georgia, but still first-rate. We shall talk . . . You will tell me of your life in Petersburg, won't you?"

"Really, I have nothing to tell, my dear Maksim Maksimich . . . And now I must say good-by, time for me to leave, I am in a hurry. Thanks for not forgetting me," he added, taking him by the hand.

The old man frowned. He was sad and cross, though he tried to conceal it. "Forgotten!" he growled. "I, for one, haven't forgotten anything. Well, do as you please. This is not the way I thought we would meet again. . . ."

"Oh come, come," said Pechorin with a friendly embrace. "Am I not the same as of old? What's to be done? To each his own road. God alone knows if we shall have another chance to see each other . . ." Speaking thus, he was already sitting in his carriage, and the coachman had already begun to gather up the reins.

"Wait, wait," suddenly shouted Maksim Maksimich, clutching at the door of the carriage. "It almost escaped my mind. You left some of your papers with me, Grigoriy Aleksandrovich. I lug them along with me—thought I might find you in Georgia —and see now where the Lord has us see each other. What shall I do with them?"

"Whatever you like," answered Pechorin. "Good-by."

"So you are off to Persia? . . . and when will you be back?" Maksim Maksimich shouted after him.

The carriage was already far, but Pechorin made a sign with his hand which might have been interpreted as most likely never! and besides what for? . . .

The jingling of the shaft bell and the clatter of the wheels on the flinty road had long ceased to be heard, but the poor old fellow still stood in the same place, deep in thought.

"Yes," he said at last, trying to assume an indifferent air, although a tear of vexation would still sparkle from time to time on his lashes, "of course, we used to be friends, but what is friendship in our times? What can I mean to him? I have neither wealth nor rank, nor am I at all his mate in age. Look what a dandy he has become after revisiting Petersburg. What a calash! How much luggage! And such a haughty valet!" These words were uttered with an ironic smile. "Tell me," he continued, turning to me, "now, what do you think of it? What devil now is sweeping him off to Persia? Absurd, by Jove, it's absurd! Matter of fact, I knew all along that he was a volatile fellow on whom one could not rely. Still, it's a pity that he will come to a bad end . . . could not be otherwise! It's something I have always said, there's no good in him who forgets his old friends!" At this he turned away to conceal his agitation and began to walk in the yard around his carriage, pretending to examine its wheels, while his eyes, every moment, filled with tears.

"Maksim Maksimich," I said, going up to him, "what are those papers that Pechorin left with you?"

"Goodness knows! Some sort of memoirs."

"And what are you going to do with them?"

"What, indeed? I'll have them made into cartridges."

"Better give them to me."

He looked at me with surprise, muttered something through his teeth, and began to rummage in a suitcase; presently he took out a notebook and threw it on the ground with contempt; a second, a third and up to a tenth book received the same treatment. There was something childish about his resentment; I began to feel both amused and touched.

"Here they are, all of them," he said, "congratulations on your find. . . ."

"And I may do with them all I wish?"

"You may even publish them in the gazettes. What do I care? One would think I was some kind of friend or relative of his. True, we did live for a long time under one roof . . . But haven't I had any number of roommates?"

I seized the papers and hastened to carry them away, fearing lest the captain might repent. Soon after, we were informed that the convoy would start in an hour. I ordered the horses to be harnessed. The captain entered the room when I had already put on my cap; it seemed he was not getting ready to go; there was something cold and constrained about his appearance.

"And you, Maksim Maksimich, aren't you coming?"

"No, sir."

"Why so?"

"Well, I haven't yet seen the commandant; there is some government property that I have to hand over."

"But haven't you been to see him?"

"I did go, of course," he said falteringly, "but he was not in . . . and I did not wait."

I understood him. The poor old fellow had, perhaps for the first time in his life, abandoned official business for what in the parlance of paperdom is termed "a private necessity"—and how he had been rewarded!

"I am very sorry," I said, "I am very sorry, Maksim Maksimich, that we have to part sooner than the term set."

"How can we, unschooled old fellows, keep up with you? You are young men of fashion, you are haughty. It may be all right while one is together here under Circassian fire . . . but meet you later and you're ashamed to shake hands with one of us."

"I have done nothing to justify such reproaches, Maksim Maksimich."

"Well, I just happened to mention it; however, I wish you all possible happiness and a merry trip."

We parted rather drily. My good Maksim Maksimich had turned into a stubborn and grumpy junior captain! And why? Just because Pechorin, out of absent-mindedness or for some other reason, proffered his hand while Maksim Maksimich wanted to throw himself on Pechorin's neck! It is sad to see a youth lose his fondest hopes and dreams, when the rosy tulle, through which he had looked upon the acts and feelings of men, is torn aside before him, even though there is hope that he will replace his old delusions by new ones, no less fleeting but also no less sweet. But by what can one replace them at Maksim Maksimich's age? No wonder that the heart hardens and the soul folds up.

I drove off alone.

# Introduction to Pechorin's Journal

I LEARNED not long ago that Pechorin had died on his way back from Persia.[58] This news gladdened me very much, it gave me the right to publish these notes, and I took advantage of the opportunity to sign another man's work with my own name. God grant that readers do not castigate me for such an innocent forgery.

I now must explain somehow the reasons that prompted me to deliver to the public the innermost secrets of a man whom I had never known. It might have been all right had I been his friend—the perfidious indiscreetness of a true friend is intelligible to anyone—but I saw him only once in my life, on the highway, and consequently cannot harbor for him that ineffable detestation which, concealed under the mask of friendship, only awaits death or misfortune to befall the beloved object in order to break out over his head in a hail of reproach, advice, gibes, and lamentations.

While reading over these notes, I became convinced of the sincerity of this man who so mercilessly exhibited his own failings and vices. The history of a human soul, be it even the meanest soul, can hardly be less curious or less instructive than the history of an entire nation—especially when it is the result of self-observation on the part of a mature mind, and when it is written without the ambitious desire to provoke sympathy or amazement. Rousseau's *Confessions*[59] have already the defect of his having read them to his friends.

Thus, solely the desire to be useful compelled me to print excerpts from a journal that came accidentally into my possession. Although I altered all proper names, those people of whom it tells will probably recognize themselves, and possibly they will find some justification in regard to actions for which, until now, they blamed a man who, henceforth, has nothing in common with our world—we nearly always excuse what we can understand.

I have included in this book only that which refers to Pechorin's sojourn in the Caucasus. There still remains in my possession a fat notebook wherein he narrates all his life. Some day it, too, will be presented to the judgment of the world, but for the present there are important reasons why I dare not assume such a responsibility.

Perhaps some readers will want to know my opinion of Pechorin's character. My answer is the title of this book. "But this is wicked irony!" they will say.

I wonder.

# Taman

TAMAN IS the worst little town of all the seacoast towns in Russia. I almost died of hunger there and, moreover, an attempt was made to drown me. I arrived late one night with post horses, in a small springless carriage. The driver stopped his tired troika at the gate of the only stone house in Taman, at the town entrance. The sentinel, a Black Sea Cossack,[60] startled in his sleep by the jingle of the harness-bell, yelled out in a wild voice "Who goes there?" A sergeant and a corporal appeared. I explained to them that I was an officer going on official business to join a detachment on active duty, and demanded governmental quarters. The corporal took me over the town. Every hut we drove up to proved taken. The weather was cold; I had not slept for three nights, I was worn out, and was beginning to get angry. "Take me somewhere, you rascal!" I cried. "Let it be the devil's, but lead me to the place." "There is one more *fatéra* [quarters]," replied the corporal scratching the back of his head, "but your honor won't like it, it's an evil place!" I did not understand the exact sense of that word and ordered the man to go ahead. After wandering for a long time along dirty alleys where, on both sides, I could see nothing but decrepit fences, we drove up to a shanty on the very edge of the sea.

The full moon shone on the rush roof and the whitewashed walls of my new abode; in the yard, within an enclosure of cobbles, there stood, all awry, a second hut, smaller and more ancient than the first. Almost at its very walls, the shore fell abruptly toward the sea, and below, with an incessant murmur, the dark-blue waves plashed. The moon mildly surveyed the element, both restless and submissive to her, and by her light, I could distinguish, far from the shore, two ships, whose motionless black rigging was outlined, gossamer-like, against the pale horizon. "There are ships in the harbor," I said to myself. "Tomorrow I'll set out for Gelendzhik."[61]

I had in my service, as orderly, a Cossack from a line regiment. I told him to take out my valise and to dismiss the coachman. Then I began calling the landlord. Silence. I knocked. Silence again. Funny situation. Finally a boy of fourteen or so crept out of the hallway.[62]

"Where is the landlord?" "No landlord." "How's that? None at all?" "None." "And what about a landlady?" "Gone to the settlement." "Then who'll open the door for me?" I asked, and gave it a kick. The door opened of itself, a whiff of dampness came from within. I lit a sulphur match and brought it close to the lad's very nose; it illumined two white eyes. He was blind, totally blind from birth. He stood motionless before me and I began to examine his features.

I confess, I have a strong prejudice against those who are blind, one-eyed, deaf, mute, legless, armless, hunchbacked, and so forth. I have observed that there always exists some strange relationship between the appearance of a man and his soul, as if

with the loss of a limb, the soul lost one of its senses.
And so I began to examine the blind lad's face,
but what can one read in a face that lacks eyes? For
a long time, I kept looking at him with involuntary
pity, when all of a sudden a hardly perceptible smile
ran over his thin lips, and for some reason it made
on me a most unpleasant impression. There was
born in my mind the suspicion that this blind lad
was not as blind as it seemed; in vain did I try to
persuade myself that those white eyes could not be
faked—and what would have been the purpose? But
I could not help wondering. I am often inclined to
prejudice.

"Are you the landlady's son?" I asked him at last.
"No." "Who are you then?" "An orphan, a cripple."
"And does the landlady have any children?" "No.
There was a daughter, but she's run off across the
sea with a Tatar." "What Tatar?" "The evil one
knows! Some Tatar from the Crimea, a boatman,
from Kerch."

I entered the shanty; two benches and a table,
plus a huge trunk by the stove, made up all its
furniture. Not one ikon hung on the wall—a bad sign!
The sea breeze kept blowing through the broken
windowpane. I took out of my suitcase a bit of wax
candle and, having lit it, began to unpack my things.
I placed in one corner of the room my sword and
rifle, laid my pistols on the table, spread my felt
cloak on one bench, my Cossack spread his on the
other: ten minutes later, he began to snore, but I
could not fall asleep, the white-eyed lad kept hovering before me in the dark.

About an hour passed in this way. The moon
shone in the window and one beam played on the
earthen floor of the shanty. Suddenly, upon the
bright band that crossed the floor, a shadow flicked

by. I raised myself and glanced through the window; once again someone ran past and vanished, God knows where. I could not suppose that this creature had run down the steep slope of the shore; however, there was no other place for it to have gone. I got up, put on my *beshmet*, buckled my dagger on, and as softly as possible stepped out of the shanty: the blind lad appeared before me. I huddled beside the fence, and he went by me with a firm but cautious step. He carried a bundle under his arm; turning toward the harbor, he began to go down the narrow steep path. "On that day the dumb shall cry out and the blind shall see,"[63] I thought, as I followed him at a distance which allowed me not to lose sight of him.

Meanwhile, the moon had begun to clothe herself in clouds and above the sea a mist had risen; through it, a lantern glimmered on the stern of the nearer ship. Close to the beach, there gleamed the foam of the breakers[64] which threatened to flood it any minute. Descending with difficulty, I groped my way down the precipitous slope, and this is what I saw: the blind lad stopped for a moment, then turned to the right at the bottom of the slope; he walked so close to the water, that it looked as if any moment a wave might seize him and carry him away; but evidently this was not the first time he took this walk, judging by the assuredness with which he stepped from stone to stone and avoided holes. Finally, he stopped as if listening to something, sat down on the ground and laid down the bundle beside him. I followed his movements as I stood concealed behind a projecting part of the rocky coast. After a few minutes, a white figure came in sight, from the opposite direction. It advanced toward the blind lad and sat down beside him. From time to time, the wind brought me snatches of their conversation.

"Well, blind one?" said a woman's voice. "The storm is heavy; Yanko will not come." "Yanko does not fear the storm," the other replied. "The mist is getting thicker," the woman's voice retorted with a note of sadness.

"A mist is best for slipping past the patrol ships," was the answer. "And what if he drowns?" "Well, what of it? You'll go to church Sunday without a new ribbon."

There followed a silence; one thing, however, had struck me: to me, the blind lad had spoken in the Ukrainian dialect, now he expressed himself in perfect Russian.

"You see, I was right," spoke the blind lad again, clapping his hands together. "Yanko is not afraid either of the sea or the winds or the mist or the coast guards. Listen! That is not water splashing— one cannot deceive me—it's his long oars!"

The woman jumped up and began to peer into the distance, with an air of anxiety.

"You're dreaming, blind one," she said, "I don't see anything."

I confess that no matter how I strained to make out, in the distance, anything resembling a boat, my efforts were in vain. Some ten minutes elapsed; then, amid the mountains of the waves, a black dot appeared; it grew now bigger, now smaller. Slowly rising upon the wave crests, and rapidly coming down them, a boat was nearing the shore. He must be a valiant navigator, indeed, to venture on such a night to cross the straits, a distance of fifteen miles; and it must be an important reason that induced him to do so! These were my thoughts as, with an involuntary throbbing of the heart, I looked at the wretched boat; but she kept diving like a duck and then, with a wing-like upsweep of oars, would spring out of the abyss amid a burst of foam; and now, I thought, her impetus will dash her against the shore and she will be smashed to bits; but cleverly she turned sideways and bounded, unharmed, into a cove. A man of medium height, in a Tatar cap of sheepskin, came ashore. He waved his hand, and all three began to drag something out of the boat; the load was so great that, to this day, I cannot understand how she had not sunk. Each having shouldered a bundle, they started to walk away along the coast, and I soon lost sight of them. I had to go back to my lodgings; but, I confess, all these strange things worried me, and I had a hard time awaiting the morning.

My Cossack was much surprised when, upon waking, he saw me all dressed; I did not, however, tell him the reason. After admiring, for a while, from the window, the blue sky strewn with torn cloudlets, and the distant shore of the Crimea which extended in a lilac line and ended in a rock on the summit of which a lighthouse loomed white, I made my way to Phanagoria⁶⁵ Fort to find out from the commandant the hour of my departure for Gelendzhik.

But, alas, the commandant could tell me nothing definite. The ships that lay in the harbor were either patrol ships or merchantmen that had not even begun to load. "Maybe within three or four days the mailboat will come," said the commandant, "and then we shall see." I returned home, gloomy and cross. In the doorway my Cossack met me with a frightened face.

"It's a bad business, sir," he said to me.

"Yes, my friend, the Lord knows when we shall get out of here!" At this he became even more perturbed and, bending toward me, said in a whisper: "It's an evil place!" Today, I met a Black Sea sergeant; he's a friend of mine who was in our detachment, last year. The moment I told him where we were quartered, he said to me: 'Brother, it's an evil place, those are bad people!' And, true enough, what kind of a blindman is this? Goes alone everywhere, to the market, to get bread, to get water . . . seems all are used to it around here. . . ."

"Well, at least, did the landlady show up?"

"When you were out today, there came an old woman, and her daughter."

"What daughter? She has no daughter."

"The Lord knows who she is then if she is not her daughter. Anyway, the old woman is in her hut now."

I entered the smaller hut. The stove had been thoroughly heated, and in it, a dinner was cooking, fairly luxurious for paupers. To all my questions, the old woman replied that she was deaf, could not hear me. What was I to do with her? I turned to the blind lad who sat before the stove, feeding the fire with brushwood. "Well now, you blind little devil," I said, taking him by the ear, "out with it . . . where did you go prowling last night with that bundle . . . hey?" All at once my blind lad began to weep, to shriek, to moan. "Where did I go? Nowhere at all . . . With a bundle? What bundle?" This time the old woman did hear, and began to grumble: "What things people will make up! And about a poor cripple, too! Why are you after him? What has he done to you?" I got tired of this and left, firmly resolved to obtain the key to this riddle.

I wrapped myself in my felt cloak and, seating myself on a stone beside the fence, fell to looking idly afar. In front of me, there spread the sea, stirred up by last night's storm, and its monotonous sound, akin to the murmur of a city settling down to sleep, reminded me of past years, and carried my thoughts northward, toward our cold capital. I was troubled by memories and lost myself in them. Thus passed an hour, perhaps even more. Suddenly, something resembling a song struck my hearing. It was, indeed, a song, and the limpid young voice was that of a woman—but where did it come from? I listened; the tune was bizarre, now slow and sad, now fast and lively. I turned—there was no one around; again I listened—the sounds seemed to fall from the sky. I raised my eyes; on the roof of my hut, stood a girl in a striped dress, her hair hanging loose, a regular water nymph. Shading her eyes from the rays of the sun with the palm of her hand, she fixedly peered afar, now laughing and reasoning with herself, now singing her song.

I memorized that song, word for word:

> Over the free franchise
> of the green sea
> good ships keep going,
> white-sailed.
>
> Among those good ships
> is my own small boat,
> a boat unrigged,
> two-oared.
>
> Let a storm run riot:
> the old ships
> will lift their wings
> and scatter over the sea.
>
> To the sea I shall bow
> very low:
> "You, bad sea, do not touch
> my small boat.

My small boat carries
costly things;
it is guided through the dark night
by a bold daredevil."

Involuntarily, the thought struck me that last
night I had heard the same voice: I was lost in meditation for a moment, and when I looked again at the
roof, the girl was no longer there. All at once, she
ran past me, singing some other snatch and then,
snapping her fingers, ran into the old woman's hut,
upon which a dispute arose between them. The old
woman was furious, the girl laughed loudly. Presently, I saw my undine[67] skip out again. On coming
up level with me, she stopped and looked fixedly
into my eyes as if she were surprised at my presence; then she turned away casually and slowly
walked toward the harbor.

This was not the end: all day long she hovered
about my dwelling; her singing and skipping did
not cease for one minute. What an odd creature she
was! Her face showed no signs of insanity; on the
contrary, her eyes rested upon me with brisk perspi-
cacity. Those eyes, it seemed, were endowed with
some kind of magnetic power, and every time they
looked, they seemed to be waiting for a question.
But barely did I begin to speak, than she would run
away, with a crafty smile.

Really, I had never seen such a woman! She was
far from beautiful, but I have my preconceptions in
regard to beauty, too. She revealed a good deal of
breeding . . . and breeding in women, as in horses,
is a great thing: *les Jeunes-France*[68] are responsible
for this discovery. It (that is, breeding, not Young
France) is most visible in the gait, in the hands and
feet; the nose is especially significant. In Russia, a

straight nose is rarer than a small foot. My song-stress did not appear to be more than eighteen. The extraordinary suppleness of her figure, a special inclination of the head, peculiar to her alone, her long auburn hair, a kind of golden sheen on the slightly sun-tanned skin of her neck and shoulders, and, especially, her straight nose—all this was enchanting to me. Although I detected in her oblique glances something wild and suspicious, and although there was an odd vagueness about her smile, still such is the force of preconception; her straight nose drove me crazy. I imagined I had discovered Goethe's Mignon[69]—that extravagant product of his German imagination—and indeed, there was a lot in common between them: the same rapid transitions from intense restlessness to complete immobility, the same enigmatic accents, the same capers and strange songs.

Toward nightfall I accosted her by the door, and started the following conversation with her:

"Tell me, my pretty girl," I said, "what were you doing today on the roof?"

"Oh, just tried to see whence the wind was blowing."

"What is that to you?"

"Whence the wind comes, happiness comes, too."

"So you were inviting happiness with your song?"

"Where there are songs, there is happiness."

"And what if you chance to sing sorrow in?"

"What of it? Where it will not get better, it will get worse, and then again, it is not far from bad to good."

"And who taught you that song?"

"Nobody taught me, I sing when I feel like singing; he who is meant to hear it, will hear, and he who is not, will not understand."

"And what's your name, my songstress?"

"The one who christened me knows."

"And who christened you?"

"How should I know?"

"What reticence! Yet look, there is something I've found out about you." (Her face did not change, her lips did not move, as if I were not speaking of her.) "I've found out that you went down to the shore last night." At this point I very solemnly related to her all I had seen, expecting she would be taken aback. Not in the least! She burst into roars of laughter. "You've seen much, but you know little," she said. "And whatever you do know, you'd better keep under lock."

"And what if, for instance, I took it into my head to inform the commandant?"

At this point, I assumed a very serious, even severe, expression. Suddenly, off she hopped, broke into song and vanished like some little bird that has been flushed out of the shrubbery. My last words had been entirely out of place: at the time, I did not realize all their importance, but later had a chance to regret them.

It had just got dark; I ordered the Cossack to heat the tea kettle, bivouac-fashion, lit a candle and sat down at the table, quietly puffing at my traveling pipe. By the time I was finishing my second glass of tea, the door creaked, suddenly, and I heard, behind me, the light rustle of a dress and the sound of steps: I started and turned around—it was she, my undine. Softly, silently, she sat down, facing me across the table, and fixed me with her eyes, and I do not know why, but her look seemed to me wondrously tender;[70] it reminded me of those gazes which, in past years, so despotically toyed with my life. She seemed to be waiting for a question, but I

remained silent, filled with an ineffable confusion. A
dull pallor, betraying inner agitation, covered her
face, her hand strayed over the table aimlessly, and
I noticed a slight tremor in it; now her bosom would
rise high, and now she would seem to be holding
her breath. This comedy was beginning to bore me,
and I was prepared to break the silence in a most
prosaic way—that is, to offer her a glass of tea—when
she suddenly jumped up, twined her arms around
my neck, and a moist, burning kiss[71] sounded upon
my lips. Everything turned dark before my eyes, my
head swam, I crushed her in my embrace with all
the force of youthful passion, but she, like a snake,
glided between my arms, whispering in my ear:
"Tonight, when everybody is asleep, come onto the
shore," and, like an arrow, sped out of the room. In
the hallway, she overturned the kettle and a candle
which stood on the floor. "That she-devil!" cried the
Cossack, who had made himself comfortable on
some straw and had been looking forward to warm-
ing himself with the remainder of the tea. Only then,
did I come to my senses.

Some two hours later, when everything had
quieted down in the harbor, I roused my Cossack.
"If I fire my pistol," I told him, "come down to the
shore, as fast as you can." His eyes bulged and he
answered automatically: "At your orders, sir." I
stuck a pistol in my belt and went out. She was waiting for me at the edge of the declivity; her garment
was more than light, a flimsy kerchief girded her
supple figure.[72]

"Follow me!" she said, taking me by the hand,
and we started to walk down. I wonder that I did
not break my neck: once below, we turned right and
went along the same road along which I had tracked
the blind lad on the previous night. The moon had

not yet risen, and only two little stars, like two guiding beacons, sparkled in the dark-blue vault. Heavy waves rolled rhythmically and evenly one after the other, hardly raising the lone boat that was moored to the shore. "Let's get into the boat," said my companion. I hesitated—I am no amateur of sentimental promenades on the sea—but this was not the moment to retreat. She jumped into the boat, I followed, and had barely recovered my senses when I noticed that we were adrift. "What does this mean?" I said crossly. "It means," she said, making me sit on a bench, and winding her arms around my waist, "it means that I love you." Her cheek pressed mine and I felt, on my face, her flaming breath. Suddenly, something fell into the water, with a noisy splash; my hand flew to my belt—my pistol was gone. Ah, what a terrible suspicion stole into my soul! The blood rushed to my head; I looked around—we were a hundred yards from the shore, and I could not swim! I tried to push her away, but she clung to my clothes like a cat, and suddenly a powerful push almost precipitated me overboard. The boat rocked, but I regained my balance, and a desperate struggle started between us; my rage gave me strength, but I soon realized that, in agility, I was inferior to my adversary. "What do you want?" I cried, squeezing her small hands hard. Her fingers crunched, but she did not cry out; her serpent nature withstood this torture.

"You saw," she replied, "you will tell!" And with a superhuman effort she brought me crashing down against the side of the boat; we both hung over from the waist up; her hair touched the water; it was a decisive moment. I braced my knee against the bottom of the boat; with one hand I seized her by the hair, with the other got hold of her throat; she released my clothes, and I instantly shoved her into the waves.

By that time it was rather dark: once or twice, I glimpsed her head amid the foam, and then I saw nothing more. . . .

At the bottom of the boat, I found one half of an old oar, and, after protracted efforts, somehow managed to reach the landing place. As I made my way along the shore toward my hut, I could not help peering in the direction where, on the eve, the blind lad had waited for the nocturnal navigator. The moon was already riding the sky, and it seemed to me that someone in white sat on the shore: egged on by curiosity, I stole close up and lay in the grass on the brink of the steep shore. Sticking out my head a little, I could clearly see from the cliff all that took place below, and was not much surprised, but felt almost glad, to recognize my mermaid. She was wringing the wet foam out of her long hair; her wet shift outlined her supple figure and raised breasts. In the distance, there soon appeared a boat; quickly it approached; out of it, as on the night before, there stepped a man in a Tatar cap, but with his hair cut in the Cossack fashion, and a large knife sticking out of his leather belt. "Yanko," she said, "all is lost!" After this, their conversation continued, but in such low tones that I could not make out a word of it. "And where is the blind one?" Yanko said at last raising his voice. "I sent him on an errand," was the answer. A few minutes later the blind lad appeared hauling, on his back, a sack which they put into the boat.

"Listen, blind one," said Yanko, "you watch that place . . . know what I mean? . . . there are some rich wares there . . . Tell (I did not catch the name) not to count on my services any longer.

Things have gone wrong, he will not see me again; it is dangerous now. I'll go to look for work at some other place, but he will never again find such a bold fellow. Also tell him that if he had paid me better for my labors, then Yanko would not have left him: as for me I'll always find an open road wherever the wind blows and the sea sounds!" After a silence, Yanko continued: "She'll go with me, she can't stay here. And tell the old woman that I guess it is time for her to die, she's lived too long, one ought to know when to quit. As to us, she won't see us again."

"And what about me?" said the blind lad in a piteous voice.

"What use are you to me?" was the answer.

Meanwhile, my undine had jumped into the boat and signaled with her hand to her companion; he put something in the blind lad's hand, saying: "Here, get yourself some gingerbread." "Is that all?" said the blind lad. "Well, here's some more,"—and a fallen coin rang against a stone. The blind lad did not pick it up. Yanko got into the boat; the wind blew offshore; they hoisted a small sail and sped away. For a long time, the white sail glanced in the moonlight amid the dark waves; the blind lad kept sitting on the shore, and presently I heard something resembling a sob, and indeed, the blind little fellow was crying. He cried for a long long time . . . I felt sad. What business did fate have to land me into the peaceful midst of *honest smugglers?* Like a stone thrown into the smooth water of a spring, I had disturbed their peace, and like a stone, had very nearly gone to the bottom myself!

I returned to my lodgings. In the hallway, the burned-down candle sputtered in a wooden plate, and my Cossack, despite my orders, lay sound asleep, holding his rifle in both hands. I left him in peace, took the candle and went into the interior of the hut. Alas! My traveling box, my sword chased with silver, my Dagestan dagger—a present from a pal—all had disappeared. It was then that I realized the nature of the things that the confounded blind lad had been hauling. Upon rousing the Cossack with a rather uncivil push, I scolded him and vented my anger a little, but there was nothing to be done! Really, would it not be absurd to complain to the authorities that I had been robbed by a blind boy, and had almost been drowned by an eighteen-year-old girl? Fortunately, next morning it proved possible to continue my journey, and I left Taman. What became of the old woman and of the poor blind lad I do not know. And besides, what do I care about human joys and sorrows—I, a military man on the move, and holder, moreover, of a road-pass issued to those on official business!

# Princess Mary

YESTERDAY, I arrived in Pyatigorsk[74] and rented lodgings on the outskirts of the town, at its highest point, at the foot of Mount Mashuk: when there is a thunderstorm, the clouds will descend down to my roof. At five this morning, when I opened the window, my room was filled with the perfume of flowers growing in the modest front garden. The branches of cherry trees in bloom look into my window, and the wind occasionally strews my desk with their white petals. The view on three sides is marvelous: to the west, the five-peaked Besh Tau looms blue like "the last thundercloud of a tempest dispersed";[75] to the north, Mount Mashuk rises like a shaggy Persian fur cap and closes off all that part of the horizon; to the east, the outlook is gayer; right below me, lies the varicolored, neat, brand-new little town, the medicinal springs babble, and so does the multilingual crowd; and, beyond the town, amphitheatrical mountains pile up, ever bluer and mistier, while on the edge of the horizon there stretches a silver range of snowy summits, beginning with Mount Kazbek, and ending with the bicephalous Mount Elbruz.[76] It is gay to live in such country! A kind of joyful feeling permeates all my veins. The air is pure and fresh, like the kiss of a child, the sun is bright, the sky is blue—what more, it seems, could one wish? Who, here, needs passions, desires, regrets? However, it is time. I shall go to the Elizabeth Spring: there, I am told, the entire spa society gathers in the morning.

.    .    .    .    .    .    .    .    .[77]

Upon descending into the center of town, I followed the boulevard where I came across several melancholy groups that were slowly going uphill. These were mostly families of landowners from the steppe provinces: this could be inferred immediately from the worn-out, old-fashioned frock coats of the husbands and the elaborate attires of the wives and daughters. Obviously they had already taken stock of all the young men at the waters for they looked at me with tender curiosity. The St. Petersburg cut of my military surtout misled them, but soon, recognizing the epaulets of a mere army officer,[78] they turned away in disgust.

The wives of the local officials, the hostesses of the waters, so to speak, were more favorably disposed; they have lorgnettes, they pay less attention to uniforms, they are used to encountering in the Caucasus, an ardent heart under a numbered army button, and a cultivated mind under a white army cap. These ladies are very charming, and remain charming for a long time! Every year, their admirers are replaced by new ones, and herein, perhaps, lies the secret of their indefatigable amiability. As I climbed the narrow path leading to the Elizabeth Spring, I overtook a bunch of men, some civilian, some military, who, as I afterwards learned, make up a special class of people among those hoping for the action of the waters. They drink—but not water, they walk little, they flirt only in passing, they gamble and complain of ennui. They are dandies: as they dip their wicker-encased glasses into the well of sulphurous water, they assume academic poses: the civilians wear pale-blue neckerchiefs, the military men allow ruffles to show above their coat-collars. They profess a profound contempt for provincial houses and sigh after the capitals' aristocratic salons where they are not admitted.

At last, there was the well. Near it, on the terrace, a small red-roofed structure was built to house the bath, and a little further, there was the gallery where one walked when it rained. Several wounded officers sat on a bench, their crutches drawn up, looking pale and sad. Several ladies walked briskly back and forth on the terrace awaiting the action of the waters. Among them there were two or three pretty faces. In the avenues of vines that cover the slope of Mount Mashuk, one could glimpse now and then the variegated bonnets of ladies partial to shared isolation, since I would always notice, near such a bonnet, either a military cap or one of those round civilian hats that are so ugly. On a steep cliff where the pavilion termed The Aeolian Harp is built, the lovers of scenery perched and trained a telescope on Mount Elbruz: among them were two tutors with their charges, who had come to have their scrofula treated.

I had stopped out of breath on the edge of the hill and, leaning against the corner of the bath-house, had begun to survey the picturesque landscape, when suddenly I heard a familiar voice behind me:

"Pechorin! Have you been here long?"

I turned around: it was Grushnitski! We embraced. I had made his acquaintance in a detachment on active duty. He had been wounded by a bullet in the leg and had left for the waters about a week before me.

' Grushnitski is a cadet. He has been in the service only one year; he wears, following a peculiar kind of foppishness, a soldier's thick coat.[79] He has a soldier's St. George's Cross. He is well built, swarthy and black-haired; judging by his appearance, one might give him twenty-five years of age, although he is hardly twenty-one. He throws his head back when he speaks, and keeps twirling his mustache with his left hand since he uses his right for leaning on his crutch. His speech is rapid and ornate; he is one of those people who, for every occasion in life, have ready-made pompous phrases, whom unadorned beauty does not move, and who solemnly drape themselves in extraordinary emotions, exalted passions, and exceptional sufferings. To produce an effect is rapture to them; romantic provincial ladies go crazy over them. With age they become either peaceful landowners, or drunkards; sometimes, both. Their souls often possess many good qualities, but not an ounce of poetry. Grushnitski's passion was[80] to declaim; he bombarded you with words as soon as the talk transcended the circle of everyday notions: I have never been able to argue with him. He does not answer your objections, he does not listen to you. The moment you stop, he launches upon a long tirade apparently having some connection with what you have said, but actually being only a continuation of his own discourse.

He is fairly witty; his epigrams are frequently amusing, but they are neither to the point nor venomous; he will never kill anyone with a single word; he does not know people and their vulnerable spots, since all his life he has been occupied with his own self. His object is to become the hero of a novel. So often has he tried to convince others that he is a being not made for this world and doomed to suffer in secret, that he has almost succeeded in convincing himself of it. That is why he wears, so proudly, that thick soldier's coat of his. I have seen through him, and that is why he dislikes me, although outwardly we are on the friendliest of terms. Grushnitski has the reputation of an exceptionally brave man. I have seen him in action: he brandishes his sword, he yells, he rushes forward with closed eyes. Somehow, this is not Russian courage!

I don't like him either: I feel that one day we shall meet on a narrow path, and one of us will fare ill.

His coming to the Caucasus is likewise a consequence of his fanatic romanticism. I am sure that on the eve of his departure from the family country seat, he told some pretty neighbor, with a gloomy air, that he was going to the Caucasus not merely to serve there, but that he was seeking death because . . . and here, probably, he would cover his eyes with his hand and continue thus: "No, you must not know this! Your pure soul would shudder! And what for? What am I to you? Would you understand me? . . ." and so forth.

He told me himself that the reason which impelled him to join the K. regiment would remain an eternal secret between him and heaven.

Yet during those moments when he casts off the tragic cloak, Grushnitski is quite pleasant and amusing. I am curious to see him with women: that is when, I suppose, he really tries hard!

We met like old chums. I began to question him about life at the spa and its noteworthy people.

"Our life here is rather prosaic," he said with a

sigh. "Those who drink the waters in the morning are insipid like all invalids, and those who drink wine in the evening are unbearable like all healthy people. Feminine society exists, but there is little comfort therein: these ladies play whist, dress badly and speak dreadful French! From Moscow this year, there is only Princess Ligovskoy with her daughter, but I am not acquainted with them. My soldier's coat is like a seal of rejection. The sympathy that it arouses is as painful as charity."

At that moment, two ladies walked past us in the direction of the well: one was elderly, the other young and graceful. Their bonnets prevented me from getting a good look at their faces, but they were dressed according to the strict rules of the best taste: there was nothing superfluous. The younger one wore a pearl-gray dress closed at the throat, a light silk fichu twined around her supple neck, shoes, *couleur puce*, so pleasingly constricted at the ankle her spare little foot, that even one uninitiated into the mysteries of beauty would have certainly uttered an exclamation, if only of surprise. Her light, yet noble, gait had something virginal about it that escaped definition, but was comprehensible to the gaze. As she walked past us, there emanated from her that ineffable fragrance which breathes sometimes from a beloved woman's letter.

"That's Princess Ligovskoy," said Grushnitski, "and with her is her daughter, Mary, as she calls her after the English fashion. They have been here only three days."

"And yet you already know her name?"

"Yes, I happened to hear it," he answered flushing. "I confess, I do not wish to meet them. Those proud aristocrats look upon us army men as savages. And what do they care whether or not there is a mind under a numbered regimental cap and a heart under a thick army coat?"[81]

"Poor coat," I said with a smile. "And who is the gentleman going up to them and so helpfully offering them tumblers?"

"Oh, that's the Moscow dandy Raevich. He is a gamester: it can be seen at once by the huge, golden watch chain that winds across his sky-blue waistcoat. And what a thick walking stick—like Robinson Crusoe's; and his beard and haircut à la moujik[82] are also characteristic."

"You are embittered against the whole of humanity?"

"And there is a good reason for that."

"Oh, really?"

At this point the ladies moved away from the well and came level with us. Grushnitski had time to assume a dramatic attitude with the help of his crutch, and loudly answered me in French:

"*Mon cher, je hais les hommes pour ne pas les mépriser, car autrement la vie serait une farce trop dégoûtante.*"[83]

The pretty young princess turned her head and bestowed a long curious glance upon the orator. The expression of this glance was very indefinite, but it was not derisive, a fact on which I inwardly congratulated him with all my heart.

"This Princess Mary is extremely pretty," I said to him. "She has such velvety eyes—yes, velvety is the word for them. I advise you to appropriate this term when you speak of her eyes: the upper and lower lashes are so long, that the pupils do not reflect the rays of the sun. I like this kind of lusterless eyes: they are so soft, they seem to stroke you. However, this seems to be the only nice thing about her face. And her teeth, are they white? This is very important! Pity she did not smile at your pompous phrase."

"You talk of a pretty woman as of an English horse," said Grushnitski with indignation.

*"Mon cher,"* I answered trying to copy his manner, *"je méprise les femmes pour ne pas les aimer, car autrement la vie serait un mélodrame trop ridicule."*

I turned and walked away from him. For about half an hour, I strolled along the viny avenues, the limestone ledges, and the bushes hanging between them. It was getting hot, and I decided to hurry home. When passing the sulphurous spring, I stopped at the covered walk to draw a deep breath in its shade, and this provided me with the opportunity to witness a rather curious scene. This is how the actors were placed. The elderly princess and the Moscow dandy sat on a bench in the covered walk, and both seemed to be engrossed in serious conversation. The young princess, probably having finished her last glass of water, strolled pensively near the well. Grushnitski stood right beside it; there was no one else on the terrace.

I drew closer and hid behind a corner of the walk. At this moment, Grushnitski dropped his glass upon the sand and tried hard to bend down in order to pick it up. His injured leg hampered him. Poor fellow! How he exerted himself while leaning on his crutch, but all in vain. His expressive face reflected real pain.

Princess Mary saw it all even better than I. Lighter than a little bird, she skipped up to him, bent down, picked up the glass, and handed it to him with a movement full of inexpressible charm. Then she blushed dreadfully, glanced back at the covered walk, but having convinced herself that her mamma had seen nothing, appeared at once to re-

gain her composure. When Grushnitski opened his
mouth to thank her, she was already far away. A
minute later, she left the gallery with her mother
and the dandy, but as she passed by Grushnitski,
she assumed a most formal and dignified air, she did
not even turn her head, did not even take notice of
the passionate glance with which he followed her
for a long time until she reached the bottom of the
hill and disappeared beyond the young lindens of
the boulevard. Presently, however, her bonnet could
be glimpsed crossing the street; she hurried through
the gate of one of the best houses in Pyatigorsk. Her
mother walked in after her, and at the gate gave
Raevich a parting nod.

Only then did the poor passionate cadet notice
my presence.

"Did you see?" he said firmly gripping me by the
hand. "A very angel!"

"Why?" I asked, with an air of the most genuine
naïveté.

"Didn't you see?"

"I did: she picked up your glass. Had an attend-
ant been around, he would have done the same
thing, and with even more alacrity since he would
be hoping for a tip. However, one can quite understand that she felt sorry for you: you made such an
awful face when you shifted your weight onto your
wounded leg."

"And you did not feel at all touched looking at her
at the moment her soul shone in her face?"

"No."

I lied, but I wanted to infuriate him. Contradic-
tion is, with me, an innate passion; my entire life
has been nothing but a chain of sad and frustrating
contradictions to heart or reason. The presence of an
enthusiast envelops me with midwinter frost, and I

think that frequent commerce with an inert phleg-
matic individual would have made of me a passionate dreamer. I further confess that a nasty but familiar sensation, at that moment, skimmed over my
heart. This sensation was envy: I boldly say "envy"
because I am used to being frank with myself in
everything, and it is doubtful if there can be found a
young man who, upon meeting a pretty woman who
has riveted his idle attention and has suddenly given
obvious preference to another man equally unknown
to her, it is doubtful, let me repeat, that there can be
found a young man (provided, of course, that he has
lived in the *grand monde* and is accustomed to in-
dulge his vanity), who would not be unpleasantly
struck by this.

In silence, Grushnitski and I descended the hill
and walked along the boulevard past the windows
of the house into which our charmer had vanished.
She was sitting at the window. Grushnitski jerked
me by the arm, and threw upon her one of those
blurrily tender glances which have so little effect
upon women. I trained my lorgnette on her and
noticed that his glance made her smile, and that my
insolent lorgnette angered her in no uncertain way.
And how, indeed, does a Caucasian army officer
dare to train his quizzing-glass on a young princess
from Moscow?

*May 13th*

This morning my doctor friend called on me: his
surname is Werner, but he is Russian. Why should
this be surprising? I used to know an Ivanov who
was German.

Werner is a remarkable man in many respects. He
is a sceptic and a materialist, like almost all medical

men, but he is also a poet, and this I mean seriously. He is a poet in all his actions, and frequently in his utterings, although in all his life he never wrote two lines of verse. He has studied all the live strings of the human heart in the same way as one studies the veins of a dead body, but he has never learned how to put his knowledge to profit: thus sometimes an excellent anatomist may not know how to cure a fever. Ordinarily, Werner made unobtrusive fun of his patients, but once I saw him cry over a dying soldier. He was poor; he dreamt of becoming a millionaire but would never have taken one additional step for the sake of money. He told me once that he would rather do a favor for an enemy than for a friend, because in the latter case it would mean selling charity, whereas hatred only grows in proportion to an enemy's generosity. He had a caustic tongue: under the label of his epigram, many a kindly man acquired the reputation of a vulgarian and a fool. His competitors, envious resort doctors, once spread the rumor that he drew cartoons of his patients—the patients became infuriated—and almost all refused to be treated by him. His friends, that is to say, all the really decent people serving in the Caucasus, tried in vain to restore his fallen credit.

His appearance was[84] of the kind that, at first glance, impresses one unfavorably but attracts one later, when the eye has learned to decipher in irregular features the imprint of a dependable and lofty soul. Examples are known of women falling madly in love with such people and of not exchanging their ugly exterior for the beauty of the freshest and rosiest Endymions. Women must be given their due: they have a flair for spiritual beauty. This may be why men like Werner are so passionately fond of women.

Werner was of small stature, thin and frail like a child. One of his legs was shorter than the other, as in the case of Byron; in proportion to his body, his head seemed enormous; he cropped his hair; the bumps of his skull, thus revealed, would have amazed a phrenologist by their bizarre interplay of contradictory inclinations. His small black eyes, never at rest, tried to penetrate your mind. His dress revealed taste and tidiness; his lean, wiry, small hands sported light-yellow gloves. His frock coat, neckcloth and waistcoat were always black. The younger men dubbed him Mephistopheles. He pretended to resent this nickname, but, in point of fact, it flattered his vanity. We soon came to understand each other and became pals—for I am not capable of true friendship. One of the two friends is always the slave of the other, although, often, neither of the two admits this to himself. I can be nobody's slave, while to assume command in such cases is tiresome work because it has to be combined with deceit. I, moreover, am supplied with lackeys and money. We became pals in the following way: I first met Werner in the town of S——, among a numerous and noisy group of young men. Toward the end of the evening, the conversation took a philosophic and metaphysical turn; convictions were discussed; everyone was convinced of something or other.

"As for me, I am convinced of only one thing," said the doctor.

"Of what?" I asked, wishing to learn the opinion of this man who up to now had been silent.

"Of the fact," he answered, "that, sooner or later, one fine morning, I shall die."

"I'm better off than you," I said. "I've one more conviction besides yours, namely that one miserable evening I had the misfortune to be born."

Everybody found that we were talking nonsense, but, really, not one of them said anything more intelligent than that. Henceforth, we distinguished each other in the crowd. We would often see each other and discuss, together, with great seriousness, abstract matters, until we noticed that we were gulling each other. Then, after looking meaningly into each other's eyes, we began to laugh as Roman augurs[85] did, according to Cicero, and having had our fill of mirth, we would separate well-content with our evening.

I was lying on the divan, with eyes directed at the ceiling and hands clasped under my head, when Werner entered my room. He sat down in an armchair, placed his cane in a corner, yawned, and declared that it was getting hot out of doors. I answered that the flies were bothering me, and we both fell silent.

"Observe, my dear doctor," said I, "that without fools, the world would be a very dull place . . . Consider: here we are, two intelligent people; we know beforehand that one can argue endlessly about anything, and therefore we do not argue; we know almost all the secret thoughts of each other; one word is a whole story for us; we see the kernel of our every emotion through a triple[86] shell. Sad things seem to us funny, funny things seem to us melancholy, and generally we are, to tell the truth, rather indifferent to everything except our own selves. Thus, between us there can be no exchange of feelings and thoughts: we know everything about each other that we wish to know, and we do not wish to know anything more. There remains only one solution: telling the news. So tell me some piece of news."

Tired by my long speech, I closed my eyes and yawned.

He answered, after a moment's thought: "Nevertheless, your drivel contains an idea."

"Two ideas," I answered.

"Tell me one, and I'll tell you the other."

"All right, you start!" said I, continuing to examine the ceiling and inwardly smiling.

"You'd like to learn some details about some resort guest, and I have already an inkling as to the subject of your concern, because there have already been inquiries about you in that quarter."

"Doctor! It is definitely impossible for us to converse: we read in each other's souls."

"Now, the other idea. . . ."

"Here is the other idea: I wanted to make you relate something or other—in the first place, because to listen is less fatiguing; in the second place, because a listener cannot give himself away; in the third place, because one can discover another's secret; and in the fourth place, because such intelligent people as you prefer an audience to a storyteller. Now, to business! What did the old Princess Ligovskoy say to you about me?"

"You are quite sure that it was the old princess and not the young one?"

"I'm absolutely sure."

"Why?"

"Because the young princess asked about Grushnitski."

"You've a great talent for putting two and two together. The young princess said she was sure that that young man in the soldier's coat had been degraded to the ranks for a duel."

"I hope you left her under this pleasant delusion."

"Naturally."

"We have the beginning of a plot!" I cried in delight. "The denouement of this comedy will be our concern. Fate is obviously taking care of my not being bored."

"I have a presentiment," said the doctor, "that poor Grushnitski is going to be your victim. . . ."

"Go on with your story, doctor."

"The old princess said that your face was familiar to her. I observed to her that no doubt she had met you in Petersburg, at some fashionable reception. I told her your name. The name was known to her. I believe your escapade caused a big sensation there. The old princess started to tell of your exploits, adding her own remarks to what was probably society gossip. Her daughter listened with curiosity. In her imagination, you became the hero of a novel in the latest fashion. I did not contradict the old lady, though I was aware she was talking nonsense."

"My worthy friend!" said I, extending my hand to him. The doctor shook it with feeling, and continued:

"If you wish, I'll introduce you. . . ."

"Mercy!" said I, raising my hands. "Does one introduce heroes? They never meet their beloved other than in the act of saving her from certain death."

"And so you really intend to flirt with the young princess?"

"On the contrary, quite on the contrary! Doctor, at last I triumph: you do not understand me! This, however, saddens me, doctor," I went on, after a moment of silence. "I never disclose my secrets myself, but I am awfully fond of having them divined, because that way I can always repudiate them if necessary. But come, you must describe to me the mamma and the daughter. What sort of people are they?"

"Well, in the first place, the mother is a woman of forty-five," answered Werner. "Her digestion is excellent, but there is something wrong with her blood; there are red blotches on her cheeks. She has spent the latter half of her life in Moscow, and there, in retirement, has grown fat. She likes risqué anecdotes and sometimes, when her daughter is not in the room, says improper things herself. She announced to me that her daughter was as innocent as a dove. What do I care? I was on the point of replying that she need not worry, I would not tell anybody. The mother is being treated for rheumatism, and what the daughter's complaint is, goodness knows. I told them both to drink two glasses of oxysulphuric water daily, and take a diluted bath twice a week. The old princess, it seems, is not used to command; she has great respect for the intelligence and the knowledge of her daughter, who has read Byron in English[87] and knows algebra. It seems that in Moscow young ladies have taken to higher education, and, by Jove, it's a good thing! Our men, generally speaking, are so boorish that to coquet with them must be unbearable for any intelligent woman. The old princess is very fond of young men; the young princess looks at them with a certain contempt—a Moscow habit! In Moscow, all they enjoy is the company of forty-year-old wags."

"And you, doctor, have you been in Moscow?"

"Yes, I had a fair amount of practice there."

"Go on with your story."

"Well, I seem to have told you everything . . . Oh yes! One more thing: the young princess seems fond of discussing sentiments, passions, and so forth. She spent one winter in Petersburg, and did not like it, especially the society there: probably she was given a cool reception."

"You saw no one at their house today?"

"On the contrary, there was one adjutant, one stiff-looking guardsman, and a lady who has recently arrived, a relative of the princess by marriage, a very pretty woman but a very sick one, it seems . . . Didn't you chance to meet her at the well? She's of medium height, a blonde, with regular features, her complexion is consumptive, and she has a little black mole on her right cheek. Her face struck me by its expressiveness."

"A little mole!" I muttered through my teeth. "Really?"

The doctor looked at me and said solemnly, placing his hand on my heart: "She is someone you know! . . ." My heart, indeed, was beating faster than usual.

"It is now your turn to triumph," I said, "but I rely on you; you will not betray me. I have not seen her yet, but I am sure that I recognize, from your depiction, a certain woman whom I loved in the old days. Don't tell her a word about me; should she ask, give a bad account of me."

"As you please!" said Werner with a shrug.

When he left, a dreadful sadness constrained my heart. Was it fate that was bringing us together again in the Caucasus, or had she come here on purpose, knowing she would meet me? And how would we meet? And, anyway, was it she? Presentiments never deceive me. There is no man in the world over whom the past gains such power as it does over me. Every reminder of a past sorrow or joy painfully strikes my soul and extracts from it the same old sounds . . . I am stupidly made, I forget nothing . . . nothing!

After dinner, around six, I went out onto the boulevard: there was a crowd there; the princess sat with her daughter on a bench, surrounded by young men who vied in paying attention to them. I sat down on another bench some way off, stopped two officers of the D. regiment whom I knew, and began telling them something; apparently, it was amusing, because they began laughing like mad. Curiosity attracted to me some of those who surrounded the young princess; little by little, they all abandoned her and joined my group. I never ceased talking; my stories were clever to the point of stupidity, my raillery, directed at the freaks who passed by, was wicked to the point of frenzy. I went on entertaining my audience till sunset. Several times, the young princess and her mother passed by me, arm in arm, accompanied by a little old man with a limp; several times her glance, falling upon me, expressed vexation while striving to express indifference.

"What has he been telling you?" she inquired of one of the young men who had returned to her out of politeness. "Surely, a very entertaining story . . . his exploits in battles?" She said this rather loudly and probably with the intention of pin-pricking me. "Aha," I thought, "you are angry in earnest, my dear princess; just wait, there is more to come!"

Grushnitski watched her like a beast of prey and never took his eyes off her: I bet that tomorrow he will beg somebody to introduce him to her mother. She will be very pleased, because she is bored.

*May 16th*

During the last two days, my affairs have advanced tremendously. The young princess definitely hates me: people have already reported to me two or three epigrams aimed at me, fairly caustic, but at the same time very flattering. She finds it awfully strange that I, who am used to high society and am on such intimate terms with her Petersburg female cousins and aunts, do not try to make her acquaintance. Every day, we run into each other at the well or on the boulevard; I do my best to lure away her admirers, brilliant adjutants, pallid Moscovites and others—and almost always, I succeed. I have always hated to entertain guests at my house. Now, my place is full every day; people dine, sup, play cards, and, alas, my champagne triumphs over the power of her magnetic young eyes![88]

Yesterday, I saw her in Chelahov's store: she was bargaining for a wonderful Persian rug. The young princess kept begging her mamma not to be stingy; that rug would be such an adornment for her dressing room! I offered forty roubles more and outbid her; for this I was rewarded by a glance in which glittered the most exquisite rage. About dinner time, I purposely ordered my Circassian horse to be covered with that rug and led past her windows. Werner was with them at the time, and told me that the effect of that scene was most dramatic. The young princess wants to preach a crusade against me: I have even noticed that already two adjutants in her presence greet me very drily, although they dine at my house every day.

Grushnitski has assumed a mysterious air: he walks with his hands behind his back and does not seem to recognize anybody; his leg has suddenly got well, he hardly limps at all. He has found the occasion to enter into conversation with the old princess and to pay a compliment to her daughter. The latter is apparently none too choosy, for since then she has been acknowledging his salute with the prettiest of smiles.

"You are sure you do not wish to make the acquaintance of the Ligovskoys?" he said to me yesterday.

"Quite sure."

"Oh come! Theirs is the pleasantest house at the spa! All the best society here. . . ."

"My friend, I am dreadfully sick of the best society which is not here. And you . . . do you go there?"

"Not yet. I have talked to the young princess a couple of times, and more.[89] It is kind of embarrassing to fish for an invitation, you know, though it is done here . . . It would have been another matter, if I wore epaulets. . . ."

"Oh come! You are much more intriguing this way! You simply don't know how to take advantage of your lucky situation. In the eyes of any sentimental young lady, your soldier's coat is bound to make a hero of you, a martyr."

Grushnitski smiled smugly.

"What nonsense!" he said.

"I'm sure," I went on, "that the young princess is already in love with you."

He blushed to the ears, and puffed out his chest.[90]

O vanity! you are the lever by means of which Archimedes wished to lift the earth!

"You always joke!" he said, feigning to be cross. "In the first place, she knows me so little as yet."

"Women love only those whom they do not know."

"But I have no pretension whatever to make her fond of me, I simply want to gain access to a pleasant house, and it would have been quite absurd if I had any hopes . . . Now you people, for example, are another matter; you St. Petersburg lady-killers, you have only to look . . . and women melt . . . By the way, Pechorin, do you know what the young princess said about you?"

"Really? Has she already started to speak to you about me?"

"Wait—there is nothing to be glad about. The other day I entered into conversation with her at the well, by chance. Her third word was: 'Who is that gentleman with that unpleasant oppressive gaze? He was with you when . . .' She blushed and did not want to name the day, remembering her charming gesture. 'You don't have to mention the day,' I replied to her, 'it will always remain in my memory.' Pechorin, my friend! I do not congratulate you; you are on her black list. And this, indeed, is regrettable because [my][91] Mary is a very charming girl!"

It should be noted that Grushnitski is one of those people who, when speaking of a woman whom they hardly know, call her *my Mary, my Sophie,* if she had the fortune to catch their fancy.

I assumed a serious air and replied to him:

"Yes, she is not bad . . . But beware, Grushnitski! Russian young ladies, for the most part, nourish themselves on platonic love, without admixing to it any thought of marriage: now, platonic love is the most troublesome kind. The young princess seems to be one of those women who want to be amused: if she is bored in your presence for two minutes together, you are irretrievably lost. Your silence must excite her curiosity, your talk should never entirely satisfy it; you must disturb her every minute. She will disregard convention, publicly, a dozen times for your sake, and will call it a sacrifice, and, in order to reward herself for it, she will begin to torment you, and after that she will simply say that she cannot stand you. Unless you gain some ascendency over her, even her first kiss will not entitle you to a second: she will have her fill of flirting with you, and in two years or so she will marry a monster out of submissiveness to her mother, and will start persuading herself that she is miserable, that she loved only one man, meaning you, but that Heaven had not wished to unite her with him because he wore a soldier's coat, although under that thick gray coat there beat a passionate and noble heart. . . ."

Grushnitski hit the table with his fist and started to pace up and down the room.

I inwardly roared with laughter, and even smiled once or twice, but fortunately he did not notice.

It is clear that he is in love, for he has become even more credulous than before: there even appeared on his finger, a nielloed, silver ring of local production. It looked suspicious to me. I began to examine it, and what would you think? . . . The name *Mary* was engraved in minuscule letters on the inside, and next to it was the day of the month when she picked up the famous glass. I concealed my discovery. I do not wish to force a confession from him, I want him to choose me for a confidant himself—and it is then that I shall enjoy myself! . . .

　　•　　•　　•　　•　　•　　•　　•　　•

Today I rose late; when I reached the well, there was already nobody there. It was getting hot; furry white clouds were rapidly scudding from the snowy mountains with the promise of a thunderstorm; the top of Mount Mashuk smoked like an extinguished torch; around it there coiled and slithered, like snakes, gray shreds of cloud, which had been delayed in their surge and seemed to have caught in its thorny brush. The air was pervaded with elec-

tricity. I plunged into a viny avenue that led to a
grotto; I was sad. I kept thinking of that young
woman with the little birthmark on her cheek of
whom the doctor had been talking. Why was she
here? And was it she? And why did I think it was
she? And why was I even so sure of it? Were there
not many women with little moles on their cheeks!
Meditating in this fashion, I came close to the grotto.
As I looked in, I saw in the cool shade of its vault, on
a stone bench, a seated woman, wearing a straw hat,
a black shawl wrapped around her shoulders, her
head sunken on her breast: the hat screened her
face. I was on the point of turning back, so as not to
disturb her revery, when she looked up at me.

"Vera!" I cried involuntarily.

She started and grew pale.

"I knew that you were here," she said.

I sat down near her and took her hand. A long-
forgotten thrill ran through my veins at the sound
of that dear voice: she looked into my eyes with her
deep and calm eyes; they expressed distrust and
something akin to reproachfulness.

"We have not seen each other for a long time," I
said.

"Yes, a long time, and we have both changed in
many ways!"

"So this means that you do not love me any
more? . . ."

"I am married! . . ." she said.

"Again? Several years ago, however, the same reason existed, and yet. . . ."

She snatched her hand out of mine. And her
cheeks flamed.

"Perhaps you love your second husband. . . ."

She did not answer and turned away.

"Or is he very jealous?"

Silence.

"Well? He is young, handsome, he is, in particular, rich, no doubt, and you are afraid . . ." I glanced at her and was shocked: her face expressed profound despair, tears sparkled in her eyes.

"Tell me," she whispered at last, "do you find it very amusing to torture me? I ought to hate you. Ever since we have known each other, you gave me nothing but sufferings . . ." Her voice trembled; she leaned toward me to lay her head on my breast.

"Perhaps," I thought, "this is exactly why you loved me: one forgets joys, one never forgets sorrows. . . ."

I embraced her warmly, and thus we remained for a long time. At last our lips came close together and merged in an ardent rapturous kiss; her hands were as cold as ice, her brow was burning. Between us, started one of those conversations which have no sense on paper, which cannot be repeated and which one cannot even retain in one's mind: the meaning of sounds replaces and enhances the meaning of words, as in the Italian opera.

She definitely does not wish that I meet her husband, that little old gentleman with the limp whom I glimpsed on the boulevard: she married him for the sake of her son. He is rich and suffers from rheumatism. I did not allow myself a single jibe at him: she respects him as a father—and will deceive him as a husband. What a bizarre thing, the human heart in general, and a woman's heart in particular!

Vera's husband, Semyon Vasilievich G——v, is a distant relation of Princess Ligovskoy. He lives near her: Vera often visits the old princess. I gave her my word that I would get acquainted with the Ligovskoys and court the young princess in order to divert attention from Vera. In this way, my plans

have not been upset in the least, and I shall have a
merry time. . . .

Merry time! Yes, I have already passed that stage
of the soul's life when one seeks only happiness,
when the heart feels the need to love someone
strongly and passionately. At present, all I wish is to
be loved, and that by very few: it even seems to me
that I would be content with one permanent attach-
ment, a pitiful habit of the heart!

One thing has always struck me as strange: I
never became the slave of the women I loved; on the
contrary, I have always gained unconquerable
power over their will and heart, with no effort at all.
Why is it so? Is it because I never treasured anything too much, while they incessantly feared to let
me slip out of their hands? Or is it the magnetic
influence of a strong organism? Or did I simply
never succeed in encountering a woman with a stubborn will of her own?

I must admit that, indeed, I never cared for
women with wills of their own; it is not their department.

True, I remember now—once, only once did I love
a strong-willed woman, whom I could never con-
quer. We parted enemies—but even so, perhaps, had
our meeting occurred five years later, we would
have parted differently.

Vera is ill, very ill, although she will not admit it:
I fear she may have consumption, or that disease
which is called *fièvre lente*,[92] a completely non-Russian disease, for which there is no name in our language.

The thunderstorm caught us in the grotto and detained us there for an extra half hour. She did not
make me swear that I would be true to her, did not
ask if I had loved other women since we had parted.

She entrusted herself to me again with the same un-concern as before—and I will not deceive her. She is the only woman on earth whom I could not bear to deceive. I know that we shall soon part again—perhaps, forever; that each of us will go his separate way, graveward. But her memory will remain in-violable in my soul: I have always repeated this to her, and she believes me, although she says she does not.

At last, we separated: for a long time, I followed her with my gaze until her hat disappeared behind the shrubs and cliffs. My heart painfully contracted as after the first parting. Oh, how that feeling glad-dened me! Could it be that youth with its beneficial storms wants to return to me again, or is it merely its farewell glance—a last gift to its memory? And yet it's absurd to think that in appearance I am still a boy: my face is pale but still fresh-complexioned, my limbs are supple and svelte, my thick hair curls, my eyes sparkle, my blood is ebullient.

When I returned home, I got on my horse and galloped out into the steppe. I love to gallop on a spirited horse through tall grass, against the wind of the wilderness; avidly do I swallow the redolent air and direct my gaze into the blue remoteness, trying to distinguish the nebulous outlines of objects that become, every minute, clearer and clearer. What-ever sorrow may burden my heart, whatever anxiety may oppress my mind, everything is dispersed in a moment: the soul feels easy, bodily fatigue van-quishes mental worry. There is no feminine gaze that I would not forget at the sight of mountains covered with curly vegetation,[93] and illumined by the southern sun, at the sight of the blue sky, or at the sound of a torrent that falls from crag to crag.

I think that the Cossacks yawning on the top of

their watchtowers, upon seeing me galloping without need or goal, were for a long time tormented by this riddle, for I am sure they must have taken me for a Circassian because of my dress. Indeed, I have been told that when riding in Circassian garb, I look more like a Kabardan than many a Kabardan. And, in point of fact, as regards that noble battle garb, I am an absolute dandy: not one bit of superfluous braid; costly arms in plain setting; the fur of the cap neither too long nor too short; leggings and boots fitted with the utmost exactitude; a white *beshmet;* a dark-brown *cherkeska*[94]. I have studied, for a long time, the mountain peoples' style of riding: there is no better way of flattering my vanity than to acknowledge my skill in riding a horse in the Caucasian fashion. I keep four horses: one for myself, three for pals, so as not to feel dull while ranging the fields alone: they take my horses with alacrity, and never ride with me. It was already six in the evening, when I remembered that it was time to dine. My horse was worn out; I came out onto the road which led from Pyatigorsk to the German settlement where the spa society frequently went for picnics. The road ran winding among bushes, and descending into small ravines where noisy creeks flowed under the shelter of tall grasses; all around rose an amphitheatre of blue masses—Besh Tau, Snake Mountain, Iron Mountain and Bald Mountain. Upon descending into one of these ravines, called *balkas*[95] in the local dialect, I stopped to water my horse. At that moment, there appeared on the road a noisy and resplendent cavalcade, the ladies in black or light-blue riding habits, and the gentlemen in costumes representing a mixture of Circassian and Nizhni-Novgorodan:[96] Grushnitski rode in front with Princess Mary.

Ladies at Caucasian spas still believe in the possibility of Circassian attacks in broad daylight: presumably, this is why Grushnitski had hung a sword and a brace of pistols onto his soldier's coat. He was rather absurd in this heroic attire. A tall shrub hid me from them, but through its foliage I could see everything and could guess from the expressions on their faces that the conversation was sentimental. Finally, they drew close to the declivity; Grushnitski took the princess' horse by the bridle, and then I heard the end of their conversation:

"And you wish to remain for the rest of your life in the Caucasus?" the princess was saying.

"What is Russia to me?" answered her companion, "a country where thousands of people will look on me with contempt because they are richer than I am —whereas here—here this thick soldier's coat has not prevented me from making your acquaintance. . . ."

"On the contrary . . ." said the princess, blushing.

Grushnitski's face portrayed pleasure. He went on:

"My life here will flow by noisily, unnoticeably, and rapidly under the bullets of the savages, and if God would send me, every year, one radiant feminine glance, one glance similiar to the one. . . ."

At this point they came level with me; I struck my horse with my riding crop and rode out from behind the bush. . . .

"*Mon Dieu, un Circassien!* . . ." cried the princess in terror.

In order to dissuade her completely, I answered in French, bowing slightly:

"*Ne craignez rien, madame—je ne suis pas plus dangereux que votre cavalier.*"

She was embarrassed—but why? Because of her

mistake, or because my answer seemed insolent to her? I would have liked my second supposition to be the correct one. Grushnitski cast a look of displeasure at me.

Late this evening, that is to say around eleven, I went for a stroll in the linden avenue of the boulevard. The town was asleep: only in some windows lights could be glimpsed. On three sides, there loomed the black crest of cliffs, offshoots of Mount Mashuk, on the summit of which an ominous little cloud was lying. The moon was rising in the east; afar glittered the silvery rim of snow-covered mountains. The cries of the sentries alternated with the sound of the hot springs, which had been given free flow for the night. At times, the sonorous stamp of a horse was heard in the street, accompanied by the creaking of a Nogay[97] wagon and a mournful Tatar song. I sat down on a bench and became lost in thought. I felt the need of pouring out my thoughts in friendly talk—but with whom? What was Vera doing now, I wondered. I would have paid dearly to press her hand at that moment.

Suddenly I heard quick irregular steps—Grushnitski, no doubt. So it was!

"Where do you come from?"

"From Princess Ligovskoy," he said very importantly. "How Mary can sing!"

"Do you know what?" I said to him, "I bet she does not know that you are a cadet; she thinks you have been degraded to the ranks."

"Perhaps! What do I care?" he said absently.

"Oh, I just happened to mention it."

"Do you know, you made her dreadfully angry today? She found it an unheard-of insolence. I had a lot of trouble convincing her that you are too well brought up and that you know the *grand monde* too well to have had any intention of insulting her: she says that you have an impudent gaze and that, no doubt, you have the highest opinion of yourself."

"She is not mistaken . . . Perhaps you would like to stand up for her?"

"I regret that I do not have that right yet. . . ."

"Oh, oh!" I thought, "I see he already has hopes."

"Well, so much the worse for you," Grushnitski continued, "it would be difficult for you to make their acquaintance now; and that's a pity! It is one of the most pleasant houses that I know of."

I smiled inwardly.

"The most pleasant house for me is now my own," I said yawning, and got up to go.

"But first confess, you repent?"

"What nonsense! If I choose, I shall be at the old princess's house tomorrow evening. . . ."

"We shall see. . . ."

"And even, to oblige you, I shall flirt with the young princess. . . ."

"Yes, if she is willing to speak to you. . . ."

"I shall only wait for the moment when your conversation begins to bore her . . . Good-by."

"And I shall go roaming; I could never fall asleep now . . . Look, let's better go to the restaurant, there is gambling there . . . tonight I require strong sensations. . . ."

"I wish you bad luck."

I went home.

*May 21st*

Almost a week has passed, and I still have not made the acquaintance of the Ligovskoys. I am waiting for a convenient occasion. Grushnitski, like a shadow, follows the young princess everywhere;

their conversations are endless: when will he begin to bore her at last? Her mother does not pay any attention to this because he is not an "eligible" young man. That's the logic of mothers for you! I have observed two or three tender glances—an end must be put to it.

Yesterday, Vera appeared for the first time at the well. Since our meeting in the grotto, she has not been out of the house. We dipped our glasses simultaneously and, bending, she said to me in a whisper:

"You don't want to get acquainted with the Ligovskoys? It's the only place where we could see each other."

A reproach! How dull! But I have deserved it. . . .

Apropos, tomorrow there is a subscription dance in the ballroom of the restaurant, and I am going to dance the mazurka with the young princess.

*May 22nd*

The restaurant's ballroom was transformed into that of the Club of the Nobility. By nine o'clock, everybody had arrived. The old princess and her daughter were among the last to appear: many ladies looked at her with envy and ill will because Princess Mary dresses with taste. Those ladies who regard themselves as the aristocrats of the place concealed their envy and attached themselves to her. What can you do? Where there is feminine society, there will appear at once a higher and a lower circle. Outside the window, in a crowd of people, stood Grushnitski,[98] pressing his face to the windowpane and never taking his eyes off his goddess: as she passed by, she gave him a hardly perceptible nod. He beamed like the sun. The dancing began with a polonaise; then the band began to play a waltz. Spurs tinkled, coat tails flew up and whirled.

I stood behind a stout lady: her head was crowned with pink plumes; the luxuriance of her dress recalled the times of farthingales, and the variegation of her rough skin, the happy era of black taffeta patches. The largest wart on her neck was concealed by the clasp of a necklace. She was saying to her dancing partner, a captain of dragoons:

"That young Princess Ligovskoy is an intolerable little thing! Fancy, she bumped into me and never apologized, but in addition turned around and looked at me through her lorgnette . . . *C'est impayable!* . . . And what is she so proud of? She ought to be taught a lesson. . . ."

"No trouble in getting that done," answered the obliging captain, and went into the next room.

I immediately went up to the young princess and engaged her for the waltz, taking advantage of the easy local customs which allow one to dance with ladies to whom one has not been introduced.

She could hardly force herself not to smile and not to hide her triumph: she managed, however, rather soon to assume a completely indifferent and even severe air. She nonchalantly dropped her hand on my shoulder, slightly inclined her pretty head to one side—and off we went. I do not know a waist more voluptuous and supple! Her fresh breath touched my face; sometimes a curl that had become separated in the whirl of the waltz from its fellows, would brush my burning cheek. I made three turns (she waltzes amazingly well). She was out of breath, her eyes were dim, her half-opened lips could hardly murmur the obligatory "Merci, monsieur."

After several moments of silence, I said to her, assuming a most submissive air:

"I hear, princess, that despite my being completely unknown to you, I have already had the misfortune to earn your displeasure . . . that you've found me insolent . . . Can this be true?"

"And now you would like to confirm me in this opinion?" she replied with an ironic little grimace, which incidentally was very becoming to her mobile features.

"If I had the insolence to offend you in any way, then allow me to have the still greater insolence to beg your pardon. And truly, I would wish very much to prove to you that you are mistaken about me."

"You will find this rather difficult."

"Why so?"

"Because you do not come to our house, and these balls will probably not take place very often."

"This means," I thought, "that their door is closed to me forever."

"Do you know, princess," I said with some vexation, "one should never turn down a repentant criminal: out of sheer despair he may become twice as criminal as before, and then. . . ."

Laughter and whispering among the people around us made me turn and interrupt my sentence. A few steps away from me stood a group of men, and among them was the Captain of Dragoons who had declared hostile intentions against the charming young princess. He was particularly satisfied with something; he rubbed his hands, he laughed and exchanged winks with his companions. Suddenly out of their midst emerged a person in a dresscoat, with a long mustache and a florid face and directed his unsteady steps straight toward the young princess: he was drunk. Having come to a stop in front of the

disconcerted princess, and clasping his hands behind his back, he fixed her with his bleary, gray eyes
and uttered in a hoarse, treble voice:

"Permetay . . . oh, what's the use of that! . . . I
simply engage you for the mazurka. . . ."

"What do you want?" she uttered in a trembling
voice, as she cast around her an imploring glance.
Alas! her mother was far away, and in her vicinity
she could see none of the gentlemen she knew. One
adjutant, I think, witnessed it all, but hid behind
the crowd so as not to be involved in a row.

"Well?" said the drunk, winking at the Captain of
Dragoons, who was encouraging him with signs,
"don't you want to? Here I am again requesting the
honor of engaging you *pour mazurque*[99] . . . You
think, perhaps, that I am drunk? That does not matter! One is much freer that way, I can assure you."

I saw that she was about to swoon from fear and
indignation.

I went up to the drunk, took him rather firmly by
the arm and looking steadily into his eyes, asked
him to go away, because, I added, the princess had
long ago promised to dance the mazurka with me.

"Well, nothing to be done! . . . Some other time!"
he said with a laugh, and went off to join his abashed
companions, who immediately led him away into
the other room.

I was rewarded by a deep, wonderful glance.

The princess went up to her mother and told her
everything: the latter sought me out in the crowd
and thanked me. She informed me that she used to
know my mother and was on friendly terms with
half a dozen of my aunts.

"I do not know how it happened that we have not
met before now," she added, "but you must admit
that you alone are to blame for this; you shun every-

body: I have never seen anything like it. I hope that the atmosphere of my drawing room will dissipate your spleen . . . Am I right?"

I said to her one of those phrases which everyone should have in store for such occasions.

The quadrilles dragged on for a terribly long time.

At last, the mazurka resounded from the upper balcony. The young princess and I seated ourselves.

Never once did I allude either to the tipsy man, or to my former behavior, or to Grushnitski. The impression that the unpleasant scene had made upon her gradually dissipated. Her pretty face bloomed, she joked very charmingly, her conversation was witty, without any pretention to wit, it was lively and free; her observations were sometimes profound. I gave her to understand, by means of a very involved sentence, that I had long been attracted to her. She inclined her young head and colored slightly.

"You're a bizarre person!" she presently said, raising upon me her velvety eyes and laughing in a constrained way.

"I did not wish to make your acquaintance," I continued, "because you were surrounded by too dense a crowd of admirers, and I was afraid of getting completely lost in it."

"Your fears were unfounded: all of them are most dull. . . ."

"All! Are you sure you mean all?"

She looked at me intently, as if trying to recall something, then she slightly blushed again, and finally uttered resolutely: *"all!"*

"Including even my friend Grushnitski?"

"Why, is he your friend?" she said, revealing some doubt.

"Yes."

"He does not enter, of course, into the category of dull people."

"Rather the category of unfortunate ones," I said laughing.

"Of course! You find it funny? I wish you were in his place."

"Well, I used to be a cadet myself and indeed it was the very best time of my life!"

"But is he a cadet? . . ." she said quickly, and then added: "I thought that. . . ."

"What is it you thought?"

"Nothing! . . . Who is that lady?"

Here the conversation took another direction, and did not return to that subject any more.

The mazurka came to an end, and we parted—until our next meeting. The ladies left. I went to have supper and ran into Werner.

"Aha!" he said, "so that's the way you are! Didn't you intend not to make the princess's acquaintance in any other way than by saving her from certain death?"

"I did better," I answered him, "I saved her from fainting at a ball. . . ."

"How's that? Tell me. . . ."

"No, try and guess—you, who can guess all things in the world!"

*May 23rd*

Around seven tonight, I was out strolling on the boulevard. Grushnitski, on seeing me in the distance, came up to me: a kind of absurd exaltation shone in his eyes. He gripped my hand and said in a tragic voice:

"I thank you, Pechorin . . . You understand me?"

"No; but whatever it is, it is not worth gratitude,"

I answered, having indeed no charitable action on my conscience.

"But what about last night? You can't have forgotten? . . . Mary told me everything. . . ."

"Do you two have everything in common now? Even gratitude?"

"Look," said Grushnitski very importantly, "please do not make fun of my love, if you wish to remain my pal . . . You see, I love her to distraction. And I think, I hope, that she loves me too . . . I have a favor to ask of you. You are going to visit them tonight: promise me to observe everything. I know you are experienced in these matters, you know women better than I do . . . Women! Women! Who will understand them? Their smiles contradict their glances, their words promise and lure, while the sound of their voices drives us away. One minute they comprehend and divine our most secret thought, and the next, they do not understand the clearest hints. Take the young princess, for instance, yesterday her eyes blazed with passion when they rested upon me, today they are dull and cold. . . ."

"This, perhaps, is due to the effect of the waters," I answered.

"You see in everything the nasty side . . . you materialist," he added contemptuously. "Let us switch, however, to another matter." And pleased with this poor pun, he cheered up.

Around half past eight, we went together to the princess's house.

Walking past Vera's windows, I saw her at the window. We threw each other a fleeting glance. She entered the Ligovskoys' drawing room soon after us. The old princess introduced me to her as to a relation of hers. Tea was being served; there were many visitors; the conversation was general. I endeavored to ingratiate myself with the old princess; I jested, I made her laugh heartily several times: the young princess also wanted to laugh more than once, but she restrained herself so as not to depart from the role she had assumed. She finds that a languorous air suits her, and perhaps she does not err. Grushnitski was apparently very glad that my gaiety did not infect her.

After tea, we all went into the music room.

"Are you pleased with my obedience, Vera?" I said as I passed her.

She threw me a glance full of love and gratitude. I am now used to those glances, but there was a time when they made my bliss. The old princess had her daughter sit down at the piano: everyone was asking her to sing something. I kept silent and, taking advantage of the hubbub, I drew away toward a window with Vera, who wanted to tell me something very important for both of us. It turned out to be nonsense.

Meanwhile, my indifference was annoying to the young princess, as I could conjecture by a single angry, blazing glance . . . Oh, I understand wonderfully that kind of conversation, mute but expressive, brief but forcible! . . .

She started to sing: her voice is not bad, but she sings poorly. I did not listen, however. In compensation, Grushnitski, with his elbows on the piano, facing her, devoured her with his eyes and every minute kept saying under his breath: *"Charmant! Délicieux!"*

"Listen," Vera was saying to me, "I do not want you to meet my husband, but you must, without fail, please the old princess. It is easy for you; you can achieve anything you want. We shall see each other only here. . . ."[100]

"Only here? . . ."

She colored and went on: "You know that I am
your slave; I never was able to resist you . . . and for
this I shall be punished. You will cease to love me.
I wish, at least, to save my reputation . . . not for
my own sake: you know that very well! Oh, I be-
seech you, do not torment me as before with empty
doubts and feigned coldness. I shall die soon, perhaps. I feel myself getting weaker every day . . .
and, in spite of that, I cannot think of a future life, I
think only of you . . . You men do not understand
the delights of a glance, of a handshake . . . while
I, I swear to you, I, when listening to your voice, I
experience such deep, strange bliss that the most
ardent kisses could not replace it.

Meanwhile Princess Mary had stopped singing. A
murmur of praise sounded around her. I went up to
her after all the other guests and said something to
her about her voice, rather casually.

She made a grimace, protruding her lower lip and
curtsied in a very mocking manner.

"It is all the more flattering to me," she said, "since
you did not listen to me at all; but then, perhaps,
you do not like music?"

"On the contrary . . . particularly after dinner."

"Grushnitski is right in saying that you have most
prosaic tastes . . . And I see that you like music in a
gastronomic way."

"You are wrong again. I am far from being a gourmet: my digestion is exceedingly bad. But music
after dinner puts one to sleep, and sleep after dinner
is good for one's health. Consequently, I like music
from a medical point of view. In the evening, on the
contrary, it irritates my nerves too much; my mood
becomes either too melancholy, or too gay. Both
are exhausting, when there is no positive cause to be

sad or to be joyful, and, moreover, melancholy at a
social gathering is absurd, while immoderate gaiety
is improper. . . ."

She did not hear me out, moved away, sat down
next to Grushnitski, and there started between them
some kind of sentimental conversation. The young
princess, it seemed, replied rather absently and ir-
relevantly to his wise pronouncements, though she
tried to show that she listened to him with attention,
for now and then he would glance at her with surprise, trying to guess the reason for the inward
agitation that expressed itself now and then in her
restless glance.

But I have found you out, my dear princess. Beware! You want to repay me in my own coin, to
prick my vanity—you will not succeed. And if you
declare war on me, I shall be merciless.

In the course of the evening, I tried several times,
on purpose, to join their conversation, but she countered my remarks rather drily, and, with feigned
annoyance, I finally moved away. The young princess triumphed; Grushnitski, likewise. Have your
triumph, my friends, hurry—you won't triumph long!
What is to be done? I have a presentiment . . .
Whenever I become acquainted with a woman, I
always guess without fail, whether she will fall in
love with me or not.

I spent the rest of the evening at Vera's side and
talked of old times to my heart's content. What does
she love me for so much—I really don't know; particularly since she is the only woman who has completely understood me with all my petty weaknesses
and wicked passions. Can evil possibly be so attractive?

Grushnitski and I left together: when we got outside, he put his arm through mine and said after a long silence:

"Well, what do you think?"

"That you are a fool," I wanted to answer, but restrained myself, and merely shrugged my shoulders.

*May 29th*

During all these days, I never once departed from my system. The young princess begins to like my conversation. I told her some of the strange occurrences in my life, and she begins to see in me an extraordinary person. I laugh at everything in the world, especially at feelings: this is beginning to frighten her. In my presence she does not dare to launch upon sentimental debates with Grushnitski, and has several times already replied to his sallies with a mocking smile; but every time that Grushnitski comes up to her, I assume a humble air and leave them alone together. The first time she was glad of it or tried to make it seem so; the second time she became cross with me; the third time she became cross with Grushnitski.

"You have very little vanity!" she said to me yesterday. "Why do you think that I have more fun with Grushnitski?"

I answered that I was sacrificing to a pal's happiness, my own pleasure.

"And mine," she added.

I looked at her intently and assumed a serious air. After this, I did not say another word to her all day. In the evening, she was pensive, this morning, at the well, she was more pensive still. When I went up to her, she was absently listening to Grushnitski, who, it seems, was being rhapsodical about nature; but as soon as she saw me, she began to laugh (very much *mal à propos*), pretending not to notice me. I walked off some distance and stealthily watched her: she turned away from her interlocutor and yawned twice. Decidedly, Grushnitski has begun to bore her. I shall not speak to her for two more days.

*June 3rd*

I often wonder, why I do so stubbornly try to gain the love of a little maiden whom I do not wish to seduce, and whom I shall never marry? Why this feminine coquetry? Vera loves me more than Princess Mary will ever love anyone: if she had seemed to me to be an unconquerable belle, then perhaps I might have been fascinated by the difficulty of the enterprise.

But it is nothing of the sort! Consequently, this is not that restless need for love that torments us in the first years of youth, and drives us from one woman to another, until we find one who cannot abide us: and here begins our constancy—that true, infinite passion, which can be mathematically expressed by means of a line falling from a given point into space: the secret of that infinity lies solely in the impossibility of reaching a goal, that is to say, reaching the end.

Why then do I take all this trouble? Because I envy Grushnitski? Poor thing! He has not earned it at all. Or is it the outcome of that nasty but unconquerable feeling which urges us to destroy the sweet delusions of a fellow man, in order to have the petty satisfaction of saying to him, when he asks in despair, what is it he should believe:

"My friend, the same thing happened to me, and still, you see, I dine, I sup, I sleep in perfect peace, and hope to be able to die without cries and tears."

And then again . . . there is boundless delight in the possession of a young, barely unfolded soul! It is like a flower whose best fragrance emanates to meet the first ray of the sun. It should be plucked that very minute and after inhaling one's fill of it, one should throw it away on the road: perchance, someone will pick it up! I feel in myself this insatiable avidity, which engulfs everything met on the way. I look upon the sufferings and joys of others only in relation to myself as on the food sustaining the strength of my soul. I am no longer capable myself of frenzy under the influence of passion: ambition with me has been suppressed by circumstances, but it has manifested itself in another form, since ambition is nothing else than thirst for power, and my main pleasure—which is to subjugate to my will all that surrounds me, and to excite the emotions of love, devotion, and fear in relation to me—is it not the main sign and greatest triumph of power? To be to somebody the cause of sufferings and joys, without having any positive right to it—is this not the sweetest possible nourishment for our pride? And what is happiness? Sated pride. If I considered myself to be better and more powerful than anyone in the world, I would be happy; if everybody loved me, I would find in myself infinite sources of love. Evil begets evil: the first ache gives us an idea of the pleasure of tormenting another. The idea of evil cannot enter a person's head without his wanting to apply it to reality: ideas are organic creations. Someone has said that their very birth endows them with a form, and this form is action; he in whose head more ideas have been born is more active than others. This is why a genius chained to an office desk must die or go mad, exactly as a powerfully built man, whose life is sedentary and whose behavior is virtuous, dies of apoplexy.

The passions are nothing else but ideas in their first phase of development; they are an attribute of the youth of the heart; and he is a fool who thinks he will be agitated by them all his life. Many a calm river begins as a turbulent waterfall, yet none hurtles and foams all the way to the sea. But that calm is often the sign of great, though concealed, strength; the plenitude and depth of feelings and thoughts does not tolerate frantic surgings; the soul, while experiencing pain or pleasure, gives itself a strict account of everything and becomes convinced that so it must be; it knows that without storms, a constantly torrid sun will wither it; it becomes penetrated with its own life, it fondles and punishes itself, as if it were a beloved child. Only in this supreme state of self-knowledge can a man evaluate divine justice.

On re-reading this page, I notice that I have strayed far from my subject . . . But what does it matter? . . . I write this journal for myself and, consequently, anything that I may toss into it will become, in time, for me, a precious memory.

•    •    •    •    •    •    •    •    •    •    •

Grushnitski came and threw himself on my neck: he had been promoted to an officer's rank. We had some champagne. Dr. Werner dropped in soon after him.

"I do not congratulate you," he said to Grushnitski.

"Why?"

"Because a soldier's coat is very becoming to you, and you must admit that an infantry army officer's uniform, made in this watering place, will not give you any glamor. You see, up to now you were an exception, while now you will come under the general rule."

"Talk on, talk on, doctor! You will not prevent me from being delighted. He does not know," added Grushnitski, whispering into my ear: "what hopes these epaulets give me . . . Ah . . . epaulets, epaulets! Your little stars are guiding stars. No! I'm entirely happy now."

"Are you coming with us for that walk to The Hollow?" I asked him.

"I? For nothing in the world shall I show myself to the young princess till my uniform is ready."

"Do you wish me to announce the glad news to her?"

"No, please do not tell her . . . I want to surprise her. . . ."

"By the way, tell me, how are you getting on with her?"

He lost countenance and grew pensive: he wanted to boast and lie, but he was ashamed to do so, and yet it would have been mortifying to admit the truth.

"What do you think, does she love you?"

"Love me? Come, Pechorin, what notions you do have! . . . How could this happen so fast? . . . Even if she does love one, a decent woman would not tell. . . ."

"Fine! And probably, according to you, a decent man should also keep silent about his passion?"

"Ah, my good fellow! There is a way of doing things; there is much that is not said, but guessed. . . ."

"That's true . . . However, the love that is read in the eyes does not bind a woman to anything, whereas words . . . Take care, Grushnitski, she is fooling you."

"She? . . ." he answered, raising his eyes to Heaven and smiling complacently: "I pity you, Pechorin!"

He left.

In the evening, a numerous party set out on foot for The Hollow.

In the opinion of local scientists, that "hollow" is nothing else than an extinguished crater: it is situated on a slope of Mount Mashuk, less than a mile from town. To it leads a narrow trail, among bushes and cliffs. As we went up the mountain, I offered the young princess my arm, and she never abandoned it during the entire walk.

Our conversation began with gossip: I passed in review our acquaintances, both present and absent: first, I brought out their comic traits, and then their evil ones. My bile began to stir. I started in jest and finished in frank waspishness. At first it amused her, then frightened her.

"You are a dangerous man!" she said to me. "I would sooner find myself in a wood under a murderer's knife than be the victim of your sharp tongue . . . I ask you seriously, when it occurs to you to talk badly about me, better take a knife and cut my throat: I don't think you will find it very difficult."

"Do I look like a murderer?"

"You are worse. . . ."

I thought a moment, and then said, assuming a deeply touched air:

"Yes, such was my lot since my very childhood! Everybody read in my face the signs of bad inclinations which were not there, but they were supposed to be there—and so they came into existence. I was modest—they accused me of being crafty: I became secretive. I felt deeply good and evil—nobody caressed me, everybody offended me: I became rancorous. I was gloomy—other children were merry and talkative. I felt myself superior to them—but was considered inferior: I became envious. I was ready to love the whole world—none understood me: and I learned to hate. My colorless youth was spent in a struggle with myself and with the world. Fearing mockery, I buried my best feelings at the bottom of my heart: there they died. I spoke the truth—I was not believed: I began to deceive. When I got to know well the fashionable world and the mechanism of society, I became skilled in the science of life, and saw how others were happy without that skill, enjoying, at no cost to themselves, all those advantages which I so indefatigably pursued. And then in my breast despair was born—not that despair which is cured with the pistol's muzzle, but cold, helpless despair, concealed under amiability and a good-natured smile. I became a moral cripple. One half of my soul did not exist; it had withered away, it had evaporated, it had died. I cut it off and threw it away—while the other half stirred and lived, at the service of everybody. And this nobody noticed, because nobody knew that its dead half had ever existed; but now you have aroused its memory in me, and I have read to you its epitaph. To many people, all epitaphs, in general, seem ridiculous, but not so to me; especially when I recall what lies beneath them. However, I do not ask you to share my views; if my outburst seems to you ridiculous, please, laugh: I warn you, that it will not distress me in any way."

At that moment, I met her eyes: tears danced in them;[101] her arm, leaning on mine, trembled, her cheeks glowed; she was sorry for me! Compassion —an emotion to which all women so easily submit —had sunk its claws into her inexperienced heart. During the whole walk she was absent-minded, did not coquet with anyone—and that is a great sign!

We reached The Hollow: the ladies left their escorts, but she did not abandon my arm. The witticisms of the local dandies did not amuse her; the steepness of the precipice near which she stood did not frighten her, while the other young ladies squealed and closed their eyes.

On the way back, I did not renew our melancholy conversation, but to my trivial questions and jokes she replied briefly and absently.

"Have you ever loved?" I asked her at last.

She glanced at me intently, shook her head and again became lost in thought: it was evident that she wanted to say something, but she did not know how to begin. Her breast heaved . . . What would you—a muslin sleeve is little protection, and an electric spark ran from my wrist[102] to hers. Almost all passions start thus; and we often deceive ourselves greatly in thinking that a woman loves us for our physical or moral qualities. Of course, they prepare and incline their hearts for the reception of the sacred fire: nonetheless, it is the first contact that decides the matter.

"Don't you think I was very amiable today?" said the young princess to me, with a forced smile when we returned from the excursion.

We parted.

She is displeased with herself; she accuses herself of having treated me coldly . . . Oh, this is the first, the main triumph!

Tomorrow she will want to recompense me. I know it all by heart—that is what is so boring.

*June 4th*

Today, I saw Vera. She has exhausted me with her jealousy. The young princess, it seems, took it into her head to confide the secrets of the heart to Vera: not a very fortunate choice, one must admit!

"I can guess to what it all tends," Vera kept saying to me. "Better tell me now, plainly, that you love her."

"But if I don't?"

"Then why pursue her, disturb her, excite her imagination? Oh, I know you well! Listen, if you want me to believe you, then come next week to Kislovodsk: we are going there after tomorrow. The Ligovskoys remain here for a little while longer. Rent an apartment near by. We shall be living in the big house near the spring, on the mezzanine floor, Princess Ligovskoy will be on the first floor, and next door, there is a house belonging to the same proprietor, which is not yet occupied . . . Will you come?"

I promised, and on the same day sent a messenger to rent those lodgings.

Grushnitski came to see me at six in the evening, and announced that his uniform would be ready on the morrow, just in time for the ball.

"At last I shall dance with her the whole evening . . . What a chance to talk!" he added.

"When is that ball?"

"Why, tomorrow! Didn't you know? A big festival. And the local authorities have undertaken to arrange it. . . ."

"Let's go for a walk on the boulevard."

"Not for anything, in this horrid coat. . . ."

"What, have you ceased liking it?"

I went alone and, upon meeting Princess Mary, asked her to dance the mazurka with me. She seemed surprised and pleased.

"I thought you danced only out of necessity, as last time," she said, smiling very prettily.

It seems she does not notice at all Grushnitski's absence.

"Tomorrow you will be agreeably surprised," I said to her.

"What will that be?"

"It's a secret . . . You will discover it for yourself at the ball."

I finished the evening at the old princess's: there were no visitors except Vera and a very entertaining old gentleman. I was in high spirits, I improvised all kinds of extraordinary stories: the young princess sat opposite me and listened to my tosh with such deep, tense, even tender attention that I felt ashamed of myself. What had become of her vivacity, her coquetry, her whims, her arrogant mien, scornful smile, abstracted gaze?

Vera noticed it all: deep melancholy expressed itself on her sickly face: she sat in shadow, near the window, sunk in an ample armchair . . . I felt sorry for her.

Then I related the whole dramatic story of our acquaintanceship, of our love—naturally, concealing it under invented names.

So vividly did I picture my tenderness, my anxiety, my transports, in such an advantageous light did I present her actions, her character, that, willy-nilly, she had to forgive me my flirtation with the princess.

She got up, came over to us, became animated . . . and only at two in the morning did we remember that the doctor's order was to go to bed at eleven.

*June 5th*

Half an hour before the ball, Grushnitski appeared before me in the full splendor of an infantry army officer's uniform. To the third button, he had attached a bronze chainlet from which hung a double lorgnette; epaulets of incredible size were turned upward like the wings of a cupid; his boots squeaked; in his left hand, he held a pair of brown kid gloves and his cap, and with his right he kept fluffing up, every moment, his shock of hair, which was waved in small curls. Self-satisfaction and, at the same time, a certain lack of assurance were expressed in his countenance: his festive exterior, his proud gait, would have made me burst out laughing, had that been in accordance with my plans.

He threw his cap and gloves onto the table and began to pull down the skirts of his coat and to preen himself before the mirror: a huge black neckcloth that was wound over a tremendously high stiffener, the bristles of which propped up his chin, showed half an inch above his collar. He thought this was not enough: he pulled it up, till it reached his ears. This laborious task—for the collar of his uniform was very tight and uncomfortable—caused the blood to rush to his face.

"I'm told you have been flirting terribly with my princess these days?" he said rather casually, and without looking at me.

"It's not for us, oafs, to drink tea!" I answered him, repeating the favorite saying of one of the most dashing rakes of the past, of whom Pushkin once sang.[103]

"Tell me, how does the coat fit me? Oh, that confounded Jew! . . .[104] How it cuts me under the arms! . . . Have you got any perfume?"

"Good gracious, do you need any more? You simply reek of rose pomade, as it is."

"No matter. Give it here."

He poured out half of the vial between neck and neckcloth, onto his pocket handkerchief, and upon his sleeves.

"Are you going to dance?" he asked.

"I don't think so."

"I'm afraid that I shall have to begin the mazurka with the princess, and I hardly know one figure of it."

"Have you asked her for the mazurka?"

"Not yet. . . ."

"Look out, you might be forestalled. . . ."

"That's right!" he said, clapping a hand to his forehead. "Good-by . . . I'm going to wait for her at the entrance door." He seized his cap and ran off.

Half an hour later, I also set out. The streets were dark and deserted; around the club, or tavern—whichever you choose to call it—the crowd was dense; the windows shone; the sounds of the military band were brought to me by the evening breeze. I walked slowly; I felt sad . . . "Is it possible," I thought, "that my only function on earth is to ruin other people's hopes? Ever since I have lived and acted, fate has always seemed to bring me in at the denouement of other people's dramas, as if none could either die or despair without me! I am the indispensable persona in the fifth act; involuntarily, I play the miserable part of the executioner or the traitor. What could be fate's purpose in this? Might it not be that it had designated me to become the author of bourgeois tragedies and family novels, or the collaborator of some purveyor of stories for the "Library for Reading"?[105] How should one know? How many people, in the beginning of life, think they will finish it as Alexander the Great or Lord Byron, and instead, retain for the whole of their existence, the rank of titulary counsellor?[106]

Upon coming into the ballroom, I hid in the crowd of men and began to make my observations. Grushnitski stood next to the young princess and was saying something to her with great animation: she listened to him absent-mindedly, kept glancing this way and that, putting her fan to her lips. Her face expressed impatience, her eyes sought around for someone: I softly approached from behind, in order to overhear their conversation.

"You torment me, princess," Grushnitski was saying. "You have changed tremendously since I last saw you. . . ."

"You too have changed," she answered, casting upon him a swift glance, in which he failed to discern secret mockery.

"I? I have changed? . . . Oh, never! You know that it is impossible! He who has once seen you, will carry with him, forever, your divine image."

"Stop, please. . . ."

"Why then will you not listen now to what only

recently, and so often, you listened with favor?"

"Because I do not like repetition," she answered laughing.

"Oh, I've made a bitter mistake! . . . I thought, in my folly, that at least these epaulets would give me the right to hope . . . No, it would have been better for me had I remained all my life in that miserable soldier's coat to which, maybe, I owed your attention."

"Indeed, that coat suited you much better. . . ."

At this point I came up and bowed to the young princess: she blushed slightly and said quickly:

"Am I not right, Monsieur Pechorin, that the gray soldier's coat was much more becoming to Monsieur Grushnitski?"

"I disagree with you," I replied. "In this uniform, he looks even more youthful."

Grushnitski could not bear this blow: like all youths, he professes to be an old man; he thinks that deep traces of passions replace the imprint of years. He cast on me a furious glance, stamped his foot and walked away.

"Now confess," I said to the young princess, "that despite his having always been very absurd, still, quite recently, you thought him interesting . . . in his gray coat?"

She dropped her eyes and did not answer.

All evening Grushnitski pursued the young princess, either dancing with her or being her *vis-à-vis;* he devoured her with his eyes, sighed and pestered her with entreaties and reproaches. After the third quadrille, she already detested him.

"I did not expect this of you," he said, coming up to me and taking me by the arm.

"What, exactly?"

"You are dancing the mazurka with her, aren't

you?" he asked in a solemn voice. "She confessed to me. . . ."

"Well, what of it? Is it a secret?"

"Naturally . . . I should have expected this from a frivolous girl, from a flirt . . . But I'll have my revenge!"

"Blame your soldier's coat or your officer's epaulets, but why blame her? Is it her fault that you no longer appeal to her?"

"Why then give me hopes?"

"Why then did you hope? I can understand people who desire something and strive for it; but who wants to hope?"

"You have won your bet, though not quite," he said with a wrathful smile.

The mazurka began. Grushnitski kept choosing nobody but the princess, the other men chose her continuously: it was obviously a conspiracy against me. So much the better. She wants to talk to me, they prevent her—she will want it twice as much.

Once or twice, I pressed her hand: the second time, she snatched it away, without saying a word.

"I shall sleep badly tonight," she said to me, when the mazurka was over.

"It's Grushnitski's fault."

"Oh no!" And her face became so pensive, so sad, that I promised myself to kiss her hand, without fail, that evening.

People began to leave. As I handed the princess into her carriage, I rapidly pressed her small hand to my lips. It was dark, and no one could see it.

I re-entered the ballroom, well-content with myself.

At a long table, young men were having supper, and among them was Grushnitski. When I came in, they all fell silent: evidently, they had been talking about me. Many are ill-disposed toward me since the last ball, especially the Captain of Dragoons, and now, it seems, an inimical gang is actually being organized against me, under the leadership of Grushnitski. He had such a proud and courageous air.

I am very glad; I love my enemies, although not in a Christian sense: they amuse me, they quicken my pulses. To be always on the lookout, to intercept every glance, to catch the meaning of every word, to guess intentions, to thwart plots, to pretend to be fooled, and suddenly, with one push, to upset the entire enormous and elaborate structure of cunning and scheming—that is what I call life.

During the supper Grushnitski kept whispering and exchanging winks with the Captain of Dragoons.[107]

*June 6th*

This morning, Vera left for Kislovodsk with her husband. I met their coach as I was on my way to Princess Ligovskoy. Vera nodded to me: there was reproach in her glance.

Whose fault is it? Why does she not want to give me the chance to see her alone? Love, like fire, goes out without fuel. Perchance jealousy will accomplish what my entreaties could not.

I stayed at the princess's an hour by the clock. Mary did not appear; she was ill. In the evening she was not on the boulevard. The newly organized gang, armed with lorgnettes, has assumed a truly threatening appearance. I am glad that the princess is ill: they might have done something insolent in regard to her. Grushnitski's hair was all awry and he looked desperate: I think he is really distressed.

His vanity, in particular, is injured; but, oddly enough, there are people who are ludicrous even in their despair!

On coming home, I noticed a lack of something. *I have not seen her! She is ill!* Can it be that I have really fallen in love? . . . What nonsense!

*June 7th*

At eleven in the morning—the hour at which the old Princess Ligovskoy is usually sweating it out in the Ermolov bathhouse—I was walking past her house. The young princess was sitting pensively at the window. When she saw me, she rose abruptly.

I entered the vestibule, none of the servants were there, and without being announced, taking advantage of the local customs, I made my way into the drawing room.

A dull pallor was spread over the princess's pretty face. She stood at the piano, leaning with one hand on the back of an armchair: that hand trembled ever so slightly. I quietly went up to her and said:

"You are angry with me?"

She raised upon me a languid, deep gaze and shook her head; her lips wanted to utter something, and could not; her eyes filled with tears; she sank into the armchair and covered her face with her hand.

"What is the matter with you?" I said, taking her hand.

"You do not respect me! . . . Oh, leave me alone!"

I made a few steps . . . She straightened herself up in her chair; her eyes glittered.

I stopped, with my hand on the door handle, and said:

"Forgive me, princess, I have acted like a madman . . . This will not happen again: I will see to it . . . Why must you know what, up to now, has been taking place in my soul?[108] You will never learn it, and so much the better for you. Adieu."

As I went out, I believe I heard her crying.

Till evening, I roamed on foot about the outskirts of Mount Mashuk, got terribly tired and, on coming home, threw myself on my bed in utter exhaustion.

Werner dropped in.

"Is it true," he asked, "that you are going to marry the young Princess Ligovskoy?"

"Why?"

"The whole town says so; all my patients are preoccupied with this important news: that's the kind of people patients are; they know everything!"

"Grushnitski's tricks," I thought to myself.

"In order to prove to you, doctor, that these rumors are false, let me inform you in secret that tomorrow I am moving to Kislovodsk."

"And the Ligovskoys, too?"

"No; they remain here for another week."

"So you are not marrying her?"

"Doctor, doctor! Look at me: do I resemble a fiancé, or anything of the kind?"

"I do not say it . . . But you know there are cases," he added with a cunning smile, "in which an honorable man is obliged to marry, and there are mammas who do not at least avert such cases. Therefore, I advise you as a pal to be more careful. Here at the spa the atmosphere is most dangerous: I have seen so many fine, young men, worthy of a better lot, who have gone straight from here to the altar. Would you believe it, there has even been an attempt to have me marry! Namely, on the part of a provincial mamma whose daughter was very pale, I had had the misfortune to tell her that her daughter's face would regain its color after marriage. Then, with tears of gratitude, she offered me her daughter's hand and their entire fortune—fifty serfs, I believe.[109] But I answered that I was incapable of marriage."

Werner left, fully convinced that he had put me on my guard.

From his words, I note that various nasty rumors have already been spread in town about the young princess and me. Grushnitski will have to pay for this!

*June 10th*

I have been here, in Kislovodsk, three days already. Every day I see Vera at the well and at the promenade. In the morning, upon awakening, I sit down by the window and train my lorgnette on her balcony: she is already long since dressed and awaits the prearranged signal: we meet, as if by chance, in the garden, which descends from our houses to the well. The vivifying mountain air has brought back her color and strength. It is not for nothing that Narzan[110] is termed "The Fountain of Mightiness." The local inhabitants maintain that the air of Kislovodsk disposes one romantically, that here comes the denouement of all the love affairs that ever were started at the foot of Mount Mashuk. And, indeed, everything here breathes seclusion; everything here is mysterious—the dense canopies of linden avenues that bend over the torrent which, as it noisily and foamily falls from ledge to ledge, cuts for itself a path between the verdant mountains; and the gorges filled with gloom and silence that branch out from here in all directions; and the freshness of the aromatic air, laden with the emanations of tall southern grasses and white acacias;[111] and the constant deliciously somniferous babble of cool brooks which, meeting at the far end of the valley, join in a friendly race and, at last, fall into the Podkumok River. On this side the gorge widens and turns into a green glen; a dusty road meanders through it. Every time I look at it, I keep imagining that a close carriage comes there, and from the window of the carriage, there peers out a rosy little face. Many coaches have, by now, passed on that road, but never that one. The suburb beyond the fort has grown populous: in the restaurant, built on a bluff a few steps from my dwelling, lights begin to flicker in the evenings through a double row of poplars; noise and the clinking of glasses resound there till late at night.

Nowhere is there consumed so much Kahetian wine and mineral water as here.

> To mix these two pursuits, a lot of men
> Are eager—I'm not one of them.[112]

Grushnitski with his gang, every day, carouses at the tavern, and hardly nods to me.

He arrived only yesterday,[113] and has already managed to quarrel with three old men who wanted to take their baths before him: definitely —misfortunes develop in him a martial spirit.

*June 11th*

They have come at last. I was sitting by the window when I heard the rattle of their coach: my heart quivered . . . What is it then? Could it be that I am in love? . . . I am so stupidly made that this could be expected from me.

I have dined at their house. The old princess looks at me very tenderly and does not leave her daughter's side . . . That's bad! On the other hand, Vera is jealous of the young princess—this is a nice state of things I have brought about! What will not a woman do in order to vex a rival? I remember one woman who fell in love with me, because I was in love with another. There is nothing more paradoxical than a woman's mind: it is difficult to convince women of anything; you have to bring them to a point where they will convince their own selves. The sequence of proofs by means of which they overcome their prejudices, is very original: to learn their dialectic, one must overturn in one's mind all the school rules of logic. Here, for instance, is the normal method:

That man loves me; but I am married: consequently, I must not love him.[114]

Now for the feminine method:

I must not love him for I am married; but he loves me—consequently. . . .

Here come several dots, for reason does not say anything more, and what speaks mainly, is the tongue, the eyes, and in their wake, the heart, if the latter exists.

What if these notes should ever fall under a woman's eyes? "Slander!" she will cry with indignation.

Ever since poets have been writing and women reading them (for which they should receive the deepest gratitude), they have been called angels so many times, that in the simplicity of their souls, they have actually believed this compliment, forgetting that the same poets dubbed Nero a demi-god, for money.

It is not I who should speak of women with such spite—I, who love nothing in the world save them—I, who have always been ready to sacrifice to them peace of mind, ambition, life. But then, it is not in a fit of annoyance and offended vanity that I try to tear from them that magic veil, through which only an experienced gaze penetrates. No, all that I am saying about them is only a result of

The mind's cold observations,
The mournful comments of the heart.[115]

Women ought to desire that all men know them as well as I do, because I love them a hundred times better, ever since I stopped fearing them and comprehended their little weaknesses.

Apropos, the other day Werner compared women to the enchanted forest of which Tasso tells in his "Jerusalem Liberated":[116] "Only come near," said Werner: "and mercy, what horrors will come flying at you from every side: Duty, Pride, Propriety, Public Opinion, Mockery, Scorn . . . All you have to do is not look and walk straight on: little by little, the monsters disappear and before you there opens a serene and sunny meadow, in the midst of which, green myrtle blooms. On the other hand, woe to you if, at the first steps, your heart fails you and you look back!"

*June 12th*

This evening has been rich in events. Within two miles of Kislovodsk, in a canyon through which flows the Podkumok River, there is a cliff, called The Ring. This is a gateway formed by nature; it

rises from a high hill, and through it the setting
sun throws its last flaming glance on the world. A
large cavalcade set out thither to view the sunset
through that window of stone. None of us, to say
the truth, was thinking of sunsets. I was riding by
the young princess's side: on our way home, the
Podkumok River had to be forded. The shallowest
mountain streams are dangerous, especially because their bottom is an absolute kaleidoscope:
every day it changes from the pressure of the
waves. Where yesterday there was a stone, today
there is a hole. I took the princess's horse by the
bridle and led it down into the water, which was
no more than knee-deep: we started to advance
slowly in an oblique direction against the current.
It is well-known that when fording rapid streams,
one should not look at the water, for otherwise one
immediately gets dizzy. I forgot to warn Princess
Mary of this.

We were already in midstream, where the current was swiftest, when she suddenly swayed in
her saddle. "I feel faint!" she said in a weak voice.
I quickly bent toward her and wound my arm
around her supple waist.

"Look up!" I whispered to her. "It is nothing,
only don't be afraid; I'm with you."

She felt better; she wanted to free herself from
my arm, but I wound it still tighter around her
tender, soft body; my cheek almost touched her
cheek; flame emanated from it.

"What are you doing to me? . . . Good
God! . . ."

I paid no attention to her tremor and confusion,
and my lips touched her tender cheek; she gave a
start but said nothing. We were riding behind: nobody saw. When we got out onto the bank, every-

body started off at a trot. The young princess held her horse in; I stayed by her. It could be seen that my silence worried her, but I swore not to say a word—out of curiosity. I wanted to see how she would extricate herself from this embarrassing situation.

"Either you despise me, or love me very much!" she said at last, in a voice in which there were tears. "Perhaps you want to laugh at me, to trouble my soul, and then leave me . . . It would be so base, so mean, that the mere supposition . . . Oh no! Isn't it true," she added in a tone of tender trust, "isn't it true that there is nothing in me that would preclude respect? Your insolent action . . . I must, I must forgive it you, because I allowed it . . . Answer, do speak, I want to hear your voice! . . ."

In the last words, there was such feminine impatience that I could not help smiling. Fortunately, it was beginning to get dark . . . I did not answer anything.

"You are silent?" she went on. "Perhaps you wish me to be the first to say that I love you."

I was silent.

"Do you wish it?" she went on, quickly turning toward me. In the determination of her gaze and voice, there was something frightening.

"What for?" I answered shrugging my shoulders.

She gave her horse a cut of the whip and set off at all speed along the narrow dangerous road. It happened so fast, that I hardly managed to overtake her, and when I did, she had already joined the rest of the party. All the way home she talked and laughed incessantly. In her movements there was something feverish; not once did she glance at me. Everybody noticed this unusual gaiety. And the old princess inwardly rejoiced, as she looked at her daughter; yet her daughter was merely having a nervous fit. She will spend a sleepless night and will weep. This thought gives me boundless delight: there are moments when I understand the vampire . . .[117] And to think that I am reputed to be a jolly good fellow and try to earn that appellation!

Having dismounted, the ladies went to the old princess's. I was excited and galloped off into the mountains to dissipate the thoughts that crowded in my head. The dewy evening breathed delicious coolness. The moon was rising from behind the dark summits. Every step of my unshod horse produced a hollow echo in the silence of the gorges. At the cascade, I watered my steed, avidly inhaled, a couple of times, the fresh air of the southern night, and started back. I rode through the suburb. The lights were beginning to go out in the windows; the sentries on the rampart of the fort, and the Cossacks in outlying pickets, exchanged long-drawn calls.

In one of the houses of the suburb, which stood on the edge of a ravine, I noticed an extraordinary illumination: at times there resounded discordant talk and cries, indicating that an officers' banquet was in progress. I dismounted and stole up to the window: an improperly closed shutter allowed me to see the revelers and to make out their words. They were speaking about me.

The Captain of Dragoons, flushed with wine, struck the table with his fist, demanding attention.

"Gentlemen!" he said, "this is really impossible! Pechorin must be taught a lesson! These fledglings from Petersburg always give themselves airs, till you hit them on the nose! He thinks that he alone has lived in the world of fashion, just because he always has clean gloves and well-polished boots."

"And what an arrogant smile! Yet I'm sure he is a coward—yes, a coward!"

"I think so too," said Grushnitski. "He likes to jest his way out. I once said to him such things, for which another would have hacked me to pieces then and there, but Pechorin gave it all a humorous interpretation. I, naturally, did not call him out, because it was up to him. Moreover, I did not want to get entangled. . . ."

"Grushnitski is mad at him because he took away the young princess from him," said someone.

"What a notion! As a matter of fact, I did flirt slightly with her, but gave it up at once, because I do not want to marry, and it is not in my rules to compromise a young girl."

"Yes, I assure you that he is a first-rate coward—that is to say, Pechorin, and not Grushnitski. Oh, Grushnitski is a capital fellow, and moreover, he is a true friend of mine!" said the Captain of Dragoons. "Gentlemen! Nobody here stands up for him? Nobody? All the better! Would you like to test his courage? You might find it entertaining."

"We would like to; but how?"

"Well, listen, Grushnitski is particularly angry with him—he gets the main part! He will pick some kind of silly quarrel with him and challenge Pechorin to a duel . . . Now wait a bit, here comes the point . . . He will challenge him to a duel—good! All this—the challenge, the preparations, the conditions—will be as solemn and terrible as possible—I shall see to that. I shall be your second, my poor friend! Good! But now, here is the hitch: we shall not put any balls into the pistols. I here answer for it that Pechorin will funk it—I shall have

them face each other at six paces distance, by
Jove! Do you agree, gentlemen?"

"A capital plan! We agree! Why not?" sounded
from all sides.

"And you, Grushnitski?"

In a tremor of eagerness, I awaited Grushnitski's
reply. Cold fury possessed me at the thought that,
had it not been for chance, I might have become
the laughing stock of those fools. If Grushnitski had
refused, I would have thrown myself upon his neck.
But after a short silence, he rose from his chair,
offered his hand to the captain and said very
pompously: "All right, I agree."

It would be difficult to describe the delight of
the whole honorable company.

I returned home, agitated by two different emotions. The first was sadness. "What do they all hate
me for?" I thought. "What for? Have I offended
anybody? No. Could it be that I belong to the number of those people whose appearance alone is sufficient to produce ill will?" And I felt a venomous
rancor gradually filling my soul. "Take care, Mr.
Grushnitski!" I kept saying, as I paced to and fro
in my room, "I am not to be trifled with like this.
You may have to pay dearly for the approval of
your stupid cronies. I am not a plaything for you!"

I did not sleep all night. By morning, I was as
yellow as a wild orange.

In the morning, I met the young princess at the
well.

"Are you ill?" she said, looking at me intently.

"I did not sleep all night."

"Nor did I . . . I accused you . . . perhaps,
wrongly? But explain your behavior, I may forgive
you everything."

"Everything?"

"Everything . . . Only tell me the truth . . . and hurry . . . I have thought a lot, trying to explain, to justify your conduct: perhaps, you are afraid of obstacles on the part of my family . . . It does not matter. When they hear of it . . . (her voice trembled) my entreaties will convince them . . . Or is it your own situation . . . But I want you to know that I can sacrifice anything for the one I love . . . Oh, answer quick . . . have pity . . . You do not despise me, do you?"

She grasped my hand.

The old princess was walking in front of us with Vera's husband, and did not see anything, but we might have been seen by the promenading patients, of all inquisitive people the most inquisitive gossipers, and I quickly freed my hand from her passionate grasp.

"I shall tell you the whole truth," I replied to the princess, "I shall neither justify myself, nor explain my actions. I do not love you."

Her lips paled slightly.

"Leave me," she said almost inaudibly.

I shrugged my shoulders, turned, and walked away.

*June 14th*

I sometimes despise myself . . . Is this not why I despise others? . . . I have become incapable of noble impulses. I am afraid of appearing laughable to myself. Another man in my place would offer the young princess *son cœur et sa fortune;* but over me the word "marry" has some kind of magic power. However much I may love a woman, if she only lets me feel that I must marry her—farewell to love! My heart turns to stone, and nothing can warm it again. I am ready to make any sacrifice except this one. I may set my life upon a card twenty times, and even my honor—but I will not sell my freedom. Why do I treasure it so? What good is it to me? What do I prepare myself for? What do I expect from the future? . . . Indeed, nothing whatever. It is a kind of innate fear, an ineffable presentiment. Aren't there people who have an unaccountable fear of spiders, cockroaches, mice? Shall I confess? When I was still a child, an old woman told my fortune to my mother. She predicted of me "death from a wicked wife." It made a deep impression upon me then: in my soul was born an insuperable aversion to marriage. Yet something tells me that her prediction will come true,[118] at least, I shall do my best to have it come true as late as possible.

### June 15th

Yesterday there arrived here the conjurer Apfelbaum. On the door of the restaurant, there appeared a long *affiche,* informing the esteemed public that the above-named, wonderful conjurer, acrobat, chemist, and optician, would have the honor to give a superb performance at eight tonight, in the reception hall of the Club of the Nobility (in other words, the restaurant); admission two roubles, fifty.

Everybody intends to go to see the wonderful conjurer: even Princess Ligovskoy, despite the fact that her daughter is ill, took a ticket for herself.

Today after dinner, I passed under Vera's windows. She was sitting on the balcony alone. A billet fell at my feet:

"Tonight, around half past nine, come to me by

the main staircase. My husband has gone to Pyatigorsk and will return only tomorrow morning. My footmen and maidservants will not be in the house: I have distributed tickets to all of them, as well as to the princess's servants. I await you. Come without fail."

"Aha!" I thought, "at last I am having my way after all."

At eight, I went to see the conjurer. The spectators assembled shortly before nine: the performance began. In the back rows of chairs, I recognized the lackeys and the maids of Vera and the princess. Everybody was here. Grushnitski sat in the front row, with his lorgnette. The conjurer turned to him every time he needed a pocket handkerchief, a watch, a ring, and so forth.

Grushnitski does not greet me since some time ago, and tonight, once or twice, he glanced at me rather insolently. All this shall be remembered when the time comes to settle our accounts.

Shortly before ten, I rose and left.

It was pitch dark outside. Heavy, cold clouds lay on the summits of the surrounding mountains; only now and then a dying breeze soughed in the crests of the poplars around the restaurant. There was a crowd of people outside the windows. I descended the hill and, turning into the gateway, accelerated my pace. Suddenly it seemed to me that someone was walking behind me. I stopped and looked about me. Nothing could be distinguished in the darkness; however, I took the precaution to go around the house as if I were taking a stroll. As I passed under the windows of the young princess, I again heard steps behind me. A man wrapped up in a military cloak ran past me. This alarmed me: however, I stole up to the porch and swiftly ran up the dark stairs. The door opened, a small hand grasped my hand.

"No one saw you?" said Vera in a whisper, pressing herself to me.

"No one."

"Now do you believe that I love you? Oh! For a long time I wavered, for a long time I was tormented . . . But you make of me all you want."

Her heart was beating violently, her hands were as cold as ice. There began the reproaches of jealousy, plaints: she demanded of me that I confess to her all, saying she would bear, with submission, my unfaithfulness, since all she desired was my happiness. I did not quite believe this, but I calmed her with vows, promises, and so forth.

"So you are not going to marry Mary? You don't love her? And she thinks . . . do you know, she is madly in love with you, the poor thing!"

.   .   .   .   .   .   .   .   .   .   .   .

.   .   .   .   .   .   .   .   .   .   .

Around two o'clock in the morning, I opened the window and, having tied two shawls together, let myself down from the upper balcony to the lower one, holding onto a pillar. In the young princess's room, a light was still burning. Something urged me toward that window. The curtain was not completely drawn, and I could cast a curious glance into the interior of the room. Mary was sitting on her bed, her hands folded in her lap; her abundant hair was gathered under a night cap fringed with lace; a large crimson kerchief covered her slender white shoulders; her small feet hid in variegated Persian slippers. She sat motionless, her head sunk onto her breast; before her, on a little table, a book was opened, but her eyes, motionless and full of ineffable sadness, seemed, for a hundredth time, to skim over the same page, while her thoughts were far away.

At this moment, somebody stirred behind a bush. I jumped down from the balcony onto the turf. An invisible hand seized me by the shoulder.

"Aha!" said a rough voice, "you're caught! . . . I'll teach you to visit young princesses at night! . . ."

"Hold him tight!" cried somebody else, springing from behind a corner.

They were Grushnitski and the Captain of Dragoons.

I struck the latter upon the head with my fist, knocked him down, and dashed into the shrubbery. All the paths of the garden which covered the sloping ground in front of our houses were known to me.

"Thieves! Help!" they cried. A gun shot rang out; a smoking wad fell almost at my feet.

A minute later, I was already in my room; I undressed and lay down. Hardly had my valet locked the door, than Grushnitski and the captain began to knock.

"Pechorin! Are you asleep? Are you there?" the captain cried.

"I am asleep," I answered crossly.

"Get up! . . . Thieves . . . Circassians. . . ."

"I have a cold," I answered, "I'm afraid to catch a chill."

They left. I should not have answered them: they would have gone on looking for me in the garden for another hour. In the meantime, the alarm became terrific. A Cossack came, at full speed, from the fort. There was a universal stir: they started to look for Circassians in every bush—and, naturally, found nothing. But many people, probably, re-

mained firmly convinced that, had the garrison revealed more courage and promptness, at least a
score of pillagers would have remained lying about.

*June 16th*

This morning, at the well, there was nothing but
talk about the night raid of the Circassians. Having
drunk the prescribed number of glasses of the
Narzan water, and having walked the length of the
long linden avenue ten times or so, I met Vera's
husband, who had just arrived from Pyatigorsk. He
took my arm, and we went to the restaurant to have
lunch. He was terribly anxious about his wife. "How
frightened she was last night," he kept saying, "and
to think it should have happened precisely during
my absence." We sat down to lunch near a door
which led to the corner room, where a dozen young
people were assembled, including Grushnitski. For
a second time, destiny provided me with the
chance to overhear a conversation, which was to
decide his fate. He could not see me and, consequently, I could not suspect him of a deliberate
purpose; but this only increased his guilt in my
eyes.

"Could it have really been the Circassians?"
someone said. "Did anybody see them?"

"I shall tell you the whole story," answered
Grushnitski, "but please do not give me away. This
is how it was. Last night, a man, whom I shall not
name to you, came to me and told me that shortly
before ten he saw someone steal into the house
where the Ligovskoys live. I should mention to you
that the old princess was here, and the young princess was at home. So he and I betook ourselves
under their windows to waylay the lucky fellow."

I must confess that I was alarmed, although my interlocutor was very busy with his luncheon. He might have heard things that would be disagreeable to him, if Grushnitski had inadvertently guessed the truth; but being blinded by jealousy, the latter did not suspect it.

"Well, you see," Grushnitski went on, "we set out, taking a gun with us, loaded with a blank cartridge—just to frighten him. Till two o'clock, we waited in the garden. Finally—God knows where he appeared from, certainly not from the window, because it was never opened, but presumably he came out through the glass door which is behind the pillar—finally, as I say, we saw someone come down from the balcony . . . How do you like the princess's behavior, eh? Well, I must say, those Moscow misses are something! After that, what would you believe? We wanted to seize him, but he freed himself and, like a hare, dashed into the bushes. It was then I took a shot at him."

A murmur of incredulity resounded around Grushnitski.

"You do not believe me?" he continued. "I give you my honest and honorable word that all this is the very truth, and in proof, if you wish it, I shall name the gentleman."

"Tell us, tell us who he is!" resounded from all sides.

"Pechorin," answered Grushnitski.

At this moment, he raised his eyes—I was standing in the door opposite him—he flushed dreadfully. I went up to him and said slowly and distinctly:

"I regret very much that I entered after you had already given your word of honor in support of the vilest slander. My presence would have saved you from extra knavery."

Grushnitski jumped up from his seat and was about to flare up.

"I beg you," I continued, in the same tone of voice, "I beg you to retract your words at once: you know very well that it is an invention. I do not think that a woman's indifference to your brilliant qualities merits so awful a vengeance. Think well. By affirming your opinion, you lose your right to the name of a gentleman, and you risk your life."

Grushnitski stood before me, with lowered eyes, in violent agitation. But the struggle between conscience and vanity did not last long. The Captain of Dragoons, who was sitting next to him, nudged him with his elbow: he started and quickly replied to me, without raising his eyes:

"Sir, when I say something, I mean it, and am ready to repeat it. I am not afraid of your threats, and am prepared for anything."

"This last you have already proved," I answered coldly and, taking the Captain of Dragoons by the arm, I left the room.

"What is it you want?" asked the captain.

"You are a friend of Grushnitski and will probably be his second?"

The captain bowed with great importance.

"You have guessed," he answered. "I am even obliged to be his second, because the insult inflicted upon him refers also to me. I was with him last night," he added, straightening his stooping shoulders.

"Ah! So it was you that I hit so awkwardly on the head?"

He turned yellow, turned blue; concealed malevolence was expressed in his face.

"I shall have the honor to send you my second

today," I added with a very polite bow, pretending not to pay any attention to his rage.

On the porch of the restaurant, I came across Vera's husband. Apparently, he had been waiting for me.

He grasped my hand with an emotion resembling enthusiasm.

"Noble young man," he said with tears in his eyes, "I heard it all. What a scoundrel! What lack of gratitude! Who will want to admit them into a decent house after that! Thank God I have no daughters! But you will be rewarded by her for whom you risk your life. You may rely on my discretion for the time being," he went on. "I have been young myself, and have served in the military service: I know one should not interfere in these matters. Good-by."

Poor thing! He rejoices he has no daughters.

I went straight to Werner, found him at home and told him everything—my relations with Vera and with the young princess, and the conversation I had overheard, from which I had learned the intention those gentlemen had of making a fool of me by forcing me to fight a duel with pistols loaded with blanks. But now the matter was going beyond a joke: they, probably, had not expected such an outcome.

The doctor agreed to be my second; I gave him some instructions concerning the terms of the duel. He was to insist on the affair remaining as secret as possible because, although I am ready to brave death any time, I am not at all disposed to ruin, forever, my future career in this world.

After this I went home. An hour later, the doctor returned from his expedition.

"There is, indeed, a plot against you," he said.

"I found at Grushnitski's the Captain of Dragoons and yet another gentleman, whose name I do not remember. For a moment I stopped in the vestibule to take off my rubbers. They were making a lot of noise and arguing. 'For nothing in the world shall I agree,' Grushnitski was saying. 'He insulted me in public: before that, things were entirely different.' 'What business is this of yours?' answered the captain. 'I take everything upon myself. I was a second in five duels, and you may be sure I know how to arrange it. I have planned it all. Only please do not interfere. It won't do any harm to scare the fellow. But why expose oneself to danger if one can avoid it? . . .' At this moment, I entered. They were suddenly silent. Our negotiations lasted a considerable time. Finally, we decided the matter in the following way: within three miles from here there is a desolate gorge; they will drive there tomorrow at four in the morning, and we shall set out half an hour after them; you will shoot at each other at six paces—Grushnitski himself demanded this. The one who is killed is to be put down to the Circassians. Now, here are my suspicions: they, that is to say the seconds, have apparently altered somewhat their former plan and want to load, with a bullet, only Grushnitski's pistol. This slightly resembles murder, but in time of war, and especially Asiatic war, trickery is allowed. However, Grushnitski seems to be a little nobler than his companions. What do you think, should we show them that we have found them out?"

"Not for anything on earth, doctor! Rest assured, I shall not fall in their trap."

"What then do you want to do?"

"That's my secret."

"See that you don't get caught . . . Remember, the distance is six paces!"

"Doctor, I expect you tomorrow at four: the horses will be ready . . . Good-by."

Till evening I remained at home, locked up in my room. A footman came with an invitation from the old princess—I had him told that I was ill.

.   .   .   .   .   .   .   .   .   .

Two o'clock in the morning . . . Sleep does not come . . . Yet I ought to have some sleep so that my hand does not shake tomorrow. Anyway, it would be difficult to miss at six paces. Ah, Mr. Grushnitski! Your mystification will not come off . . . We shall exchange parts: it is now I who will search your pale face for signs of secret fear. Why did you designate yourself those fatal six paces? You think that I shall present my forehead to you without arguing . . . But we shall cast lots . . . and then . . . then . . . what if his luck outweighs mine? What if my star at last betrays me? . . . It would hardly be strange, it has so long served my whims faithfully. There is no more constancy in heaven than there is on earth.

Well, what of it? If I am to die, I'll die! The loss to the world will not be large and, anyway, I myself am sufficiently bored. I am like a man who yawns at a ball and does not drive home to sleep, only because his carriage is not yet there. But now the carriage is ready . . . good-by! . . .

I scan my whole past in memory and involuntarily wonder: why did I live, for what purpose was I born? . . . And yet that purpose must have existed, and my destination must have been a lofty one, for I feel, in my soul, boundless strength. But I did not divine that destination, I became enticed

by the lure of hollow and thankless passions. From
their crucible, I emerged as hard and cold as iron,
but lost forever the ardor of noble yearnings—the
best blossom of life. And since then, how many
times I have played the part of an axe in the hands
of fate! As an executioner's tool, I would fall upon
the head of doomed victims, often without malice,
always without regret. My love brought happiness
to none, because I never gave up anything for the
sake of those whom I loved. I loved for myself,
for my proper pleasure; I merely satisfied a bizarre
need of my heart, avidly consuming their sentiments, their tenderness, their joys and sufferings—
and never could I have my fill. Thus a man, tormented by hunger and fatigue, goes to sleep and
sees before him rich viands and sparkling wines;
he devours with delight the airy gifts of fancy, and
he seems to feel relief; but as soon as he awakes—
the vision vanishes. He is left with redoubled hunger and despair!

And, perhaps tomorrow, I shall die! . . . And
there will not remain, on earth, a single creature
that would have understood me completely. Some
deem me worse, others better than I actually am.
Some will say he was a good fellow; others will
say he was a scoundrel. Both this and that will be
false. After this, is it worth the trouble to live? And
yet one lives—out of curiosity. One keeps expecting
something new . . . Absurd and vexatious!

It is now a month and a half already that I have
been in the fort of N——. Maksim Maksimich is out
hunting. I am alone, I am sitting at the window.
Gray clouds have shut off the mountains to their
base: through the mist, the sun looks like a yellow
blur. It is cold: the wind whistles and shakes the

shutters . . . How dull! . . . I am going to continue my journal, which has been interrupted by so many strange events.

I read over the last page: how funny!—I expected to die: it was impossible. I had not yet drained the cup of sufferings, and I now feel that I still have many years to live.

How clearly and sharply the past has crystallized in my memory! Time has not erased one line, one shade!

I remember that, during the night before the duel, I did not sleep one minute. I could not write long: a secret restlessness had taken possession of me. For an hour or so, I paced the room, then I sat down and opened a novel by Walter Scott which lay on my table: it was *The Scottish Puritans*.[119] At first I read with an effort, but then I lost myself in it, carried away by the magic fantasy. Could it be that, in the next world, the Scottish bard is not paid for every glad minute that his book gives?

Dawn came at last. My nerves had quieted down. I looked at myself in the mirror: a dull pallor was spread over my face, which bore the traces of painful insomnia; but the eyes, although surrounded by brown shadows, glittered proudly and inflexibly. I was satisfied with myself.

After having ordered the horses to be saddled, I dressed and ran down to the bathhouse. As I immersed myself in the cold ebullience of Narzan water, I felt the forces of my body and soul return. I emerged from the bath, refreshed and braced up, as if I were about to go to a ball. Try to say after this that the soul is not dependent on the body!

Upon returning home, I found the doctor there. He wore gray riding breeches, a Caucasian overcoat and a Circassian cap. I burst out laughing at the sight of his small figure under that huge shaggy cap: his face is anything but that of a warrior, and on this occasion it looked longer than ever.

"Why are you so sad, doctor?" I said to him. "Haven't you seen people off on their way to the next world with the greatest indifference, a hundred times before? You should imagine that I have bilious fever. I may get well, and again, I may die; both are in the natural order of things. Try to see in me a patient afflicted with an illness that is still unknown to you—and then your curiosity will be roused to the highest pitch. By watching me you can now make several important physiological observations. Isn't the expectation of violent death, after all, a genuine illness?"

This thought impressed the doctor and he cheered up.

We got on our horses. Werner clutched at the bridle with both hands, and we set off. In a twinkle we had galloped past the fort by way of the suburb, and entered the gorge along which the road wound, half-choked with tall grasses, and constantly crossed and recrossed by a loud brook, which had to be forded, to the great dismay of the doctor, for every time his horse stopped in the water.

I do not remember a bluer and fresher morning. The sun had just appeared from behind the green summits, and the merging of the first warmth of its rays with the waning coolness of the night pervaded all one's senses with a kind of delicious languor. The glad beam of the young day had not yet penetrated into the gorge; it gilded only the tops of the cliffs that hung on both sides above us. The dense-foliaged bushes, growing in the deep crevices, asperged us with a silver rain at the least breath of wind. I remember that on this occasion, more than ever before, I was in love with nature. How curiously I examined every dewdrop that trembled upon a broad vine leaf and reflected a million iridescent rays! How avidly my gaze tried to penetrate into the hazy distance! There, the road was becoming narrower, the cliffs were growing bluer and more awesome, and finally, they seemed to blend in an impenetrable wall. We rode in silence.

"Have you made your will?" Werner suddenly asked.

"No."

"And what if you are killed?"

"My heirs will turn up of themselves."

"Do you mean you have not got any friends to whom you would wish to send a last farewell?"

I shook my head.

"Do you mean there is not one woman in the world to whom you would want to leave something in remembrance?"

"Do you want me, doctor," I answered him, "to open my soul to you? . . . You see, I have outlived those years when people die uttering the name of their beloved and bequeathing a tuft of pomaded or unpomaded hair to a friend. When I think of near and possible death, I am thinking of myself only: some people don't do even that. Friends who, tomorrow, will forget me or, worse, will saddle me with goodness knows what fictions; women who, while embracing another, will laugh at me so as not to make him jealous of a dead man—what do I care for them all! Out of life's storm I carried only a few ideas—and not one feeling. For a long time now, I have been living not with the heart, but with the head. I weigh and analyze my own passions and actions with stern curiosity, but without participation. Within me there are two persons: one of them lives in the full sense of the word, the other cogitates and judges him. The first will, perhaps, in an hour's time, take leave of you and the world forever, while the other . . . what about the other? . . . Look, doctor, do you see on that cliff on the right three black figures? These are our adversaries, I believe."

We set off at a trot.

In the bushes at the foot of the cliff, three horses were tied. We tied our horses there too, and clambered up a narrow path to a flat ledge, where Grushnitski was awaiting us with the Captain of Dragoons and his other second, whose name and patronymic were Ivan Ignatievich. I never learned his surname.

"We have been expecting you for a long time," the Captain of Dragoons said with an ironic smile.

I took out my watch and showed it to him.

He apologized, saying that his was fast.

For several moments there was an awkward silence: at last, the doctor broke it by addressing himself to Grushnitski:

"It seems to me," he said, "that both parties having shown their readiness to fight, and having thus satisfied the demands of honor, you might, gentlemen, talk matters over and close the affair amicably."

"I'm willing," I said.

The captain gave Grushnitski a wink, and he, thinking that I was scared, assumed a proud air, although up to then a dull pallor had been spread over his cheeks. For the first time since we had come, he raised his eyes to look at me; but in his glance there was some kind of perturbation betraying an inner struggle.

"Explain your terms," he said, "and whatever I can do for you, you may be assured. . . ."

"Here are my terms: this very day you will publicly retract your slander and will apologize to me."

"Sir, I am amazed that you dare offer such things to me!"

"What else could I offer you?"

"We shall fight."

I shrugged my shoulders.

"As you please; but consider—one of us will certainly be killed."

"My wish is that it may be you."

"And I'm convinced of the opposite."

He lost countenance, colored, then burst into forced laughter.

The captain took his arm and led him aside: for a long time, they whispered together. I had arrived in a fairly peaceable state of mind, but all this was beginning to annoy me.

The doctor came up to me.

"Listen," he said with obvious anxiety, "you must have forgotten about their plot? I do not know how to load a pistol, but in the present case . . . You are a strange fellow! Tell them that you are aware of their intention, and they will not dare . . . What is the sense of this? They'll bring you down like a bird."

"Please don't worry, doctor, and wait a bit . . . I shall arrange everything in such a way that on their side there will be no advantage whatever. Let them hugger-mugger a little."

"Gentlemen! This is becoming tiresome," I said

in a loud voice. "If we are to fight, let us fight: you had plenty of time to talk it over yesterday."

"We are ready," answered the captain. "To your places, gentlemen! Doctor, have the kindness to measure off six paces."

"To your places!" repeated Ivan Ignatievich, in a squeaky voice.

"Allow me!" I said. "There is one further condition. Since we are going to fight to the death, we should do everything possible to keep the matter secret and to avoid our seconds being held responsible. Do you agree?"

"We completely agree."

"Well, this is what I have thought up. Do you see at the summit of that sheer cliff on the right, a narrow bit of flat ground? There is a drop of about three hundred feet or more from there; below, there are sharp rocks. Each of us will take his stand on the very edge of the shelf, and in this way even a light wound will be fatal. This must be in keeping with your desire for you stipulated yourself, a distance of six paces. The one who is wounded will inevitably topple down and will be dashed to pieces; the doctor will take out the bullet, and then it should be very easy to ascribe this sudden death to an unfortunate leap. We shall draw lots to decide who is to shoot first. Let me inform you, in conclusion, that otherwise I will not fight."

"Have it your way!" said the captain after glancing meaningly at Grushnitski, who nodded in sign of consent. His face kept changing every minute. I had placed him in an awkward position. Had we fought under ordinary conditions, he might have aimed at my leg, wounded me lightly and satisfied, in this way, his thirst for revenge, without burdening his conscience too heavily. But now he had either to discharge his pistol into the air, or become a murderer, or lastly, abandon his vile plan and expose himself to equal danger with me. At this moment, I would not have wished to be in his place. He led the captain aside and began to say something to him with great heat. I saw his livid lips tremble, but the captain turned away from him with a contemptuous smile. "You're a fool!" he said to Grushnitski, rather loudly, "you do not understand anything! Let us go, gentlemen!"

A narrow trail led up the precipice between the bushes; broken rocks formed the precarious steps of this natural staircase: holding onto bushes, we started to climb up. Grushnitski was in front, behind him were his seconds, and after them came the doctor and I.

"I am amazed at you," said the doctor, giving my hand a strong squeeze. "Let me feel your pulse . . . Oho! it's feverish! . . . But nothing shows in your face . . . Only your eyes shine brighter than usual."

Suddenly, small stones noisily rolled down to our feet. What was it? Grushnitski had stumbled. The branch which he had grasped broke and he would have slid down on his back, had not his seconds supported him.

"Take care!" I cried to him. "Don't fall beforehand: it's a bad omen. Remember Julius Caesar!"[120]

Presently we reached the top of the jutting cliff: its flat surface was covered with fine sand, as if made especially for a duel. All around, melting in the golden mist of the morning, mountain summits teemed like an innumerable herd, and to the south Mount Elbruz raised its white mass, the last link in the chain of icy crests among which wispy clouds, which had blown from the east, were already roaming. I went to the edge of the natural platform and looked down: my head almost began to turn. Down below it was dark and cold as in the tomb; mossgrown jags of rocks, cast down by storm and time, were awaiting their prey.

The platform on which we were to fight presented an almost regular triangle. Six paces were measured off from the jutting angle and it was decided that he who would have to face first his foe's fire, should stand at the very apex, with his back to the chasm. If he were not killed, the principles were to change places.

I decided to give Grushnitski every advantage; I wished to test him. A spark of magnanimity might awaken in his soul—and then everything would turn out for the best; but vanity and weakness of character were to triumph! . . . I wished to give myself the full right to show him no quarter, if fate spared me. Who has not concluded similar agreements with his conscience?

"Spin the coin, doctor!" said the captain.

The doctor took out of his pocket a silver coin and held it up.

"Tails!" cried Grushnitski hurriedly, like a man who has been suddenly awakened by a friendly nudge.

"Heads!" I said.

The coin soared up and fell with a tinkle; everyone rushed toward it.

"You're lucky," I said to Grushnitski, "you are to fire first! But remember that if you do not kill me, I shall not miss—I give you my word of honor."

He colored; he was ashamed to kill an unarmed man. I was looking at him intently; for a moment it seemed to me that he would throw himself at my

feet, begging for forgiveness, but who could own
having such a villainous design? . . . Only one resource remained to him—to fire in the air. I was
sure he would fire in the air! Only one thing could
interfere with it: the thought that I should demand
another duel.

"It is time!" the doctor whispered to me, pulling
my sleeve. "If you do not tell them now that we
know their intentions, all is lost. Look, he is already
loading . . . If you do not say anything, I myself
shall. . . ."

"Not for anything in the world, doctor!" I replied,
holding him back by the arm. "You would spoil
everything. You gave me your word not to interfere . . . What does it matter to you? Perhaps, I
wish to be killed. . . ."

He glanced at me with surprise.

"Oh, that's different! . . . Only do not bring complaints against me in the next world."

In the meantime, the captain had loaded his
pistols; he handed one to Grushnitski, whispering
something to him with a smile; the other he handed
to me.

I took my stand at the apex of the platform,
bracing my left foot firmly against the rock and leaning forward a little, so as not to fall backward in
the case of a light wound.

Grushnitski stationed himself opposite me and
at a given signal began to raise his pistol. His knees
shook. He was aiming straight at my forehead.

Ineffable fury flared up in my breast.

Suddenly, he lowered the muzzle of his pistol
and, going as white as a sheet, turned toward his
second:

"I can't," he said in a hollow voice.

"Coward!" answered the captain.

The shot rang out. The bullet grazed my knee. Involuntarily, I took several steps forward so as to get away, as soon as possible, from the brink.

"Well, friend Grushnitski, it's a pity you've missed!" said the captain. "Now it's your turn, take your stand! Embrace me first: we shall not see each other again!" They embraced; the captain could hardly keep himself from laughing. "Have no fear," he added, with a sly glance at Grushnitski. "All's nonsense on earth! . . . Nature is a ninny, fate is a henny, and life is a penny!"

After this tragic phrase, delivered with appropriate dignity, he withdrew to his place. Ivan Ignatievich, with tears, likewise embraced Grushnitski, and now he was left alone facing me. To this day I try to explain to myself what kind of feeling was boiling then in my breast. It was the irritation of injured vanity, and contempt, and wrath which arose at the thought that this man, now looking at me with such confidence and such calm insolence, had tried, two minutes before, without exposing himself to any danger, to kill me like a dog, for if I had been wounded in the leg a little more severely, I would have certainly fallen off the cliff.

For several moments, I kept looking intently into his face, striving to discern the slightest trace of repentance. But it seemed to me that he was withholding a smile.

"I advise you to say your prayers before dying," I then said to him.

"Do not worry about my soul more than you do about your own. One thing I ask of you: shoot quickly."

"And you do not retract your slander? You do not ask my pardon? Think well: does not your conscience say something to you?"

"Mr. Pechorin!" cried the Captain of Dragoons, "you are not here to hear confession, allow me to tell you . . . Let us finish quickly, otherwise somebody may come driving through the gorge and see us."

"All right. Doctor, come over to me."

The doctor came. Poor doctor! He was paler than Grushnitski had been ten minutes before.

I spaced on purpose the following words, pronouncing them loudly and distinctly, the way a death sentence is pronounced:

"Doctor, these gentlemen, no doubt in their hurry, forgot to place a bullet in my pistol. Please, load it again—and properly!"

"This cannot be!" the captain was shouting, "it cannot be! I loaded both pistols: perhaps, the ball rolled out of yours . . . That is not my fault! And you have no right to reload . . . no right whatsoever. It is utterly against the rules; I shall not permit it. . . ."

"All right!" I said to the captain. "If so, you and I will have a duel on the same conditions."

He faltered.

Grushnitski stood, his head sunk on his breast, embarrassed and gloomy.

"Leave them alone!" he finally said to the captain who wanted to snatch my pistol out of the doctor's hands. "You know very well yourself that they are right."

In vain did the captain make various signs to him. Grushnitski would not even look.

Meanwhile, the doctor had loaded the pistol, and now handed it to me.

Upon seeing this, the captain spat and stamped his foot.

"Brother, you *are* a fool!" he said. "A vulgar fool!

. . . Since you've relied upon me, you should obey me in everything . . . Serve you right! Perish like a fly . . ." He turned away and, as he walked off, he muttered: "And still it is utterly against the rules."

"Grushnitski!" I said. "There is still time: retract your slander and I shall forgive you everything. You did not succeed in fooling me, and my self-esteem is satisfied. Remember, we were friends once. . . ."

His face blazed, his eyes glittered.

"Shoot!" he answered. "I despise myself and hate you. If you do not kill me, I shall cut your throat in a dark alley. There is no room in this world for the two of us. . . ."

I fired. . . .

When the smoke dispersed, Grushnitski was not on the ledge. Only dust in a light column still revolved on the brink of the precipice.

All cried out in one voice.

"*Finita la commedia!*" I said to the doctor.

He did not answer and turned away in horror.

I shrugged my shoulders and bowed to Grushnitski's seconds as I took leave of them.

On my way down the trail, I noticed, among the crevices of the cliffs, Grushnitski's blood-stained body. Involuntarily, I shut my eyes.

I untied my horse and set out for home at a walk: a stone lay on my heart. The sun seemed to me without luster; its rays did not warm me.

Before reaching the suburb, I turned off to the right, down the gorge. The sight of a human being would have been burdensome to me. I wanted to be alone. With slack reins, my head sunk on my breast, I rode a long while; at last, I found myself in a spot that was completely unknown to me. I turned my horse around and began to look for the road; the sun was already setting when I reached Kislovodsk, exhausted, on an exhausted horse.

My valet told me that Werner had called, and handed me two notes: one from Werner himself, the other . . . from Vera.

I unsealed the first one; it contained the following message:

"Everything has been arranged as well as possible: the body has been brought back in a disfigured condition, the bullet has been extracted from the breast. Everybody believes that his death had been caused by an accident; only the commandant, to whom your quarrel was probably known, shook his head, but said nothing. There are no proofs against you whatsoever, and you can sleep in peace . . . if you can . . . Good-by."

For a long time, I could not make myself open the second note . . . What could she tell me? . . . A heavy presentiment agitated my soul.

Here it is, this letter, whose every word is indelibly graven in my memory:

"I write to you with the complete certitude that we shall never see each other again. Several years ago, when parting with you, I thought the same; but Heaven chose to try me a second time. I did not withstand this trial: my weak heart submitted again to the familiar voice. You will not despise me for this, will you? This letter is going to be both a farewell and a confession: I feel obliged to tell you all that has accumulated in my heart ever since it loved you. I shall not blame you—you treated me as any other man would have done; you loved me as your property, as a source of joys, agitations and sorrows, which mutually replaced one another and without which life would have been dull and monotonous. This I understood from the first; but you were unhappy, and I sacrificed myself, hoping that some day you would appreciate my sacrifice, that some day you would understand my deep tenderness, not depending on any circumstances. Since then much time has passed. I penetrated into all the secrets of your soul . . . and realized that my hope had been a vain one. It made me bitterly sad! But my love had grown one with my soul; it became darker, but did not go out.

"We part forever; yet you may be sure that I shall never love another: my soul has spent upon you all its treasures, its tears and hopes. She, who has loved you once, cannot look without a certain contempt on other men, not because you are better than they—oh, no!—but because there is something special about your nature, peculiar to you alone, something proud and mysterious. In your voice, whatever you may be saying, there is unconquerable power. None is able to desire so incessantly to be loved; in none is evil so attractive; the gaze of none promises so much bliss; none knows better to use his advantages; and none can be so genuinely unhappy as you, because none tries so hard to convince himself of the contrary.

"I must now explain to you the reason for my hurried departure: it will seem to you of little importance, since it concerns me alone.

"This morning, my husband came into my room and related your quarrel with Grushnitski. Evidently, I looked terribly upset, for he looked long and intently into my eyes. I nearly fainted at the thought that you must fight today and that I was the cause of it: it seemed to me that I would go mad . . . But now that I can reason, I feel sure that your life will be spared: it is impossible that you should die without me, impossible! My husband paced the room for a long time. I do not know what he was saying to me, I do not remember what I answered him . . . No doubt, I told him that I loved you . . . I only remember that toward the end of our conversation, he insulted me with a dreadful word and went out. I heard him order the coach to be got ready . . . I have now been sitting at the window for three hours, awaiting your return . . . But you are alive, you cannot die! . . .[121] The coach is almost ready . . . Farewell, farewell . . . I perish—but what does it matter? If I could be sure that you will always remember me—I don't say, love me—no, only remember . . . Farewell . . . Somebody is coming . . . I must hide this letter. . . .

"You do not love Mary, do you? You will not marry her? Listen, you must make this sacrifice to me: for you I have lost everything in the world. . . ."

Like a madman, I rushed out onto the porch, jumped on my Circassian horse which was being promenaded in the yard, and galloped off, at full speed, on the road to Pyatigorsk. Unmercifully I urged my exhausted steed, which, snorting and all covered with foam, carried me swiftly along the stony road.

The sun had already hidden in a black cloud that rested on the ridge of the western mountains; it had become dark and damp in the gorge. The Podkumok River roared dully and monotonously as it made its way over stones. I galloped on, breathless with impatience. The thought of arriving in Pyatigorsk too late to find her, beat like a hammer on my heart. To see her for one minute, one more minute, say good-by to her, press her hand . . . I prayed, cursed, wept, laughed . . . No, nothing can express my anxiety, my despair! Faced by the possibility of losing Vera forever, I felt that she had become dearer to me than anything in the world—dearer than life, honor, happiness! God knows what strange, mad plans swarmed in my head . . . And meanwhile I continued to gallop, urging my horse mercilessly. And presently, I began to notice that my steed was breathing more heavily; once or twice he had already stumbled on level ground. Three miles remained to Essentuki, a Cossack settlement where I might be able to change horses.

Everything would have been saved had my horse's strength lasted for another ten minutes! But suddenly, as we emerged from a small ravine at the end of the defile where there was a sharp turn, he crashed onto the ground. I nimbly jumped off, tried to make him get up, tagged at the bridle—in vain. A hardly audible moan escaped through his clenched teeth; a few minutes later he was dead. I remained alone in the steppe, my last hope gone; I tried to proceed on foot—my legs gave way under me. Worn out by the agitations of the day and by insomnia, I fell on the wet grass and began crying like a child.

And for a long time, I lay motionless and cried bitterly, not attempting to hold back the tears and sobs. I thought my chest would burst; all my firmness, all my coolness vanished like smoke; my soul wilted, my reason was mute and if, at that moment, anyone had seen me, he would have turned away in contempt.

When the night dew and the mountain breeze had cooled my burning head, and my thoughts had regained their usual order, I realized that to pursue perished happiness was useless and senseless. What was it that I still needed? To see her? What for? Was not everything ended between us? One bitter farewell kiss would not enrich my memories, and after it, we would only find it harder to part.

Yet it pleases me that I am capable of weeping. It may have been due, however, to upset nerves, to a sleepless night, to a couple of minutes spent facing the muzzle of a pistol, and to an empty stomach.

Everything is for the best! That new torment produced in me, to use military parlance, a fortunate diversion. Tears are wholesome, and then, probably, if I had not gone for that ride, and had not been compelled to walk ten miles home, that night, too, sleep would not have come to close my eyes.

I returned to Kislovodsk at five in the morning, threw myself on my bed and slept the sleep of Napoleon after Waterloo.

When I awoke it was already dark outside. I seated myself at the open window, unbuttoned my Caucasian overcoat, and the mountain breeze cooled my breast, which had not yet been appeased by the heavy sleep of exhaustion. Far away, beyond the river, through the tops of the dense limes sheltering it, there flickered lights in the buildings of the fort and of the suburb. Around the house, all was quiet. The princess's house was in darkness.

The doctor came in; his brow was furrowed; contrary to his custom, he did not give me his hand.

"Where do you come from, doctor?"

"From the Princess Ligovskoy. Her daughter is ill—a nervous breakdown . . . However, that is not the matter, but this: the authorities are suspicious, and, although nothing can be proved positively, I would nevertheless advise you to be more careful. The princess told me today that she knows you fought a duel over her daughter. She learned it all from that little old man—what's his name? He witnessed your clash with Grushnitski at the restaurant. I came to warn you. Good-by. I suppose we shan't see each other again: you will be transferred somewhere."

On the threshold, he stopped. He would have liked to shake my hand, and had I displayed to him the slightest desire for it, he would have thrown himself on my neck; but I remained as cold as stone—and he left.

That's the human being for you! They are all like that: they know beforehand all the bad sides of an action. They help you, they advise you, they even approve of it, perceiving the impossibility of a different course—and afterwards they wash their hands of it, and turn away indignantly from him who had the courage to take upon himself the entire burden of responsibility. They are all like that, even the kindest, even the most intelligent ones.

On the following morning, upon receiving from the higher authorities the order to proceed to the fort of N——, I called on the old princess to say good-by.

She was surprised when, to her question, whether I had not anything particularly important to tell her, I answered that I wished her happiness and so forth.

"As to me, I must talk to you very seriously."

I sat down in silence.

It was obvious she did not know how to begin. Her face turned purple, her plump fingers drummed upon the table; at last, she began thus, in a halting voice:

"Listen, Monsieur Pechorin, I believe you are a gentleman."

I bowed.

"I am even convinced of it," she went on, "although your behavior is somewhat ambiguous; but you may have reasons which I do not know, and it is those reasons that you now must confide to me. You have defended my daughter from slander; you fought a duel for her—consequently, risked your life. Do not reply. I know you will not admit it, because Grushnitski is dead." (She crossed herself.) "God will forgive him, and He will forgive you, too, I hope! . . . That does not concern me . . . I dare not condemn you, since my daughter, though innocently, was the cause of it. She told me everything—I think, everything. You declared your love to her . . . she confessed her love to you." (Here the princess sighed heavily.) "But she is ill, and I am certain that it is no ordinary illness! A secret sorrow is killing her; she does not admit it, but I am certain that you are its cause . . . Listen, you may think, perhaps, that I am looking for rank, for huge riches. Undeceive yourself! I seek only my daughter's happiness. Your present situation is not enviable, but it can improve: you are a man of means. My daughter loves you; she has been brought up in such a way that she will make her husband's happiness. I am rich, she is my only child . . . Tell me, what holds you back? . . . You see, I should not have been saying all this to you, but I rely on your heart, on your honor . . . Remember, I have but one daughter . . . one. . . ."

She began to cry.

"Princess," I said, "it is impossible for me to answer you. Allow me to talk to your daughter alone."

"Never!" she exclaimed, rising from her chair in great agitation,

"As you please," I answered, preparing to go.

She lapsed into thought, made me a sign to wait, and left the room.

Five minutes passed; my heart was beating violently, but my thoughts were calm, my head cool. No matter how hard I searched my breast for one spark of love for the charming Mary, my efforts were in vain.

Presently the door opened, and she came in. Good Lord! How she had altered since I saw her last—and had that been so very long ago?

On reaching the middle of the room, she swayed; I jumped up,[122] gave her my arm and led her to an armchair.

I stood facing her. For a long time we were silent. Her great eyes, filled with ineffable sadness, seemed to seek in my eyes something resembling hope; her pale lips vainly tried to smile; her delicate hands, folded in her lap, were so thin and diaphanous, that I felt sorry for her.

"Princess," I said, "you know that I laughed at you? You must despise me."

A feverish rosiness appeared on her cheeks.

I went on: "Consequently, you cannot love me. . . ."

She turned away, rested her elbow on a table, covered her eyes with her hand, and it seemed to me that tears glistened in them.

"Oh God!" she uttered almost inaudibly.

This was becoming unbearable: another minute, and I would have fallen at her feet.

"So you see for yourself," I said, in as firm a voice as I could and with a strained smile, "you see for yourself that I cannot marry you. Even if you wished it now, you would soon regret it. My talk with your mother obliged me to have it out with you, so frankly and so roughly. I hope she is under a delusion: it will be easy for you to undeceive her. You see, I am playing, in your eyes, a most miserable and odious part, and even this I admit—this is all I'm able to do for you. However unfavorable the opinion you may have of me, I submit to it. You see, I am base in regard to you. Am I not right that even if you loved me, from this moment on you despise me?"

She turned to me as pale as marble; only her eyes glittered marvelously.

"I hate you," she said.

I thanked her, bowed respectfully and left.

An hour later, an express *troika* was rushing me away from Kislovodsk. A few miles before reaching Essentuki, I recognized, by the roadside, the carcass of my gallant steed.[123] The saddle had been removed, probably by some passing Cossack and, instead of the saddle, there were two ravens perched on the dead beast's back. I sighed and turned away.

And now here, in this dull fort, I often scan the past in thought, and wonder why I had not wanted to tread that path, which fate had opened for me, where quiet joys and peace of mind awaited me? No, I would not have got used to such an existence! I am like a sailor born and bred on the deck of a pirate brig. His soul is used to storms and battles, and, when cast out on the shore, he feels bored and oppressed, no matter how the shady grove lures him, no matter how the peaceful sun shines on him. All day long he haunts the sand of the shore, hearkens to the monotonous murmur of the surf and peers into the misty distance. Will there not appear there, glimpsed on the pale line separating the blue main from the gray cloudlets, the longed-for sail, at first like the wing of a sea gull, but gradually separating itself[124] from the foam of the breakers and, at a smooth clip, nearing the desolate quay?

# The Fatalist

I ONCE HAPPENED to spend two weeks at a Cossack settlement on our left flank. An infantry battalion was also stationed there and officers used to assemble at each other's quarters in turn, and play cards in the evening.

On one occasion, having tired of boston and thrown the cards under the table, we sat on for a very long time at Major S——'s place. The talk, contrary to custom, was entertaining. We discussed the fact that the Moslem belief in a man's fate being written in heaven finds also among us Christians many adherents; each related various unusual occurrences in proof or refutation.

"All this does not prove anything, gentlemen," said the elderly major. "I take it, none of you witnessed the strange cases with which you corroborate your opinions?"

"None, of course," said several, "but we heard it from reliable people. . . ."

"It is all humbug!" said someone. "Where are those reliable people who have seen the scroll where the hour of our death is assigned? And if predestination actually exists, why then are we given free will and reason, and why must we account for our actions?"

At this moment, an officer, who had been sitting in a corner of the room, got up and, slowly coming up to the table, surveyed all present with a calm and solemn gaze. He was of Serbian origin, as was apparent from his name.

Lieutenant Vulich's looks corresponded perfectly to his nature. A tall stature, a swarthy complexion, black hair, black piercing eyes, a large but regular nose, characteristic of his nation, and a sad chill smile perpetually wandering on his lips—all this seemed to blend in such a way as to endow him with the air of a special being, incapable of sharing thoughts and passions with those whom fate had given him for companions.

He was brave, spoke little but trenchantly; confided in none the secrets of his soul or of his family; drank almost no wine; never courted the Cossack girls (whose charm is hard to imagine for those who have never seen them). It was said, however, that the colonel's wife was not indifferent to his expressive eyes; but he would get seriously annoyed when one hinted at it.

There was only one passion of which he made no secret—the gaming passion. Once seated at the green table, he forgot everything, and usually lost; but continuous bad luck only served to exasperate his obstinacy. It was rumored that, one night, while on active duty, he dealt out the cards at stuss on his pillow; he was having formidable luck. All of a sudden, shots were heard, the alarm was sounded, there was a general scamper for weapons. "Set your stake for the whole bank," cried Vulich, without rising, to one of the keenest punters. "All right, I set it upon a seven," answered the other, as he rushed off. Despite the general confusion, Vulich went on dealing all alone, and the seven came up for the punter.[125]

When he reached the front line, the firing there was already intensive. Vulich paid no attention either to the bullets or the swords of the Chechens: he was in search of his fortunate punter. "The seven turned up on your side," he shouted on seeing him at last in the firing line, which was beginning to force the enemy out of the forest, and, on coming closer, took out his purse and his wallet and handed them to the lucky gamester, despite the latter's protest that this was not an appropriate place for payment. Upon acquitting himself of this unpleasant duty, he dashed forward, carrying the soldiers with him, and most coolly kept exchanging shots with the Chechens to the end of the engagement.

When Lieutenant Vulich approached the table, everybody fell silent, expecting some eccentric stunt from him.

"Gentlemen!" he said (his voice was quiet though a tone below his usual pitch). "Gentlemen, what is the use of empty arguments? You want proofs? I offer you to try out on me whether a man may dispose of his life at will or a fateful minute is assigned to each of us in advance . . . Who is willing?"

"Not I, not I," came from every side. "What an odd fellow! Who would think of such a thing! . . ."

"I offer you a wager," I said in jest.

"What kind of wager?"

"I affirm that there is no predestination," I said, pouring onto the table a score of gold coins—all there was in my pocket.

"I accept," answered Vulich in a toneless voice. "Major, you will be umpire. Here are fifteen gold pieces. The other five you owe me, and you would do me a favor by adding them to the rest."

"All right," said the major, "but I don't understand, what it is all about? How are you going to settle the argument?"

Vulich without a word walked into the major's bedroom: we followed him. He went to the wall where there hung some weapons, and among pistols of various caliber, he, at random, took one down from its nail. We still failed to understand, but when he cocked it and poured powder into the pan, several officers, with involuntary exclamations, seized him by the arms.

"What do you want to do? Look here, this is madness!" they cried to him.

"Gentlemen," he said slowly, freeing his arms, "who is willing to pay twenty gold pieces for me?"

All were silent and stepped aside.

Vulich went to the other room and sat down at the table: we all followed him there. With a sign he invited us to take seats around him. He was obeyed in silence: at that moment, he had acquired some mysterious power over us. I looked fixedly into his eyes,[126] but he countered my probing glance with a calm and steady gaze, and his pale lips smiled; but despite his coolness, I seemed to decipher the imprint of death upon his pale face. I had observed —and many a seasoned warrior had confirmed this observation of mine—that often the face of a man who is to die within a few hours bears the strange imprint of his imminent fate, so that an experienced eye can hardly mistake it.

"Tonight you will die," I said to him. He turned to me quickly, but answered slowly and calmly.

"Maybe yes, maybe no . . ." Then, addressing himself to the major, he asked: "Is there a ball in the pistol?" The major, in his confusion, could not remember properly.

"Oh come, Vulich," somebody exclaimed, "surely it's loaded if it was hanging at the head of the bed. Stop fooling!"

"A foolish joke!" another joined in.

"I'll bet you fifty roubles to five that the pistol is not loaded!" cried a third.

New bets were made.

I became bored with this long procedure. "Listen," I said, "either shoot yourself or hang the pistol back in its place and let's go home to bed."

"That's right," many exclaimed, "let's go home to bed."

"Gentlemen, please stay where you are!" said Vulich applying the muzzle of the pistol to his forehead.

Everybody sat petrified.

"Mr. Pechorin," he added, "take a card and throw it up into the air."

I took from the table what I vividly remember turned out to be the ace of hearts and threw it upwards. Everyone held his breath; all eyes, expressing fear and a kind of vague curiosity, switched back and forth from the pistol to the fateful ace which quivered in the air and slowly came down. The moment it touched the table, Vulich pulled the trigger . . . the pistol snapped!

"Thank God!" many cried. "It was not loaded. . . ."

"Let's take a look, anyway," said Vulich. He cocked the pistol again, took aim at a cap that was hanging above the window. A shot resounded—smoke filled the room. When it dispersed, the cap was taken down. It had been shot clean through the middle, and the bullet had lodged deep in the wall.

For some three minutes, no one was able to utter a word. With perfect composure, Vulich transferred my gold pieces into his purse.

A discussion arose as to why the pistol had missed fire the first time. Some maintained that the pan must have been clogged; others said in a whisper that at first the powder must have been damp and that afterwards Vulich added some fresh powder; but I affirmed that this last supposition was wrong because I had never taken my eyes off the pistol.

"You're a lucky gambler!" I said to Vulich.

"For the first time in my life," he answered, smiling complacently. "This is better than faro or stuss."

"But then, it's a bit more dangerous."

"Bye-the-bye, have you begun to believe in predestination?"

"I believe in it, but I cannot understand now why it seemed to me that you must certainly die tonight."

This very man, who only a moment before had calmly aimed a pistol at his own forehead, now suddenly flushed and looked flustered.

"Well, enough of this!" he said, rising up. "Our bet has been settled, and I think your remarks are out of place now." He took his cap and left. This appeared odd to me—and not without reason.

Soon after, everyone went home—commenting variously upon Vulich's vagaries, and probably, in unison, calling me an egoist for having made a bet against a man who was going to shoot himself, as if without me he would not be able to find a convenient occasion! . . .

I was walking home along the empty alleys of the settlement. The moon, full and red, like the glow of a conflagration, began to appear from behind the uneven line of roofs; the stars shone calmly upon the dark-blue vault, and it amused me to recall that, once upon a time, there were sages who thought that the heavenly bodies took part in our trivial conflicts for some piece of land or some imaginary rights. And what happened? These lampads, lit, in the opinion of those sages, merely to illumine their battles and festivals, were burning as brightly as ever, while their passions and hopes had long been extinguished with them, like a small fire lit on the edge of the forest by a carefree way-farer! But on the other hand, what strength of will they derived from the certitude that the entire sky with its countless inhabitants was looking upon them with mute but permanent sympathy! Whereas we, their miserable descendants, who roam the earth without convictions or pride, without rapture or fear (except for that instinctive dread that com-presses our hearts at the thought of the inevitable end), we are no longer capable of great sacrifice, neither for the good of mankind, nor even for our own happiness, because we know its impossibility, and pass with indifference from doubt to doubt, just as our ancestors rushed from one delusion to an-other. But we, however, do not have either their hopes or even that indefinite, albeit real, rapture that the soul encounters in any struggle with men or with fate.

And many other, similar, thoughts passed through my mind. I did not detain them, since I do not care to concentrate on any abstract thought; and, indeed, what does it lead to? In my early youth, I was a dreamer; I liked to fondle images, gloomy or iridescent by turn, that my restless and avid im-agination pictured to me. But what was left me of it? Nothing but weariness, as from a night battle

with a phantom, and a vague memory full of regrets. In this vain struggle, I exhausted the ardency
of soul and the endurance of will, indispensable for
real life. I entered that life after having already
lived it through in my mind, and I became bored
and disgusted, like one who would read a poor
imitation of a book that he has long known.

The event of the evening had made a rather
deep impression upon me and had irritated my
nerves. I do not know for certain if I now believe in
predestination or not, but that night I firmly believed in it: the proof was overwhelming, and despite my laughing at our ancestors and their obliging astrology, I had involuntarily slipped into their
tracks. But I stopped myself in time on this dangerous path; and as I have, for rule, never to re-
ject anything decisively, nor trust blindly in anything, I brushed metaphysics aside and began to
look under my feet. Such a precaution proved
much to the point: I very nearly fell, having stumbled over something fat and soft, but apparently
inanimate. Down I bent. The moon now shone
right upon the road—and what did I see? Before
me lay a pig, slashed in two by a sword. Hardly
had I time to inspect it, when I heard the sound
of footfalls. Two Cossacks came running out of a
lane; one of them came up to me and asked if I
had not seen a drunken Cossack chasing a pig. I
informed them that I had not encountered the Cossack, and pointed to the unfortunate victim of his
frenzied valor.

"The rascal!" said the second Cossack. "Every
time he drinks his fill of *chihir'*,[127] there he goes
cutting up everything that comes his way. Let's go
after him, Eremeich;[128] he must be tied, or
else. . . ."

They went off; I continued my way with more caution and, at length, reached my quarters safely.

I was living at the house of an old Cossack sergeant, whom I liked for his kindly disposition, and especially for his pretty young daughter, Nastya.

As was her custom, she was waiting for me at the wicket, wrapped up in her fur coat. The moon illumined her sweet lips, now blue with the cold of the night. On seeing it was I, she smiled; but I had other things on my mind. "Good night, Nastya!" I said, as I went by. She was on the point of answering something, but only sighed.

I closed the door of my room, lit a candle and threw myself on my bed; however, sleep made me wait for it longer than usual. The east was already beginning to pale when I fell asleep, but apparently it was written in heaven that I was not to get my fill of sleep that night. At four in the morning, two fists began to beat against my window. I jumped up: what was the matter? "Get up, get dressed!" shouted several voices. I dressed quickly and went out. "Do you know what's happened?" said, with one voice, the three officers who had come to fetch me. They were as pale as death.

"What?"

"Vulich has been killed."

I was stupefied.

"Yes, killed," they continued. "Let's hurry."

"Where to?"

"You'll find out on the way."

Off we went. They told me all that had happened with an admixture of various remarks regarding the strange predestination which had saved him from inevitable death, half an hour before his death. Vulich had been walking alone in a dark street. The drunken Cossack, who had hacked up the pig, happened to pitch into him, and would, perhaps, have gone on without taking notice of him, had not Vulich stopped short and said: "Whom are you looking for, man?" "You!" answered the Cossack, striking him with his sword, and cutting him in two, from the shoulder almost down to the heart. The two Cossacks who had met me and who were on the lookout for the murderer, came along; they picked up the wounded officer, but he was already breathing his last and said only three words: "He was right!" I alone understood the obscure meaning of these words: they referred to me. I had unwittingly foretold the poor fellow's fate; my intuition had not betrayed me; I had really read upon his altered face, the imprint of his imminent end.

The assassin had locked himself up in an empty hut on the outskirts of the settlement: we proceeded thither. A great many women ran, wailing, in the same direction. Here and there, some belated Cossack rushed out into the street fastening on his dagger, and passed us at a run. The commotion was terrible.

When we finally got there, we saw a crowd surrounding the hut: its doors and shutters were locked from within. Officers and Cossacks were eagerly discussing the situation; women were wailing, lamenting and keening. Among them I noticed at once the striking face of an old woman which expressed frantic despair. She sat on a thick log, her elbows propped on her knees and her hands supporting her head: it was the murderer's mother. Now and then her lips moved . . . Was it a prayer they whispered or a curse?

Meanwhile, some decision had to be taken, and

the criminal seized. No one, however, ventured to be the first to take the plunge.

I walked up to the window and looked through a chink in the shutter. White-faced, he lay on the floor, holding a pistol in his right hand; a blood-stained sword lay beside him. His expressive eyes rolled dreadfully; at times he would start and clutch at his head as if vaguely recollecting the events of the night. I did not read strong determination in this restless gaze and asked the major why he did not order the Cossacks to break down the door and rush in, because it would be better to do it now than later when he would have fully regained his senses.

At this point an old Cossack captain went up to the door and called him by his name: the man responded.

"You've done wrong, friend Efimich," said the captain. "There's no way out except to submit."

"I will not submit!" replied the Cossack.

"Have fear of the Lord! Think, you're not a godless Chechen, but a decent Christian. Well, if sin has led you astray, there is nothing to be done; one can't avoid one's fate."

"I will not submit!" fiercely cried the Cossack, and one could hear the click of a cocked pistol.

"Hey, my good woman," said the captain to the old woman, "talk a bit to your son, maybe he'll listen to you . . . All this only angers God. And look, the gentlemen have been waiting for two hours now."

The old woman looked at him fixedly and shook her head.

"Vasily Petrovich," said the captain, going up to the major, "he will not surrender—I know him; and if we break the door open, he will kill many of our men. Hadn't you better give the order to shoot him? There is a wide crack in the shutter."

At that moment, an odd thought flashed through my mind. It occurred to me to test my fate as Vulich had.

"Wait," I said to the major, "I shall take him alive." Telling the captain to start a conversation with him and, having stationed three Cossacks at the door, ready to break it in and rush to my assistance at a given signal, I walked around the hut and went close to the fateful window. My heart beat violently.

"Hey you, cursed heathen!" the captain was yelling, "are you laughing at us? Or do you think we shall not be able to subdue you?" He began to knock on the door with all his might. My eye against the chink, I watched the movements of the Cossack who did not expect an attack from this side. Suddenly, I wrenched off the shutter and flung myself through the window, headfirst. A shot sounded above my very ear, a bullet tore off one of my epaulets; but the smoke that filled the room prevented my adversary from finding his sword which lay beside him. I seized him by the arms; the Cossacks burst in, and three minutes had not passed before the criminal was bound and removed under guard. The people dispersed. The officers kept congratulating me—and indeed, there was reason enough.

After all this, how, it would seem, can one escape becoming a fatalist? But then, how can a man know for certain whether or not he is really convinced of anything? And how often we mistake, for conviction, the deceit of our senses or an error of reasoning? I like to have doubts, about everything: this inclination of the mind does not impinge upon resoluteness of character. On the contrary, as far as I am concerned, I always advance with greater courage, when I do not know what awaits me. For nothing worse than death can ever occur; and from death there is no escape!

After my return to the fort, I related to Maksim Maksimich all that had happened to me and what I had witnessed, and I desired to know his opinion regarding predestination. At first, he did not understand the word, but I explained it to him as best I could; and then he said significantly shaking his head:

"Yes, sir! this is, of course, a rather tricky matter! . . . However, those Asiatic pistol cocks often miss fire if they are not properly oiled or if you do not press hard enough with the finger. I must say, I also do not like Circassian rifles. Somehow, they don't seem to be suitable for the likes of us: the butt is so small you have to be careful not to get your nose burnt . . . But then, those swords they have—ah, they're really something!"

Then he added after some thought:

"Yes, I'm sorry for the poor fellow . . . Why the devil did he talk to a drunk at night! . . . However, this must have been what was assigned to him at his birth!"[129]

Nothing more could I get out of him: he does not care, generally, for metaphysical discussions.

# Notes

1. The English (London) versions known to me—all bad—are:

1854    Wisdom and Marr, *A Hero of our own Time* (reprinted as *The Heart of a Russian,* 1912).

1854    Pulszky, *The Hero of our Days.*

1888    Lipman, *A Hero of our Time.*

1928    Merton, *A Hero of our Time* (with a most unfortunate foreword by Prince Mirski).

1940    Paul, *A Hero of our Times.*

And there have been others.

2. These chameleonic effects are nothing in comparison to the colorations of facial elements in the sloppier sort of French fiction of the time. I quote from Balzac's *La Femme de Trente Ans* (see note 54): "*Ses yeux de feu, ombragés de sourcils épais et bordés de longs cils, se dessinaient comme deux ovales blancs entre deux lignes noires*" ("His fiery eyes shaded with thick eyebrows and bordered with long lashes appeared as two white ovals between two black lines"), Part I, description of Colonel Victor d'Aiglemont. Or: "*Et tout à coup une rougeur empourpra ses joues* / those of Hélène d'Aiglemont /, *fit resplendir ses traits, briller ses yeux, et son teint devint d'un blanc mat*" ("And suddenly a flush encrimsoned her cheeks, caused her features to glow resplendently, made her eyes shine, and her complexion turned a dull white"), Part V.

3. The MS. title had been: *One of the Heroes of the Beginning of the Century.* The work was begun probably in 1838, was completed in 1839, and was first published in April 1840, after "Bela," "The Fatalist," and

"Taman" had appeared as separate stories in a magazine (*Otechestvennie Zapiski*, 1839, issues 2 and 6; 1840, issue 8). The author's introduction was written a year later for the second edition (1841), where it incongruously headed vol. 2, which, equally incongruously, contained the "Second Part" ("Princess Mary" and "The Fatalist"). Except in the position of the Introduction, Russian editions still follow this purely fortuitous arrangement: Part First: I "Bela,": II "Maksim Maksimich"; Introduction to Pechorin's Journal; I "Taman"; Part Second: II "Princess Mary"; III "The Fatalist."

The Russian text I have used is Eyhenbaum's edition (Mihail Yurievich Lermontov, *Polnoe Sobranie Sochineniy*, vol. 4, OGIZ, Leningrad, 1948). The map (which the reader is urged to consult at every turn of the story) is one composed on the basis of various Russian, English, and American sources. It has been adapted by Raphael Palacios from an original by my son.

4. I was traveling: Lermontov, or his representative, is traveling back from Georgia to Russia. The time is autumn, 1837. He is taking the so-called Military Georgian road from Tiflis, capital of Georgia, to Vladikavkaz, a distance of about 80 mi. as the crow flies, but actually around 135 mi. At first, he drives north along the Aragva River, which rises northwest of the Pass of the Cross (almost 8,000 ft.) and flows south to the Kura. He enters Koyshaur Canyon some 40 mi. north of Tiflis and, after having traversed the pass, reaches the village of Kobi (6,500 ft.), and pushes on north, through the villages of Kazbek and Lars to the town of Vladikavkaz (40 mi. from Kobi) along the Terek River. Stavropol, whither he is to proceed via Ekaterinograd, lies 160 mi. northwest of Vladikavkaz.

5. Springless carriage: the word for this primitive traveling contraption was, in Lermontov's time, still the old *telezhka* (which now means simply any small cart) or *telega* (now only connoting a peasant's wagon for hay, etc.).

6. A region in Southern Caucasus bounded by the Black Sea on the west and the Dagestan region on the east, with Tiflis (now Tbilisi), the capital.

The gradual annexation of the Caucasus by Russia went on intermittently from the capture of Derbent

(1722) by Peter I, to the capture (in 1859) of the chieftain and religious leader of the Lezgians, Shamil. The advance of the Russian Empire was realized by various means, from voluntary integration (e.g. Georgia in 1801) to a fierce war with the mountaineers, of whom the various Circassian tribes offered the toughest resistance. The war (mainly in Chechnya and Dagestan) was in full progress during the years Lermontov served in the Caucasus (1837, and 1840–41).

7. Aleksey Petrovich Ermolov (1772–1861), a celebrated Russian general, who, from 1818 on, conducted military operations in Chechnya, Dagestan, and elsewhere in the Caucasus, and built several forts along the northeast stretch of the Terek. He proved an able administrator. Retired in 1827.

8. *Shtabs-kapitan*. Maksim Maksimich's rank is between lieutenant and captain, and corresponds to the ninth rank (titulary councillor) in the civil service (see note 106). The lowest commissioned officer's rank in the military scale (corresponding to the one before last, thirteenth, in the civil service) is *praporshchik*, which is usually translated as ensign. This was Pechorin's rank when Maksim Maksimich first met him (see note 31).

9. A group of lavatic volcanic peaks, the tallest of which is 12,140 ft. high, southwest of Gudaur.

10. I do not know if this place really existed, but I have marked it on the map where Maksim Maksimich's fort should be, according to the scant data in "Bela."

11. Webster spells it "boza" in English. It is a fermented drink made of hemp seed and darnel meal; but the word may also mean any kind of new wine.

12. *Mirnoy knyaz'*. This term designated a local chieftain who took no sides in the war between the Caucasian tribes and the Russians.

13. It will be noted that the story Maksim Maksimich eventually tells has little to do with his promise of it here, just as farther on (p. 14) the fact of Kazbich's wearing a coat of mail is not significant in the sense at which Maksim Maksimich darkly hints.

14. Although most of the Caucasus (deemed by Russians an Asiatic region) was by that time already "Russia" in a political sense, the term is limited here to Eu-

ropean Russia, the great plains extending northward
from the Black Sea to the White Sea.

15. Pechorin: Maksim Maksimich refers to him as
"Grigoriy Aleksandrovich" here and elsewhere. Pechorin
is Gregory, son of Alexander, and the junior captain
(whose surname we never learn) is Maxim, son of
Maxim (to anglicize these names). Maksim Maksimich's
patronymic is a familiar contraction of Maksimovich.
The "Maksimich" is pronounced something like Mak-see-
much, with the stress on "see." The mutual address between people in Russia is the use of name and patronymic as here. This is not inconsistent sometimes with
an informal "thouing." There is a faint indication (p. 58)
that Pechorin and Maksim Maksimich had switched to
the familiar second person, and that Pechorin forgot its
fraternal establishment between them when they met
again.

16. Consecrated friend, convive, chum, buddy. It
comes from the word for "guest" in Turkic dialects. One
is supposed to do anything for one's *kunak,* share with
him one's home, and, if need be, avenge him. Maksim
Maksimich does not live up to his "kunakship."

17. Meaning merely a Moslem in this context.

18. Probably, *shicha-pshina.*

19. Here and elsewhere, the Russian word is *baranï*
which specifically means "rams." I suspect it is loosely
used for "sheep." "Mutton" in Russian is *baranina,* and
for a Caucasian a sheep is merely animated mutton,
sheathed in useful wool.

20. That is to say west and north of Kuban River which
takes its rise in a glacier at the foot of Mount Elbruz
and flows north and west to the Sea of Azov, a distance
of 560 mi.

21. Native bandits, dedicated breaknecks, guerrillas.

22. A kind of smock made of silk or cotton, generally
belted and worn by Caucasians over the shirt. Over this,
come two or three other garments, loosely opened and
thus revealing the *beshmet.*

23. Neither this, nor the "I recalled the coat of mail"
(p. 15) is followed up.

24. Karagyoz or Karagöz: I suspect that the name of
the horse is meant to mean "Black Eye" in Turkish.

25.  One should assume that Kazbich's situation in the ravine was on higher ground than the open country, where his horse was being pursued.

26.  To this "ancient song" (rendered by Lermontov in dactylic tetrameter with rhymes *bbaaccee*) the author appended the following note: "I must apologize to my readers for transposing into rhymed lines Kazbich's song which was given to me, of course, in prose; but habit is second nature."

The "I" here (Narrator One, Lermontov's representative) is supposed to record faithfully not only the mannerisms of Maksim Maksimich's speech, but Maksim Maksimich's rendering of the mannerisms of other speakers (Pechorin, Azamat, Kazbich, etc.). In the case of this "ancient song," however, it is Narrator One improving on the version supplied by Narrator Two (Maksim Maksimich).

27.  Here and elsewhere, the listener's eagerness is a little overdone.

28.  Maksim Maksimich seems to have forgotten that Kazbich (pronounced "Kahz-beech" with the stress on the second syllable) never bothered to tie his beautifully-trained steed (see p. 14).

29.  There is some error in the Russian text at this point.

30.  North of the eastern reach of that river. This was "beyond" for a Circassian, while the region south would be "beyond" for a Russian.

31.  *Gospodín práporshchik!* We do not know if Pechorin was reduced to this lowest commissioned officer's rank in the infantry for his mysterious St. Petersburg escapade (before the events described in "Taman") or for his duel with Grushnitski in "Princess Mary."

32.  Pronounced something like "Meets-kah" with the accent on the first syllable. A vulgar abbreviation of "Dmitri."

33.  Either Maksim Maksimich means that these Moslemized Circassians used a Turkic dialect allied to Turkish, or the author means that Maksim Maksimich called "Tatar" (in the loose sense of "Asiatic") any Caucasian language. (In the original sense, Tatars were Mongols.) The language of the Circassian tribes belongs to the Iberian-Caucasian group and is not related to Turkish,

though certain familiar terms have been borrowed from the Turkish. One feels that Lermontov himself was not too well acquainted with these distinctions.

Further on (pp. 38 and 43) Kazbich is twice said to cry out "something in his own tongue." Maksim Maksimich's remark that he knows "their" language when relating the visit to the neutral chieftain is not very convincing since we are not told what language is meant.

34. A town in northeastern Caucasus on the left (north) bank of the eastern reach of Terek River, in the Caspian depression, some 30 mi. west of the Caspian Sea.

35. Bela (the name means "grief" in Turkish) is apparently a Circassian (*cherkeshenka*, "Cherkes girl"). Webster defines "Circassian" as "an individual of a group of tribes in the Caucasus of Caucasian race, but not of Indo-European speech, noted for their physical beauty. They are tall, amiable and brave. The chief tribes are the Circassians proper and the Kabardians."

36. Meaning Moslem girls of tribes living south of the Caucasian Mountains, and in Dagestan.

37. The phrase I have rendered as "dances of stars" is in the original *horovodi zvyozd,* "the choral dances of stars," a formula stemming from Pushkin's "Eugene Onegin," Two, XXVIII, 4 (1826).

38. This is, of course, a romanticist notion. It is completely untrue.

39. The allusion is to a blunder committed by Jacques François Gamba, French consul in Tiflis, who, in his work *Voyage dans la Russie méridionale et particulièrement dans les provinces situées au-delà du Caucase, fait depuis 1820 jusqu'au 1824,* 2 vols., Paris, 1826, translated *Krestovaya* as "of Christopher" instead of "of the cross."

40. Names of cities in Central Russia that connote backwood, in-the-sticks provincialism.

41. The nickname of a mighty whistler appearing in Russian folk tales. He is a monstrous highwayman whose imitation of animal cries can overpower an army.

42. Peter I drove through the Caucasus in 1722 (see note 6).

43. The full name of this Moscow club (founded in

1783) was, since 1810, The Russian Club of Nobility (*Rossiyskoe blagorodnoe sobranie*). It was also known as *Dvoryanskiy Klub* or *Club de la Noblesse*. Its palatial white-pillared ballroom is often referred to in memoirs of the time.

44. The second half of September or the beginning of October, if we take into account the twelve-day lag of the Julian calendar ("Old Style"), used at the time in Russia, behind the universal Gregorian ("New Style").

45. Lermontov seems to employ here the word *polyana* (which really means "small field," "clearing," "lawn") in the wrong sense of the Fr. *plaine*. Throughout the book, he has trouble finding the right words for natural objects—rocks, shrubs, streams, and so forth, hence the curious abstract quality of his landscapes, despite the presence of color words. The "golden snows," for instance, are borne out by his own pictures of apricot-tinged, snow-capped mountains; and the adjective "lilac" (Crimean shoreline) which occurs in "Taman" was a new epithet in 1840.

46. There seems to be a misprint, or a reading based on an initial misprint, in the 1948 edition. I have used here Dudïshkin's otherwise unreliable edition of 1863. Unfortunately I have not been able to procure, for reference, the first and second editions (1840, 1841).

47. The good reader will note that there is no retrospective intimation here of the romantic adventures which Pechorin had with Mary and Vera only a few months before the "Bela" episode. At the time, Lermontov had not yet written "Princess Mary."

48. A Circassian tribe inhabiting the northwestern coastal area.

49. Terek River (365 mi.) has its source from a small glacier in the Central Chain, on Mount Kazbek. It skirts the Kazbek group and flows turbulently in a general easterly direction, through a series of gorges (of which the most famous is the Daryal Canyon), along which the Military Georgian Road runs. Below Vladikavkaz, the Terek collects the waters of various mountain streams, flows north toward steppe country, then turns resolutely east and continues its course to the Caspian Sea (see map).

50. The reference is to a Roman Catholic *mitra simplex* of white silk or linen.

51. The shrewd and disgruntled valet in Beaumarchais's comedy, *Le Mariage de Figaro*, (1785).

52. I have translated as "sacks" Lermontov's vague term *kotomki*. According to an English traveler (E. D. Clarke, "Travels," vol. 2, p. 48), who sampled Circassian mountain honey in 1800, it is "sewed up in goatskin with the hair on the outside."

53. The "medium height" probably implies a small man by our standards, as it seems to do a small woman in Vera's case (p. 97). Otherwise this descriptive item would be pointless. It is curious to note that in other fragments of fiction, Lermontov repeats this epithet. He was physically of smallish stature, with velvety eyes, broad shoulders and bowlegs.

54. The allusion is to *La Femme de Trente Ans* in *Scènes de la Vie Privée*, 1828–44, a vulgar novelette, ending in ridiculous melodrama, by the overrated French writer, Balzac. The Marquise d'Aiglemont reaches thirty in Part Three, and, when Charles de Vandenesse sees her for the first time, part of the description runs: "*Ce reste de coquetterie / "les soins minutieux qu'elle prenait de sa main et de son pied"/se faisait même excuser par une gracieuse nonchalance . . . [La] courbure de son cou, le laisser aller de son corps fatigué mais souple qui paraissait élégamment brisé dans le fauteuil, l'abandon de ses jambes, l'insouciance de sa pose, ses mouvements pleins de lassitude, tout révélait une femme sans intérêt dans la vie*", etc.

A little further, occur the famous, but actually insipid and commonplace pages ("*Son silence est aussi dangereux que sa parole*", etc.), wherein Balzac analyzes the woman of thirty. No wonder Vandenesse "*resta silencieux et petit [?] devant cette grande et noble femme*".

55. See note 15.

56. Oddly enough, Maksim Maksimich forgets that, as he had said himself (see p. 48), Bela was not to be mentioned.

57. It is hardly necessary to remind the good reader that these unrealistic blanchings and blushings, slight or

otherwise, are mere code words used by novelists to convey one character's awareness of another character's emotion. Even Tolstoy, despite his incomparable genius for the vivid rendering of the physical, was not above the "grew-slightly-pale" device which in the long run goes back to French novelistic formulas.

58.   We never learn exactly how Pechorin died. His digestion was poor and his bile excessive, but otherwise he had a remarkably strong constitution. One suspects that the death he encountered on his way home from Persia was a violent one, and that Lermontov withheld the mystery to make an additional story of it in some later volume (see also note 118).

59.   *Les Confessions de Jean Jacques Rousseau*, Genève, 1782 and 1789.

60.   These "Black-Sea Cossacks" (not to be confused with the other Cossacks mentioned in the book) were descendants of Ukrainians removed by Empress Catherine II from beyond the cataracts of the Dniepr to the Kuban region in order to repel the incursions of Caucasian and Turkish tribes.

61.   Gelendzhik: A port on a small bay of the Black Sea about 80 mi. SE of Taman, in the extreme NW corner of the Caucasus. Taman village is a small port in Taman Gulf, an eastern inlet of Kerch Strait, about 250 mi. NW of Suhum.

62.   The hallway (or covered porch) of the second, smaller, cottage.

63.   "Then the eyes of the blind shall be opened. . . . And the tongue of the dumb sing." Isaiah, XXXV, 5–6. (The Revised Standard Version of 1952 adds "for joy.")

64.   The word used here is *valuni* (sing., *valún*), which means "boulders," not "breakers," as indicated by the context. Lermontov's odd application of the word may have been influenced by a similarity to *volni* or *vali* (German, *Wellen*), "waves," "billows." These *valuni* reappear as breakers on p. 181, in a poetical metaphor that links up the end of "Princess Mary" with the "Taman" seascape.

65.   Ruins of an ancient Greek colony in the vicinity northeast of Taman village.

66.   The Russian epithet *nechisto* implies some devilry;

the "evil" shades into the "uncanny" and "haunted." "There is something wrong about the place." *Nechisto*, in its absolutely literal sense, means "not clean," which is the way Pechorin first interprets it. It is interesting to note that the Cossack corporal practically repeats line 15 of Zhukovski's *Undina* (see next note).

67. A buoyant and frisky maiden meant to be eerie, a changeling of mermaid origin, well-known to Russian readers from Zhukovski's adaptation in unrhymed dactylic verse (1833–36) of a romance by the German writer, La Motte Fouqué (*Undine*, 1811).

68. *Yunaya Frantsia*, in the Russian text. The *Jeune-France* was the Parisian dandy of 1830 who copied the London dandy of 1815. The movement (not to be confused with a later political organization, 1848) had but few repercussions in the literature of 1830–40. Eccentricity of language and manners, detestation of bourgeois smugness, a desire to scandalize people, etc., marked this rather sterile post-romanticist fad.

69. A reference to the fey Italian girl in Goethe's romance *Wilhelm Meisters Lehrjahre* (1795–96).

Lermontov knew French perfectly, German passably, and seems to have had a little more English than his master in poetry and prose, Pushkin (1799–1837).

70. Pechorin borrows this epithet from Pushkin's novel-in-verse *Eugene Onegin* (Five, XXXIV, 9) where Onegin gives Tatiana a "wondrously tender" look.

71. Borrowed from the poem, *Le Déjeuner*, by the French elegiast, Millevoye (1782–1816):

> *Un long baiser . . .*
> *Vient m'embraser de son humide flamme*

72. Pechorin's description of the girl's attire is romantically vague. That kerchief or scarf was not her *only* garment.

73. I have left the dates as they are, in Old Style. They lag twelve days behind ours.

74. A famous mineral-springs resort in northern Caucasus (see map). Another spa, Kislovodsk, is some 40 mi. to the west of it.

The Pyatigorsk mountains mentioned in the course of the story are: 1. Iron Mountain, Russian, *Zheleznaya Gora* (2,795 ft.); 2. Snake Mountain, *Zmeinaya Gora* or

*Zmeyka* (3,261 ft.); 3. Besh Tau or Mount Besh (4,590 ft.); 4. Mount Mashuk (3,258 ft.); and 5. Bald Mountain (2,427 ft.). These mountains are situated north and east (Bald Mountain) of Pyatigorsk.

To the south, in the western part of the Central Chain (running from parallel 44° in NW Caucasus to parallel 41° in SE Caucasus), some 50 mi. south of Pyatigorsk, loom Mount Elbruz, the highest mountain in Europe (about 18,500 ft.), and Mount Kazbek (about 16,500 ft.).

75. The opening line of an allegorical short poem by Pushkin, *The Cloud* (1835), in amphibrachic tetrameter.

76. Here and elsewhere, the style of Pechorin's descriptions of Caucasian mountain views does not differ in any way from Lermontov's own prose rhythm (p. 5 and elsewhere).

77. The line of dots (here and elsewhere) was a stylistic device of the time denoting an interruption or pause, or ineffable things, with nonchalant or romantic connotations.

78. There existed a great social distinction between officers of the Guard and those of the Army.

79. A deleted passage in the draft corroborates one's suspicion that Pechorin in 1833 (like Lermontov in 1840) was expelled to the Caucasus because of a duel. Officers of the Guard were demoted to low ranks in the Army (Pechorin has sunk to the lowest degree of commissioned officer in "Bela") for escapades of that kind, and Grushnitski poses as a romantic exile by wearing a soldier's overcoat. Actually, he has not yet been promoted from cadet to officer. On the other hand, the much-prized soldier's St. George's Cross that Grushnitski sports does imply some act of courage in battle.

80. This sudden switch to the past tense is symptomatic (see note 84).

81. Grushnitski's aphoristic remark might seem, at first blush, to be meant by Lermontov as an echo of a similar observation by Pechorin on a previous page (p. 85); actually, of course, Pechorin, in tabulating the events of the day, jots down that phrase (p. 85) *after* his conversation with Grushnitski (p. 87). This shifting of sequential levels of sense is typical of Lermontov's manner.

82. A kind of masculine bob.

83. A few moments after Grushnitski has delivered himself of this aphorism ("I hate men in order not to despise them, since otherwise life would be too disgusting a farce."), Pechorin will deliberately echo it ("I despise women in order not to love them, since otherwise life would be too ridiculous a melodrama.").

84. It would seem that Pechorin (who at the time may have thought of turning novelist) is experimenting, here and elsewhere, with the past tense, in an attempt to make of Werner a character in a story.

85. Lermontov, and other Russian authors before him, had a strange predilection for this trite Gallicism, an old cliché of French journalism, *Les augurs de Rome qui ne peuvent se regarder sans rire*. Cicero (in *De divinatione, Liber Secundus, XXIV*) says that Cato wondered "how one diviner (*aruspex,* a soothsayer who foretold the future from an examination of the entrails of animals) could see another without laughing."

86. 1. The sadness of sad things; 2. Their absurdity; 3. Our indifference to them.

87. At the height of Byron's vogue in Russia (1820–40), most educated people in Russia, where French was incomparably more widespread than English, read Byron's works in the prose versions of Amédée Pichot. These are wretchedly inexact, but read "smoothly."

88. This theme is not followed up.

89. *I bolee.* One wonders if this should not be *ne bolee* (no more).

90. *Nadulsya.* This has two possible meanings, the French *il se rengorgea* (as I think it is here) and the more usual "he went into a huff."

91. The omission of "my" in the editions I have consulted is possibly based on an initial misprint.

92. This is defined by Littré as "*fièvre continue, peu intense dans ses symptômes, et qui suit une marche chronique. Souvent le mot est synonyme de fièvre hectique*" which is "*accompagnée d'amaigrissement progressif [et] survient assez souvent aux maladies du poumon.*"

93. Pechorin evidently means the oak scrub and juniper

(or, as we say in America, "cedar") that covers mountains at comparatively low elevations.

94. A kind of longish tunic worn by Circassians over
the *beshmet* (see note 22).

95. The word (which is exactly rendered by the Spanish, "*barranco*"), is of Tatar (Turkic) origin and was
used all over southern Russia.

96. This is a familiar reference to a passage in Griboe-
dov's great comedy-in-verse *Woe from Wit* (*Gore ot
Uma*), completed in 1824, first edition published in
1833. The passage comes from Scene VII, Act One.
Chatski, returning after three years from abroad, asks
Sofia about current fashions in Moscow, 1819:

> Does there still reign . . .
> At grand assemblies a confusion
> Of tongues, French and Nizhni-Novgorodan?

97. The Tatar population of the southern Russian
steppes. Also the Nogay steppes in East Caucasus.

98. Grushnitski's absence from the ball is due not to
his wound, but to his not yet having got his commission.

99. Eyhenbaum's edition has *mazure*, which seems
pretty meaningless, even for a Russian drunk. In Dudïshkin's edition of 1863, the word is spelled *mazurc*. The
MS. and the 1840–41 editions should be consulted.

100. It would have been rather difficult for Pechorin simultaneously to frequent the old princess, as Vera wants
him to do, and to avoid meeting there Mr. G——, who
was a relation of the Ligovskoys. In fact, by p. 153
(three weeks later), Pechorin and Vera's husband are
good friends.

101. *Begali slyozï v glazakh.* The same oddly un-Russian
locution occurs in Chapter Four, lines 18–19, of Zhukovski's *Undina* (see note 66).

102. *Ruka* as used here, in a not too felicitous image,
may mean in Russian either "hand" or "arm." The context suggests a middle course.

103. The reference seems to be to Pavel Kaverin
(1794–1855), hussar, man-about-town, and Goettingen
graduate, whom Pushkin, in an inscription to his portrait, in 1817, characterized thus:

> In him there always boils the heat of punch and war;
> A warrior fierce he was in fields of Mars;

'Mid friends, staunch friend, tormentor of the fair,
And everywhere hussar!

He is also mentioned as a pal of the fictitious protagonist in *Eugene Onegin* (One, XVI, 6).

104.  Jews in Russia were restricted in the choice of trade or profession; many of them became tailors; Grushnitski's crack belongs to the stock-in-trade of literature.

105.  *Biblioteka dlya Chteniya,* a magazine (1834–48), edited by Osip Senkovski on the lines of the Parisian *Bibliothèque Universelle.* It contained, among other stuff, Russian adaptations of foreign novels.

106.  An average rank in the civil service, the ninth in a scale where the lowest rung (fourteenth) is a Collegiate Registrator and the highest (first) a Chancellor (*Kantsler*), corresponding to Field Marshal in military service.

107.  The whole interplay between Grushnitski and the Captain of Dragoons is extremely unconvincing. Lermontov does not seem to have bothered about finding the right words here and keeps using the first comedy device that occurred to him.

108.  Another curious link between Grushnitski and Pechorin, who utters here, with practically the same intonation, a dramatic phrase that on p. 85 he assigned to Grushnitski as an example of the latter's post-Byronic style.

109.  The owner of only fifty slaves was a needy landlord in pre-Emancipation Russia (i.e. before 1861), where a rich man might own a thousand peasants or more.

110.  A carbonate mineral water, the name of which comes from *nart-sane,* which means, in the Kabardan dialect, "the drink of the giants" (Narts, mythical heroes sung by the tribes of the Northern Caucasus).

111.  What is called in Southern Russia "white acacia," and what Lermontov means here, as well as in the description of Bela's grave, is not the true acacia but the American Black Locust, *Robinia pseudoacacia* of Linnaeus, introduced into Europe by the French herbalist Robin in the Seventeenth century.

112.  This is from Griboedov's *Woe from Wit* (see note

96), Act Three, Scene III, Chatski's retort to the toady Molchalin (but reads there somewhat differently than Pechorin has it):

When I have work to do, I hide from gaieties;
When it is fooling time, I fool:
To mix these two pursuits, a lot of men
Are apt. I am not one of them.

113. "Grushnitski every day carouses . . . He arrived only yesterday . . ." A strange discrepancy.

114. Tomashevski (*Literaturnoe Nasledstvo*, issue 43–44, v. 1, 1941) has traced this and a few other passages in our book to the French novel *Gerfaux* (1838) by a disciple of Balzac, the forgotten writer, Charles de Bernard du Grail de la Villette (1804–50), whose name the otherwise admirable Russian commentator gives neither in full nor in French.

115. Pechorin quotes from *Eugene Onegin* the two closing lines of the Prefatory Piece, which first appeared, as a dedication of Chapters Four and Five, in 1828.

116. The allusion is to *La Gerusalemma liberata* (1581) by the Italian poet Torquato Tasso. He was read by Russians in French versions such as that of Prince Charles Lebrun, 1774.

117. The reference is to "The Vampyre, a Tale," first published anonymously in the *New Magazine*, April, 1819, and attributed to Byron, in a separate edition, as a novel in July of the same year, but actually written by his physician, Dr. John William Polidori. It was read by Russians in the French version of Chastopalli (joint pseudonym of Amédée Pichot and Euzèbe de Salle), who placed it among the *Oeuvres de Lord Byron* in their 1819 and 1820 editions of his works, after which it was dropped.

118. One wonders if perhaps Lermontov had planned to have Pechorin marry in Persia.

119. The reference is to Defauconpret's French version, under the title *Les Puritains d'Ecosse* (Paris, 1817 and later editions), of *Old Mortality* by Walter Scott who, like all other English writers, was read by Russians in French.

120. An allusion to the various omens that preceded Caesar's assassination as related in Plutarch's *Parallel*

*Lives* (circa 100 A.D.), known to Russians in the French of Amyot's *Vies des hommes illustres* (1559).

121. The technical difficulty of having the lady leave Kislovodsk before the issue of her lover's duel is known, and of having her, simultaneously, be satisfied that he is spared is not solved here any too neatly.

122. Odd behavior! Should we believe that Pechorin, a fashionable man, had remained seated after Mary had come in?

123. Cf. this to Pechorin's noticing Grushnitski's corpse (p. 171).

124. *Otdelyayushchey, otdelyayushcheysya.* It is just like Lermontov and his casual style to let this long and limp word appear twice in the same, final, sentence.

125. In Lermontov's day, the fashionable banking game (*bank*) was a German variation of faro called *Stoss* (Russ., *shtoss*) or stuss. The player or "punter" chose a card from his pack, put it down on the card table, and set his stake. The dealer or "banker" unsealed a fresh pack and proceeded to turn the cards up from its top, one by one, the first card on his right hand, the second on his left, and so on, alternately, until the whole pack was dealt out. The dealer won when a card equal in points to that on which the stake had been set came up on his right hand, but lost when it was dealt to the left. When a doublet occurred—two similar cards turning up in the same coup—the punter lost half his stake at faro, the whole of it in stuss.

126. This scene curiously echoes that of the duel in "Princess Mary" (p. 164), and there are other echoes further on (cf. p. 158, "this is becoming a bore," and p. 186, "I became bored with the long procedure").

127. Caucasian new red wine, or must.

128. The second Cossack addresses the first by his patronymic ("son of Eremey"), and the same folksy familiarism is used on p. 192 by the Cossack captain in addressing the murderer (Efimich, "son of Efim"). "Vulich," which ends similarly, is, however, a surname.

129. It will be marked that Maksim Maksimich closes the book with much the same remark as the one he makes about Pechorin at the beginning (p. 11).

# ANCHOR BOOKS

## BRITISH FICTION

CONRAD, JOSEPH  The Secret Agent, A8
——  The Shadow-Line, Typhoon and The Secret Sharer, A178
——  Under Western Eyes, ed. Zabel, A323
——  Victory, A106
——  Youth, Heart of Darkness and The End of the Tether, A173
KIPLING, RUDYARD  The English in England: Short Stories by Rudyard Kipling, ed. Jarrell, A362
——  In the Vernacular: The English in India, ed. Jarrell, A363
MISH, CHARLES C., ed.  Anchor Anthology of Short Fiction of the Seventeenth Century, AC1
SNOW, C. P.  The Masters, A162
WEINTRAUB, STANLEY, ed.  The Yellow Book: Quintessence of the Nineties, A421

## CONTINENTAL FICTION

ALAIN-FOURNIER, HENRI  The Wanderer, A14
CHEKHOV, ANTON  Ward No. 6 *Six Russian Short Novels*, ed. Jarrell, A348
COLETTE  My Mother's House *and* The Vagabond, A62
DOSTOEVSKY  Three Short Novels of Dostoevsky, A193
FLORES, ANGEL, ed.  Nineteenth Century German Tales, A184
GOGOL, NIKOLAI  The Overcoat *Six Russian Short Novels*, ed. Jarrell, A348
JARRELL, RANDALL, ed.  Six Russian Short Novels, A348
LERMONTOV, MIHAIL  A Hero of Our Time, A133
LESKOV, NIKOLAI  The Lady Macbeth of the Mtsensk District *Six Russian Short Novels*, ed. Jarrell, A348
MERWIN, W. S., trans.  The Life of Lazarillo de Tormes, A316
SERGE, VICTOR  The Case of Comrade Tulayev, A349
TOLSTOY, LEO  The Death of Ivan Ilych *and* Master and Man *Six Russian Short Novels*, ed. Jarrell, A348
TURGENEV, IVAN  A Lear of the Steppes *Six Russian Short Novels*, ed. Jarrell, A348

## ORIENTAL LITERATURE

KAI-YU, HSU, trans. & ed.  Twentieth Century Chinese Poetry—An Anthology, A413
KANG-HU, KIANG  The Jade Mountain—Being Three Hundred Poems of the T'ang Dynasty 618–906, trans. Bynner, A411
MURASAKI, LADY  The Tale of Genji, trans. Waley
Vol. I—A55
SCOTT, A. C.  Literature and the Arts in Twentieth Century China, A343
TSAO HSUEH-CHIN  Dream of the Red Chamber, trans. Wang, A159

A 2a

H

# ANCHOR BOOKS

## AMERICAN HISTORY AND STUDIES

## AMERICAN FICTION

# ANCHOR BOOKS

## EUROPEAN HISTORY

A 6Ba

PRINTED IN U.S.A.

GAYLORD

---------------★---------------

"Dada!"

She realized that Nicky's insistent shriek was coming from behind the half-closed door of the master bedroom. "Nicky?" she called. Her heart in her throat, she pushed the door open and stepped into the room. The nauseating stench was far stronger here.

The scene that greeted her was almost too much to take in all at once. Too small to climb up on the king-size bed by himself, Nicky stood at its edge, yanking on the blue-and-yellow flowered bedspread with both of his small fists.

She forced herself to look at the bed a second time.

There, lying on his back across its center, ashen-faced and still, was Dylan. The butcher's knife Annabel had stashed in the bookcase headboard for protection protruded from the center of his chest.

---------------★---------------

*Previously published Worldwide Mystery title by*
*NANCY BAKER JACOBS*

**STAR STRUCK**

Nancy Baker Jacobs

# RICOCHET

**W🌐RLDWIDE**®

TORONTO • NEW YORK • LONDON
AMSTERDAM • PARIS • SYDNEY • HAMBURG
STOCKHOLM • ATHENS • TOKYO • MILAN
MADRID • WARSAW • BUDAPEST • AUCKLAND

**RICOCHET**

A Worldwide Mystery/February 2006

First published by Five Star.

ISBN 0-373-26554-9

**Printed in U.S.A.**

# RICOCHET

# ONE

As SHE PULLED HER Honda into the driveway and shut off the motor, Annabel noticed the man in the driver's seat of the dark green Toyota parked across the street. Another lost tourist trying to decipher a map, she figured. Carmel was overrun with vacationers this time of year—folks from Michigan or South Carolina or Idaho who would start searching for Clint Eastwood's Mission Ranch or a shortcut to Monterey's Cannery Row, only to become hopelessly lost on the town's winding streets. Many had no qualms at all about knocking on a local's door to ask for directions, or even to use the bathroom. But if she hurried inside, maybe this one would bother one of her neighbors instead of her.

She reached across the seat to grab her shoulder bag, pushed open her door, and swung her long legs onto asphalt raised and cracked by the roots of adjacent cypress trees. *Damn*. The man was getting out of his car and heading in her direction. She was in no mood, today of all days, to play tour director for some confused tourist. After two hours in the lawyer's office, all she wanted was to lie back in a hot bath and pretend she was somewhere else. Maybe even, for a few minutes, pretend she was some*body* else.

"Excuse me, ma'am."

The man caught up with her before she could remove the door key and escape into her bougainvillea-covered cottage. He wore dark rumpled pants with a white shirt and maroon-striped tie and held a clipboard. Maybe not a tourist after all, she decided; possibly a salesman, or somebody proselytizing for some oddball religion, although the Bible-pushers generally traveled in pairs.

"I'm looking for Dylan Nettleton," he said.

Startled, Annabel jerked the key out of the lock and stared openly at her portly visitor. She hadn't expected *that*—nobody had ever come looking for her husband before, not once in their entire eighteen months of marriage. Not here in Carmel, or in any of the other four places they'd lived. "I'm Mrs. Nettleton," she said. *But maybe not for long.* "My husband's not home right now."

"When do you expect him back?"

"Hard to say. He's out of town, probably for another day or two, but I couldn't swear." Dylan didn't share that sort of thing with her; that was part of the problem.

The stranger's gaze dipped toward the clipboard. "The man I'm looking for is Dylan Baez Nettleton," he said, "born September twelve, nineteen sixty-eight in San Francisco."

The sharp edges of the key dug into Annabel's fingertips as her grip on it tightened. "Why? Who are you?" Maybe this middle-aged man was a cop. Or a DEA agent. Her husband could be a drug runner, without her even knowing it; that would explain his strange absences and his secretiveness, maybe even his insistence that they move to a new town every few months.

"I'm Jeff Link, investigator specializing in locating missing persons. May I come in for a few minutes and explain? Might be worth something to your husband." He handed her his business card. It listed his name and a Chicago address and phone number. "Discreet Investigations" was printed in blood-red type across the top, with "Locator of Missing Heirs" in black just below.

Maybe Dylan wasn't about to be arrested. Relieved and curious, Annabel stuffed the card into the pocket of the one good suit she'd bought since losing her pregnancy weight and reassured herself that Louise wouldn't mind keeping the baby next door for a little while longer. He would be napping by now, anyway. She unlocked the front door and led the way into the living room.

"You can have a seat over there," Annabel told the investigator, indicating the green wicker sofa angled toward the window to catch a glimpse of the Pacific through a screen of pines. The morning fog had burned off and the water was now a brilliant, white-capped blue. She supposed she should offer Jeffrey Link a cup of coffee or at least a glass of water, but that would only keep him here longer, and she didn't want to impose much more on her neighbor's willingness to babysit.

"Nice place you've got here."

"Thanks." Lucky she'd taken time to tidy up the house before leaving for her meeting, Annabel thought, and that she'd put Nicky's toys into his bedroom toy chest. But her effort had also stripped the place of any personal touches, except for the salmon-colored lilies on the dining room buffet, bought at Tuesday's Farmer's Market, and her small gallery of family photos—not one picture from Dylan's side—on the lamp table. Like all the places where she and Dylan had lived together, this cottage was a vacation rental property, fully furnished by the leasing company, right down to dishes and linens.

She hung her purse on a hook by the front door and smoothed the wrinkles from her teal raw silk skirt. Now that she'd risked inviting a strange man into her home, she couldn't help wishing the skirt were a little longer, that it didn't reveal quite so much leg. She lowered herself as modestly as possible into an old oak rocking chair opposite her guest. "Now, what's this about?" she asked.

"Ever hear of Oliver Nettleton, Nettleton Metalworks?" he asked, settling back against the sofa's green plaid upholstered cushions.

"No. Should I have?"

Jeff Link shrugged his shoulders. "If your husband's the right Dylan Nettleton—"

"You got his birthday right. He was born September twelfth, sixty-eight."

"In San Francisco?"

"Right."

"And his middle name's Baez?"

Annabel nodded.

"Well, then, not likely there'd be two Dylan Baez Nettletons born on the same day in the same city, right? Oliver Nettleton's your husband's grandfather."

Annabel was confused. "But all my husband's relatives are dead, so if you're looking for this Oliver guy, I'm afraid we can't—"

Link shook his balding head. "No, no, you don't understand. It's not *Oliver* who's missing, it's Dylan. Missing from Oliver's point of view, anyway. I was hired to find Dylan. Chances are your husband doesn't know much about his grandfather—they've never met."

Annabel's green eyes narrowed. "I don't under—?"

"Seems there was some bad blood between your husband's mother, Eleanor Nettleton, and her father." The private eye flipped a page on his clipboard and consulted his notes. "Eleanor left home in sixty-seven, when she was only seventeen. Family says she ran off with some hippie friends. Gave birth to a son a year later—that'd be Dylan. Wrote home just once after the baby was born, to tell her father he had a grandchild and that she'd named him Dylan Baez—after her two favorite protest singers. But Oliver was still mad at her. Probably more steamed than ever, 'cause Eleanor didn't bother to marry the baby's father, didn't even identify the guy on the kid's birth certificate. Midwesterners didn't go for that sort of thing, at least not back in the sixties. So Oliver ignored his daughter's letter."

Annabel bristled. "What about Eleanor's mother? Didn't she care about her daughter and grandson, either?" She couldn't imagine herself acting so unforgiving toward her own daughter, assuming she ever had one. But, of course, times had changed when it came to tolerating a variety of sexual behaviors.

"The mother was dead," Link explained. "Died of cancer when Eleanor was in grade school. There were no other kids, so it was just the girl and her father left. Don't know if Oliver ever tried to contact Eleanor after she wrote him that one time, but he got a note five or six years later from a pal of hers. Told him his daughter had died from drugs and her friends had scattered her ashes at sea. Letter was postmarked San Francisco, but there was no return address."

San Francisco—the same place Eleanor's child, Dylan Baez, was born. Annabel wondered whether the young mother had stayed in San Francisco the entire time, maybe hanging out with the hippies in the Haight. The old clock on the fireplace mantle struck two with an annoyingly tinny sound. "So why now?" she asked, feeling increasingly irritated by the story she was hearing. "Why didn't Oliver Nettleton try to find Eleanor while it might have done the two of them some good? Or at least look for Dylan right after his mother died, instead of letting the poor kid end up in all those horrible foster homes?" Didn't the man realize how precious blood kin were, how you had to cling to them with everything you had and, even then, they could just slip away from you? Annabel herself had almost died twice—she had the scars to prove it—

doing whatever she could to keep her own family going. Yet this self-righteous old man hadn't even bothered to put pen to paper to save his. Hell, she thought, it was probably as much old man Nettleton's fault as anybody's that Dylan was so screwed up, letting him spend his childhood being shuffled from one temporary home to the next. Was it any wonder that now her husband couldn't bear to stay in one place for more than a few months? Or that he never really trusted anyone, not even his own wife?

Link's voice took on a defensive edge. "Maybe Oliver did try to find his daughter and grandson, I don't know. All I know is that now he's dying—in the final stages of Parkinson's disease and failing fast. He's pretty much paralyzed, so he hasn't got much longer. Obviously, Mr. Nettleton had a change of heart and decided he wanted to leave his estate to his grandson, if he could be found. Seems he's trying to make amends for the past."

Annabel wanted to ask how much those amends were worth in dollars, but she held back. It probably wasn't any of her business. Instead, she warned, "I'm not sure how my husband's going to feel about being asked to run off to Chicago or wherever to see a dying old man who didn't give a damn about him until now." Certainly she was in no hurry to bundle up Nicky and haul him off to see this newly discovered great-grandfather, even if he did plan to leave Dylan a few dollars.

"You don't understand," Link said, a smirk crawling onto his lips. "Oliver Nettleton isn't expecting visitors. Or love, or dedication, or anything like that. This is just about his estate. His *money*."

Annabel shifted in her seat. "What do you mean?"

Link's face broke into a broad grin. "Oliver Nettleton is a very rich man. Sold Nettleton Metalworks maybe ten years ago, and invested the money in the stock market. His holdings have been up and down some since then, but mostly up. On a good day, his estate is worth somewhere in the area of forty million after taxes."

Annabel felt like she'd been punched in the chest. "Forty million *dollars?*"

Link nodded, grinning broadly now. "And every cent goes to Oliver's grandson—Dylan."

Annabel sagged back against the rocker. Forty *million dollars!* Things like this just didn't happen to people like her, or to anyone she'd ever known. Not even most lottery winners ended up with that kind of money, did they? Her mind whirled as she tried to process what this unexpected windfall might mean. Not that money had ever been a really big a problem for her and Dylan…or had it? She knew virtually nothing about their finances. Since their wedding day, her husband had deposited cash into her checking account each week, money for groceries, clothing, Nicky's care, whatever she needed to cover their living expenses. There'd always been plenty available and she was a thrifty person, so she'd never had to ask for more. She hadn't had to return to the workplace after they'd married, either. In fact, Dylan had insisted she not even look for a job.

How this inheritance would change things between them, *if* it would change things, would require some analysis. The fear that immediately pierced Annabel's heart was that now Dylan would have an endless supply of money to fight her for custody of Nicky. Providing she went ahead with her plan to divorce him, of course. Obviously, she would have to talk to the attorney again before she actually confronted Dylan with her plan. She only hoped that Dylan's good luck wouldn't turn into her bad luck.

"How can Dylan reach you when he gets back?" Annabel asked, turning her attention back to her visitor.

"I'm at the Pine Lodge here in town for another day or two. After that, he can get me at my Chicago number."

"And if he wants to visit his grandfather before he dies?" For that kind of money, who knew what Dylan might feel obligated to do? If he wanted to, he could go directly from Salt Lake City to Chicago without returning to Carmel in between—providing he bothered to call her before showing up at home.

Jeff Link seemed to choose his words carefully. "If your husband thinks it's important for him to see his grandfather, I'm sure no one would object. But I'm afraid Mr. Nettleton no longer recognizes people, and he can't talk. The disease has affected both his memory and his speech, so it really won't make any difference to him whether your husband makes the trip or not."

"I don't get it. I thought you said Oliver Nettleton hired you to find Dylan."

"No, no. Mr. Nettleton changed his will to benefit Dylan at least a year ago, but he didn't do anything about finding him. I was hired just last month by his late wife's nephew, Warner Schuman. Mr. Schuman runs the household and handles the dying man's business affairs, now that Mr. Nettleton can't do it himself. Mr. Schuman wants the lawyers to be able to find Dylan quickly when the inevitable happens."

"I see." Annabel stood up. "I'll have Dylan contact you then, as soon as I hear from him." She ushered Jeff Link out, closing the door tightly after him, then pressed her shaking hands and her forehead against the door's smooth, cool wood for a long moment, considering the new form of upheaval that suddenly promised to intrude upon her life.

"THAT DIDN'T TAKE LONG," Warner Schuman said when Jeff Link called to tell him the news.

"Anybody can find 'em, Discreet Investigations can." Jeff was pleased with himself. This was the part of his job he liked best, bringing long-lost relatives back together. Telling people they were coming into an unexpected inheritance sure beat skip-tracing deadbeat debtors, like he'd done when he first became a PI.

"Sure you've got the right guy?" Schuman asked.

"Haven't met Dylan himself yet," Jeff confessed, "but his wife confirms his middle name's Baez, and the date of birth is right. He's got a California driver's license as Dylan B. Nettleton, too, same DOB. I always recommend a DNA test if you have any doubts. The kind of money you're talking about, you want to be a hundred percent certain." The really rich people always wanted scientific proof, Jeff knew, and the sooner those test results were in, the faster he'd see the fat bonus he'd been promised for locating Oliver Nettleton's heir. It would be enough to cover his next year's spousal support payments to Jane, plus his son's freshman year tuition at Northwestern, with maybe enough left over for a few months' car payments. "I've got a good lab I can recommend," he offered.

"I'll handle that part. You just keep an eye on the wife and the house, make sure we don't lose Dylan once he gets home. Don't approach him directly. I'll do that when I get out there. And I'll handle getting him to verify his identity."

"Well, sure, if that's the way you want to work things." This guy was more suspicious than most of Jeff's clients. Did Schuman suspect him of calling in a ringer to earn his bonus or maybe even of trying to siphon off the inheritance for himself? If that's the way his Chicago boss wanted to play it, Jeff could be cool. He'd never cheated a client in his life and he wasn't about to start now. But that didn't mean he was a sucker. "Gotta remind you the meter's still running, Mr. Schuman," he said. "Have to keep charging you by the day, plus expenses, if you want me to hang around here now that I've located Dylan." Hell, if the man wanted to pay him to spend a few more days here in vacation land, Jeff was game. He could manage to put up with sipping a Corona or two and sucking on barbecued spareribs while he watched the sunset from the terrace of the Mission Ranch. A few runs a day past the Nettleton cottage to see if Dylan had returned would fulfill his contract; the rest was a windfall, an all-expenses-paid holiday, courtesy of Oliver Nettleton.

"No problem," Warner said. "Just keep an eye on things out there and keep track of your expenses. Don't forget receipts. I'll catch a plane out as soon as I'm sure Uncle Oliver'll be okay while I'm gone."

"So WHAT ARE you going to do now?" Louise Zuckerman asked as she refilled Annabel's iced tea glass. Nicky Nettleton and Louise's own toddler, Jason, napped in the bedroom while she and Annabel chatted in the kitchen of her modern, ocean-view house.

"Darned if I know." Annabel crumbled a gingersnap between her fingers; despite skipping lunch, she had no appetite. "When I left the lawyer's office, I thought I had everything all straight in my mind. I even rehearsed what I was going to say to Dylan when he got home—how I was going to lay it all out about our settling down here and going to marriage counseling if he didn't want me to go ahead with the divorce, everything. But this really messes things up. Now I don't know what to do."

Louise lowered her fashionably skinny body into the chair opposite Annabel's. "Tell you what I'd do if it was me," she said, "I'd wait it out, let the son of a bitch inherit all that money, and then I'd go for half of it in court."

"That's not even an option," Annabel explained. "Inherited

money isn't community property, so whatever Dylan gets
from his grandfather is his alone. Besides, I don't want money
that doesn't belong to me."

"Yeah, right. And I don't want to win the lottery."

"No, I'm serious, and even if I did want some of this
money, I'm not legally entitled to it. Sure, I want to live com-
fortably, to be able to give Nicky whatever he needs. Who
wouldn't? But I don't need millions of dollars." She dunked
an ice cube in her glass with the tip of one finger. "I've never
been afraid to work, to earn my own way. Used to be a travel
agent before I met Dylan. I could always do that again."

Louise made a face. "Don't be a fool, Annabel. You must
know how much it costs to live like this." She gestured around
at her own house with its panoramic ocean view, tiny backyard
guest house, and furnishings right out of *House Beautiful*.

"I'm not greedy, Louise, I—"

"I'm not talking about greedy. I'm talking about survival,
about you and your son living the way your husband has accustomed you to living."

"So? I don't need any forty million to do that."

"You need a hell of a lot more than you can earn selling
airline tickets." Louise poured herself another cup of coffee
as she warmed to her subject. "I bet you don't even know how
much Dylan earns each year, do you?"

"Well—"

"That's what I thought. So how can you possibly end up
with a fair deal?"

Annabel twirled a lock of her long blond hair around a finger. This conversation was beginning to make her nervous,
although she could see that Louise had a point. "I hired a
good lawyer…I think. It's his job to see I don't get screwed
financially."

Louise made a snorting sound. "Right. Put your trust in

lawyers and see what it gets you. What it got me was the shaft."

Annabel bristled. "I'm not you, Louise."

"Thank your lucky stars for that." Louise smiled. "I'm not trying to be bossy, hon, I'm just trying to help. Take my advice and don't let Dylan off too easy. I walked away from my first husband with custody of Missy, five hundred a month in child support, and half our debts. A year later, he was pulling down half a mil a year while Missy and I were living in a rented apartment and buying our clothes at Sears. Found out years later that the SOB had hidden money all over town while he was telling me he was dead broke. By that time, I'd already married Sid, so I couldn't even go back to court to get alimony."

"I don't even know if I want alimony. Child support, sure, but alimony? Sort of retro, isn't it?"

Louise rolled her eyes and sighed. "How much did you earn when you worked in the travel agency?"

"Twenty-four, almost twenty-five thousand a year."

"Ha! That wouldn't even pay the rent on your house. Look, Dylan has to be pulling down good money. I mean, it costs a fortune to pull up roots every few months and move the way you've been doing, right?"

Annabel nodded, feeling stupid. The truth was, she had no idea how much money Dylan had, and she wasn't even certain how he earned his living. He'd told her he was a free-lance headhunter, that his profession was finding top jobs for other people, a service for which somebody— whether employee or employer, she didn't know—paid him generous commissions. Except when he was off on one of his mysterious business trips, he spent a couple of hours every day shut away in the spare bedroom he used as an office, working on his computer. But as far as she knew, he never made phone calls during his office hours and she'd never run across even one piece of business mail. Could he really run the kind of business he'd described, communicating only through e-mail? On the few occasions when she'd invaded his private space, she'd observed nothing but his computer and a shelf bulging with books about financial investing. "Look, I admit I don't know much about Dylan's money or his business, Louise, but the truth is, I haven't a clue how to find out. Whenever I ask him about money or his work, he clams up, gets hostile, tells me to butt out."

"Typical male reaction, especially when the marriage is rocky."

Annabel wasn't sure she bought into Louise's cynical philosophy. Besides, her fear wasn't that Dylan was being a typical male; it was that he had something to hide, something far beyond how much money he had, something that wouldn't bear scrutiny. That was why she'd been worried that Jeff Link might be a DEA agent or some other kind of cop, someone who'd come to arrest her husband. "It's not that Dylan's cheap, Louise, really it isn't. Anything I need or want, all I ever have to do is ask him." Not that she asked very often; Annabel was used to living on a shoestring. She sighed, staring at her hands. "I guess I never should have married him."

"So why did you?"

Annabel raised her head and looked Louise straight in the eye. "I got pregnant. Very soon after we met, I'm rather embarrassed to say."

"Oh." Louise took a beat. "Talk about retro."

"Most women my age would have had the sense to use birth control."

"Or had an abortion if it failed." Louise was eight or nine years older than Annabel and the concept of the shotgun marriage was passé in her own circle. "Not that I'm being judg-mental. Obviously, it was your decision."

Annabel had her own reasons for not having an abortion, none of them particularly religious, and she'd long since ad-mitted to herself that subconsciously she'd wanted to become pregnant. She wanted someone to love, someone who wouldn't leave her. "I really, really wanted this baby," she ad-mitted. "And my doctor told me I shouldn't wait too long to get pregnant if I ever wanted kids. Because I've got only one kidney left, he thought pregnancy would be harder on my body, the older I was."

Louise already knew that Annabel had donated one of her kidneys to save her brother, who'd suffered from kidney dis-ease since birth. But both the Lindberg siblings had con-tracted staph in the hospital. Annabel eventually had recovered, but Erik had been unable to fight off the virulent infection and he'd died. "So when I ended up pregnant, there was no way I even considered doing anything but having the baby," Annabel said.

"I can understand wanting a baby, particularly in your cir-cumstances," Louise said, "but nowadays you don't really have to marry your kid's father, do you?"

Annabel nodded. "I was completely prepared to have my baby and raise it on my own, but Dylan said no kid of his was going to grow up a bastard, that we'd have to do the right thing and get married. I knew he'd spent a lot of years in foster homes when he was a kid and, after what that private detec-tive told me today, I can see why he felt so strongly. His own mother never got married, apparently didn't even know who his father was.

"I—I thought marriage might actually work for us if we really tried. Damn it, Louise, the truth is I was lonely. My brother and I'd been so close. I guess I was as much a mother to him as a sister after our folks died, and when he died even after— I was just so alone and Dylan seemed so, so glamorous. Guess I was just a fool."

"So you had a fairytale wedding and lived happily ever after."

With an ironic laugh, Annabel said, "Which is why I went to see a lawyer about a divorce this morning."

Louise leaned over and patted her new friend's shoulder. "Happens to the best of us, hon."

"At least Dylan's crazy about Nicky. I've got to give him that. If only he loved me half as much as he loves our son—"

Louise looked at her neighbor. "Look, Annabel, truth is I'd kill to have legs like yours, or hair. You're a good-looking woman, and you're no dope, either. You've got guts and you're a survivor. I can tell. If Dylan Nettleton doesn't love you, he's a damn fool, that's all I can say."

Annabel's eyes began to fill and she blinked to keep a tear from spilling onto her cheek. It had been so long since anyone had said anything kind or supportive to her that Louise's unexpected praise touched her. "Thanks," she replied. "I've tried to make the best of things, but I just don't think I can live like this much longer. It's not that Dylan hates me, but I don't think he loves me, either. Truth is, he doesn't think of me at all, except maybe as Nicky's mother or the person who cooks his meals and packs the boxes whenever he decides he wants to move on. Hell, I might as well be the guy from United Van Lines."

It was another of Dylan's snap decisions to move—decisions he made without even asking her input—that had prompted the visit to the lawyer this morning. He'd called last night from Salt Lake City to tell her to pack up, that he'd found a house for them there, that they'd be moving in less than two weeks. But Annabel was sick of moving, of having no roots, of having no friends who weren't superficial, of having no control over her own life.

"So what are you going to do?" Louise asked.

"We're back to that, aren't we?"

"Square one."

"I—I guess I'll wait it out for a few days, see what happens with this inheritance thing." As she spoke, Annabel realized she'd made up her mind. "It's not that I want to cash in. It's just that I'm so scared I'll lose Nicky."

"Why on earth would you lose Nicky? You're his mother and Dylan's hardly ever even home."

"You don't know him, Louise. He'll never willingly give up his son and now, with all this money, he'll be able to afford any lawyer in the world to fight me for custody. What chance will I have against that?" Annabel swallowed hard. "How did I get myself into this? All I ever really wanted was a happy—" Her throat constricted and tears stung her eyes. She bent her head to hide her sudden outburst of emotion from her neighbor. *What am I doing here?* she asked herself. She'd known this woman only a few weeks and here she was, discussing all these intimate details of her life. Was it because Louise had paid her a compliment? The truth was that about the only things the two of them really had in common were the neighborhood and the fact that they both had baby sons. If only she hadn't let herself become so isolated, so lonely, Annabel thought, she'd be handling things so much better, the way the old Annabel always did, before she began to fall apart. Before she met Dylan Nettleton.

Annabel wiped at her cheek. "I'd better get home," she said, carrying her glass to the sink. "I'll go get Nicky."

"There's no rush—"

"Thanks for babysitting, Louise. I really appreciate it."

"No problem. Anytime I'm free, or Missy is—I've been letting her sit for her baby brother after school since she turned thirteen, and she's doing great. We're glad to help out, really, and Nicky's good company for Jason."

Annabel tiptoed into the bedroom and lifted her sleeping son from the nest he'd made for himself in Jason's playpen. He stirred only slightly, his eyelids fluttering and closing again, the pale blond hair he'd inherited from her plastered damp against his scalp. "Come on, sweetie, we're going home," Annabel whispered as he nestled against her shoulder. This was what made it all worthwhile, she told herself. Even if her marriage went completely sour, she would still have Nicky. He was all that really mattered to her now.

ANNABEL WAS IN her nightgown, washing off her makeup when she heard the front door slam.

"Annie? I'm home."

"Back here," she stage-whispered from the bathroom as she recognized her husband's voice. She wiped her face dry on a striped hand towel, then grabbed her old yellow flannel robe, tied it tight around her waist, and met him in the hallway. "Nicky just got to sleep," she said, holding a warning finger against her lips. "How was your flight?"

As Dylan planted a quick, perfunctory kiss on her cheek, she caught a faint whiff of liquor on his breath. "Bumpy getting into Monterey. Those box kites they fly in and out of this town are a real pain in the ass." He barged past her and threw open the door to the baby's bedroom. "How's my boy?" Crossing over to the crib, he leaned down and gently stroked the sleeping child's hair.

"Hey, don't wake him up. He got way over-excited tonight and it took me forever to get him settled down for bed."

"Hell, you coddle the kid too much, Annie." He leaned down

and planted a kiss on his son's forehead. "You act like it's a crime for a dad to want to see his son." The little boy stirred in his sleep and sucked his thumb harder, but didn't waken.

Annabel felt herself bristling. Dylan hadn't been home two minutes and already he was criticizing her mothering technique. "Just let him sleep, will you? It's already after ten and we've got things to talk about."

Dylan straightened up and shot his wife a cold look. "That right? Such as?"

"Come on. Not here." She grabbed Dylan's sleeve and ushered him out of the room, firmly closing the door behind them. He wasn't going to wake Nicky again if she could help it. "A man came looking for you today," she told him after they'd reached the living room and Dylan had poured himself two fingers of Black Bushmills. She wondered how many he'd had on the plane ride home.

His face froze. "What do you mean?"

"Don't look so worried. It's *good* news." Now that Dylan was finally home, she was trying to act excited about his pending good fortune. Maybe it would improve things between them, she'd tried to convince herself, maybe it would give Dylan an added reason to settle down and stop traveling so much, an incentive to be a husband to her as well as a father to Nicky. Handing him Jeff Link's business card, she sat down on the sofa, pulling her feet up under her, and described the encounter she'd had earlier in the day.

"You could inherit forty million dollars, Dylan, can you believe it?" she concluded. "You won't have to travel so much anymore, maybe we could buy a house, stay in one place, and be a real family for once."

Dylan had listened without comment or visible reaction as Annabel talked. Now he stared at the business card gripped tightly in his hand, his knuckles white. "This is bull."

Her excited smile disappeared from her face. "What? Why do you say that?"

"How many times do I have to tell you, Annie? I don't have family, I don't have relatives... none, zero, zip... least of all some rich old man who's going to leave me his fortune out of the clear blue. This is a hundred percent bogus." He crumpled the card in his fingers and tossed it angrily onto the coffee table.

"But why? From what Mr. Link said, your mother had a falling out with her father—your grandfather—when she was just a girl, and now that he's dying, the old man's had a change of heart. Why is that so impossible to believe?"

"You don't know anything about me or my mother. Her family was all dead years ago, before I was born. That's a goddamned fact."

"Maybe your mom just told you that because she didn't get along with her family and she didn't want you asking her about them. I mean, you were only a kid when she died, right? So how do you really know?"

"That's crap!" He drained his glass and quickly refilled it. "Whoever hired this private eye, it sure as hell wasn't any long-lost grandfather who's going to hand me forty million bucks."

"But why else would—"

"He's got the wrong guy."

"But Mr. Link had your correct birth date and he knew your middle name and—"

"What did you tell him?" Dylan slammed the glass down on the table and took a step toward Annabel.

"About what?"

"About me, of course. What did you tell him about me, Annie?"

Annabel pressed back against the cushions until she could

hear the wicker creak. Dylan's face reddened as his anger grew and she felt a tiny sting of fear—her husband was a large man, given to sudden flares of temper. Yet she felt strangely energized as well. If she'd had any lingering doubts about leaving this man she'd married so impulsively, they quickly were being erased by his bizarre reaction to what she'd thought would be outstandingly good news. "I told Mr. Link you were out of town and that I didn't know when you'd be back," she said carefully, keeping her voice even and emotionless. "I told him precisely the truth."

Dylan began to pace the floor. "How'd he find me?" he demanded. "That's what I want to know."

"What? How would I know? How do people like that find anybody?"

He reached down and grabbed Annabel's arm, yanking her up off the sofa. "How did he find me, Annabel?"

"Let go of me. That hurts!"

Dylan's grip on her arm tightened as his voice rose. "You tell me! We've moved every few months, we always have unlisted phone numbers, new bank accounts, new driver's licenses in every goddamned state. So how in hell did this creep find me?"

Her heart racing, Annabel pried her husband's fingers off her arm. At a full five feet ten, she was not a small woman, but Dylan had a good four inches and seventy-five pounds on her. This close, his liquor breath was nearly overpowering. "I—I don't know," she said. "If the man knew somewhere to start, he probably just had to check with the post office or something. That's what I'd do if—"

"What about the post office?"

"Forwarding addresses. He probably just checked them."

*"You left forwarding addresses at the post office?"* A vein in Dylan's forehead began to throb noticeably.

Annabel tried to step back, but her legs butted against the sofa and she staggered. "Sure, why not?" *What was going on here?* From the way Dylan was reacting, you'd think she'd committed some unpardonable sin.

"You stupid bitch! You stupid, stupid bitch! I never told you to do that!"

He had no right to speak to her that way! "You don't tell me what to do and what not to do." Annabel was yelling now, too. "Maybe it comes as a shock, but I'm *not* your slave. I might have been stupid enough to marry you, but I can fix that real easy, and I will. Just watch me."

Dylan drew back his big hand and slapped Annabel hard across the mouth. She stumbled and fell backward onto the sofa, stunned. Her husband had raised his voice to her before, more than once. He'd even grabbed her by her slender arms a time or two before tonight, squeezed them in his beefy hands and left red finger-marks on her pale skin. But he'd never actually struck her before. Tears of anger and shock as well as pain burned her eyes. She ran her tongue over her rapidly swelling lip and tasted the saltiness of her own blood. Sliding off the sofa onto the floor, she crawled away from Dylan's reach, then pushed herself to her feet. "Stay away from me!" she warned, sprinting for the kitchen.

As the door swung shut behind her, Annabel heard Dylan's glass shatter against it. If the door hadn't intervened, she realized, the flying tumbler might have hit her. Racing across the room, she grabbed the telephone off the wall and frantically punched in 9-1-1. Loud crashes and bangs echoed from the living room as Dylan's angry fists slammed against the walls, the table, the door.

As her husband pushed through the doorway into the kitchen, his eyelids narrowed and his fists clenched, Annabel grabbed the butcher knife from the magnetic knife rack on the wall above the cutting board and thrust it in front of her in self-defense. "I already called the police, Dylan. Stay back!" she screamed.

Dylan stared at Annabel as she pressed the phone to her ear with one shaking hand and waved the knife at him with the other. Like a cornered animal checking all potential escape routes, he shifted his gaze between her and the doorway.

"I need help!" she cried into the telephone as soon as the police dispatcher answered. "My husband—he—he hit me. Please help me!"

"Try to calm down, ma'am. I'm sending two officers over right away." The woman's voice on the phone was calm, even, reassuring. "Is your husband there in the room with you?"

"Yes, yes he is."

Dylan swept a long arm along the counter, sending the toaster and coffee maker crashing to the hard tile floor, then strode back into the living room while the terrified Annabel confirmed that the dispatcher's computer had her correct street address.

When the police barged through the unlocked front door less than five minutes later, she was still gripping both the telephone and the knife. Wakened by the sirens' shriek, Nicky began to cry in the bedroom.

But Dylan was gone. Neither he nor his car were anywhere to be found.

# TWO

WHEN ANNABEL AWOKE, she felt like she'd hardly slept at all. Her head throbbed and her knees ached from crawling around on the kitchen's Spanish tile floor until two o'clock, wiping up every last shard of glass from its hard, bumpy surface. Now she sat upright in bed and listened to the house, half-expecting to hear Dylan in another room. But Nicky's cheerful morning call of "Mama! Mamamamama!" from his crib was the only sound that broke the silence. Putting on her yellow robe, she spotted the butcher knife still in the bookcase built into the headboard, where she'd stashed it in case she needed it for protection during the night. Still fearful that Dylan could have returned without waking her, she carried the knife as she did a quick pass through the cottage. She found no one else there but the baby.

"Mommy'll be right back, sweetie," she reassured Nicholas, heading back to her bedroom. She quickly slid the knife back between the books in the headboard and went to get her son up and dressed for the day.

Last night, Annabel had told Sergeant Eileen Kopek, the female and senior half of the police team who'd taken her assault report, that she would consider applying for an official restraining order against Dylan first thing this morning. But now that the swelling of her lip had gone down and the house was clean again, a restraining order seemed like overkill. Hadn't she read that restraining orders seldom worked the way they were supposed to anyway? A piece of paper wouldn't do much good if Dylan intended her harm. That butcher knife in the bedroom would be far more protection. A gun would be even better, but she would never risk having a gun in the house where her child lived.

On edge all morning, Annabel was relieved when Dylan did not return. By afternoon, she had half-convinced herself that he was using this time away from his family to analyze his bizarre behavior of the previous night, that he would decide to change his ways and vow to make his marriage a success.

When Dylan still had neither called nor returned by dinnertime, however, Annabel began to worry.

If he had decided to end their marriage, she could and would live with that. The truth was that she would be relieved to have such a momentous decision taken out of her hands. Still, if Dylan had decided to move out for good, maybe head for Salt Lake City on his own, why hadn't he bothered to tell her, or even to come back for his clothes and his computer? He'd left in such a rush he hadn't taken so much as a toothbrush or change of underwear with him.

That Dylan could ignore her for a day or two was not difficult for Annabel to imagine. But his staying away from Nicky was entirely different. Whenever the man was home, he spent hours and hours with his baby son, taking visible pride in the child's first steps, in his first words, building endless towers of blocks for him to knock down or patiently teaching him to roll a ball across the floor. Dylan had always been a model father; she had to give him that much.

When the doorbell rang at nine o'clock on the night after her husband's abrupt departure, Annabel answered it with a feeling of trepidation. For the second time, she found Sergeant Eileen Kopek standing on her doorstep.

"I decided I didn't really need a restraining order," Annabel told her, feeling a bit defensive. There was no law that said she had to take the policewoman's advice, was there?

"I didn't come about that, Mrs. Nettleton," Kopek told her. "May I come in and talk to you a minute?"

Annabel ushered the officer inside, offering her a seat in the living room. The sergeant was about Annabel's age, but almost four inches shorter and fuller-figured. Her starched and pressed navy blue uniform strained against her ample breasts and hips as though it had been designed for a man's physique and couldn't quite adjust to her feminine curves. Her nose was flat and broad and her face below frizzy brown hair was not particularly pretty, but her smile was friendly and Eileen Kopek seldom had trouble putting others at ease.

Consulting the piece of paper in her hand, the policewoman said, "Your husband has a new red BMW convertible, California license plate JMCK3409, registered to him."

Annabel's attempt at a welcoming smile evaporated. Had Dylan been in a car accident? That would explain why he hadn't returned. "He owns a red BMW," she agreed, "but I don't know the license number offhand. That could be right. Has something happened?"

"We're not really sure yet," Sergeant Kopek told her, leaning forward with an expression of concern on her face. "About an hour ago, we got a call from the County Sheriff's office. They'd been alerted by the ranger station at Point Lobos State Reserve." Annabel had been to the Point Lobos park several times since moving here. It was a rugged, steep sliver of land jutting into the sea about three miles south of Carmel. Breathtakingly beautiful with its craggy cliffs and deep turquoise coves, a local legend said that, when he lived here, author Robert Louis Stevenson had used Point Lobos as the model for his fictional *Treasure Island*. "The ranger on patrol at Point Lobos found your husband's BMW in one of the parking lots there after the park closed for the day," the cop explained. "The car was unlocked and Mr. Nettleton's wallet, car keys, and wristwatch were lying on the front seat. The rangers searched the immediate area for him before it got too dark, but they didn't find him."

"That's weird. Where could he have gone?"

"Thought you might have an idea about that."

Annabel shook her head. "I suppose he could have gone hiking on one of the trails—he liked to do that sometimes—but why would he leave his identification in his car? Or leave the car unlocked and the keys inside? That's not like Dylan—he's a real fanatic about that car. We can't even go out to dinner without him insisting on setting the car alarm." Annabel hated car alarms, considered them the worst kind of noise pollution, but this was only one of many minor battles she'd lost during her marriage to Dylan. Eventually she'd learned to keep her mouth shut about his precious alarm—to save her breath for more important disagreements—even when the ear-splitting siren was triggered accidentally, disturbing the whole neighborhood.

"Your husband doesn't have any kind of neurological condition that might make him forget where he was or who he was, does he?"

"Uh uh, Dylan's perfectly healthy."

"No health problem that might cause him to pass out unexpectedly?"

Annabel shook her head no.

"Figured that'd be the case. We've had a few elderly people who just wandered off for no apparent reason, but those were Alzheimer's cases. Only time it ever happened with a young man, he'd been on a three-day drug orgy and got some bad heroin. But I'm sure that's not your husband's situation."

"I've never known Dylan to take drugs," Annabel said stiffly. *And I'd hardly tell the police if he did.*

The policewoman sighed. "Hate to have to ask you this, Mrs. Nettleton, but is there any possibility at all your husband could have been feeling suicidal? I know you two had a fight last night and—"

"Dylan suicidal?" Annabel's jaw dropped. "I can't imagine he'd ever kill himself." *Certainly not over me.* "He'd have no reason to. Especially not now."

"Why especially not now?"

"First of all, he's downright crazy about Nicky, our son, way more than most men are with babies. He'd never, ever do something like that to Nicky. And second, there's a good chance Dylan's about to inherit an absolute fortune." Annabel told the cop about the visit from Jeff Link, the locator of missing heirs.

"That's incredible," Kopek said. "I once knew a woman who inherited a few thousand dollars from a long-lost uncle, used it to take her whole family, including the grandkids, to Hawaii for two weeks. But forty million from a grandfather he never even heard of? That really takes the prize."

"I guess I should have known Dylan would have trouble believing that kind of good fortune would just drop from the sky. It could all be some kind of hoax, I suppose. But the investigator knew all about Dylan's mom and her father, and he definitely went to an awful lot of trouble to find him, coming all the way from Chicago that way."

"I hope things turn out well for you," Eileen Kopek said. "And I have to agree—this hardly sounds like the time when a person would decide to kill himself. You know, we've had a couple of missing persons cases where married men with problems just decided one day to disappear and start a new life somewhere else without telling their families, but again, it's hard to believe your husband would do that *now*."

"Would you, if you were about to inherit millions of dollars?"

Kopek smiled and raised an eyebrow. "Let you know, if I ever have to make that decision. Jeff Link's staying at the Pine Lodge?"

"That's what he said. Gave me his card with his Chicago address, too, but Dylan must have taken it. Couldn't find it when I cleaned up the house. Maybe he figured he'd go see Mr. Link after he cooled off."

The sergeant made a few notes. "I'll check and see if Mr. Nettleton ever did get in touch with him." She stood up. "If your husband calls you or comes home tonight, Mrs. Nettleton, please call the station right away and let us know," she said, handing Annabel her card. "If we don't hear from you by dawn, the Coast Guard will begin searching the coastline near Point Lobos."

"The Coast Guard?" Annabel swallowed hard. This really was serious business. "What kind of search?"

"Helicopters, a rescue ship, whatever it takes. Just in case he had an accident or—"

"You think Dylan's—that Dylan's *dead?*"

"No, no, not necessarily. He could've been climbing on the rocks, maybe fell someplace where nobody could spot him from up above. A couple of times a year, somebody falls down a cliff at Point Lobos. Same thing happens down in Big Sur, too, even more often." She placed a reassuring hand on Annabel's shoulder. "If your husband did fall, we want to find him as soon as possible, get him to the hospital."

Annabel was almost afraid to ask. "What happened to all those other people who fell?"

Officer Kopek hesitated a moment before answering. "One woman last May, I remember she ended up with only a broken leg. Went back home to Arkansas or somewhere with her leg in a cast and an exciting story to tell her friends."

"And the others?"

"Depends on where they fell and how fast we found them. But it won't do any good to worry about that. Every case is different. With luck, we'll find your husband fast and he'll be all right. Or better yet, maybe he just hitched a ride back to town with somebody he met at Point Lobos and you'll hear from him before morning."

*Sure, and he left his wallet, wristwatch, and car keys behind.* But Annabel was grateful to the policewoman for doing what she could to keep her hopes up. "I'll call you first thing if I hear from Dylan," she promised, closing the door behind her departing visitor.

As she watched the squad car's taillights disappearing down the tree-lined street, Annabel knew she was in for another sleepless night. If only she had a friend to call, somebody she could talk all this over with. She wished her brother were still alive. Erik would have done anything to help her through this baffling situation. Even with all his physical problems, he'd always been there for her emotionally. She'd never felt so alone in her life.

Before she climbed into bed, Annabel tiptoed into Nicky's room and watched him sleep for a while. If something terrible had happened to Dylan, how would it affect her precious little Nicholas? Was he still young enough that he could forget his father and learn to bond with some other man, to be able to call someone else Daddy? Or would her son grow up as scarred and lonely as she had?

She pulled the blanket up and tucked it under the sleeping child's chin, then stole out of the room, leaving the door open so she could hear him if he awoke during the night. By the time she finally fell asleep for a brief time, it was late. A mere six hours remained before the Coast Guard would begin the search that could reveal whether she'd lost her husband and her son had lost his father.

IT WAS FOGGY and overcast in the morning. Annabel could hear but not see the Coast Guard helicopter as she drove up to the front gate of Point Lobos State Reserve. The ranger on duty at the kiosk directed her to the parking lot at the southern end of the park, where Dylan's car had been found the night before. When she arrived there, she found the parking lot already half full. There were two pickup trucks with the symbol of the Park Rangers on their doors, a lifeguard's vehicle, a couple of search and rescue trucks and even a fire truck. She spotted two Carmel squad cars parked on either side of Dylan's red BMW. Sergeant Kopek stood next to one, sipping coffee from a paper cup with a plastic cover. Everyone else appeared to be searching the rocky shoreline.

"You found someone to take care of your son?" Sergeant Kopek asked when Annabel climbed out of her Honda.

"My next-door neighbor, Louise. Her daughter has to leave for school early, so she was already up when I called. Told her I'd be back to get Nicky before noon." The shrieks of seagulls competed with the roar of the waves and the rhythmic thumps of the helicopter's blades as it flew low along the coastline beneath the cloud cover, then turned and repeated its examination of the shoreline from the other direction. "Do you think…?"

"Hard to say how long this'll take. Coast Guard's been at it for nearly two hours and so far, nothing. The fog seems to be lifting more now, though, so that'll help speed things along." The policewoman drained her coffee cup and placed it on the roof of her squad car. "The rangers are searching the trails they didn't get to last night, so they might find something."

Annabel walked over to Dylan's car, opened the door, and peered inside. It was empty.

"We have his wallet and watch back at the station house,"

Sergeant Kopek explained. "I've got the keys, but I'll have to hold onto them until we decide whether to impound the car."

"Why would you do that?"

The policewoman shrugged. "Only if something turns up that indicates foul play. Otherwise, you can probably take the car home sometime this afternoon."

Was the woman implying that someone could have kidnapped Dylan and left his car here, where it would be found quickly and reported to the police? Annabel couldn't fathom a motive for such a thing. It seemed far more likely that somebody would car-jack the BMW and leave Dylan behind. Unless someone knew of his impending inheritance and planned to hold him for ransom. Still, this wasn't Italy or Colombia, and Dylan didn't have an extra cent yet, as far as she knew. Maybe he never would. "I'll have to get somebody to drive me over to pick up the car," Annabel said. "Or maybe take a cab." It was easier to focus on the logistics of getting Dylan's car back to Carmel than to imagine him lying dead in the water below one of these steep cliffs, whether the victim of an accidental fall or something far more nefarious.

"Don't worry about it. We can give you a ride when the time comes."

The sound of tires crunching on gravel interrupted the women's conversation. A van with a satellite dish on top raced across the parking lot and pulled into a space next to Annabel's Honda. A young man with styled, blown-dry hair, wearing a gray sport coat, a white shirt with a maroon tie, and khaki pants hopped out. "Hey, Eileen," he shouted over the din of the returning helicopter, "what've you got?"

"What took you so long, George?" the sergeant teased, grinning at him. "We've been here since six. Getting your beauty sleep while the rest of us work?"

"Well, hey, I *am* on-air talent. We big TV stars gotta look rested. So what's this, another tourist take a swan dive off a cliff?"

The sergeant's grin evaporated. "Man missing since sometime yesterday." She placed a hand on Annabel's shoulder. "This is his wife, Annabel Nettleton. Mrs. Nettleton, this is George Conover, Channel Nine News."

The reporter grimaced. "Hey, sorry, Mrs. Nettleton, didn't mean to sound callous. Occupational hazard, I'm afraid."

Annabel nodded, then ignored him, wandering closer to the water while Eileen Kopek filled him in. When she'd finished, George Conover directed his cameraman to take some establishing shots of the area, as well as one of Dylan's abandoned BMW.

"Mrs. Nettleton, I'd like to ask you a few questions," he said.

"Uh, I don't know. I don't really know anything, except that my husband's missing."

The reporter motioned for his cameraman to tape him and Annabel together, standing in front of the red convertible. "When was the last time you saw your husband?" he asked her, holding a microphone under her chin.

"Tuesday night." Annabel suddenly felt cornered. She had no intention of telling a television audience about the fight she and Dylan had had, or about why she'd felt compelled to call the police.

"And what happened then?"

As the wind suddenly picked up, the sounds of dozens of barking seals swimming in the sea below echoed against the cliffs. "Dylan had to go out," Annabel replied, pushing her windblown hair off her face. Conover's didn't budge, she noticed, envying him his hair spray. "That has nothing to do with this, though. As Sergeant Kopek told you, my husband's car wasn't found here until last night. I have no idea where he is, unless he went for a hike and fell or— Hey!" As a small lizard skittered across her foot, she leapt backward out of camera range. Shuddering, she said, "Sorry, that thing just scared me. I mean, I wasn't expecting it."

"Sergeant Kopek mentioned that your husband is the potential long-lost heir to a fortune," the reporter said, ushering her back into camera range. "Maybe you can elaborate on that."

This was safer ground, and the lizard had disappeared between the rocks as quickly as it had appeared. Turning her attention back to the camera, Annabel succinctly reiterated what Jeff Link had told her on Tuesday afternoon. "That's why I'm absolutely certain my husband wouldn't just disappear," she added, "and he would never kill himself. Not when he was about to become a very, very rich man."

George motioned for the cameraman to turn off the camera, grinned at Annabel, and shook her hand. "Thanks for being so cooperative, Mrs. Nettleton. By the way, do you have a photo of your husband that we could use? It might elicit a call from somebody who's seen him."

"Sure, good idea." Annabel fished her wallet out of her purse and handed over one of the few photos she had of Dylan. It was her favorite shot, one showing him smiling with pride as he held the newborn Nicholas in his arms. "That's our son Nicky. I'll want this picture back, so if you can make a copy…"

"Sure. I'll get it back to you in a day or two, okay?"

Annabel nodded.

"Thanks again."

"Sure." The reporter repositioned his cameraman, this time to shoot him alone against a background of cliffs and ocean as he did a lead-in for the tape he would edit for the noon news. "A Coast Guard helicopter and search boat are here at Point Lobos, looking for a Carmel man who disappeared sometime yesterday," he said. "Dylan Baez Nettleton, newly-found heir to the Oliver Nettleton fortune, apparently left his car, a new BMW convertible, in this parking lot…"

Annabel crept to the edge of the cliff and gazed out at the horizon, visible now that the fog was dissipating. Had she told the reporter too much? If for some unfathomable reason Dylan was relaxing in a nearby motel, would her going public with this story be the final straw for their marriage? Well, damn, if it was, it wasn't her fault. If Dylan didn't want publicity, he shouldn't have left his car here like this. He shouldn't have acted like a horse's ass the other night, either. And he definitely shouldn't have slapped her and forced her to call the cops for protection.

Truth was, Dylan Nettleton probably never should have married Annabel Lindberg and dragged her all across the country. Having a child together was not enough to make a marriage strong, to make it work. There'd been a time when she'd thought it would be, but now that seemed ages ago. Now she'd learned a few things and she knew much better.

She checked her watch. It was after eleven o'clock and the TV news van had left the parking lot. Shivering despite the sun's emergence through the cloud cover, Annabel realized she didn't want to stay here any longer, waiting and watching what appeared to be a futile search for the stranger she'd married. Returning to her car, she told Sergeant Kopek, "I have to go pick up my son. You'll let me know if—"

"Sure, don't worry. I'll contact you the minute we have any news at all. Just go home and take care of that little boy of yours."

Annabel drove out of the park, retrieved Nicky from Louise's house, and stayed inside her own cottage. Within half an hour of Channel Nine's noon news broadcast, reporters began to arrive on her doorstep. The parade didn't stop until well after dark. By then, Annabel had told what she knew about Dylan's disappearance and his pending inheritance no fewer than seven times. And she'd handed out all but one of her photos of Dylan.

If this kept up, she thought, she would have to move. Either that or hire someone to answer the door. A person could tell the same story only so many times before she went stark raving mad.

At six o'clock, she turned on the kitchen television set while she and Nicky ate supper. There she was, the lead local story on the "Channel Nine News," standing at Point Lobos answering George Conover's questions. Her long honey blond hair was windblown and disheveled, she saw, poking it self-consciously as she watched, and her face was drawn and pale beneath her freckles. Her casual jacket and jeans were hardly the outfit she'd have chosen if she'd known she would be on television, either. But at least her lip didn't look bruised on camera and her answers to the reporter's questions sounded reasonably coherent.

The enterprising reporter hadn't stopped with her interview. Following Annabel's clip was one in which he'd questioned Jeff Link.

"I find on average seventy-five or eighty missing heirs each year," the private investigator explained as he sat in an overstuffed chair in the lobby of the Pine Lodge. "Usually they're due anywhere from several hundred to a few thousand dollars. Until now, the largest estate I handled was in the neighborhood of two million dollars—the heir of a reclusive Wisconsin man who'd put every spare penny in the stock market while he'd lived for years in an old house with a leaky roof and bad plumbing."

In response to George Conover's questions, Link revealed that "Dylan Nettleton, assuming he's found alive, is going to be the richest missing heir I've ever managed to locate—by far."

"And if he's not found alive?" the reporter probed. "What happens to the Nettleton family fortune then?"

Link furrowed his brow. "I'd have to check the will to be

absolutely certain, but generally it would go, first, to any children Dylan has. If there aren't any children to inherit, the will probably specifies other more distant relatives, or perhaps some charities."

The photo of Dylan that Annabel had given the reporter came onto the screen for the second time in the segment. "The police and Coast Guard haven't given up hope that Dylan Nettleton, shown here holding his son, Nicholas, will be found alive," George Conover said. "Chances are this little fellow would far prefer having his father home safe to any amount of money he himself might inherit."

A telephone number flashed on the screen. "If you have seen Dylan Nettleton in the last twenty-four hours, please call the Carmel Police Department at the number you see on your television screen." The shot reverted to the reporter at the Pine Lodge. "George Conover reporting for Channel Nine News," he concluded.

AS THE NEWSCAST shifted to a report of a three-car collision on Highway 1 earlier in the day, Annabel reached over and turned off the TV, then sank back into her chair.

"Mamamamama," said Nicky, waving his spoon at the TV set.

"Mama's right here, big Nick," Annabel replied. "Still hungry?" She guided the small hand gripping the spoon toward the remaining mashed carrots, but he shook his head decisively. "No!" Pointing the spoon once more at the now-dark screen of the TV set, he demanded, "Da? Dada? Dadadada!"

Annabel sighed. "Right, Nicky. That was Daddy's picture on TV. Yours, too, right after you were born." She wanted to reassure the little boy that his father would come back to him soon, but would he? She didn't want to lie. So instead she handed him a cookie and tried to distract him.

"Come on, tiger," she said, lifting him out of the high chair.

"It's a nice warm bath for you, then Mommy'll read you *Pat the Bunny* before bedtime."

HUNDREDS OF MILES to the north in Seattle, Peter Hoy sipped his first cup of coffee of the day as he read the morning newspaper. He was working his way back toward the classified ads where he planned to search for a job, maybe another waiter gig to replace the one from which he'd been fired last Saturday night, when his eye caught an Associated Press story datelined Carmel, California. "Holy—!" he whispered to himself, then grabbed the telephone. "Gil, page three of the *Times*," he shouted when his friend answered. "Check out the missing heir story."

"I'm already late for work." Gil Collier sounded harried, as usual. He always had been the least organized of the old crew.

"Do it. Now. It's important."

"Shoot, if I lose this job, Pete, I'll friggin' kill you."

"Like selling shoes to yuppie wannabes is a big deal."

"It is for me. Can't afford to lose this one."

"How far we've sunk, eh?" From the top of the world to nearly destitute ex-cons grateful for a crappy job selling shoes or waiting tables in a Chinese restaurant. But maybe that was about to change. "Trust me, Gil, look at the goddamned newspaper like I told you, and I guarantee you won't give a crap about how many wingtips and loafers you can sell today."

"Okay, okay."

As he ran his fingers nervously through his thick, straight black hair, Peter could hear the sound of Gil's newspaper rustling over the phone line.

"Page three?" Gil asked.

"Right. 'Missing Heir Found, Now Missing Again,' right there in the top right-hand corner. See it?"

"Yeah, I've got it."

"Look real careful at that picture, Gil, tell me what you see."

"A guy, a baby… Jesus, Pete! Is that—?"

"Sure as hell looks like it to me."

"Son of a bitch!"

"Still feel like selling shoes today?"

"Got a better idea?"

"Count on it." Peter grinned broadly. Hell, this was beginning to feel like the good old days.

"Be right over."

"Bring your suitcase."

"Gimme an hour." Gil slammed down the phone.

After Pete hung up, he finished his coffee, then tore the story out of the *Times* and tossed the rest of the paper into the trash. He wouldn't need the classified ads today. If the plan he was forming worked out right, he would never need them again. He and Gil would be back in fat city, right where they belonged.


IN PHOENIX, Nell Verducci was watching CNN as she baked sweet bread. It was a hot day and the air conditioning in her apartment wasn't working right, spewing out a stream of tepid-to-warm air. A fleshy, middle-aged woman, she wiped beads of sweat off her brow with the sleeve of her yellow T-shirt as her muscular hands kneaded the dough for the final time, then separated it into three sections to roll into the strips she would braid into a loaf. As she laid out the strips and lapped one over another, she dusted them with cinnamon sugar, stuffing odd leftover pieces of raw dough into her mouth and savoring their yeasty sweetness as they dissolved on her tongue.

Nell loved to bake—it seemed so elementary somehow, so basic and necessary a skill, that it always filled her with a sense of well-being. Yet she chastised herself now for starting this latest project on such a hot day. After she turned on the oven, her small apartment would become completely unbearable.

As she set the braided loaf aside for its final rising and rinsed the flour off her hands, an edited version of George Conover's story came on the television.

"…a Carmel man who disappeared sometime yesterday," the eager young reporter was explaining from a foggy beach-side location that reminded Nell of her younger days at the ocean. "Dylan Baez Nettleton, newly found heir to the Nettleton Metalworks fortune, apparently left his car…"

The yellow-and-white checkered dishtowel slipped through Nell's fingers onto the kitchen floor as she stood riveted in place, her brilliant blue eyes trained on the television set. "What the—?" she asked no one in particular.

A deep, physical kind of fear she hadn't experienced in years washed over her, leaving her chilled to the bone, despite the oppressive heat surrounding her. *How could this possibly be happening?* She'd thought she'd left it all behind, with the drugs and the booze, with the long string of anonymous sex partners, with her two failed marriages, with her years of self-destruction, followed by decades of corrosive self-hatred. But now it all came rushing back in a flash.

She hadn't buried her fears after all. She hadn't buried the past. Not deep enough, anyway.

She should have known she'd never be able to escape Dylan. Now she realized she hadn't. As badly as she wanted to keep the past behind her, she couldn't ignore this, she didn't have it in her to pretend she'd never seen this story.

Carmel, Nell thought. She'd known the little town well, once upon a time. If she drove straight through, she could be there by sometime tomorrow.

She took her unbaked loaf of bread, quickly wrapped it in foil, and stuffed it into the freezer. Then she went to pack her suitcase.

THE CHICAGO NEWSPAPERS melded the AP story with background information on critically ill local tycoon Oliver Nettleton and his business career. At his massive cherry-wood desk in his Nettleton mansion office, Warner Schuman read the full story in the morning newspaper, his anger rising with every word he read. Why had he ever hired an idiot like Jeff Link for this job? The PI had located Dylan quickly enough, but the complete ignoramus had no idea of discretion, no common sense at all about when to keep his flapping mouth shut!

Warner had known the story would be in the morning papers and on the television and radio news shows as well. The phone at the mansion had started ringing late yesterday afternoon, as soon as the copy came across the wires into local newsrooms. He finally stopped answering the calls, hitching up a phone machine with a message informing callers that no one at the Nettleton household would make any comment about Dylan or anything else. Luckily, Oliver was well beyond being able to make any comments of his own. The old man was too far out of it to realize he and his impending death had become the center of a national feature story.

Unless Warner was wrong, this whole thing would become fodder for talk radio before the day was out. He could already hear the insipid questions the dim-witted hosts would pose to their listeners:

"What would you do if you learned you were about to inherit millions?"

"Why would a man who was about to become rich beyond his wildest dreams suddenly disappear?"

"Is this just a tragic accident, or has Dylan Baez Nettleton met with foul play? If so, who wanted him dead?"

The publicity that would follow was mind-boggling, and troubling in the extreme. This unexpected turn of events could completely scuttle Warner's well-laid plans, unless he could make some quick adjustments.

Folding the newspaper and wedging it under his long, thin arm, he slipped down the thickly carpeted hallway and into the old man's bedroom. It was a lavishly furnished room that now smelled faintly of urine and decay despite a thorough daily cleaning by the staff of maids. He found his uncle as he always did lately, lying back in the adjustable hospital bed, his head slumped to one side and drool escaping from a corner of his mouth while oxygen was pumped through a plastic tube into his nose. His faded blue eyes stared straight ahead with no sign that he saw anything in particular. The once-forceful business leader had become a living corpse.

A nurse in a starched white uniform sat in an easy chair next to the bed, reading a romance novel. "Good morning, Mr. Schuman," she said, closing her book and placing it on the nightstand.

Warner nodded his balding head without smiling. "How's he doing today, Lucille?"

Never one to risk a dying patient's overhearing her discussing him, she rose and ushered Warner out of the room, where she spoke in a whisper. "No real change, Mr. Schuman. Last night was a little easier than the night before, and Mr. Nettleton ate almost a whole bowl of oatmeal for breakfast. That's always a good sign."

As good a sign as one could expect under the circumstances, he knew. "I have to go out of town rather unexpectedly," he told her. Half of him hated to leave right now, when Uncle Oliver could die at any minute. Yet he could see no real choice, not given everything that had occurred in the past couple of days. Warner couldn't afford to delay heading for Carmel a moment longer. "It's an emergency and I might have to be gone for a few days, but it can't be helped. Do you think—?"

The nurse shrugged her shoulders. "I've seen patients in Mr. Nettleton's condition live for several weeks. Then others—" She didn't finish her sentence, knew it wasn't necessary.

"I'll have a temporary help service send in a girl to answer the phone. It's going to be ringing quite a bit for the next few days," he said, gesturing with the rolled newspaper, "until this whole fiasco blows over. I don't want you or the other nurses taking time away from Uncle Oliver to answer it. And no comments to any reporters, understood?" If he were away in California, he couldn't leave the phone machine on; he wouldn't be able to get his own calls through, he wouldn't be able to reassure himself that Uncle Oliver was still breathing.

The nurse bristled. "I've never discussed any of my patients with the press and I'm hardly about to start now," she said testily. "All of us nurses employed by Cleghorn Medical Services are trained to exercise the utmost discretion."

"No offense intended, Lucille. I just wanted to make sure we understand each other."

Her sharp chin jutted into the air. "No offense taken."

"I'll stop in again before my cab gets here, to say goodbye to my uncle." Warner glanced back into the sickroom. The oxygen machine was still humming and Oliver Nettleton had not moved. *Where has your mind gone?* Warner wondered as he looked at the old man. *What do you know about everything that's happened?* If Uncle Oliver was lucky, he was living in some better, long-ago place when his body and mind still functioned normally. If not, the old bastard had to be living in his own hell on earth.

Either way, Oliver Nettleton wouldn't be living at all for much longer. Warner only hoped he would survive until he managed to locate the elusive grandson the old man had never seen. And, it now was clear, his newly discovered great-grandson, as well.

# THREE

THE PUBLICITY SURROUNDING DYLAN Nettleton's disappearance impacted upon the Carmel Police Department as well as upon Annabel and the Nettleton household in Chicago. At the police chief's behest, and with the help of a few colleagues, Sergeant Eileen Kopek spent much of her time fielding calls from news media across the country, trying to act as though she were on top of the situation when in fact she was beginning to fear she didn't have a clue. As yet, there was no proof any crime actually had taken place, so she remained largely responsible for investigating the case...providing there actually *was* one. After finding no trace of the young husband and father during a full day's examination of the coastline, the Coast Guard had given up its search and the other agencies were merely keeping an eye out for Nettleton. If he'd met his end in the sea, his body would eventually wash ashore. In any case, if he'd fallen from a Point Lobos cliff and was still in the water, he now was well beyond saving.

The TV and newspaper coverage prompted eighty-six calls from people claiming to have seen Nettleton anywhere from drinking at Paradiso's bar on Cannery Row to hitchhiking on Highway 68, halfway to Salinas. Eileen and a few colleagues checked out most, but each eventually came to a dead end without their locating the missing man.

At home in the evening, lounging in her comfortable terrycloth robe and sipping a beer, Eileen pored over both the day's local and national news coverage of the case, hoping for some lead she'd overlooked. Back at work the next morning, she knew she would feel even more pressure to come up with a solution to the mystery than she had the day before.

The Carmel P. D. had decided to keep Dylan's BMW for the time being and to run some tests on it. This case was too bizarre not to at least consider that someone, for whatever unknown reason, had murdered Dylan Nettleton and tried to make his vanishing from Point Lobos look like either a suicide or voluntary disappearance. So his red convertible, which had been towed from Point Lobos to the station house, was inspected thoroughly for fingerprints by the expert technician assigned to Carmel by neighboring Monterey's larger police force.

"Car's completely clean inside, except for the ranger's prints," technician Greg Lucas reported to Eileen after spending more than two hours dusting it.

She shook her head in disbelief. "How could it possibly be clean? There have to be *some* prints, from the steering wheel or the glove box or somewhere. Somebody drove that car to Point Lobos."

"Well, either that somebody wore gloves, or he wiped the entire car down after he got there. The only prints besides the ranger's and tow truck driver's are on the exterior of the driver's side door, and they're too small to be a grown man's, at least one of Nettleton's size, so I figure they're a woman's, or maybe a child's."

"Could be the wife's when she looked the vehicle over at Lobos. What about the gas cap? You check that for prints?" Eileen tried to think of any other easy-to-miss spots that might harbor evidence, although she still wasn't sure evidence of what.

Greg gave her an exasperated look. "Do seals shit in the sea?"

Eileen ignored the casual profanity. "What if Nettleton

had his car washed before he drove it to Lobos?" she asked. "Could that account for the lack of fingerprints?"

Greg removed his rubber gloves and tossed them into the trash. "Don't know about you, Sarge, but I've never had my car washed that thoroughly. I'm lucky if they bother to smear the dirt around on the inside of my windshield, never mind wipe down the whole interior like this. Even if they did clean everything, I'd still have to figure on picking up prints from whatever car jockey worked on it. Those guys have their hands wet all day long, and I've never yet seen one wearing gloves."

"Me, either," Eileen had to admit. "So the only logical explanation is that somebody didn't want us finding fingerprints on Nettleton's BMW."

"Question is, who?"

"Which is my problem, not yours. Thanks for trying, Greg."

"I need the wife's prints so I can compare them to those on the outside of the car."

"I'll call her to come in and give a statement this afternoon. We can print her then."

"Give me a holler when you've got them."

WHEN SERGEANT KOPEK requested that Annabel come to the police station to have her fingerprints taken, she agreed readily, providing that either Louise Zuckerman or her teenage daughter Missy would be able to babysit Nicky. The policewoman's explanation that they needed her prints to eliminate them from those found on the BMW made sense to her, and nobody wanted this mystery resolved more than Annabel did.

After she'd been printed, Kopek asked her to step into an interview room to help clear up a few loose ends, offering her a chair across the table from her own. Within less than a minute, a gray-haired man with black-rimmed glasses and a paunch joined them. "This is Sergeant Kline," Eileen said. "He's going to sit in for a few minutes."

Kline plopped down next to Eileen as she reached for a tape recorder and placed it in the center of the table. "I'm going to tape our little talk, Mrs. Nettleton, just to make sure we get everything straight afterward," she said. She pushed a red button on the recorder and Annabel heard a whirring sound.

She looked around the compact, institutional-green room and felt her tension increasing. Should this "little talk" concern her? And why was the stern-looking Sergeant Kline "sitting in?" Maybe she should call a lawyer. The only one Annabel knew was Maxwell Garrity, the man she'd consulted about divorcing Dylan, and she had no idea whether he handled criminal cases...assuming this was a criminal case. But surely, she told herself, nobody suspected her of any crime. She was merely the missing man's wife—the victim, not some kind of criminal.

Eileen Kopek raised her eyes from her notes. "On Tuesday night, Mrs. Nettleton, you and your husband had a fight. He punched you in the face, prompting you to call the police. Right?"

"Slapped, not punched. Like I told you at the time." Sergeant Kopek had been there, had taken the call; Annabel wondered why she was being asked to go over this again.

"Slapped, then. Hard enough to bloody your lip."

Annabel ran her tongue across the inside of her lower lip. It was still tender where her teeth had cut into it, but her lipstick now hid the remnants of the bruise on the outside. "Like I said on Tuesday, Sergeant, Dylan never hit me before. I guess he just lost it this time, but I—well, I wasn't about to put up with being slapped like that, I just wasn't." Annabel had seen too many other women—neighbors, a cousin, her mother's best friend—put up with being beaten by their men.

Sergeant Kline cut in. "What sent your husband over the top this time? I mean, what made this time different from the other times you fought?"

"There weren't really all that many other times," Annabel said defensively. She caught a glimpse of her face reflected in the mirrored wall facing her—a tall, blond woman with dark circles under her bloodshot eyes. The past few days had aged her; she looked closer to forty than thirty. She wondered whether the mirror was one of those one-way jobs, like they always had on television cop shows, and whether still more cops were observing them from the other side. "It's not like Dylan and I fought all the time," she added, thinking that she probably hadn't fought with him nearly often enough, hadn't stood up for herself the way she should have.

"I'm not implying you did," Kline said. "Every couple has disagreements. I just wondered what made this time special, or different."

"I—I'm not sure, really. Dylan started ranting about how that private eye, Jeffrey Link, found him so easily. He was very upset about that, but I have no idea why."

"You've moved quite a bit since your marriage, haven't you?" Eileen leaned back in her chair. Her expression remained friendly, encouraging.

Annabel nodded. "We met and got married in Maine, where I'm from. Then Dylan wanted to move to Florida and I didn't really protest—Portland holds a lot of sad memories for me—"

"Such as?"

Was this really relevant? Annabel wondered, glancing at the tape recorder. Yet she had nothing to hide; she'd always been an open person. "My younger brother died two months before I met Dylan—he'd had kidney failure since he was little." She swallowed hard. "He had a transplant, but it didn't work. And my parents—our folks had both been dead for many years. I had a job and I knew the people I worked with, of course, but I didn't have many friends in town anymore, not since high school." *No real friends, anyway.* "Most New Englanders pretty much keep to themselves and—well, I'd spent a lot of time at home with Erik, my brother—raised him, really, after our folks died."

Lately, Annabel had begun to wonder whether she was the kiss of death to those she loved. First her parents, dead in that horrible head-on collision on the interstate, then Erik, despite her giving him one of her own kidneys. Now, maybe Dylan was dead, too.

"What kind of job did you have?" Eileen asked her.

"Travel agency. Started as the secretary and worked my way up to travel agent." As a girl, she'd had ambitions of becoming a dancer on Broadway or in the movies, but after her parents died, she'd put aside her dream of moving to New York City to study dancing so she could care for Erik. She was far too tall, anyway, she'd chided herself. Who ever heard of a five-foot-ten-inch female dancer, at least outside Las Vegas? She certainly had never wanted to be a chorus girl.

Eileen smiled encouragingly. "Working as a travel agent sounds like fun. Bet you got to see a lot of the world."

Annabel began to trace a crack in the table with her index finger. "Truth is, I've probably seen more new places since I married Dylan than I did when I worked for TravelWorld," she said. "Only real trip I took before I was married was right after my brother died. Spent a whole month in Norway and Sweden, looking up distant relatives and seeing the towns our family came from a hundred years ago. Then I ran out of money and had to go back to work."

"And that's when you met your husband."

Annabel nodded, recalling the day Dylan had walked into

the TravelWorld, looking so tall and tanned, seeming so suave and self-confident compared to the boys she'd known back in high school. She could see he had money and class, just by the way he carried himself and the elegant clothes he wore. She'd booked a flight to Tampa for him, as well as a rental car and hotel room. When he mentioned he was considering moving to Florida if he could find a suitable house to lease there, she figured she'd never see him again. Still, when he suggested it, she agreed to go out for a drink with him after work. The drink led to a lobster dinner at the pier, which led to a romantic evening at his apartment.

Afterward, Annabel was forced to admit to herself that the only reason she'd been willing to spend the night with a virtual stranger was because she'd been so lonely for so long. She'd never done anything so risky before and she vowed she'd never do it again.

Before meeting Dylan, she'd never dated much; her life had been restricted to work and home, to earning a living and taking care of Erik. After he died, that home became as quiet as a tomb and she found herself starving for companionship, for all the good times she'd missed, for a man of her own to love. But even more than that, she needed a friend, someone she could really talk to. It was no mystery why she'd been so vulnerable to the charms of the handsome stranger who'd walked into the travel agency on that crisp fall day.

Unfortunately, her one moment of weakness had had heavy if predictable consequences, but that was no one's fault but her own.

By the time Dylan returned from Tampa three weeks after their first date, Annabel'd already begun to suspect she might be pregnant. Two weeks later, her suspicions were confirmed and, within two months of their meeting, she was married to Dylan and expecting his child. The day after their City Hall wedding—a quickie, impersonal ceremony with not one friend of either the bride or the groom in attendance—she quit her job, gave her landlord notice, donated her meager furnishings to charity, and packed her clothes to move to Tampa.

Three months later, the Nettletons moved again, to Minneapolis. Then, despite her advancing pregnancy, which by that time was plagued by medical problems, Dylan insisted upon moving again, this time to Denver. Just two weeks after they arrived, suffering from skyrocketing blood pressure, Annabel gave birth to Nicholas by emergency cesarean section. As soon as she was physically able, they moved to Santa Fe for a few months, and finally here to Carmel.

By the day of the fight and Dylan's disappearance, she had made another resolution—that she'd uprooted herself and her son for the last time. If Dylan wanted to move again, he would have to do so alone. Yet Annabel hadn't had a chance to issue her ultimatum. Instead, Dylan had gone ballistic over Jeff Link and stomped out the door.

The policewoman leaned forward, her elbows on the table. "Mrs. Nettleton," she asked, "with all the moving around, didn't it ever occur to you that your husband might be running away from something? Or somebody?"

"I—not at first. Maybe recently, I guess. I don't know. He always made it sound like he was just dissatisfied, like he hadn't found the perfect place yet, the place where he wanted to settle down and stay, but that someday he would."

Unsmiling, Sergeant Kline began asking questions. "But it's possible he was hiding from something, isn't it?"

"Anything's possible." Annabel had been forced to come to the same conclusion herself, yet she didn't want to admit it to this intrusive cop. "Look, if Dylan was running away, I haven't the foggiest idea what or who from. Could be anything from a messy divorce to some sort of crime, I suppose.

All I know is that he never told me." Her tired eyes began to mist. Dylan had never told her much of anything, and he never became that friend, that soul mate, she'd wanted so badly. Even as a married woman, she still didn't really have anybody to talk to.

Kline grabbed the file folder from his partner, turned a page, and quickly read something. "You planned to divorce Dylan, didn't you, Annabel?" he asked.

Annabel's head jerked upward. "I don't—maybe, I wasn't really sure."

"But you went so far as to consult a lawyer about it."

*How did this cop know about that?* "That's personal," she said, bristling. "I don't want to discuss it with you." *Louise, of course. Louise must have told her.* "You've been talking to my neighbors about me, haven't you?"

"It's our job, Annabel," Eileen said, her voice gentle and her expression sympathetic.

What was this, Annabel thought, a game of good cop-bad cop?

Kline charged again. "The truth is, Mrs. Nettleton, you went to see a lawyer about a divorce on the very day your husband hit you, didn't you?"

"That's *not* what caused the fight. All that stuff about his grandfather came up before I could even tell him about the lawyer. I never mentioned divorce, not once. After meeting Mr. Link, I decided to wait a while, to see if Dylan's inheritance changed things between us. There was no reason to rush into things."

Kline glared at her, his pale blue eyes icy. "You mean you decided to wait and see if you could get your hands on some of your husband's new-found money."

Annabel recoiled as though she'd been slapped again, this time by a cop. "Maybe I'd better call my lawyer," she said.

"If your husband is dead, all that money goes straight to your son, doesn't it, Annabel?"

Annabel grabbed her purse from the table and fished through it for her car keys.

"Which means it might as well be your money, right? Completely different than if you divorced Dylan and had to settle for mere spousal and child support."

Annabel shoved back her chair, screeching it across the scuffed green linoleum floor, and rose to her feet. "I'm leaving," she said. "I don't need to sit here and listen to you insult me."

Eileen Kopek shot her more aggressive partner a warning glance. "We're really not trying to insult you, Mrs. Nettleton. It's just that this is a challenging case and we have to consider every angle. It's our job."

"You have to admit you've got plenty of reason to want your husband dead," Kline added. "Forty million reasons, to be specific—particularly when you planned to end your marriage anyway."

Annabel swallowed an angry retort, threw open the door and charged out of the room. She managed to hold in her tears until she'd reached her car. Then she drove home to get Nicky, becoming angrier and angrier as she wound her way through the tree-lined streets of Carmel. She would give Louise Zuckerman a piece of her mind, too. Some friend she was, blabbing to the cops about her personal business that way.

# FOUR

"Just couldn't keep your mouth shut, could you?" After his red-eye flight from Chicago and long layover in San Francisco, followed by a change of planes and a short flight into Monterey Airport, an exhausted Warner Schuman was fuming at his private investigator. "I suppose it's too much to expect that people in your profession might actually have a code of ethics."

Jeff Link was sweating despite the cool, foggy morning air that had crept through the open doorway of the Pine Lodge's lobby, where the two men were talking. "Look, Mr. Schuman, if I'd known this thing was supposed to be such a big secret, I never would've talked to the press. But Dylan's wife had already spilled the whole—"

"You idiot! You confirmed everything she said and added a helluva lot more. You made what started out as an insignificant little local story into a national gossip frenzy, all because you couldn't keep quiet about Oliver Nettleton's private business. Business for which he's paid you quite handsomely, I might add." He began to pace across the lush Berber carpet, his long fingers squeezed tightly together in front of him. If he didn't keep his hands occupied, he feared, he would use them to throttle the chubby little incompetent standing before him.

An elderly woman leading a miniature greyhound on a leash walked slowly through the hotel lobby, pausing briefly to glance at the two men. Jeff turned his face away from her, worried that she had recognized him from his recent television appearance. Or maybe her interest had been piqued by Schuman's raised voice. His employer's criticism was patently unfair, Jeff thought. He *had* done his job, and he'd done it well. He'd envisioned the national publicity as a major coup for Discreet Investigations, a rare opportunity to attract lucrative future business. But now he could see the whole thing blowing up in his face, even his bonus evaporating if he didn't manage somehow to calm down his angry client. "I'm really very sorry you're displeased with me, Mr. Schuman," he said. "But I did the job you hired me to do—I found Dylan Nettleton—and I found him in record time."

"You found his *wife,* Link. You've never laid eyes on Dylan himself."

Link stiffened and tried to put the best possible face on the situation. "Technically, maybe, but I know where he lives and he'll turn up there sooner or later, count on that."

His arms now folded across his chest, Warner sighed with exasperation. "How can you possibly know that?"

Jeff lowered his voice. "This disappearing act started with a family squabble. It'll blow over. I talked to the Nettletons' next door neighbor, a Mrs.—" He pulled a slender notebook from his inside jacket pocket and consulted it. "—Louise Zuckerman. She told me there's been trouble lately between the Nettletons, that Mrs. Nettleton had consulted a lawyer about a divorce on the very morning I talked with her. Seems Dylan and Annabel—that's the wife—they had some kind of blowup when he got back from his business trip. He lost his temper and hit her. She called the police. By the time the cops got there, Dylan had split."

"Nice piece of gossip, Link, but that doesn't explain the abandoned car, or where Dylan is."

"My theory is he split because he didn't want to deal with

the cops. Understandable. Next day, he probably figured to throw a scare into the wife, you know—make it look like he met with an accident, or took a suicidal dive off the cliffs or something. Probably thought he'd show up a few hours later and she'd be so glad to see him she'd take him back, all is forgiven, that sort of thing. But it got out of hand. Story made the evening news and now he feels trapped. He'll come home eventually, but my guess is he's waiting for things to cool off."

"Interesting theory, but that's all it is. Tell me this, if you've got the situation all figured out—with all the publicity, why hasn't somebody seen Dylan and turned him in to the authorities?"

"Who says he hasn't been spotted? Thing like this, the cops get dozens of calls, sometimes hundreds, from people who claim they've seen the guy. It's not like Dylan's a mass murderer or something, so checking out every lead that's called in isn't going to get real high priority. By the time the cops get to wherever the guy was spotted, he'll already have moved on." Jeff began to relax. He could see his client's anger starting to dissipate as the tale he was spinning off the top of his head began to sound more and more plausible. "And don't forget, Mr. Schuman, this isn't Chicago. Carmel's a small town with just a few cops and they've got their hands full with other stuff."

Warner's surge of nervous energy was spent and suddenly he was bone-tired. He dropped onto the black leather sofa, perched his elbows on his knees, and lowered his balding head into his hands. If Dylan was still alive and planning to return, it had to be soon. The clock was ticking—old Oliver could die at any minute—and if he hadn't located Dylan before then… And now it seemed that Dylan wasn't the only possible heir. "Why didn't you tell me about the child?" he demanded, rubbing his aching eyes.

Jeff lowered himself onto the opposite end of the sofa. "Dylan's son?"

Warner shot a disgusted glance at Link. "No, the Baby Jesus, you idiot. Of course, Dylan's son—the baby in the newspaper photo."

"What about him?"

Warner's spine stiffened and he bolted upright as his anger surged back more forcefully than ever. "The child is a potential heir, Link. You didn't think that little fact was relevant?"

"I didn't know there was a kid until I saw the photo myself. I mean, the wife was alone in the house when I talked with her, and there weren't any toys or anything in the living room, nothing to tell me a child lived there." Jeff was tiring of Warner Schuman's harangue. The man was paying him to do a job, but he acted like he'd bought his soul rather than his services. "You hired me to find Dylan," he said testily, "so that's what I did."

"Need I repeat myself? From where I sit, it appears Dylan is still missing."

"So, I'll find him. It's just a matter of time."

"Time is precisely what we do not have," Warner replied. Locating Dylan before Uncle Oliver died was imperative. The baby was meaningless if Dylan was still alive. Unless the baby could be used in some way to lure its father back... Time was passing quickly. "I'm going to get myself a room here and get cleaned up. I've had a long, tiring trip. In the meantime, you're not going to find Dylan by sitting here, waiting for him to walk through this doorway."

"I'll head back over to the house, see if there's any sign of him. I can check the rest of the neighbors, too, see if anybody else might know where he's gone."

"I don't give a damn what you do or how you do it, Link. Just find Dylan."

THREE DOORS DOWN from the Nettleton house, Nell Verducci sat in her old silver Volvo with its Arizona license plates. She'd been positioned here for the past two hours, having moved her car around the block and changed parking places twice during the night, then chosen still another spot when she returned from a trip to town for breakfast. She'd felt safe enough sleeping in the car overnight—she always kept a rusty old crowbar under the front seat, just in case anybody tried to bother her—and this town had no street lights, so it was easy enough to hide in the dark. Actually, the remote chance of having to fight off a mugger or rapist in this sleepy burg didn't really worry Nell. What worried her was the police. The last thing she needed was to be hassled by cops wanting to know what she was doing here, yet she had to see things for herself. So she'd compromised by moving her car every few hours and hoping nobody would spot her surveillance.

This morning she'd used the breakfast shop's restroom to freshen up, but the night in the car had taken its toll. Her back hurt, she had cramps in her legs, and she still felt grimy. At fifty, she told herself, she was getting too damned old for this sort of thing.

So far, she'd observed the young woman she'd seen on the CNN report—unusually tall, blond, and pretty in a tired-looking sort of way—carrying a tow-headed toddler and a diaper bag into the house next door. The toddler must be the infant the man CNN identified as Dylan Nettleton had been holding in the photograph, Nell concluded. She saw the blond woman leave alone in a blue Honda a few minutes later, then return after slightly more than an hour.

When the blond parked in her driveway, Nell got out of her car and walked down the street, hoping to pass for a tourist on a casual stroll. It felt good to stretch her legs after the long hours in the car, and she wanted a closer look at her target. But before she reached the Nettleton cottage, the younger woman disappeared into her neighbor's house once more. As Nell headed back toward her car, she could hear raised female voices coming from an open window in the second house.

"...right do you have?" one demanded. "...my private life and it's none..."

"...the police, Annabel," replied the second voice. "Maybe I shouldn't have talked to them, but they scared me...made it sound like I didn't have any choice, so..."

Nell's stroll led her out of earshot and back to her Volvo just as a green Toyota pulled into the curb directly ahead of her. She climbed into her driver's seat and shut the door as a pudgy middle-aged man emerged from the second car. He glanced at her, walked up the path to the Nettletons' front door, and rang the bell. Nell recognized him as Oliver Nettleton's private investigator, the man who'd been interviewed by the television reporter about the inheritance. Briefly, she considered approaching him, telling him what she knew, but quickly changed her mind. She'd made her decision years ago, burned that bridge as a matter of sheer self-preservation. For now, she dared do no more than observe from a distance, un less and until she was forced to make a move.

So she started her car and drove away slowly. She needed a bathroom, and a quick bite to eat would do her good, too. Maybe by the time she got back, Nell thought, the private eye would be gone.

"BUT DADDY, you promised you'd take me to the aquarium to see the otters!" Ten-year-old Katie Garrity's round freckled face was pink with frustration and her blue eyes were moist. Like many local girls her age, Katie was obsessed with sea otters. Her room was decorated with posters of the furry creatures and she had far more stuffed otters on her shelves and bed than dolls. Now, in anticipation of today's promised outing, she was wearing her favorite sweatshirt, the one with the words, "Monterey Bay Aquarium," stenciled across the back and a picture of a cuddly-looking sea otter floating in a kelp bed on the front. "I've been waiting all week."

A wave of guilt washed over attorney Maxwell Garrity. "I know I did, sweetheart, but this is an emergency. My client is in trouble and I really have to help her out." Ever since his wife had died of ovarian cancer three years earlier, Max had tried to spend every evening and weekend with his only daughter and she'd come to expect large amounts of his personal attention as her birthright. That he was forced to go back on a promise today troubled him greatly. "Maybe we can go tomorrow," he suggested.

"But the aquarium's always too crowded on Sundays, and everybody pushes to stand by the glass. I won't even get close enough to see them feed the otters."

"We can go real early, before the crowds arrive."

"But—"

"Katie, I'm sorry, but we just can't go today." Max was beginning to lose patience. "My client is coming to talk to me about some very important business that simply can't wait. You have to understand."

Katie curled a lock of red hair several shades brighter than her father's more subdued color around her index finger. "You always have to work," she said, sticking out her lower lip.

"That's not true and you know it, young lady."

"If Mommy was here, she'd take me—"

"Kate, stop it!" Max knew his daughter was using her final weapon in an effort to make him change his mind, but he'd been unable to deny Annabel Nettleton's desperate plea for legal advice. He compromised by having his client come here to the house instead of to his office. His housekeeper-nanny, Consuela, worked only weekdays, so seeing Annabel at the office would have required finding a last-minute sitter for Katie.

The doorbell rang.

"You're just being mean, Daddy!" Katie yelled as she stomped out of the room and down the hallway. Just before the door to her bedroom slammed shut, the child muttered something that sounded like, "I hate you!" but Max told himself he'd misheard her. He opened the front door.

"Sounds like I've come at a bad time." Annabel stood on the doorstep with Nicky balanced on her hip.

"No, no, it's all right. My daughter had a little disappointment, nothing major. Although, when you're ten, I guess everything's major." He smiled and held the door open. "Come on in," he said, standing aside while Annabel entered.

"I hope it's okay I had to bring Nicky along," she said. "I didn't have a sitter." There was no way she was going to leave her son with Louise Zuckerman again this afternoon, not after learning that her neighbor had blabbed her private business to the police.

"No problem. Believe me, I know how hard finding a good sitter can be."

"Hi!" shrieked Nicholas, holding out a chubby fist. "Hi hi hi hi."

"Well, hello, young man." He shook the baby's small hand and grinned at his smiling face. "Good to meet you, Nick. Maybe my Katie's got some toys you can play with. What do you think of that?" Max hung Annabel's coat and Nicky's jacket on the coat tree in the entryway.

"Please don't bother your wife to entertain Nicky," Annabel said. "I brought a few things along to keep him occupied."

"Katie's my daughter," Max replied, "and it's no trouble. Betsy, my wife, she…she died three years ago." The words were still difficult to say. Not a single day passed that Max didn't miss her.

"Oh, I'm sorry." Annabel said. "I know how hard it is, losing someone you love."

Max turned and called down the hall, "Kate…Katie! Come out here a minute, please."

A moment later, a door opened and Katie ventured out of her bedroom, her eyes puffy and her round face streaked with tears. She clutched a stuffed brown otter against her thin chest.

"This is Mrs. Nettleton, Katie. She brought her son, Nicky, and I thought you might have some toys he could play with. Maybe you could show him your otters?"

"Hi hi!" Nicky called to the girl holding the cuddly toy.

Katie sniffled, then ventured closer. "Hello, Mrs. Nettleton," she said politely. "Hello, Nicky."

"Nice to meet you, Katie," Annabel said, pretending not to notice that the girl had been crying. She leaned over and put Nicky down on the floor.

"How old is he?"

"Just turned one," Annabel replied.

The girl crouched down in front of the little boy. "This is my friend, Ollie," she told him, holding out the otter. "Ollie likes little kids." She wagged the toy in front of the younger child. "Want to hold him?"

Nicky stretched out a hand and stroked the otter's soft plush fur for a moment, then grabbed it.

"I can take him back to my room and show him the rest of my collection," Katie offered.

"That'd be nice, sweetheart." Max reached over and ruffled his daughter's hair affectionately. Kate might be a little spoiled, he thought, but she was basically a good kid. "Okay with you, Annabel?"

"Uh, sure, I suppose, if Katie doesn't mind."

"Come on, Nicky," Katie said, taking the boy's hand. "Let's go see Ollie's friends."

Nicholas shot a worried look at his mother.

"It's okay, tiger. Mommy ll be right here."

The two children disappeared down and hall and into Katie's bedroom.

"She'll take good care of him," Max said. "Katie loves babies and this will give us some privacy." He led the way into his home office and offered Annabel a seat facing his large oak desk. "Now, start at the beginning and tell me everything that happened this morning."

Annabel described her visit to the Carmel police station and the way in which her interview had deteriorated to the point where she'd nearly been accused of murdering her husband. "I didn't know who else to call," she concluded, "so I called you. I don't know if you handle criminal cases, or even if this is a criminal case, but you're the only lawyer I know."

"I'm a general practice attorney. I've handled a few criminal cases in my time," Max said. He didn't add that his experience to date had been limited to defending half a dozen drunk drivers and a chronic shoplifter. The bulk of his practice involved family law, wills and estates, and property disputes. He probably should refer her to a lawyer who specialized in criminal law, he knew, but he wouldn't, at least not yet. There was something about Annabel Nettleton that made him want to keep her as his own client. Or maybe it was simply that her predicament stimulated a response from deep within him, a youthful enthusiasm he hadn't felt since law school. Annabel Nettleton seemed to have faith that his knowledge of the law could save her, and her faith was beginning to make a believer of him.

"So far it sounds like the police are just on a fishing expedition," he told her. "For all they know, your husband is alive and well and gambling in Las Vegas or surfing in Maui. But I don't want you to answer any more of their questions without me, understand?"

Annabel nodded. "There's one other thing…" she began, hesitating.

"What's that?"

"I don't know when I can pay you. I stopped by the bank this morning and it looks like I've got only a few hundred dollars in my checking account. If Dylan doesn't come home soon, I—I guess I'll have to get a job to pay the bills. Not that I mind—I always worked before I was married and I can work now—but it'll take me a while to find employment and daycare for Nicky and to start bringing in a paycheck."

Max couldn't help empathizing with his client. Whatever was going on with her husband, it certainly wasn't her fault. From what Annabel had told him when she'd consulted him about divorcing Dylan Nettleton, the man was a real control freak. Now the son of a bitch had left this poor woman in a terrible position—broke, plagued by national publicity, and under police suspicion—possibly for no better reason than because he'd been afraid of being charged with spousal battery. If there was one thing Max Garrity couldn't condone, it was men who beat up on women or children, and Dylan Nettleton was one of those men.

"Paying me is the last thing I want you to be worrying about right now, Annabel," he told her. "If anything else happens, if the police want you to so much as give them your name, you call me right away, agreed?" Although he didn't tell his client, Max thought there was a good chance that Dylan Nettleton really was dead by now, either a suicide or the victim of someone he'd been fleeing during all his moving around the country, and he was afraid Annabel might be railroaded on a bogus murder charge.

"Thanks, Max, really. I don't know many people here and it means a lot to me that—" Annabel took a deep breath, then coughed before going on. "It—it's been hard lately and this just means a whole lot."

"Don't mention it," Max said, getting up. He walked around the desk and placed a comforting hand on her shoulder. "Just take good care of little Nick and I'll do what I can to take care of you, legally speaking."

After Annabel and Nicky had left, Max praised Katie for being so kind to the toddler.

"It's okay, Daddy. He's cute and he really, really liked my otters."

"I've been thinking, Kate," Max said. "You were such a big help with the baby, and you and I didn't get to go to the aquarium like I promised. How about we go out and get a pizza for dinner?"

Katie's face lit up. "With extra cheese and mushrooms?"

"And onions and artichokes."

"And sausage, too, but no pineapple. That pineapple we had last time was yucky."

"No pineapple." Max held out his hand, palm up. "Deal?"

Katie slapped it. "Deal," she agreed, and ran to get her coat.

IT WAS DUSK by the time Peter Hoy and Gil Collier had located the Nettleton house. Gil drove the rental car slowly past the flower-covered cottage, then parked it out of sight in the next block. They shoved the remains of their takeout fried chicken into a box in the backseat and headed out on foot.

"With our luck, somebody's slobbering German shepherd will jump out of the bushes and we're history," Gil complained as they made their way carefully down the darkening street. There were no sidewalks in this part of Carmel and no streetlights anywhere in the quaint village, so they were forced

to walk along the street's uneven, cracked pavement in semi-
darkness broken only by the occasional house's porch light.

"Hey! At least we found the goddamned place."

Draped windows glowed with light at the front of the Nettleton cottage as the two men approached it. Avoiding the front
walk, Peter crossed the lawn, sidled up to the living room window, and peered in at the edge of the closed curtains. He
could see a blond woman in jeans and a green sweatshirt
lying on the floor, helping a small boy in a yellow blanket
sleeper build a tower of blocks. As the child added a final red
block onto the stack of blue and green and yellow rectangles,
the tower crumbled and crashed to the floor.

"Down!" the child shrieked, gleefully. "Bocks go boom!"

The woman smiled at her child. "Those blocks sure did go
boom, sweetie. Can you help Mommy put them away?" She
rose to a kneeling position and began to toss blocks into a
brightly colored circular carton. The boy quickly became
caught up in the task, throwing the blocks at the container with
abandon. More than half of his throws went well wide of
their mark, but he didn't seem to care. Cheerfully, he toddled
to retrieve each errant block to toss it again and again until
he'd accomplished his goal.

Gil pushed his way closer to the window so he could share
his friend's view, crushing a low bush against the side of the
house as he moved. "Is that—" he began in a whisper, but
Peter silenced him with an impatient gesture.

Peter moved slowly away from the window and motioned
for Gil to follow him around the side of the house. They
peered through the darkened windows of the unoccupied
kitchen and dining room before reaching a high redwood
fence. Finding it unlocked, Peter pushed the latch on the
fence's gate up slowly, then shoved the gate inward, entered
the backyard, and held the gate open for Gil to follow.

The two men stole across the damp grass and around the back of the house, where all of the windows were dark. Through the first one, they could see a baby's crib and dresser, along with the usual child's paraphernalia. They crept past it and peered through the window into another room, where they could barely make out a desk and bookcase along the north wall, with a computer table opposite. Suddenly the lights flashed on in the baby's bedroom, casting a brilliant white trapezoid onto the close-cropped grass. The two men quickly dropped into a crouch and hid in the shadows along the side of the building. As they waited, they could hear the woman's voice speaking to the child once more as she pulled the curtains tightly shut across the window, closing off their view.

Peter and Gil crawled along the damp grass beneath the baby's window and made their way back toward the front of the house. As they pulled the gate shut, it squeaked once, then the latch fell back into place. Sprinting across the front lawn, they reached the relative safety of the dark street.

"Damnit, Pete, he's not back yet. What're we gonna do now?"

"Patience, my man, patience. Asshole's gotta know the story hit the national news, so he's probably gonna lie low till he thinks the heat's off. For all we know, he's watching the place himself, to see if the coast's clear."

Gil swiveled his head around as though he might spot his quarry standing nearby, observing him. "Yeah, well, so what next, Einstein?"

"If I were him, I'd wait until well after dark so there'd be no chance the neighbors would see me."

"You don't think his wife knows where he is? We could break in there, sweat her a little. I bet she gives him up fast enough."

Peter shook his head. "Whoa, man, prison really did screw you up!"

Gil bristled and punched Peter's shoulder. "Hey, I didn't get a goddamned country club like you, asshole. Where they sent me, I had to watch some greaser knife my brother, and don't you forget it."

"Sorry, man. You know how I feel about what happened to Cliff. I miss him, too. All I meant is we can't start off roughing up a woman, certainly not one with a little kid. Hell, from what the newspaper said, she doesn't have a clue where he is, anyway. What we need to do is keep an eye on the house and watch for him to come home."

"What makes you think he'll come back?"

"Hunch, plus the kid. Remember how psycho he used to be about kids?"

Gil shrugged. "I guess."

"Well, I do. One time we were standing in line in the Safeway and we saw this man slap his kid in the face for sassing him or whatever. Superman takes it on himself to defend the kid and, shoot, I had to stop him from tearing the father's throat out. Trust me, Gil. This guy's never gonna walk out on his own kid. The woman, sure, in a nanosecond, but not the boy."

"Screw it, Pete, you damn well better know what you're talking about. We'll try it your way, but if he doesn't show pretty damn soon, I say we find out what the blond knows."

The two men continued arguing the point as they crept down the street and back around the corner toward their car. They never noticed the woman watching them from the old Volvo parked under the broad-branched cypress across the street.

THE RHYTHMIC whooshing sounds of the dialysis machine echoing in the background, Annabel crept silently into the hospital room, carrying a vase filled with daisies, irises, and pink roses she'd picked from the garden that morning. Erik lay motionless in the crisp white bed, tubes in his arms and his deep green eyes tightly closed against the daylight. His face wore a bluish-gray tint that reminded her of the sea in early winter. She set the flowers on the nightstand and took her brother's still hands in her own, rubbing briskly to warm them, but they remained icy to her touch. As she bent closer and kissed his cheek, she felt no puff of breath against her face.

"No! No!" she shouted to no one listening. "Help! Please help him!"

She ran out of the room, into the hallway, in search of someone—doctor, nurse, anyone—who could bring her brother back to her. But the hospital quickly disappeared, metamorphosing into the house where she and Erik had grown up, the one she'd later sold to pay the astronomical medical bills. The whooshing noise persisted here—wind whistling through the window screens. Yet Erik still lay motionless on his bed, his long, difficult fight lost at last. And, when she looked down, she saw blood gushing from a slash across her own abdomen, flowing in little rivers down her legs, flooding the floor around her feet. She began to feel weak, lightheaded. The whoosh-whoosh-whoosh became the beating of her own heart, as it rhythmically pumped her body dry.

ANNABEL AWOKE with a start, shaking, her breathing fast and her heart pounding. It had been weeks since she'd dreamed of Erik, of her futile battle to save her brother. He'd also been her best friend, maybe her only friend during those last few months. As she forced in a deep breath and felt her heartbeat slow, she lay still and listened to the sounds of the house. The wind had come up during the night, whipping the branches of the pines in the backyard and whistling around the eves of the cottage. *Whoosh! Whoosh!* The whooshing sounds must have triggered her subconscious thoughts of Erik. The familiar noises, plus the fact that the overpowering sense of help-lessness she'd felt as Erik declined toward death was now back. She felt helpless again, in her current predicament, as events careened out of her control and there was nothing she could do to stop them. She had no more power over Dylan and whatever game he was playing than she'd had in fighting the final infection that coursed through Erik's exhausted young body.

As Annabel lay in the dark, mourning the past and lament-ing the present, she heard another sound. Not a whistle this time, but a creak followed by a sharp click. Certainly that wasn't the wind, she thought. Was it the old house settling? She sat up in bed and switched on the bedside lamp.

Pulling on her bathrobe and lowering her feet over the edge of the bed into her slippers, she crept out of the bedroom and down the hall to check on Nicky. Had he called out in his sleep, waking her from her nightmare? Or perhaps rattled the slats of his crib? Another creak, followed by several clicks. If she didn't know better, Annabel would think there was some-one else in the house—another adult, not her tiny son. She told herself that she had to be hearing the night wind after all.

The door to Nicky's room stood wide open. She peeked in. By the glow of the nightlight, she saw her son sleeping on his tummy, three fingers clutching a corner of his favorite blan-ket as he sucked his thumb, the picture of toddler contentment. She'd lost Erik and probably Dylan as well, but she still had Nicky; for that she would be eternally grateful.

As she pulled the door partially shut behind her, Annabel heard a loud thump from the back of the house. *This was no wind.* Her heart racing again, she closed the door to the baby's bedroom and ran for the trusty knife still stashed in her book-case headboard. Her eye fell on the bedside telephone. For an instant, she considered calling the police. But the police were no longer her friends. And what if there was no real threat here, nothing more than a marauding raccoon or the wind toying with a loose cedar shake on the roof?

With the slight reassurance provided by her weapon, Annabel crept back down the hall, past Nicky's closed door, toward the third bedroom, the one used as Dylan's office. The door was closed, although she felt certain she'd left it standing ajar when she went to bed. Holding her breath, she twisted the doorknob and threw the door open.

The room was empty, but the window sash was raised and cold night air permeated the small space. *Someone has been here.* Her hands were clammy against the knife handle. She hadn't opened that window since well before Dylan's disappearance; in fact, she'd checked to see that every door and window in the house was locked before she went to bed.

Feeling frightened and violated, Annabel closed the window, then turned on lights throughout the house as she explored each room to see if anything had been disturbed or stolen. Could a random burglar have invaded her home? But how? There was no sign that either the front or rear doors had been forced, and there was no way the lock on the office window could have been opened from the outside, not without breaking the glass.

After checking that Nicky was still sleeping peacefully, Annabel returned to her husband's home office. Nothing seemed out of place here, either. But as she stood still in the center of the room, she heard a faint whirring noise, like a small fan running. Her eye fell on the computer. The monitor's screen was black, but the top of the machine felt warm to her touch. She depressed the monitor's "on" button and watched as yellow letters flashed across its screen: "It is now safe to turn off your computer."

Dylan, she thought. *Dylan was here, using his computer.*

*Either Dylan or someone who has his extra house key and his computer password.*

Should she could call the police? No, Annabel decided. She had no actual proof her husband had returned and, for all she knew, the cops wouldn't believe her. More likely, they'd think she was trying to create a phony alibi for herself, to convince them that Dylan was still alive. Better, she decided, to wait until morning and call Max Garrity for help. He would know what to do.

For now, Annabel carried a blanket and pillow from her bed and laid them out on the floor of Nicky's nursery. Wrapping herself in the blanket against the chill of the night air, she lay down, listening to the sounds of the house and gripping the butcher knife tightly, until the first faint light of dawn crept through the window.

# FIVE

AS NELL SLUMPED sideways in the driver's seat, trying to make herself as invisible as she could, her elbow smacked the container of Pepsi she'd propped on the passenger's seat. "Damn it!" she cried out loud as a full ten ounces of sticky, icy liquid soaked through the sleeve of her sweater and spilled onto the upholstery. She grabbed a small handful of paper napkins and sopped up the wet mess as best she could, but the sweet odor of Pepsi-Cola now permeated the car and her right arm was chilled to the bone.

That's what happens when you live in a car at your age, Nell told herself. She berated herself for the next five minutes. Had this impulsive expedition of hers resulted in her learning one damn thing of any value? She'd probably lost her job back in Arizona by now, after leaving her boss scrambling for a relief waitress to cover her shifts. And she had next to nothing to show for it.

One of the few things she'd learned over the past few days was that the blond woman and her child were living alone in the Carmel cottage—the husband still hadn't returned. And her hours of observation had convinced Nell that several other people were keeping an eye on the place as well. The private eye was easiest to spot; he'd been back three or four times since she'd begun watching the house. On each occasion, he simply marched up the front walk and rang the doorbell. If the blond woman was home, he questioned her for a few minutes. If not, he usually climbed back into his car and drove away.

Then there were the two younger men—one black-haired with Asian eyes and the other taller, brown-haired, with a wiry build—who had peered through the windows, then stolen around the back of the house, before escaping down the street.

At two different times this afternoon, Nell had spotted a somewhat older man whose face always seemed to be turned away from her. Impeccably dressed in a pinstriped gray suit, white shirt, and blue paisley-patterned tie, he parked his black Cadillac across from the house and strolled down the block and back again several times as his eyes furtively scanned the flower-covered cottage. His observation was far from subtle, but he never actually approached the door of the cottage. She couldn't help wondering who he was and what business he had there.

Nell didn't think any of the male observers had noticed her, or at least they'd given no sign that they had. Their attention had been on the small house and the woman and child living there. If they had seen her sitting in her old Volvo, Nell thought, they'd probably taken her for a homeless woman, a street person. With her messy, graying hair badly in need of a shampoo, her Pepsi-soaked sweater, and the litter that was quickly accumulating inside the Volvo, that assessment wouldn't be far from wrong. Ironically, she figured, masquerading as a car-dweller probably wasn't all that bad a disguise; homeless women were as invisible in today's America as anyone could possibly be.

Nell pulled off her sweater, rolled it into a ball, and tossed it into the back of the car. She dried her cold, sticky arm with Kleenex, praying that it was far too dark for anyone to see a brassiere-clad matron in a parked Volvo. As she yanked a dry blue-and-green-striped sweater out of the duffel bag on the backseat, she caught a quick motion in her peripheral vision. She turned to see a man sneaking along the opposite side of the street. Panicked that a cop was about to catch her half-naked at two o'clock in the morning on a stakeout she couldn't explain, she thrust her head through the neck of the striped sweater, then shoved her hand through the first sleeve. She heard the unmistakable sound of something ripping as the ring on her left hand caught on a loose piece of yarn and the sweater's sleeve began to unravel. "Damn!" she exclaimed again, this time more quietly. She yanked the sleeve free of her ring and frantically pushed her arm through it.

Should she start the Volvo's engine and drive away from her post or hope that the approaching cop hadn't seen her?

Before Nell had a chance to decide, the man, a tiny flash-light in his hand, strode past the parked Volvo with no sign that he'd noticed her. Maybe he wasn't a cop after all, she thought; at closer inspection, he didn't really look much like one—he was dressed in black from head to toe and that little light he was holding wasn't the half-weapon, half-flashlight sort the police always carried. She watched him move along the front walk, peek through the cottage's living room windows, then pull something—a key?—from his pocket and unlock the door. He quickly disappeared inside, pulling the door shut behind him.

Was this the man she'd been waiting for, or simply a burglar with a lock pick? Nell stiffened in her seat, not sure what to do next in either event. So she settled for watching and waiting. The house remained dark, despite the man's bold entry through the front door. Obviously, she concluded, he didn't want to wake the house's occupants. She watched the clock on her dashboard as it ticked past two-ten, two-fifteen, two-twenty, and finally two-twenty-five.

A light flashed on in the back of the small house. A minute or two later, Nell saw someone charge through the gate in the cottage's backyard fence and run toward the center of the street. She recognized the black-clad man who'd entered the house earlier. Now lights were coming on throughout the cottage. Had the woman awakened and scared off the intruder? Nell felt a pang of sympathy for her, alone in the house with her little son. At least the young mother was safe, she reassured herself; if she was walking from room to room, turning on lights, she obviously hadn't been raped and murdered in her bed.

Nell reached over and checked to see that her car doors were securely locked, then ducked down out of sight and grabbed her crowbar, just in case, as the man in black moved past her parked car and back in the direction from which he'd come.

But as the intruder reached the street corner, she sat up again and saw the ceiling light in another car flash on as two men threw open their doors and leapt out. She sat mesmerized while the two silently jumped the first man, forced him to the ground, then threw him into the trunk of their car, and drove away with their headlights dark. From assault to escape had taken less than three minutes.

Were the assailants the same two young men she'd seen sneaking around the cottage earlier? Or the PI and an accomplice? Or possibly the well-dressed older man with a cohort? The action was too far away for Nell to tell.

She felt a quick jolt of guilt. She'd obviously witnessed some sort of abduction. Surely, a responsible citizen would call the police. But not Nell Verducci. The police would have too many questions she couldn't answer, not without throwing away the entire life she'd created.

So she waited until a few minutes after the abductors had driven away with their quarry. Then she headed her Volvo out of town, turning south on Highway 1 and searching until she found a spot near the beach where she could park safely for the rest of the night.

If anyone else had seen the attack on the man in black and reported it, or if the blond woman had called the cops when she discovered her house had been invaded, Nell wanted to be sure she was nowhere near the area when sirens pierced its dark night air.

ANNABEL OPENED the door a fraction of a second after Max Garrity rang the doorbell. She'd been waiting anxiously for his arrival ever since phoning him at eight o'clock, the earliest hour she'd felt she decently could disturb him on a Sunday. He stood on the steps, holding his daughter Katie by the hand.

"Hi, Max, Katie. Thanks for coming," Annabel said, standing aside so the two could enter. "I'm really sorry I had to ask you to come on Sunday morning."

"No problem. You said you needed my help," Max said, as though he'd do the same for any of his clients. "Hope it's okay I brought Katie along. I promised her we'd go to the Aquarium this morning, and—"

"We didn't get to go yesterday, because you had that *other* emergency," the red-haired girl announced. "Daddy promised me we could go as soon as it opened this morning. This isn't gonna take too long, is it? 'Cause the Aquarium gets crowded real early, and I—"

*"Kate, please!"* This wasn't the first time his daughter's penchant for saying exactly what she thought had embarrassed Max, to say nothing of the mortification he could see appearing on Annabel's pretty face.

"I'm so sorry, Katie," she said, wringing her hands. "I didn't realize. I—I'll try not to keep your dad too long, okay?"

Obviously angry with her father for chastising her—*he* was the one who kept breaking promises, not her!—Katie stared sullenly at the floor. "I guess," she mumbled, her freckled face growing red.

"I'm sure Nicky will be glad to see you again," Annabel told her.

"I s'pose."

The girl pouted as Annabel led them into the living room, where Nicky had his blocks spread out across the floor. "Boom…boom…boom!" he said as he crashed a small toy car into a mass of red, yellow, and blue blocks, over and over again. "Boom…boom…boom!" The game was his version of bumper cars.

Annabel had managed to change Nicholas' diaper and feed him his breakfast before the Garritys' arrival, but the toddler was still wearing the yellow blanket sleeper he'd had on last night. Anxious to consult her lawyer about last night's trauma as quickly as possible, she'd called Max, then rushed through her own shower, thrown on a pair of brown jeans and a camel-colored sweater, and pinned her hair back with a heavy gold clip while her attorney was driving to her house. Her makeup was limited to lipstick and a hint of blush to hide a complexion pale from lack of sleep. "Look who's here to see you, Nicky," she said.

When his mother called his name, the little boy glanced up from his play. His face lit up as he recognized his young friend from the previous evening. "Hi!"

"Hi, Nicky."

"Katie, you'd be a really big help if you could keep Nicholas entertained here for a few minutes while I talk with Mrs. Nettleton," Max suggested. "That'd help me get my work done a whole lot faster."

"I guess." Katie dropped to her knees and began to balance some yellow blocks on top of the blue ones. "Come on, Nicky, let's me and you build a castle."

"Thanks, Kate," Max said. He turned to Annabel. "Why don't you show me the room where the break-in took place?"

She led the attorney down the carpeted hallway and toward the back of the house, quickly and concisely describing the events of the previous evening, but deleting her vivid nightmare and later unsuccessful attempt to sleep on the floor of the nursery. "I don't think the man came in through the open window," she explained when they reached the office, "I'm sure I locked it and the glass wasn't broken. I think he came in one of the doors and escaped through the window when I turned on my bedroom light."

"But you didn't call the police."

Annabel shook her head. "After my last experience with them, I want to stay as far away from cops as I can."

"Okay." Max nodded with understanding. "You're absolutely sure the window was locked properly?"

"Positive. I checked before I went to bed. But I couldn't find any sign that somebody had forced the outside doors open, either, so whoever was here must've used a key."

"I'll take a look at the doors myself, but you're probably right about the key. It could've been somebody using a pick on the lock, but that's probably looking for a zebra where a horse will do." Max stood in the doorway of Dylan's home office, rubbing his chin and marveling at the room's starkness. This place bore no resemblance whatsoever to his own home office—always a bastion of clutter and dust, despite the fact that he did most of his legal work downtown. What kind of business could the missing man possibly have run from here without generating a single visible scrap of paper? There wasn't so much as a desk calendar or telephone pad on top of the desk.

Annabel sighed. "I figure, if it wasn't Dylan, it had to be somebody who has his extra key."

"Has anybody cleaned this room since your husband disappeared?" Max asked.

Annabel shook her head. "He didn't like me to touch anything in here, so I pretty much stayed out." She blushed slightly. "I have to confess that I tried to access his computer the other night, when he didn't come home. But I couldn't get into it—I don't know the password."

Max found the woman's obvious embarrassment over her minor infraction rather charming. If he were Annabel, married to a secretive man like Dylan Nettleton, he'd hardly have waited for the bastard to disappear before he started snooping around in that computer. In his opinion, this "business office" looked fishy as hell. "Where'd Dylan keep that extra house key?" he asked.

"He had this little magnetic key box hidden in the engine compartment of his BMW."

"Know whether it was still there when the police towed the car into the garage?"

"I didn't think to ask. But Dylan must've taken the key out of the box before he left the car at Point Lobos, assuming he used it to sneak in here last night."

"Or somebody else took it." Max thought for a moment. "It's possible the police found the key in the car and used it themselves, although I don't really think it's likely. If they had grounds to search Dylan's computer, they'd get a search warrant. And anything they found by breaking in here wouldn't be admissible in court, anyway."

"There was a house key on the ring Dylan left in the car with his car keys," Annabel pointed out. "If the cops wanted a key to break in here, they could've used that one."

"Right, I forgot. So if the extra key is still hidden in the box in the car, that might tell us something. I'll check."

"There's one more thing I just thought of," Annabel said. "Dylan rented this house from a vacation rental company, so the real estate agent must have a key. Maybe some of the previous renters do, too, unless they change all the locks every time somebody new moves in."

"I doubt it. But why would somebody like that break in here without stealing anything? You said nothing was taken, right?"

"Not as far as I can tell."

Max switched on the computer. "Looks like we have to assume whoever was here last night wanted something out of this puppy." The machine made a whirring sound as it booted up. "What passwords did you try?" he asked.

"Just the obvious ones, I'm afraid—Dylan's name and date of birth, my name and Nicky's, Dylan's mother's name—Eleanor. None of them worked."

Max tried BMW, Carmel, California, each of the other towns and states in which Dylan and Annabel had lived during their short marriage, then all the days of the week and months of the year. "Could take forever like this," he admitted when nothing clicked. "If your husband was computer savvy and really into secrecy, he probably chose a password that isn't a real word at all, just a random combination of letters, or even a combination of both letters and numbers. There are programs that run all possible letter and number combinations until they finally locate the right one. That's how hackers manage to break into university records and Pentagon files and the like." He shut off the computer. "Would it be all right if I took this to an expert I've used in the past, let him see if he can get into it?"

Annabel hesitated. "You mean move the computer out of here?"

"Just for a few days."

She shot a guilty look over her shoulder, as though Dylan might be watching her. "What if my husband comes back while it's gone?"

"Tell him you're having someone examine the computer because you thought it might help you find him."

"I guess that makes sense." Annabel asked herself what she really had to lose. Even if Dylan did come back home and, predictably, got angry that she'd let her lawyer go off with his computer, did she still care? Surely he wouldn't dare become violent with her a second time, not when he knew she wouldn't hesitate to call the cops. "Why not?" she said. "Go ahead, see what your guy can find out."

Max carried the computer out to his car, which was parked in the driveway behind Annabel's Honda, and locked it in the trunk. When he returned to the house, he examined both outside doors carefully but, like his client, he couldn't detect any evidence that they'd been forced.

"You feel safe staying here?" he asked her.

"I—I don't know. I don't have anywhere else to go, really, not with so little money left in the bank."

Max felt a sudden impulse to lend Annabel enough cash for her and Nicky to move to a motel for a few days, but he quickly rejected it. He had to let her keep her pride and, besides, chances were already pretty good that he'd never be paid for representing her. How far into the hole could he afford to go on this case? "How about having a locksmith change the locks?" he suggested.

"I'll call the real estate company and ask them to do it." That way, Annabel figured, she wouldn't have to shell out what little cash she had to a locksmith.

"Call right away, promise?"

"Promise." She chewed on her lower lip.

"I'd like to have a private eye I sometimes work with dust that office for fingerprints, too." If the elusive Dylan had something to hide, Max figured, his fingerprints just might help them learn what it was. If he'd been hiding from the authorities, he undoubtedly had a rap sheet somewhere, and the PI he had in mind would find it. Dusting the room for prints might also tell them whether somebody other than Dylan had been there last night.

"Sure, when?" Annabel felt a little lighter as Max began shouldering part of her burden, taking charge of the situation, and suggesting ideas that either hadn't occurred to her or that she knew no way to implement on her own.

"I'll let you know—probably sometime tomorrow. My investigator's name is Benny Everhardt, used to be a cop in Monterey. Real compulsive about his work—plan on him staying a while—but he's the best there is around here." Max placed a reassuring hand on his client's shoulder; he could feel her trembling. "Don't worry, Annabel. We'll figure this out," he told her. "In the meantime, if I know what's good for me, I'd better get my own little compulsive personality over to the Aquarium before she misses the otters' feeding time." He flashed a smile and was pleased to see Annabel try to return it.

"I really appreciate your coming over so fast," she told him.

"It's what I do." Which wasn't completely true in his mundane law practice. But it was Annabel Nettleton's plight that was giving him a sense of satisfaction, a feeling of being useful, plus a much-needed rush of adrenaline, just now. "Come on, Katie," he said as they reentered the living room. He glanced at his watch. "If we hurry, we can still make the noon feeding."

"*Okay!*" Katie leaned over and planted a fast kiss on Nicky's cheek. "Sorry, Nicky, me and my dad gotta go."

"Da?" Nicky asked, looking around. "Dada?"

"Katie means *her* daddy, not yours," Annabel explained.

"Dada!" Nicky demanded as Katie and Max headed for the door. "Dada!" He placed a final block atop the half-finished castle he and his red-haired pal had been building. Instantly, the structure crashed to the floor, scattering blocks in all directions. The little boy's face crumpled. He turned and saw his playmate rushing away from him, escaping through the front door, then looked around once more for his daddy, but he was nowhere in sight.

With his immediate world crashing down around him, Nicholas burst into tears.

"TWO FIFTY," said the clerk the next morning, when Annabel showed him the bread she'd selected from the baker's rack.

Expensive, but she rationalized that the loaf of Il Fornaio's still-warm, flour-dusted *ciabatta* was her indulgence for the day, a small dose of mouth-watering luxury to help her forget the weekend's break-in and the nervous hours following it. She'd left a message for the vacation rental service yesterday, explaining that she wanted the locks on the cottage changed as quickly as possible. If they did it today, undoubtedly she would sleep more easily tonight than she had for the last two. Fishing two singles and a couple of quarters from her wallet and handing them over to the sales clerk, she realized with a pang that she now had less than ten dollars left in her purse.

With Nicholas perched on her hip and the bag of bread dangling from her hand, Annabel left the bakery and headed for the cash machine down the street, just outside her bank. Using the machine instead of standing in line to cash a check would save time and she wanted to get back home to see if the rental agency had returned her call. And Benny Everhardt, Max's PI, was due at two o'clock to fingerprint Dylan's office.

After lowering her son to the sidewalk to free her hands, she inserted her bank card in the cash machine's slot, punched in her identification number, and requested a hundred dollars. There should be about four hundred left in the checking account, she recalled, an amount she would have to budget very carefully if she and Nicky were to survive until she found a job.

The machine emitted its customary clicks and whirs before spitting out five twenty-dollar bills. She thrust them into her wallet, feeling temporarily flush again.

She punched "no" when the machine asked her if she wished a second transaction, then "yes" when it asked if she wanted a receipt. Whenever she made a cash machine withdrawal, Annabel took the receipt and inserted it among the bills in her wallet as a reminder to record the transaction in her checkbook. The last thing she needed right now was to forget to record a withdrawal and end up bouncing checks.

"Dog!" Nicholas screeched, as he spotted a passing gray poodle on a leash. "Doggy, Mama, doggy!"

As Annabel grabbed the slip of paper from the machine, Nicholas took off after the poodle.

"Nicky, stop!" The receipt and the loaf of bread dropped to the pavement as Annabel spun around and dashed after her son. "Stop!"

Not for the first time, Annabel was grateful for her long legs. She managed to catch Nicky by the hood of his jacket before he'd gotten six feet away from her. Trembling a bit, she let go of the little jacket and grasped Nicholas' hand to keep him from escaping again. The incident was minor, but it reminded her how easily she could lose her son. In other circumstances, the six feet he'd traveled before she caught him might have gotten him hit by a car or snatched by a kidnapper. She crouched down beside him. "You have to stay with Mommy, Nicky." His attention still riveted to the dog, he tried to pull away.

"Here, miss. You dropped these." A silver-haired man in a charcoal business suit, three library books tucked under his arm, bent down and retrieved Annabel's bread and cash receipt.

"Oh—thanks a lot." She stood up and took her things from the man's outstretched hand. "I appreciate it."

The silver-haired man grinned at Nicholas. "Your little guy looks like a real handful."

"He loves dogs." And squirrels and cats and rabbits and just about any other creature you could name, she thought but didn't say. She tightened her grip on Nicholas' wrist as he continued trying to twist away and resume his pursuit of the poodle.

"Doggy," he said.

"My son was the same way—curious about everything and practically fearless when he was small. His mother wanted to put him in one of those harness and leash things, but I wouldn't allow it. 'A child is not an animal,' I told her."

"You have a point." But privately Annabel wondered whether something like that was really so bad if it kept your child safe and alive.

"When he grew up, our Alex became a fighter pilot." The man's smile faded. "Went to Vietnam."

Annabel wasn't sure what to say. Had the man's son never returned from Vietnam? If so, she felt sorry, but she had her own share of troubles right now and she was in no mood to start taking on a stranger's. "Well, thanks again," she said, lifting Nicky back onto her hip. "Come on, kiddo, it's almost lunch time." She turned and smiled at her helper. "Bye now."

"Take good care of that boy," he replied. "They grow up far too fast." His smile turned wistful. "And then they're gone."

As Annabel walked back to her car, she glanced at the cash machine receipt to double-check her bank balance and stopped short. There had to be some mistake. When she'd last withdrawn cash, last Thursday before heading to the grocery store, she was certain the balance had been slightly more than four hundred dollars; now it should be the same amount over three hundred.

*But the balance printed on her receipt was $50,317.29.*

She spun on her heel and headed back to the bank. This time she pushed through the door and waited in line. Nicky squirmed on her hip, but Annabel refused to let him down. If she had to chase him again, she would lose her place in line and have to start over again, and she wanted to get home.

"I'd like to verify this balance," she said, when her turn at the counter finally came. She handed the small slip of paper to the teller, a painfully thin young man with huge hands and an acne-scarred complexion. A rectangular plastic tag clipped to the pocket of his white shirt identified him as Miles Vanderbilt—an oddly aristocratic name for such a gawky young man, Annabel thought.

He typed something on his computer keyboard. "That balance is correct," he told her a moment later.

"But it can't—I mean, could you check the last deposit, please?" How could an extra fifty thousand dollars have shown up in her account over the weekend?

More typing. "Here it is, Mrs. Nettleton," Miles Vanderbilt said, swiveling the computer monitor around so that Annabel had a partial view of the screen, "Wire deposit of fifty thousand dollars received at three o'clock Sunday morning and credited to the account first thing this morning. Bank policy is to credit the account on the first business day after the wired funds are received."

Shocked, Annabel couldn't think what to say. Could she really be fifty thousand dollars richer? If so, she wouldn't have to find a job immediately after all. And she could pay Max Garrity a retainer, too. But what if this was a mistake? Or even worse, some kind of cruel joke?

"Is there anything else I can help you with, Mrs. Nettleton?" the teller asked.

His words brought Annabel back from her reverie. "I

guess—I mean—" She hesitated. She wanted this money terribly—it seemed the answer to a prayer. But if this deposit had been meant for someone else's account, she knew she couldn't keep it. If she spent money that wasn't legally hers, she might even end up in jail, and then what would happen to Nicky? "Can you check where the wired money came from?" she asked.

The print on the screen scrolled down as the teller read through it. "Foreign transfer," he said, "just like all these others. Only difference seems to be the size—the previous deposits to this account were all under ten thousand dollars."

Annabel vaguely remembered hearing somewhere that banks were required to report deposits above ten thousand dollars to some government agency, maybe the IRS or the police or possibly even the DEA. The policy was designed to catch money launderers or tax cheats or something—she hadn't paid much attention at the time, but now she wished she had.

"Is there something wrong?" Miles Vanderbilt asked, eyeing the lengthening line of customers behind her.

"Uh, no, thanks," Annabel said. "I just wanted to make sure when I could start writing checks on this money."

"That's no problem—right away. Wire transfers are the same as cash deposits, so there's never a bank hold."

As she stumbled out of the bank and back onto the street, Annabel's thoughts were a jumble and she felt numb all over. She barked her hip on one of the news boxes lined up on the sidewalk and a sharp physical pain jolted her out of her mental fog. Nicky began to whine and wiggle to be let down and she realized she'd been squeezing the child's leg unconsciously. "Sorry, Nick," she said, loosening her grasp. "Let's go home."

It had to be Dylan, she thought, as she buckled Nicholas into his car seat. That's why he'd wanted access to that computer. He'd obviously used it somehow to transfer money from—from where? Nowhere she knew about. This was money he'd hidden from her, hidden somewhere he could access it by computer.

He could have transferred it from a business account, she told herself, a legitimate business account. But something the teller had said put the lie to that theory. What was it? Oh, yes—this was a *foreign* transfer.

*"Just like all these others."*

She was married to a man who hid money in foreign accounts and transferred it into the U.S. in amounts below what the bank was required to report to the authorities.

Not for the first time, Annabel had to acknowledge that she was married to a man about whom she knew next to nothing.

She started the car and drove back across town toward the cottage. At least now she could pay next month's rent, and buy groceries and gas for the car, she told herself. She should be grateful and, at some level, she was. Maybe this was Dylan's way of providing for her and Nicholas while he was away—wherever he'd gone. Or his method of using whatever savings he had to support his family until he received that big inheritance from his dying grandfather.

But the newfound money didn't really make Annabel feel particularly relieved. She couldn't help thinking about what could happen when the bank reported that large deposit to whomever it was required to tell about such things.

All she could think about right now was what she would do or say when some authority or other came knocking on her door, demanding that she explain the source of that mysterious fifty thousand dollars.

WHEN SHE PULLED the Honda into the driveway of the cottage, Annabel found no locksmith waiting. With luck, she thought, the rental agency could still get one here this afternoon.

She and Nicky entered the house through the kitchen door. She set the bread on the table, then removed Nicky's jacket and her own. As she hung them in the coat closet, she noticed a foul odor in the air. "I think you need your pants changed, little man," she said, wrinkling her nose.

Nicky looked up at her and laughed.

"Think it's funny, do you?" She laughed back at him, planting a quick kiss on his nose. "I'll take care of you as soon as I check the phone."

Nicky toddled off down the hall while Annabel returned to the kitchen and picked up the telephone receiver. She dialed her voice mail number and learned that she had one new message, but it was from Max's private investigator, saying he wouldn't be able to fingerprint Dylan's office before tomorrow morning. Feeling annoyed about that delay as well as the vacation rental agency's lack of response to her request, she resolved to call the agency again after lunch. Now that she had the fifty thousand, of course, she could hire her own locksmith if she had to. But she didn't like being ignored, and she'd never been one to squander her money—the circumstances of her life had always forced her to be careful with a dollar. If there was any way she could get the real estate agency to take responsibility for changing the locks, she would.

After this morning's visit to the bank, however, the home security project she'd discussed with Max no longer seemed quite so urgent. Annabel now felt certain her intruder the other night had been none other than Dylan. That knowledge made her feel a little safer—better her own husband, no matter what their differences, than some stranger entering her house in the middle of the night. She had no idea what game he was playing, but at least now it seemed obvious that Dylan hadn't fallen off a cliff at Point Lobos, or even left town—at least not prior to early Sunday morning.

"Dada!"

As she headed toward the nursery, Annabel heard Nicky's singsong voice. It was as though the child had read her thoughts, had sensed she was thinking about Dylan.

"Dada!" Nicky said again.

What was the boy up to? "Nicky, come on," she called to him. "We've got to get your diaper changed." The foul odor had begun to permeate the entire house. She hoped her son didn't have a sudden case of diarrhea. Caring for a sick child right now would be an added burden she just didn't need.

"Dada, Dada pay."

Annabel had to smile. Unable to pronounce the letter L, Nicky pronounced "play" and "pay" exactly the same way. The toddler's unintentional pun amused her. Daddy might indeed *pay*—as evidenced by the fifty grand he'd deposited into the checking account—but he wasn't likely to *play* with his son anytime soon.

Unless— *He couldn't be back, could he?* Her smile died and she felt a strong sense of foreboding as she rushed down the hall.

*"Dada, pay!"*

Annabel glanced into the nursery, but it was empty.

*"Dada!"*

She realized that Nicky's insistent shriek was coming from behind the half-closed door of the master bedroom. "Nicky?" she called. Her heart in her throat, she pushed the door open and stepped into the room. The nauseating stench was far stronger here.

The scene that greeted her was almost too much to take in all at once. Too small to climb up on the king-size bed by himself, Nicky stood at its edge, yanking on the blue-and-yellow flowered bedspread with both of his small fists. As her mind grasped why, Annabel's hand flew across her mouth and she had all she could do not to lose her breakfast on the plush egg-shell-colored carpeting. She grabbed Nicholas by the arm and dragged him away from the bed.

*"Dada!"* he screamed, fighting her.

*"Nicky, no!"*

She forced herself to look at the bed a second time. There, lying on his back across its center, ashen-faced and still, was Dylan. The butcher knife Annabel had stashed in the bookcase headboard for protection protruded from the center of his chest.

"Dear God," she muttered, swallowing bile. From the strong odor in the room, there was no question that Dylan was dead, and probably had been for some time.

Scooping up Nicky, she ran out of the room, yanked the door shut after her, and set the child down in the hallway. With her small son's wrenching pleas for his father echoing in her ears, Annabel fled into the bathroom and fell to her knees in front of the toilet bowl, vomiting food and fear until she collapsed on the floor in exhaustion.

# SIX

AFTER SHE PHONED MAX, Annabel stayed in the kitchen. With the windows wide open for ventilation and the door to the rest of the house closed, the stench of death wasn't quite so strong. Her hand trembling, she peeled a banana and cut it into chunks, then nearly dropped the peanut butter jar on the tile floor as she tried to open it. Willing herself to calm down, she barely managed to spread peanut butter and apple jelly on bread to make a sandwich for Nicky's lunch.

The sight and odor of the food nauseated her all over again. There was no way she could force anything into her own stomach, but Nicky had to eat. Luckily, she thought, the poor little guy didn't realize what he'd witnessed, and he was so young that the sight of his father's dead body wouldn't haunt him for the rest of his life. Would it? She'd read somewhere that people didn't retain memories from their lives before the age of three. She prayed that piece of trivia was true. If not—well, she didn't even want to think about that.

She heard footsteps on the front walk and the doorbell rang. She stiffened and caught her breath—what if it was the locksmith? *Get a grip,* she told herself. If the locksmith had arrived, she'd simply have to send him away, tell him she was ill or something. Actually, that much was true. Her symptoms might be a hundred percent psychological, but she felt sicker now than she had in years, including those last difficult days of her pregnancy.

She saw that Nicky was secure in his high chair, busily stuffing pieces of bread into his mouth. Peanut butter and jelly were stuck to his fingers and smeared across his face. He would need a bath before his nap, but he couldn't nap in this house, not when his father lay— Annabel pushed that problem out of her mind; she would have to deal with it later. "Mommy'll be right back, sweetie," she said. "I'm just going to answer the door."

For a moment, Nicholas stared after his mother anxiously, then he returned his attention to his lunch as the kitchen door closed behind her.

With relief, Annabel saw that her visitor was Max Garrity. She opened the door wide and stood aside as the attorney entered.

"Thank God you're here," she said, meaning it. "I was too afraid to call the police—they're going to blame this on me, I just know they are."

Max placed a comforting arm around his client's shoulders. "Let's take this one step at a time," he said. "You were right to call me. I'll notify the police as soon as I assess the situation."

Annabel glanced toward the back of the house. "Do I have to go back in there?" she asked. She felt like a coward, but she didn't care—she just couldn't make herself look at Dylan's dead body again, not unless she absolutely had to. Maybe she was ready to divorce him—at times she'd even come to hate him. But Dylan Nettleton was still the man she'd once cared for, the man with whom she'd once planned to spend the rest of her life, the father of her child. And now he was dead, brutally murdered in their marriage bed. She didn't have to see him there again—the sight of his prone body, the butcher knife in his chest, would be branded on her memory forever.

She noticed Max looking at her, a quizzical look in his deep blue eyes, and felt embarrassed by her weakness. "It's just that

I—I left Nicky alone in the kitchen," she said, "and I don't like to leave him in his high chair when I'm not with him. He could try to climb out and fall or—"

"It's okay, Annabel. You don't have to come with me. Go be with your son." He squeezed her shoulder quickly and released her. "I'll check things out myself."

Relieved that Max once again seemed to be taking charge of a difficult situation, that she could defer to someone who knew how to handle it, Annabel rushed back into the kitchen, shutting the door behind her.

MAX PULLED a handkerchief from his pocket and held it over his nose and mouth as he headed toward the rear of the house. He passed the nursery and office that he'd seen yesterday. The closed door had to be the master bedroom. He could have let his nose lead him there, he thought, using the handkerchief to keep his fingerprints off the doorknob while he opened the door.

As he spotted the corpse on the bed, Max nearly turned around and left. No matter how much he'd tried to prepare himself for this moment after receiving Annabel's frantic phone call, it hadn't worked. He'd never seen a real murder victim up close before—he was no Johnny Cochran or Vince Bugliosi. He hadn't even seen all that many dead people during his lifetime. There were his parents and his wife, of course, but they had died in clean white hospital beds. They hadn't smelled like this, either, not when he saw them. The only other dead bodies he'd seen were at funeral home visitations, where the corpses were embalmed and painted and coifed and dressed in their holiday best and the viewing rooms were filled with fragrant lilies. This was not the same at all.

The knife—the one Annabel admitted she'd kept for protection—was impossible to miss. Its black handle protruded at least six inches from the corpse's chest. At first glance it seemed obvious that his client's missing husband had been stabbed to death.

Yet as Max stared at the body, he could see that there was no obvious pool of blood around it. He leaned closer, fighting not to gag from the sight and smell. The knife was thrust through the sweater the corpse wore, a thick light blue crewneck style, probably cotton, but there was no visible red stain surrounding its handle. Could someone be stabbed to death in this manner and suffer only internal bleeding? Maybe the fact that Nettleton was lying on his back made a difference, or maybe the bedding and mattress beneath the body had soaked up all the blood. Max didn't know.

But one thing he did know, if only from reading mysteries and watching crime movies—this man had been dead far longer than the couple of hours Annabel said she'd been away from the house this morning. No corpse only an hour or two old could possibly stink this badly. The odor in this room— which was quickly wafting throughout the entire house—was the unmistakable odor of human decay.

Either this body had been moved into the house well after death, or—Max hesitated to consider the other alternative, but he had to. If this man had died where he now lay, Annabel had to be lying. And, if she was lying about when she found the body, he figured, she was lying about killing her husband as well. Had the dead man been lying here yesterday morning while Max was inspecting the office down the hall? While Katie played with Nicky in the living room? If so, Annabel was some kind of monster, and he simply couldn't believe the vulnerable-looking young woman he was getting to know could possibly fit that description.

Finally averting his eyes from the corpse, Max surveyed the rest of the bedroom. Nothing seemed out of place, as far as he could tell. A framed baby picture, a small jewelry chest, and an earring tree rested neatly on the dresser top. To the attorney's eye, all the earrings displayed on the tree appeared to be tasteful but inexpensive, probably not worth stealing. The dresser drawers were all closed, as were those of the two nightstands. The closet door was shut as well. Max opened it, careful not to leave fingerprints. The right side of the closet held women's clothing while the left held men's. Shoes were neatly lined up on the floor beneath the hanging items.

The bedroom window was locked—as in the earlier invasion of the house, whoever had brought the body here undoubtedly entered through a door, using a key. There seemed to be no sign that the bedroom had been searched or that anything had been removed.

To Max, the only significant thing here was not what might have been taken away. It was what had been added.

Relieved to leave the room at last, he pulled the door closed behind him and quickly moved on to Dylan Nettleton's home office. The room looked as pristine as it had yesterday morning. More so, in fact, because the computer now was gone, leaving the top of the computer table bare.

He needed to call Harry, see if the electronics expert had been able to come up with Nettleton's password and open the computer's files. The police were certain to confiscate the machine as soon as Annabel told them about the break-in, and Max wanted to know what it contained before they did. There was a chance that Harry would have some results by now—he'd had the computer since late yesterday afternoon and had promised to start working on it right away.

Again being careful not to leave fingerprints, Max picked up the phone and dialed Harry's number, but got only his voice mail. "Harry, it's Max," he said into the phone. "Listen, I don't mean to rush you, but I need to know whether you got into that computer I left with you yesterday. Going to want a printout of everything that's in it, too, ASAP. And expect a call from Benny Everhardt. I want him to see if he can find fingerprints on the computer, so try to keep your hands off everything but the keyboard. Page me as soon as you get this and give me a status report." He left his pager number and hung up, then dialed Benny to tell him this afternoon's appointment at the Nettleton house was off, directing him to Harry's computer shop instead.

Finally, straightening his shoulders, he dialed the Carmel Police Department and asked to speak to Sergeant Kopek.

WITH NICKY PERCHED on her hip, his small mouth still smeared with peanut butter and jelly, a frantic Annabel pounded on her neighbor's front door.

When Louise opened it and saw who was there, her face froze. "Didn't expect to see *you* again anytime soon," she said coldly, starting to close the door again.

Annabel burst into tears. "Please!" she cried, now abjectly sorry she'd read Louise the riot act after finding out she'd told the cops details about her personal life. "I'm sorry I got so upset with you the other day, Louise. It's just that—" She wiped her eyes with the back of her hand, aware that Nicky was picking up on her distress and had begun whimpering. "Can I come in? *Please*. Something awful has happened. I really need help and I don't know where else to go."

Louise's manner thawed slightly. She opened the door and motioned for the mother and child to enter. "This better be good," she said.

After sending Nicky to play in the nursery with Jason, Annabel followed Louise into the kitchen, where she detailed the morning's events.

"My God! What are you going to do?" Louise asked, her eyes wide with horror.

"I don't have any idea. Just try to get through this, I guess. The police are sure to be here any minute and there's no way I can let Nicky witness that," Annabel said. "For all I know, they'll arrest me for murder. But I didn't do it, Louise, I swear I didn't!" Tears now cascaded down Annabel's cheeks.

Louise put her arm around her taller neighbor's waist and waited until her sobs had subsided. "Don't worry," she said. "I believe you. And Nicky can stay here as long as it takes to straighten this thing out. Now you'd better pull yourself together before you have to face the police."

"I—I know. Mind if I use your bathroom to splash some cold water on my face?"

"You know where it is."

When she returned to the kitchen, which now smelled of freshly brewed coffee, Annabel felt slightly more composed and her face wasn't so red. At least Nicky won't have to witness me being hauled off to jail in handcuffs, she thought, or have to live in some foster home while I stand trial for murder.

"How about a cup of coffee to fortify yourself before you go back over there?" Louise asked, pouring a stream of dark, steaming liquid into a heavy blue mug.

Annabel shook her head. "Thanks, but my stomach's so queasy I don't think I could keep it down. I better get back before my lawyer thinks I've become a fugitive."

Louise walked Annabel to the door. "About the other day," she said, "I'm sorry, too. I'm plenty old enough to know how to keep my mouth shut, but every so often I guess I have to be reminded."

"Let's just forget about it. And thanks for taking Nicky, Louise. Honestly, I don't know what I'd have done without…" Annabel's eyes began to fill again.

"Hey, no more waterworks," Louise said with a nervous smile. "Just go back home and deal with the police. Nicky's safe and sound with us for as long as it takes." She squeezed Annabel's hand in encouragement. "And if you need a place to stay for a while, you're welcome to use our guest house."

Louise's sudden generosity made Annabel a bit uncomfortable. She didn't like being beholden to people, but she didn't have much choice right now. She had to think of Nicky and the future. "Thanks," she said, "I really appreciate it."

"Hey, Sid's leaving for a three-week sales trip to China in the morning. It'll be lonely around here. I can use the company."

As Annabel left the Zuckerman house, she saw two Carmel police cars now parked on the street and an unmarked sedan with official license plates being jockeyed into a parking spot. She straightened her spine, took a deep breath, and headed back to what had once been her home but now had turned into a house of horrors.

"SORRY, THAT'S all my client has to say, folks," Max said after Annabel had explained that she'd been out all morning with her small son and returned to find her husband's dead body in their bed. "If you have anything else to ask, you can ask her through me." Under Max's direction, the brief discussion had been limited to today's events; nothing had been revealed about the earlier break-in. He wanted a chance to find out what was in that computer before the police learned of its existence.

When the cops had arrived at Annabel's house in response to his call, Max was relieved to learn that the sharp-tongued and suspicious Sergeant Kline was busy with another case. Instead, Rupert Morrison, the tiny village of Carmel-by-the-Sea's sole detective had accompanied Sergeant Eileen Kopek. Morrison was a fiftyish man with a fringe of graying brown hair surrounding his shiny bald pate. Everyone called him Morrie. Now the four of them were sitting in Annabel's kitchen, the windows wide open to air out the putrid odor emanating from the bedroom. In the rest of the small house, a forensics team borrowed from the nearby larger city of Salinas was hard at work.

"Mrs. Nettleton'll be better off if she tells us everything she's got to say right now," Morrie advised. "You know the spouse is always a major—"

"But," Annabel began to protest, "I don't *know* any—"

"*I'll* speak for you from now on, Annabel," Max reminded her. He turned to the police. "This poor woman has been through more than enough for one day. She just found her husband dead, for God's sake. I don't want her questioned anymore, not until she's had a good rest. I'll let you know when that is. Trust me, you're not going to find any grounds to arrest her for anything…particularly once the coroner realizes how long Mr. Nettleton's been dead. Annabel couldn't possibly have killed him, so I suggest you let it go for now."

Max watched as Eileen and Morrie exchanged looks. He wasn't at all sure about the truth of what he'd just told them, but he hoped the cops would have no choice but to accept his bluff, at least for now. And he knew that they had no proof— not yet, anyway—that Annabel had done anything illegal.

"You're making a mistake here, Max," Morrie warned, but he let it drop for the moment. "Mrs. Nettleton, you'll have to move out of the house—it's a crime scene now and it's going to be closed off for at least a few days."

"No problem." Annabel shuddered and hugged herself for warmth. "There's no way I'm ever going to sleep in that bedroom again anyway."

"You'll have to find someplace here in town," Morrie told her. "You'll let us know where she is, right, Max." His stern tone let Max know it wasn't a question.

"Of course. Annabel's not running away. She wants to know what happened to her husband as much as you do."

"My neighbor said I could use her guest house," Annabel offered. "I'll be right next door." She thought a moment. "Can I take some of my clothes with me?" she asked. "And some things for my son?"

"Eileen, go with her and let her take a few items of clothing," Morrie ordered. "But see to it she doesn't remove anything that might be evidence."

Under the policewoman's watchful eye, Annabel quickly filled a shopping bag with some of Nicky's clothes and a few of his favorite toys from the nursery. But as she approached the master bedroom, she hesitated. Dylan's body still lay on the bed while a forensics photographer took photos and two technicians in white jumpsuits and rubber surgical gloves surveyed the scene, collecting and bagging anything that might turn out to be evidence.

"I can't make myself go back in there," Annabel told Eileen. "Could you go and get a few of my things for me?"

"Just tell me what you need." Eileen took an empty shopping bag and returned a few minutes later. It was now filled with underwear, a nightgown and robe, and an extra pair of shoes. She held three changes of clothes still on hangers in her other hand, all of which she'd carefully checked for bloodstains before selecting them.

"Thanks," Annabel said, taking the clothes. "I appreciate it."

A few minutes later, her arms loaded down with the clothes and bags and gulping fresh air, she hurried back across the sidewalk to Louise's house.

NELL SPENT a midday hour at the Monterey Sports Center, grateful to take a real shower and wash her hair for the first time since she'd driven in from Phoenix. She'd picked up a sandwich and soft drink at the French bakery and planned to spend the afternoon at a laundromat washing her clothes. But

first, she figured, she might as well make one more drive past
the little house where Annabel and her son lived. As she
turned her old Volvo into the street, Nell spotted the collection of police vehicles parked in front of the house and her
heart skipped a beat. Now what? Had they found the husband?
Surely it was too late for the cops to be investigating the
strange events of a few nights earlier. If the wife had called
them about that, they'd have been here long ago.

Nell drove past the cottage and parked around the corner.
She waited a few minutes, then decided there was no good reason a tourist couldn't be walking along this street. She got out,
locked her purse in the car's trunk with her other belongings,
put her keys in the pocket of her last pair of clean blue jeans,
and walked back toward the spot where the police were
parked.

By now three of the neighbors were standing on the sidewalk across the street, staring at the small house. "What's
going on?" Nell asked one of them, a frail, elderly man leaning on a cane.

"Heard there's a dead guy over there," he said.

"A dead guy? Who?"

"Dunno, but it wasn't no heart attack, I can tell you that
much. My nephew was with the cops, till he retired, and he says
they don't send those folks over from Salinas unless it's some
kinda crime scene." He shook his bony finger in the direction
of the flower-covered cottage. "Real strange people over there."

Nell swallowed hard. If this old man was right, what had
happened? Was there really a dead man inside the house, possibly the victim of foul play? Was that what the police were
investigating? Or, if the old man had his genders mixed up,
the blond woman could have been killed. She hoped not. That
cute little boy needed his mom. And she couldn't even stand
to think it might be the child who was dead.

Maybe the husband had come back and somebody'd killed him, she thought. It hardly seemed like there'd been enough time, though. Nell had parked down the street earlier in the day to watch the house and she'd seen the blond wife leave in the blue Honda, with her little tow-headed son. There'd been some sort of delivery only a few minutes afterward—a truck with a couple of delivery guys who unloaded some sort of appliance, maybe a washer or dryer or a new stove. Whatever it was, it was packed in a large cube-shaped cardboard box that required a dolly for the men to get it through the front door. At first, Nell had wondered why they were making the delivery when the woman wasn't home. But then she remembered what she'd read in the newspaper—that this place was a vacation rental house. Most likely some appliance had failed and it was up to the rental agency, not the tenant, to replace it promptly. That had to be it. These guys had a key to the front door because they worked for the rental agency.

It was when she saw the deliverymen that Nell had decided to head for the Sports Center and get cleaned up. Clearly the wife and child were gone for the morning and now somebody was in the house installing a new appliance. Nothing significant was going to happen in the short time it would take for her to shower and wash her hair.

"Live around here?" the old man asked, eyeing Nell curiously.

"Got a motel room on the edge of town," Nell replied.

"Funny, could've sworn I'd seen you in this neighborhood."

"Maybe somewhere in town," Nell said, becoming worried. "Restaurant or something, or maybe on one of my walks. I like to take long walks. Been visiting here a few days now." Had her surveillance drawn the attention of the neighbors? Concerned, she decided she'd best be on her way before these neighbors got any snoopier.

As she broke away from the group and continued walking

down the street, Nell saw the tall blond woman leave the house carrying two shopping bags and some clothes on hangers. She took them to the house next door. Something obviously was very wrong here. And where was the little boy? Her gaze still fixed on the scene down the street, Nell stepped off the curb and began to cross to the other side.

The loud screech of tires suddenly claimed her attention. Her head jerked around and she managed to step back up on the curb just in time to avoid being run down by Channel Nine's news van, which was turning the corner in a hurry.

Good, she told herself when her heart rate had returned to normal. Whatever was going on in the rental cottage would be on the evening news. She walked around the block and approached her parked car from a different direction. She would spend the afternoon at the laundromat as she'd planned, then watch the evening news on one of the display sets at Circuit City or in some local bar.

"THE DEAD MAN has been identified as Dylan Baez Nettleton," reporter George Conover said to Channel Nine's camera a few hours later. "His wife, Annabel Nettleton, told police that she found her husband's body upon returning from a morning shopping trip with the couple's young son. Nettleton had been stabbed in the heart with a knife police said came from the house."

In front of the bank of television sets at the Circuit City store in nearby Sand City, Nell watched as the video switched from a shot of Conover standing outside the crime scene to file footage.

"Dylan Baez Nettleton is thought to have been the long-lost heir to the Oliver Nettleton steel fortune, estimated at approximately forty million dollars," the reporter said. "The dead man first came to national attention last week, when he disappeared shortly after he was located by private investigator Jeffrey Link. Nettleton's car was found abandoned at Point Lobos State Reserve, just south of his Carmel home. He quickly became the target of an unsuccessful search effort by the Coast Guard, park rangers, and local law enforcement."

Conover recapped his earlier story, showing portions of the original tape of Annabel and the dead man's BMW at Point Lobos, as well as the reporter's later interview with Jeffrey Link. Finally, the video switched to the photograph of Dylan holding his newborn son. "With his father dead, will this little boy, now a year older than in this photograph, be the heir to all those millions?" Conover asked. "Sources tell Channel Nine that the Nettleton marriage was a troubled one, and that Dylan's widow, Annabel, might have preferred that the huge inheritance go to her son rather than her husband. That information, coupled with the fact that Annabel Nettleton is the one who claims to have discovered her missing husband's dead body in their bed, makes her the chief suspect in this brutal murder mystery."

Shuddering, Nell stepped back from the TV sets. Were they actually going to arrest Annabel for murder? Perhaps she should go to the police right away, tell them what she'd observed at the cottage that morning. Now that she thought about it, it was possible that those deliverymen hadn't been installing a new dishwasher or clothes dryer at all. That big cardboard box easily could have held the husband's drugged or dead body. Perhaps that delivery was nothing more than an attempt to frame Annabel for murder.

But if Nell went to the police, would they even believe her? And was what she'd seen really enough to clear Annabel? At the very least, Nell would have to explain what she'd been doing outside the cottage, why she'd been watching it. And if her statement became public… It would, of course; with all the millions of dollars involved, this had become a national story. There was also the danger that nosy neighbor she'd met on the street this afternoon might put two and two together and cause her no end of trouble.

If there was anything Nell Verducci didn't need in her life, now or ever, it was more trouble.

No, she rationalized. According to Channel Nine's report, Annabel had not even been arrested for anything. Not yet, anyway. It was far too early for Nell to consider sticking her own neck out to prevent something that might never even happen. Still, she felt some responsibility. She didn't want to see that little boy's mother go to prison for a murder she didn't commit. She didn't want to see another family end in tragedy.

Nell weighed what she knew, then came up with a compromise she felt she could live with. She would not go to the police *unless and until* there was no other way to clear Annabel.

Obviously, somebody—*who?*—had killed Annabel's husband, then tried to frame her for that murder. *Why?* And, if that ploy didn't work, would that unknown somebody next try to kill the young mother? Or her tiny son? If the police thought Annabel was guilty of murder, Nell figured, they certainly wouldn't bother providing her with protection from the real killer. The young mother and child might be in terrible danger right now.

No, Nell would not go to the police, at least not this soon. But there was no reason she couldn't keep watch over the young family.

Her decision made, she left the store, climbed into her old car, and headed back to Carmel.

# SEVEN

"LOOK, I DON'T CARE how you do it, just keep him alive," Warner said into the telephone. "I don't want him to die tonight."

He listened for a moment as Oliver Nettleton's nurse repeated the old man's current health status—his breathing had become more labored and he wasn't expected to survive more than a few hours.

"I heard you the first time," Warner said, feeling sweat begin to bead up on his brow. Oliver *couldn't* die now, not when he was so close… "Put him on a ventilator, give him CPR, adrenaline, whatever it takes. Use your whole bag of medical tricks if you have to, but keep him alive for a few more days."

"Look, Mr. Schuman, I know you'd like to have time to get back here and say your good-byes to your uncle—" the nurse sounded as though she were addressing a five-year-old "—but the truth is, he wouldn't know you were here. My agency gave me clear instructions that Mr. Nettleton has both Do Not Resuscitate and Do Not Intubate orders in place. Clearly, he does not want to be kept alive by extraordinary measures."

Warner took a deep breath and tried to calm his rapid heartbeat. God, he hated these officious nurses! "Your orders do not impress me," he barked at her. "Listen to me and listen to me carefully. *I* am the one who hired your agency, *I* pay your salary, and *I* am the one who's going to make the decisions. If my uncle dies before I get back to Chicago and you haven't

done everything humanly and medically possible to keep him
alive, I promise you I'll sue you and your agency out of existence. Is that clear?"

Warner heard the nurse inhale sharply.

*"Is that clear?"*

"Y-yes, it's clear," she said.

"Good." Warner looked around his room at the Pine
Lodge. The TV set still flickered in the dim light, but he'd
muted the sound of the remainder of the newscast while he
made his call. "I'll check back in the morning and I expect
to find my uncle still with us." He slammed down the phone,
stormed down the hall to Jeffrey Link's room, and pounded
on the private eye's door.

Link opened the door with a bottle of Budweiser in his
hand and a sheepish look on his face. He was standing in his
stocking feet and Warner noticed that the buttons of his cheap
plaid shirt were straining over his bulging belly. The television set was on.

"So you saw it, too," Warner said, pushing his way into
the room.

Jeff took a quick step backward to avoid being bowled over
by the taller, thinner man. "You mean the news about Dylan?"

"No, the weather forecast for Moscow. *Of course,* Dylan's
murder, you idiot! Plus the replay of your illuminating comments of last week." Warner pushed the door shut.

Jeff flinched at his employer's heavy sarcasm. "Hey, how
was I supposed to know the wife would murder him and the
story would be all over the news again? Hell, Mr. Schuman,
I've been going over to that house at least a couple of times
a day, doing my best to find Dylan, the way we agreed. I talked
to the wife, I talked to the neighbors, I talked to the cops. I
don't know what else you think—"

"No, I'm sure you don't, not with your limited intellect."

Warner stared at the beer Jeff was holding and shook his head in disgust. "You'd better be sober, Link. I've got a job for you. I want it done now and I want it done right."

"Only had a couple of gulps," Jeff said, setting the bottle on top of the dresser.

"Well, pour the rest down the sink. You're going to need what little wit you have. I want you to get over to that neighborhood and find out exactly where the woman and the baby are right now. Their house will be closed up by the police, so they'll have had to move somewhere else."

Jeff's face hardened for a moment and he looked ready to defend himself, either physically or verbally. But after what Warner suspected was a brief inner struggle, won by the private eye's desire for money, Link looked at the floor and answered sullenly, "If that's what you want." He plopped down on the edge of the bed and began to pull on his shoes.

"The news report didn't say anything about the woman's being arrested," Warner added, "so chances are the boy's still with her, not off in foster care somewhere." He began to pace the room nervously. "That should make it easy enough to find him. I want to know where that child is and I want to know tonight."

"Sure, sure." Jeff tied his shoelaces. "I'm on it."

"And one more thing," Warner said as he walked over to the door, opened it, and checked the hallway. There was no one in sight.

"What's that?"

"See if you can't be a little discreet for a change. Don't just go ask the officer guarding the crime scene or one of the reporters hanging around the place. I don't want the whole world to know we're looking for the woman and the boy."

Warner saw a puzzled look cross the private investigator's face and realized some kind of explanation was called for.

"One thing you obviously need to learn, Link—when you work for the very wealthy, you don't blab their private business to cops and reporters. You play things close to your vest and preserve your employer's privacy at all times. Understand?"

"Yeah, uh, sure. No problem."

"I'll be in my room, waiting for your report. I want it tonight, no matter what time you get back."

ANNABEL TIPTOED around the Zuckermans' small guest house, trying her best not to wake Nicky as she stored the few belongings she'd carried over from next door. Placing Nicky's favorite stuffed bear next to him as he slept in Jason's borrowed Port-a-Crib, she felt her hands shaking again, an outward sign of the inner turmoil that seemed more and more a part of her lately. Glancing at the daybed across the room, where soon she would try to sleep, she envied her son's innocent slumber. She wasn't sure she'd ever again be able to relax enough to sleep that soundly. And, if she did manage to doze off, the prospect of the dreams that awaited her was terrifying.

The guest house in Louise's backyard was a detached studio, one large room with a minute wall kitchen that offered a bar-size refrigerator, hot plate, microwave, and small sink. The daybed had a pull-out mattress beneath it to accommodate a second adult. In the remainder of the square room were a small round table with two wooden chairs, a television set, and a blue plaid upholstered loveseat. The bathroom was also tiny, with a toilet, a sink, and a stall shower the size of a phone booth. Annabel wasn't sure how she was going to manage bathing a toddler in that Lilliputian shower. She looked around the place for a plastic infant tub, but didn't find one. She'd have to ask Louise if…

She stopped herself, realizing she was doing it again. She was obsessing about minutia to keep her mind off the big terrifying facts—that she was suddenly a widow, that she was being framed for her husband's murder, that she could lose her son and maybe even her life. How she was going to bathe Nicky in this guest house surely was the least of her worries.

During the daytime, the large picture window at the back of the guest house offered a view of the ocean. But it was already dark outside and all Annabel could see was blackness, so she'd closed the draperies for privacy. The last thing she wanted was someone out there in the dark, watching her. The high, small bathroom window faced her own house next door. Pulling aside the pink flowered curtains and peering through, she could see lights still blazing at the cottage where her husband's body lay. Or did it? Perhaps, she thought, the coroner already had removed it and Dylan now lay naked on a cold slab in the morgue, waiting to be carved up. Shuddering, she looked away, letting the curtain slip back into place.

With trepidation, she thought about what might become of her and Nicky. She easily could end up in prison and Nicky in foster care—Dylan's worst fear had been that a child of his would become one of society's discards, as he had in his own childhood years. From the start, Annabel had known that fear was the reason Dylan had been so adamant about marrying her—she was pregnant with his child, a child he desperately wanted. Still, she'd believed he would grow to love her, too, and that theirs eventually would become the sort of family she'd always wanted. She'd wanted *so badly* to believe… Maybe, too, she had to admit, part of what had appealed to her about Dylan was the challenge he presented, the certain knowledge that she would have to work hard to earn his love. She simply hadn't known just how impossible a task that would turn out to be.

Wrinkling her nose as she caught a faint whiff of a now-familiar foul odor, she hung up a pair of her jeans in the two-foot-wide closet next to the bathroom. Had the smell of death permeated her clothing so quickly, or was her mind playing tricks on her? She closed the closet door, a vision of Dylan lying dead on their bed once again dancing before her eyes.

She had more to worry about than ending up in prison, she realized as she thought about the day's terrible events. Somebody had killed her husband, probably at least a day or two ago, if what Max told her about the body's decomposition was correct. Then the murderer had watched the house, waiting for her and Nicky to leave before bringing Dylan in, positioning him on the bed, and stabbing him in the chest with her knife. Who would do such a thing? Why? And would the murderer be content with framing Annabel for his deed? If he failed to shift the blame for the murder onto her and send her to prison, would he simply kill her instead? And what about Nicky? She felt a strong yet indefinable threat continually hovering over her and her child, but clearly she could expect no help from the police—they seemed to want to pin her husband's murder on her every bit as badly as the killer did.

If only she could figure out who had wanted Dylan dead, and why, she might have a fighting chance of protecting what was left of her family. Surely, she thought, Dylan's murder had something to do with his unexpected inheritance. Or with his hidden past. Or maybe both things were somehow interrelated.

Yet, it was also possible, she realized, that Dylan had done something here in Carmel that had gotten him murdered. Maybe he'd recognized somebody who didn't want to be recognized, or pulled some sort of con game on the wrong man. Or perhaps he'd become involved in some kind of drug deal that went horribly wrong. Certainly murders were committed over drugs and drug money somewhere in America every day of the week. Maybe Dylan knew he was in trouble he couldn't handle and that was why he was in such a hurry to move away from here.

Knowing so little about the man whose name she bore, Annabel felt completely in the dark. Until she knew more—a great deal more—there was no way she could assess what kind of further risk, if any, she and Nicky were facing.

She sank onto the daybed and rested her aching head in her hands. Maybe this was all her own fault, she thought. If only she hadn't gotten pregnant…if only she'd refused Dylan's proposal of marriage…if only she hadn't protested moving to Salt Lake City. If only…if only…if only… For the millionth time in her life, she examined her conscience and found herself deficient.

Like many people who'd grown up in a chaotic home, Annabel frequently found herself attempting to control her fate by taking personal responsibility—and, by corollary, the blame—for everything short of the weather. Whenever, during their marriage, Dylan threw one of his not infrequent tantrums, she told herself that she must have done something to cause it; therefore, if she simply changed her own behavior, she'd be able to prevent Dylan's displays of temper, to control her husband's actions.

Now, past her thirtieth birthday, she finally was learning a hard lesson—that her game of self-blaming in an attempt to feel in control of her life generally did little, if anything, to alter its most significant events. Despite everything from pleading to hiding his liquor, she'd never been able to control her father's alcoholism…and he and her mother had been killed in a car crash in which he was at fault. She'd been unable to save her brother's life…despite her own sacrifice. And she'd been unable to make her marriage work…no matter how hard she'd tried to placate a man who was incapable of loving her.

Now, would she be powerless to keep herself from going to prison for a murder she hadn't committed? Or to keep her small son from reliving his father's short, tragic life?

*Not without a fight,* Annabel vowed. She might not be able to control her own fate or Nicky's, but she'd never been a quitter. If she went down again, it would be only while fighting back with everything she had.

As Nicky began to stir fitfully in the crib, she walked over and planted a light kiss on his forehead. Here was the reason she could never completely regret her relationship with Dylan Nettleton, she knew. Despite its horrific ending, it had produced her precious son, and for that she would be forever grateful.

She prayed that maybe someday there'd be another man for her, someone she would know far, far better than she'd known Dylan when she married him, a good man, a man able to love her as much as she loved him. But first, she knew she would have to go through a period of mourning—if not for Dylan himself, then for her dead dreams, for her shattered hopes of being part of that elusive fantasy, a truly happy family.

She tucked the blanket around Nicky's small curled form and gently pulled his thumb from between his puckered pink baby lips. She checked that the door between their little retreat and the threatening darkness outside was securely locked. Then, for good measure, she took one of the wooden chairs and braced it under the doorknob.

Finally, she pulled back the covers on the daybed, turned off the lamp, lay down, and stared at the ceiling, trying to shut off her turbulent thoughts and quiet her shaking hands long enough to fall asleep.

"THE WIFE AND SON are staying in the next-door neighbor's guest house," Jeff reported when he returned to the Pine Lodge. He'd been gone less than forty-five minutes and felt pleased with his efficiency. Surely his difficult, insulting employer would be impressed with his work this time, maybe even enough to forget about his being on the news for the second time in less than a week. "Zuckerman's the neighbor's name. Big white house on the south side."

Warner nodded. "Good." He narrowed his eyes at the private detective. "How'd you come up with this piece of information?"

Jeff bristled, holding up both palms in protest. "Hey, I listened to you, Mr. Schuman. I didn't ask the cops and I didn't ask the press, so don't sweat it. Just talked up the neighbors some, until I located the woman and kid. Interviewed this Mrs. Zuckerman a time or two before now, so she knows me, knows I'm trying to see to it that the Nettletons get their inheritance. Told me right off they're staying with her until this whole thing with Dylan's murder gets straightened out."

Warner nodded and ushered Jeff further into his hotel room. "Have a seat, Link," he said, indicating the two chairs angled toward each other in the bay window.

Jeff plopped his ample form into one, leaned back, and stretched his aching legs out in front of him. He was disappointed that Schuman seemed to want more than the address where the Nettletons were now living. It was late and he wanted nothing more than a stiff drink in the bar, followed by a good night's sleep.

"What kind of guest house is it?" Warner asked, sitting down in the other chair.

Jeff straightened up. "What do you mean? A guest house is a guest house, right?" Was there no satisfying this pompous asshole? Why wouldn't Warner just chill out and let him do his job, for godsake? Which of them was the damn detective here, anyway?

Warner sighed in the way he always seemed to just before he called Jeff an idiot or something worse. "No, a guest house is *not* always just a guest house. Is this one a separate building or is it attached to the main house? Is it big or small? Is it behind locked gates? What kind of security system does it have?"

"Why do you want to know?" Jeff asked, his investigator's instincts suddenly aroused. "You want to talk to Mrs. Nettleton, just go on over to the Zuckermans' and ring the doorbell. It's not like you're the enemy, right?"

Warner paused a moment, shook his head in apparent disgust, then spoke in his best schoolteacher voice. "Look, Link, this is a complicated situation. Somebody killed Dylan, right?"

Jeff nodded.

"And we don't know who or why, do we? Maybe the wife killed him because she didn't like him and she believes her child will now inherit the Oliver Nettleton fortune. If so, they're probably in no real physical danger. But if Dylan was murdered by somebody else, for some unknown reason, for all we know, his widow and son might also be targets. Understand?"

"I—I guess. So you're worried they might need more security than what they've got in this guest house situation?"

"That's certainly one point."

Jeff waited for Schuman to state any other points he might want to make, but nothing was forthcoming. Reluctantly, he finally broke the silence himself. "So, you want me to bodyguard them? See to it nobody harms them?" That was the last thing he wanted to do at this hour, but if it was part of the job... He could probably negotiate a bonus for putting in extra hours.

"Are the police still working next door?" Warner asked.

"Were when I was talking to Mrs. Zuckerman."

"Then I think Mrs. Nettleton and her son should be safe enough for now. I doubt anybody's going to try to harm them right under the cops' noses."

Jeff tried not to show how relieved he was that he wouldn't

have to spend the night in his car, trying to stay awake long enough to guard the Zuckermans' guest house.

"So, tell me what you know about this guest house," Warner said again.

Jeff combed his memory. "Didn't see it tonight," he admitted. "Dark out and all. But one other time when I talked with Mrs. Zuckerman, she was nice enough to invite me inside." She'd offered him a cup of coffee and he'd made a good-size dent in the plate of cookies she set before him. He'd noticed that she didn't touch them herself. Probably couldn't eat cookies and stay as skinny as she was. "We sat in her kitchen," he recalled, "and I could see this little guest house from there. Small, squarish building, completely separate from the main house. Downhill a little from the house, way I remember. It doesn't block the ocean view."

"Is the yard fenced?"

Jeff closed his eyes and tried to picture the place in his mind. "Don't think so," he said, opening his eyes again. "Not at the back, anyway. If there's a fence at the back, it's gotta be a pretty low one. You put up one of those high privacy fences in that neighborhood, you block your ocean view and nobody wants to do that."

"Good, Link. Good work."

Jeff smiled warily at the unusual praise. He wanted to be polite but he was anxious to leave. "Okay if I go hit the sack for now?" he asked.

"Soon," Warner said, "soon. There's one more thing I need you to do tonight."

As his employer described his final task, Jeff groaned inwardly, his thirst for that stiff drink increasing by the moment. As he listened, he realized it would be probably be hours before he'd be back at the hotel again and, by then, the hotel bar was sure to be closed.

SHORTLY AFTER SHE AWOKE the next morning, Annabel heard a sharp knock on the guest house door. After she moved the chair and opened the locks, she found Louise, still in her bathrobe and looking disheveled, standing outside in the morning fog. "It's Max Garrity," Louise said, handing Annabel the portable phone. "He says they want you to come down to the police station for more questioning. But tell him you're having breakfast with me first." She turned and ran back to the big house across the yard.

Annabel closed the door. "Morning, Max," she said into the telephone. She listened while he explained that the police wanted to re-question her, now that she'd had a night's rest. "I don't get it," she replied. "Do they think I'm going to change what I already told them?"

"They can always hope, I suppose, and if you don't show up, they'll think you've got something to hide. But don't worry, I'll control the situation."

"What needs controlling, Max? I didn't kill Dylan, and I really don't know a thing I haven't already told the police."

"Then there's nothing to worry about, right?"

"Nothing except maybe getting railroaded into prison for something I didn't do."

"It's my job to see that doesn't happen," Max told her. "Just let me do my job and I'll take good care of you."

Annabel found her lawyer's self-assured voice comforting. She could count on Max. Couldn't she? "What time do I have to be there?"

"Ten-thirty."

"Okay, I'll be there, providing Louise can take care of Nicky. I really don't want to take him with me, not to a police station."

"Meet you there at ten-fifteen. We can go over what's likely to happen next." After a brief good-bye, Max hung up.

Half an hour later, Annabel was sitting with Louise in her friend's kitchen, trying her best to eat a bowl of oatmeal despite her nervous stomach. Nicky was smearing his cereal around his high chair's wooden tray, occasionally managing to get a little into his mouth as well. Louise's two children were still asleep.

"Afraid I've got a hair appointment this morning, hon," Louise said, running her fingers through her dyed chestnut hair. "My roots are getting positively embarrassing. But Missy'll be home with Jason—thank God for school vacations, huh? No reason she can't watch Nicky, too."

"Are you sure?" Annabel said nervously. "*Two* toddlers? Missy's only thirteen."

Louise waved away Annabel's concern. "Hey, she's been staying with Jason since he was nine months old, whenever Sid and I go out, and she babysat for the Fillmores for the last three weekends. They've got three kids—two, three, and six—a real challenge." She refilled Annabel's coffee cup. "Missy's great with little kids and, besides, she'll probably have an easier time with Nicky to keep Jason company."

Annabel felt a bit wary, yet grateful. Surely, leaving Nicky here with Missy was a better option than taking him along to the police station, wasn't it? At least Nicky knew the girl, and maybe Annabel could bring in the Port-a-Crib and put him down for his morning nap before she left. Otherwise, he'd be cranky this afternoon. Besides, what would she do with the poor little fellow if she brought him to the police station? He wouldn't be allowed to sit on her lap while she answered questions, and she didn't want to pass him off to some strange cop for however long the interrogation might take. No, leaving him here with Missy was definitely the better option.

"Thanks, Louise," Annabel said, once she'd made up her mind. "Tell Missy I'll pay her regular babysitting rate."

"Nonsense, Annabel, that's not necess—"

"*I insist.* You've done more than enough for us already, and there's no way I'm going to ask Missy to babysit for free." She remembered how much earning a few dollars had meant to her when she was a teenager.

Louise glanced at the wall clock. "Hey, it's already after nine. I've got to get going. I'll make sure Missy's up before I leave, so don't worry about Nicky." She put her bowl and cup in the sink and headed out of the kitchen. At the doorway, she turned and said with an anxious smile, "Hey, Annabel, good luck today."

"LOOKS LIKE THE COPS are targeting the wife for the murder," Peter said, nodding with satisfaction as he handed the morning newspaper to Gil. The story of Dylan Nettleton's murder had made the front page, above the fold. The two men were sitting in the eating area of their cheap apartment motel in downtown Seaside, pigging out on onion bagels and coffee from a nearby takeout store.

"Already read it," Gil said, waving the newspaper away. "What I don't get is how that's gonna help us get our money."

"Amount of trouble the widow Nettleton's in already, you think she's gonna be in any mood to give us any crap?"

"Yeah, right." Gil got to his feet and stood menacingly over his smaller buddy. "What, Pete? Tell me how you got it figured. We go over there, knock on her door, and tell her we came to collect what her old man owes us? Her *dead* old man? Gimme a break." He slammed down his fist on the table, knocking over Peter's half-filled plastic coffee cup.

Peter grabbed a stack of paper napkins and frantically sopped up the stream of hot coffee before it could run onto the rug. "Damn," he muttered under his breath.

"Leverage, man," Gil shouted, oblivious to the spilled coffee. "We need leverage here, Pete. You tell me—what's this broad's incentive? Her husband's already a goner and, if you believe this damn newspaper, she didn't much like the son of a bitch anyway. What're we gonna do, sue her?"

"Chill the hell out, Gil," Peter said, tossing the wet napkins into the wastebasket. "We still got options."

"Such as?"

Peter ran his hand over his chin, feeling the prickle of his two-day-old beard. "Let's take a ride over there," he suggested, "check things out. I think you're right about this leverage thing and—"

"Holy crap!" Gil said, narrowing his eyes. "The brain here finally admits stupid old Gil is right about something. And he's got such a great friggin' track record himself."

Peter bristled. "Hey! I'm not the one who—"

"Screw you, Hoy!" Gil flashed Peter the bird. "You and your goddamn brilliant plans. Get me all the way down here from Seattle and what happens? I'm a helluva lot worse off than when I was selling nerdy-looking shoes to Microsoft yuppies is what!" He kicked the leg of a wooden chair, sending it flying across the room.

Peter backed up a step. He was never sure just how far the volatile Gil might go. There always seemed to be sheer rage simmering just below the surface with his longtime friend and, whenever it boiled over, there was hell to pay. He carefully picked up the chair and set it upright again. "Don't need the motel manager hearing trouble and kicking us outta here, right, pal?" He eyed Gil, holding his breath as he waited for a reaction.

But Gil's tantrum had played itself out with the overturned chair. Seemingly exhausted now, he flopped down on the threadbare couch, leaned back, and swung his feet onto the armrest.

"Don't know about you," Peter added, "but I'm not walking away from millions of my hard-earned bucks. You in or out?"

"Shoot," Gil said, sounding resigned. "You got me this far. Already screwed, so I might as well stay in." He shook his head. "Okay, Einstein, let's hear what kinda brainstorm you got *this* time."

NELL PULLED her Volvo into the curb a couple of houses away from Annabel's Carmel cottage and shut off the motor. It appeared that the police had finished their work here, at least for the moment. Now she could see an official seal taped across the cottage's front door, but the police cars were no longer around. There were several other vehicles parked along the shady street, however—four newer cars in front of various houses and a big white van a short way down the block. Annabel's Honda remained parked directly in front of the cottage. Obviously the young mother and child must have stayed the night at the neighbor's place, unless the cops had hauled Annabel off to jail.

Nervously, Nell eyed the other houses along the street, trying to determine whether anyone was watching her through their windows. Did that suspicious old man she'd talked to yesterday have her in his sights? Would he report her surveillance to the police? When she saw no movement at any of the windows, she decided to risk it. If a police car came down the street, she told herself, she'd simply drive off. Or if she became trapped into talking to the cops, she could claim she was just curious to see the house where a murder had taken place. After all, the story was all over the news. Not only was it on TV last night, but there was a detailed story, right here on the front page of the morning newspaper she'd bought outside the café where she'd had breakfast.

It wasn't long before Nell saw a fashionably thin woman,

the one who lived in the big white house where Annabel had taken refuge, drive her black Mercedes out of her garage. She was alone. Watching the woman, so elegant in her expensive designer clothes, made Nell feel like something of a cow. Her own extra twenty-some pounds, neo-hippie ponytail, and jeans topped by a University of Arizona sweatshirt seemed so dowdy in comparison. Nell felt more like the homeless woman she was becoming every day. She wondered whether she still had her job back in Phoenix. Or, if not, whether she'd be able to get a new one. Her boss probably wouldn't be inclined to give her much of a reference, not after she'd just walked off that way.

If the neighbor woman was gone for the morning, Annabel and the baby must be home alone, Nell figured. But she soon realized she was wrong. A few minutes later, Annabel came out of the big white house by herself, let the screen door slam shut behind her, climbed into her Honda, and drove off.

Should she follow her? Nell hesitated a moment, then decided it was more important to make sure the child was safe than to follow the mother. Somebody had to be inside with the little boy the news reports called Nicholas Nettleton. Surely, the blond woman wouldn't leave him alone; nothing Nell had observed so far indicated that she was one of those terrible mothers, the kind of women who ignore their children's most basic needs.

Staving off a pang of regret over the way her own life was turning out, Nell settled back in the seat with the morning's newspaper. She turned to the classified ads, thinking maybe she'd make a change, get a new job here, rent herself a small place by the ocean. It would be heavenly to be able to walk along the beach whenever she wanted to. And, if she'd already lost her job in Phoenix, what did she have to lose by moving here? It wasn't as though she had loads of friends and lovers in Phoenix…not even as though she had much of a life there.

She found numerous ads for the kind of menial work a middle-aged woman with no college degree could probably get—salesperson, home care worker, short order cook, bank clerk, grocery checker. It looked like she could earn eight or ten dollars an hour here, at least a couple of dollars an hour more than her waitress work in Phoenix had been paying her.

But her temporary enthusiasm waned as soon as she began checking the apartment rental ads. Even a modest one-bedroom apartment in Pacific Grove or Monterey—in neighborhoods not nearly as upscale as this one in Carmel—went for upwards of a thousand dollars or twelve hundred a month. After deductions for taxes and Social Security at one of these part-time, no-benefits jobs, she'd barely earn enough to pay her rent, never mind put food on the table or gas in the Volvo.

Her dreams of making a life change back on hold, at least for the moment, Nell dug a pencil out of her purse and turned to the crossword puzzle.

MISSY LAY FACE DOWN, playing with the two tow-headed toddlers on the living room floor. The three of them rolled a big blue ball amongst themselves, the two little tow-headed boys giggling with glee whenever they managed to trap it between their uncoordinated hands for an instant or two before shoving it away again.

"Come on, Jason, roll the ball to me," Missy said once more. But Jason had tired of the game by now and quickly shifted his attention to his new toy fire engine, beginning to push it across the floorboards. "Rrrrm, rrrrm, rrrrm," he said, as he ran the miniature plastic fire truck back and forth.

Nicky began to rub his eyes and his happy laugh of a few minutes earlier quickly turned into a plaintive whine. "Mama?" he asked, turning his wide blue eyes to Missy. "Mamamama?"

"Your mom had to go out," Missy explained patiently.

"She'll be back in a little bit." She picked up a big plastic hexagon with star, square, circle, oval, and triangle-shaped holes cut into its six sides. "Here, Nicky, want to try putting some shapes in here? You do it like this." She picked up a thick yellow plastic star and inserted it through the star-shaped hole. "Here." She held up a yellow square.

But Nicky batted the piece of plastic out of her hand, crawled across the floor to his favorite crib blanket and held it up to his cheek. His eyelids drooping, he stuck his thumb into his mouth.

"Tired, aren't you, little guy?" Missy pushed herself up off the floor. At thirteen, she was almost as tall as her mother, with long light brown hair she wore parted in the middle. Today she'd tied it back with a pink ribbon that matched her form-fitting T-shirt and shorts. "Come on, Nicky, time for your nap. Let's go lie down." She pulled Nicky to his feet. Holding onto one of his small hands, she led him, his blanket trailing behind, into the guest bedroom, where her mother had set up the Port-a-Crib. "Be right back, Jason," she called over her shoulder.

But Jason was absorbed in playing with his toy fire engine and hardly noticed that his sister and his playmate had left the room.

GIL AND PETER SAT in the white van, watching and waiting, not really sure for what. "Here she comes," Peter said suddenly, as Annabel left the white house next door to hers, got into her car, and drove off.

"Gonna follow her?" Gil asked.

Peter shook his head. "Nope. Doesn't matter where she's going."

"Then why the hell are we sitting here? Thought we were gonna sweat her about the money."

"Leverage," Peter reminded him. "Remember, we need a good incentive to get her to cough up the dough."

Gil formed his right hand into a fist and slammed it against his left palm. "She doesn't cooperate, I'll give her *incentivo*," he said, his expression menacing. "No way that broad's gonna cheat me out of what's mine."

"Come on," Peter said, a few minutes later as he opened the driver's side door.

"Come on where? What the hell you doing?"

"Checking out the situation over there. Let's go see what's going on."

"But what do we say if—"

"Hell, Gil, use your imagination. We're a couple of true-believing Jehovah's Witnesses looking for converts, if we have to be."

The two men sprinted from the van, along the sidewalk and up to the front door of the Zuckermans' house. As they approached, they saw that the inside door was standing open to allow the morning breeze to enter through the screen door, which was obviously custom-made. The word, "Zuckerman," was emblazoned in shiny aluminum across the middle section.

As Peter peered through the screen, his finger poised over the doorbell, he heard a telephone ring inside the house and saw a small, blond-haired boy playing on the floor just inside the door. The tot was cheerfully running a bright red fire truck into the legs of the coffee table.

"Hi, Mom," Peter heard a young girl's faint voice say from somewhere in the back of the house. "Yeah, everything's fine. How long are…"

Instead of ringing the doorbell, Peter tried the handle of the screen door. It was locked. As the girl's phone conversation continued, he pulled out his pocket knife, slit a few inches of screen along the edge of the doorframe, reached through, and unlocked the screen door from the inside. A finger held against his lips, he whispered to Gil, "That's her kid. Here, take the keys and get the van. Back it up here and get ready to drive." He handed over the keys and quietly opened the door. "Get going," he whispered. "Looks like we finally got lucky."

An instant later, Peter entered the living room, swooped down and picked up Jason Zuckerman, clapped a hand over the small boy's mouth to stifle his cry of surprise, and fled out the door with the child in his arms.

Gil leaned over and opened the passenger side door of the van so Peter could climb inside with the squirming toddler, then took off as fast as he could.

"*Now* we got us some leverage!" Gil cried as the van's tires screeched around the corner.

# EIGHT

"Is THERE ANYONE who can verify your account of where you were and what you were doing yesterday morning?" Detective Morrison asked Annabel.

"I already told you—my son Nicky was with me all morning," she said. She and Max were sitting with Detective Morrison and Sergeant Kopek in an interrogation room at the Carmel Police Department's building on Junipero Street. She'd been going over her day's activities for the past twenty minutes.

"An *adult*," Morrison said with ill-disguised impatience.

Annabel sighed, crossing and uncrossing her legs. "Like I told you, I bought bread at Il Fornaio, a loaf of *ciabatta*. Maybe the clerk will remember me," she said doubtfully— the bakery had been crowded. She tried to retrace her steps mentally. Was there anybody else? Yes, of course! "There was a nice old man on the sidewalk near the bakery. Nicky tried to chase a dog down the street and almost got away from me. When I ran after him, I dropped my bread. The man picked it up for me and we chatted for a minute or two about trying to raise active sons. I think he said his own boy died in the Vietnam War."

"What's this man's name?" Morrison asked, his pencil poised over a pad of paper as though to take notes despite the tape recorder sitting on the table between him and his prime suspect.

Annabel shook her head. "I—I don't know. I didn't ask. I could probably describe him, though." When Morrison failed to ask her for details, Annabel knew there would be no attempt made to verify her account, at least not by police combing the streets for the pleasant, silver-haired man who'd disapproved of his wife's confining their own son in a harness and leash.

"Nobody else?" the detective asked.

There was the bank teller, of course, Annabel recalled. He'd probably remember her, especially after she'd asked him to check the source of that fifty-thousand-dollar deposit. But she didn't really want the police to know about the strange origins of that money, not yet anyway. Where would she and Nicky be if the cops claimed they had no right to that cash, if they decided to confiscate it as evidence of some illegal activity she knew nothing about? She could end up in even more trouble. No, she wouldn't mention either the bank visit or the teller unless she absolutely had to.

But maybe a small part of the story would suffice. "I remember I went to the ATM on Ocean Avenue near Lincoln," Annabel offered. "I might still have the receipt." As the others watched, she plowed through her large tan leather purse and finally came up with the cash receipt. "Here it is. It's got the time and date stamped right on it."

Morrison took the slip of paper and examined it. "You keep quite a bit of money in your checking account," he observed.

"My—my husband always took care of that sort of thing," Annabel said. Had she made a mistake in showing this cop the ATM receipt?

Max stepped in. "How much money my client has in her checking account has nothing to do with her husband's murder," he said. "Nor, frankly, does where she was yesterday morning. I'm no coroner, Morrie, but even I know Mr. Nettleton had to have been dead far longer than an hour or two by the time I called you. The body was already…uh, decomposing." He shot Annabel an apologetic glance.

"The coroner's report isn't in yet," Morrison said vaguely. "But now that you mention it, I'd like to ask Mrs. Nettleton how she can prove to us that her husband's body hadn't been lying there since, say, late Saturday night?"

"It's not up to Mrs. Nettleton to prove her innocence and you know it," Max said. "But in the interest of cooperation, I personally can vouch that there was no dead body in her bed on Sunday morning."

"*Really,* Max? And just how would you know that?" Sergeant Kopek asked with a raised eyebrow and wicked leer.

Annabel bit down on her lip as she became aware of the lascivious slant the cops were putting on Max's innocent attempt to defend her. A fleeting image of herself in that bed, lying naked in Max's strong arms, invaded her thoughts and she blushed bright red.

"Katie was there with me, Eileen," Max said in a patronizing tone. "I believe you've met her—my ten-year-old daughter."

Sergeant Kopek shrugged.

"So tell us, Max, just why were you at the Nettleton house on Sunday morning?" Morrison asked. "Not exactly your usual office hours."

"You know I don't have to answer that—it's attorney-client privilege. But again, in the interest of clearing my client's name as quickly as possible, I'll tell you."

Annabel held her breath, hoping Max wouldn't mention the break-in and the missing computer—she didn't want to have to explain why she hadn't notified the police. But she quickly realized that her fear was premature. Her attorney turned out to be circumspect as well as protective.

"As you know, my client was extremely concerned about her missing husband," Max continued. "She asked me to come over and help her look through the house, see if I could find any clues to his whereabouts. You know, any small thing that might indicate whether Dylan had decided to abandon her and their son, or if he'd met with foul play or had some sort of accident."

"And what did you find?"

Max grinned. *"No dead body in the bed,* like I just told you. No dead body anywhere in the house, for that matter. So, on Sunday morning, Dylan Nettleton had to have been dead somewhere else. His body was moved into the house and positioned on the bed many hours later, while my client was out buying a loaf of *ciabatta,* using the ATM, and discussing child-rearing with an old man on the streets of Carmel."

Morrison glanced at the tape recorder, which was still running. "Sure," he said. "Assuming two very big things, Max—that you're telling the truth, and that the coroner's report jibes with your theory about the time of Dylan Nettleton's death."

"Use your own judgment on the first, Morrie—you know me—and wait for the ME's notes on the second. In the meantime, I think Mrs. Nettleton has answered enough questions." Max pushed back his chair and stood up, signaling that the interview was over. "Annabel," he said, pulling her chair out of the way as she stood and stretched her cramped legs. He turned to the two cops. "You have anymore questions, folks, don't hesitate to call me. Just don't bother Mrs. Nettleton."

The lawyer and client left the police station. As they reached their cars in the parking lot behind the compact green building, Max reached over and laid his hand gently on Annabel's upper arm. "How are you holding up, Annabel?" he asked, concern obvious on his face.

"I—I'm not sleeping well, and I worry all the time," Annabel confessed. Oddly, the unexpected human touch made her feel like crying, but she quickly stifled the impulse.

"You look tired," Max agreed. "Still gorgeous, of course, but tired." He flashed her a sympathetic smile.

Annabel was taken aback. She'd never thought of herself as gorgeous, or even particularly pretty. She had nice hair, maybe, and a few of the men she'd dated before Dylan told her she had good legs. But gorgeous? That word was reserved for movie stars and supermodels, not Annabel Nettleton. Not even her own husband had ever called her *gorgeous.* As she self-consciously stared at her shoes, she felt the second blush of the morning coloring her cheeks. She shouldn't feel flattered, she told herself. After all, Max Garrity was a lawyer, and lawyers were known for their ability to compliment and cajole virtually anybody, weren't they?

"Come have lunch with me and we'll talk about it," Max suggested.

Annabel looked up, noticing what a kind face Max had, lawyer or not. She wanted nothing more right now than to have lunch with this good, solid man, to pretend they were a normal couple like all the others in the restaurant—not an accused murderer and her defense attorney. But they weren't a normal couple, no matter how much she might wish it were so. She glanced at her watch. "Thanks, but I should be getting back. Nicky will—"

"Just a quick sandwich across the street, Annabel. It's still early. Surely your neighbor won't mind if you're gone for another forty, forty-five minutes. Call it a legal strategy session. No charge, of course, and I'm treating."

Annabel hesitated only briefly, then agreed. "My stomach's so nervous, I don't know if I can get down any lunch," she told him. "But I sure could use a shoulder to cry on."

"That much I can promise you." Max took her elbow and

guided her out of the parking lot. "Parking's always a pain in Carmel," he said, conspiratorially. "No reason we can't let the cops take care of our cars for a little while longer."

They headed to the restaurant across the street on foot.

IT ALL HAPPENED so fast, it took a moment for Nell to fully recognize what she'd seen—the abduction of a child in broad daylight. Or *was* it an abduction? Maybe one of those young men—the white guy, not the Asian—was a relative of the people who lived in the white house and had permission to take the little boy away. Assuming the man had left carrying the child who lived there, of course. But had he? What if the child who'd been snatched away in a flash was little Nicky Nettleton?

Nell quickly dismissed her idea about the man's being a relative with permission to take the child. After all, it was the Asian man who'd carried the blond boy into the van, not his Caucasian cohort. Certainly something far more nefarious had happened here.

She dropped her newspaper on the passenger seat, suddenly in a panic about what she should do next. She could knock on the door of the white house, she supposed, ask whoever was inside what was going on. But that would require explaining why she'd been watching the house and, besides, by then the white van could be almost anywhere. She hadn't even reacted quickly enough to notice its license number.

She could ignore the whole thing, she knew, pretend she'd seen nothing out of the ordinary. Yet the reason she'd been sitting here in the first place was because she'd had some vague, foolish notion about helping to help protect Annabel's little boy.

No, Nell knew she wouldn't be able to live with herself if she didn't do whatever she could to prevent something terrible from happening to a little boy. Not this time.

So she chose the third option. Starting up the Volvo's engine, she pulled away from the curb, made a U-turn at the corner, and headed down the street and around the corner after the van. With luck, it wouldn't reach the main highway before she caught up to it.

MISSY HUNG UP the phone and went to check on Nicky. He was curled up in the Port-a-Crib, sucking his thumb and sleeping peacefully. She covered him, pulling his blanket up to his tiny chin, and tiptoed out of the room, gently closing the door behind her.

Now to get Jason down for his nap, she thought, heading for the living room. If he cooperated, she'd have a good hour of privacy to phone her friends before her mom got back from having her hair done.

"Jason, nap time!" she called as she entered the living room. She looked around, spotting the bright red fire truck among the toys the boys had been playing with, but not her baby brother. "Come on, sweetie. Time to go sleepy-bye."

Missy looked behind the sofa and chairs, then pulled back the curtains. "Playing hide and seek, you little devil?" she asked, a laugh in her voice.

But when she didn't find him quickly, her playful mood turned to irritation. "Come on, Jason, I'm waiting. Come out, come out, wherever you are."

He couldn't have passed her in the hallway to the bedroom, could he? Unless maybe he'd toddled down the hall while she was on the phone with her mother. "Jason! This is so not funny!" she called. The house was deadly quiet, unusual whenever her brother was awake. Morbid news stories about small children who'd drowned in a toilet or been electrocuted when they found a hair pin on the floor and stuck it into an electric socket dancing in her head, Missy rushed down the hall to the bathroom, but Jason was nowhere to be found.

Increasingly worried, she methodically moved from room to room, looking under the beds, in the closets, in the kitchen. She knew that sometimes her brother liked to pull out her mother's pots and pans onto the kitchen floor. Maybe he'd gotten caught inside a cupboard, trying to find something new to play with. She dropped to her bare knees and crawled across the rough tiles of the kitchen floor, peering deep inside every one of the lower cupboards, but Jason wasn't there, either.

"Jason!" Missy cried, feeling panicky when she couldn't find him anywhere in the house. This was getting too weird! Could he somehow have gotten outside? She felt certain she'd locked all the doors after her mother left for the beauty shop. She checked the kitchen door and found it securely locked. The sliding doors from the family room to the patio also were closed and locked.

Back in the living room, Missy saw the front door standing ajar, as she'd left it for ventilation, and the screen door was still closed. She tried the doorknob. Her heart plummeted as the knob turned easily in her hand. The screen door was unlocked! Could Jason have done it? No way! His little fingers couldn't possibly have the coordination needed to push the tiny bolt aside. But if she'd forgotten to lock the screen door, could he have managed to turn the knob and push the door open by himself?

Missy had no idea. All she knew was that Jason wasn't in the house and the screen door was now unlocked. Somehow, her little brother must have managed to open it. Her mom was going to totally kill her when she found out!

*If* she found out, Missy rationalized. If only she could find Jason and get him back inside the house before her mother got home, nobody would ever have to know how bad she'd screwed up.

How long had he been gone? Missy checked the new pink-banded wristwatch she'd bought with her babysitting money, guessing that it had been maybe fifteen minutes, twenty at the most, since she'd left the living room to put Nicky down for his nap. How far could a one-year-old boy get in that amount of time? Surely not very far.

*Please, God, don't let him go into the street and get hit by a car,* Missy prayed as she ran into the front yard and down the street, calling her brother's name. Luckily, there was no traffic on the tree-lined road in front of her house. Just four parked cars.

For the next half hour, Missy frantically checked each neighbor's yard, behind bushes, under cars parked in driveways and on the street, in every space where a small boy might fit.

By the time she saw her mother's Mercedes turn onto the block, Missy was hysterical, now far more afraid for Jason than for herself. Tears of fear ran down her face as she sprinted toward her mother.

*"Mommy!"* she cried, feeling more like a frightened little girl than the pseudo-adult who'd been left in charge of two toddlers. "Jason got out and I can't find him anywhere!"

MAX'S PAGER vibrated in his pocket as he finished eating his grilled eggplant sandwich. He pulled it out and checked the number. "It's Harry," he told Annabel. "With luck, he's cracked into that computer and we can stop dancing around the subject with the cops." Eyeing the sign on each of the restaurant tables that dictated, "Cell Phone Use Prohibited!" he excused himself and went outside to return Harry's call from the sidewalk.

When he came back to the table a few minutes later, Annabel had finished as much of her crab salad as she could manage and was anxious to get back to Louise's. "I asked the waitress to bring us the check," she told Max indicating the black leather folder lying on the table. "What did Harry say?"

As he sat down, Max surveyed the small room to make sure nobody was listening to their conversation. When he was reassured, he leaned across the table and said in a low voice, "Harry managed to get into the computer's files. He found links to some hidden money."

Annabel wasn't surprised. Obviously, Dylan had money stashed away in a foreign account somewhere or he couldn't have used his computer to transfer that fifty thousand dollars into the local checking account. "How much money?" she asked.

Max lowered his voice even further. "Millions."

Her breath caught. *"Millions?"* she whispered.

Max nodded. "Harry says Dylan had a large account, worth something more than ten million dollars, at one of the major Internet stock brokerages. The account was closed out first thing Monday morning. Looks like a sell order was executed on Saturday night."

"Dylan must have done it when he broke into the house and used the computer," Annabel said, now more convinced than ever that the break-in had been her husband's handiwork. The larger mystery was what had happened to him after she'd scared him off and he'd fled through the office window.

"Sure looks that way," Max agreed. "The sell order directed that the account be completely liquidated as soon as the markets opened on Monday."

"But why? And where's the money from the stock sale now?"

"Let's take the second part first," Max said. "The money seems to have been transferred to a numbered bank account in the Cayman Islands. That kind of account is frequently used by drug dealers, embezzlers, con artists, anyone who doesn't want the government—or anyone else—to know their money exists, or to find it if they do know about it. Chances are Dylan already had some cash stashed away in that account. I don't think there's any way he could have opened it on Saturday night."

"Probably," Annabel said. "The bank teller told me the fifty thousand dollars that showed up in my checking account Monday morning was transferred from a foreign bank account. Must be this same account."

Max glanced at the lunch check, took three ten-dollar bills from his wallet, slid them inside the leather folder, and set it on the edge of the table with the cash protruding from the top.

"Could be," he agreed. "But, depending on what Dylan's deal was, it's possible he had several bank accounts hidden away in various places. There are quite a few friendly banking communities around the world where funny money can be hidden in numbered accounts, no names or Social Security numbers required, no questions asked the Cayman Islands, the Isle of Man, a few others."

Annabel pressed her fingertips against her throbbing temples, feeling more weary than ever. So this was why Dylan hadn't been ecstatic about inheriting his grandfather's millions—he already had millions, albeit undoubtedly dirty millions, of his own. And the prospect of all the attention being discovered as Oliver Nettleton's long-lost heir would bring made him panic. To Dylan, keeping his secret—whatever it was—had been worth forty million dollars.

Another wrinkle quickly occurred to Annabel. "The cops are going to see this money as another motive for me to have killed Dylan, aren't they?" she asked.

"Certainly isn't going to help your case," Max admitted. He paused as the waitress, a portly woman about Annabel's age, came to collect the check. "I don't need any change," he told her.

"Thanks," she said with a broad smile. "Come back soon."

Annabel waited until the waitress was out of earshot, then protested. "I didn't know a thing about this hidden money, Max. Please believe me. I didn't even know Dylan had a foreign bank account until I found that unexpected money in the checking account. I still don't know how much there is or how to get my hands on it. He never said a word to me about owning any stocks, either."

"I do believe you, Annabel. I'm just not sure the police will." Max reached across the table and rested his hand on top of his client's. "Look, we don't have to do the cops' work for them, and so far nobody's asked us about Dylan's computer. So we don't volunteer anything. Understand?"

Annabel nodded. "I've got to get back to Nicky," she said, noticing the time. "What happens next?"

"I'll stop at Harry's shop on my way back to the office, take a look at what he's found. Then maybe I'll have a better idea about what Dylan was trying to hide, and why. If we can figure that out, maybe we can figure out who killed him. In the meantime, you just take care of yourself and Nicky. Let me worry about the police. If they contact you, you have nothing to say about anything—not so much as the weather report—without your attorney present."

"Thanks, Max," Annabel said as the two left the restaurant and headed back across the street to their cars. "I don't know what I'd do without you to—well, without you."

Max waited until Annabel's car had pulled out into the street, then headed for Harry's computer shop with a combined sense of anticipation and dread.

NELL MISSED the green light at Carpenter Street and Highway 1, but at least she could see that the white van, which had made the light, was heading north on the highway. It was a long light, but traffic wasn't too heavy at this hour. With luck, she could catch up to the van before it exited from the highway and find out where it was going.

When the light finally turned green again and she made the left turn, Nell floored her old Volvo, cutting around an elderly driver in a green Cadillac who insisted on driving forty-five in the fast lane.

The speed limit quickly changed to sixty-five as Highway 1 became a freeway. Praying there were no cops with radar guns surveilling the highway, she kept her foot on the accelerator and watched as her speedometer reached seventy-five, then eighty. She tried to eyeball the exit ramp at Highway 68 west, then the ones at Munras Avenue and Aguajito Road, but didn't see the van. She kept driving north.

"Shoot," she said five minutes later, figuring she'd lost them. But just as she'd almost given up hope of finding it, she spotted the van pulling over into the right lane approaching the Highway 68 exit eastbound. A large sign marked it as the route to the local airport. Nell felt a wave of panic. Could the men be planning to fly the child out of town? Surely they couldn't expect to avoid drawing attention on a commercial flight. And if they had a private plane, she'd have no way of tracking them.

But luck was with her, at least for the moment. The van avoided the sharp right turn to the airport, instead exiting on adjacent Fremont Boulevard and heading toward Seaside. Nell followed, keeping a few cars between her and the van, in case the driver had seen her car parked on the street near Annabel's house. The last thing she wanted was to cause the two men to panic and harm the child.

She managed to make the first several stoplights on green or yellow and maintain her short distance behind the van as it passed a series of fast food joints, a large drug store, and several motels. But at Canyon del Rey, the pickup truck ahead of her stopped on the yellow and she had no choice but to hit the brakes and wait for the light to change. As she saw the van pull away and disappear into the stream of traffic turning onto Fremont at the intersection, she swore under her breath.

When the light turned green again, Nell proceeded north on Fremont, past used merchandise stores, taco shops, and a huge auto mall, to the point where the street rejoined Highway 1, but the white van had disappeared. It must have stopped or turned off of Fremont, she figured. If the driver had planned to continue north on the freeway, there was no reason to detour onto Fremont—unless he'd been checking his rearview mirror for a tail.

Instead of proceeding onto the freeway, Nell turned around and retraced her route along Fremont Boulevard, looking for the white van among the vehicles parked along the street.

But it was nowhere in sight.

WHEN ANNABEL pulled into the curb in front of the Zuckermans' house, she noticed that Louise's Mercedes was already in the driveway. Her relief that an adult was now in charge of the children, however, evaporated almost immediately.

As Annabel climbed out of her car, Louise rushed over to her and quickly explained that Jason was missing, that she and Missy were checking with all the neighbors on the block to see if anyone might have taken him in. "If we don't find him in the next ten minutes, I'm calling the police," she added, looking haggard and years older than she had this morning, despite her brand new hairdo.

"My God!" Annabel said, her spirits plummeting at the news. Then a new fear, one far closer to home, struck her. "Where's Nicky?"

"In the house, still napping," Louise said. "He's fine. I

checked on him the minute I got home. Go see for yourself, then come back outside and help us search for Jason."

Quickly agreeing, Annabel rushed into the house. She was relieved to hear Nicky whimpering in the guest bedroom, making the familiar sounds he made whenever he awakened from a nap. As she headed down the hall toward her son, the telephone rang.

"Hold on a minute, Nicky. Mommy'll be right there," she called to reassure him before detouring to the master bedroom to answer the nearest telephone. Maybe it was somebody calling about Jason.

"Hello," she said, when she'd grabbed the receiver off the nightstand. "Zuckerman residence."

"It's about time somebody answered! Put on Annabel Nettleton," a low, muffled voice demanded.

"Speaking." Who knew she would be at the Zuckermans' house? Only Max and the police, as far as Annabel knew. *"Who is this?"*

"Listen carefully, Mrs. Nettleton—only gonna tell you this once. We got your little boy. We're not gonna hurt him, long as you give us back our money and keep your mouth shut about it. Understand?"

"What? What are you talking about? Nicky's—" Annabel caught herself in mid-sentence as a terrible thought occurred to her. *The person on the phone thought he—or was it she—had Nicky, not Jason.* "What money?" she asked, hoping she hadn't already revealed too much about what quickly could become a catastrophe for poor little Jason. "I don't know what you're talking about."

"Cut the bull. Your asshole husband stole twenty mil that belongs to us and now you got it. You don't give it back, your kid is history. Your choice, lady. *And no cops.* You call the cops and your boy's as dead as his old man. Got it?"

Annabel's knees went weak and she sat down on the edge of the high king-size bed. "Yes," she said in a small, frightened voice, her hand beginning to shake so hard she could barely keep the receiver against her ear. Whoever was calling must know about the millions Dylan stashed away in that foreign account…unless the kidnapper was some nutcase who'd seen the TV coverage and thought she already had access to part of the Nettleton inheritance. Either way, she figured she'd better stall for time. Otherwise, Jason Zuckerman was going to die.

"Be at the phone booth in Del Monte Center, the one outside Macy's on the lower level, at nine tomorrow morning," the muffled voice continued. "Wait for a call. We'll be watching you. You contact the cops, we'll know it, and your kid is history." The caller hung up without waiting for a response.

Stunned and trembling, Annabel ran to the guest bedroom, lifted her son out of the Port-a-Crib, and held his small form tightly against her body. She felt a complicated mixture of emotions—unbelievable, almost shamefully strong relief that it hadn't been Nicky who'd been snatched, tempered by a deep sense of guilt that her friend's child had been taken in place of her own. This whole mess had nothing to do with Louise or her family; the Zuckermans had done nothing but try to be kind, to help during the darkest hours of her life. Now look what their generosity had gotten them.

Worst of all, Annabel was afraid she would do something wrong, that she would make some false move and inadvertently cause little Jason's death. She was terrified she wouldn't be able to act fast enough to get the kidnappers the money they were demanding, and the Zuckermans would end up paying an unthinkable price for her sins.

Did she really have the ability, the power, to get Jason back to his mother unharmed? Or was Jason's kidnapping just the latest example of what Annabel had come to consider her personal curse—the fact that almost everyone she'd ever cared about ended up dead?

*No!* She stopped her negative thought process cold—nei ther self-pity nor self-blame would do Jason a bit of good. She had no choice but to get that money out of the Cayman Islands account or accounts in time, whatever it took. She was ready to hand over every last nickel to the kidnappers in exchange for that little boy. Annabel could never keep that cash, any way, not when it obviously came from a tainted source. Money meant nothing in comparison with an innocent child's life.

If only she could stall the kidnappers long enough to fig ure out how to get the ransom and transfer it…without get ting caught by the police.

Annabel hugged Nicky to her breast, instinctively afraid to let him go. She buried her nose in his sweet-smelling hair, inhaling his reassuring baby scent. He squirmed to get down.

"Not yet, kiddo," she whispered to him. "Gotta go tell Louise." As she carried Nicky outdoors, Annabel noticed the small slit in the black mesh of the screen door. So it had been that easy, she realized. The kidnappers had made this almost invisible little cut in the screen, reached inside to unlock the door, then snatched Jason away as he played with the toys still strewn across the living room floor.

*Gone in a flash.*

If they'd been watching her and Nicky, it was understand able the kidnappers had mixed up the two boys. Jason was a couple of months older, but not much larger than Nicky. And both of the boys had white-blond hair. It was even possible the kidnappers didn't know Jason existed, that they'd had no idea Missy'd been babysitting for two toddlers.

Annabel didn't even want to think about how terrified the poor little tyke must be by now. Her heart a stone within her

chest, she carried Nicky out onto the front steps and waved
to Louise, who was still trudging down the block from one
neighbor's house to the next. "Come on back!" Annabel called
to her. "I've got news about Jason."

The look of sheer relief she saw on her friend's face as she
sprinted back toward her opulent home stabbed Annabel to
the core.

"I'LL MASSACRE the goddamned assholes!" Louise said as
soon as Annabel had sent the children back to the guest house
and told her neighbor about the kidnappers' telephone call.
"They harm one hair on Jason's head and I'll gouge their
eyes out and smash them! I'll rip their fingers off, one at a
time! Lethal injection is too damn good for scum like this. I—
I'm going to make them *suffer!*" Her eyes were narrow slits,
her thin body rigid with tension and rage.

Annabel reached over and patted Louise's shoulder. "It's
going to be okay," she said, trying as much to convince herself as much as her friend. "Nothing bad is going to happen
to Jason. As long as these people keep thinking they've got
Nicky, I can pay the ransom and we'll get him back. It'll
work out okay."

Louise's eyes burned with a wild, irrational fire. "These
jerks don't know who they're dealing with! Nobody hurts me
or my kids and gets away with it. Never again!"

"Come on, let's sit down and think this over." Startled by
her friend's outburst, Annabel shoved aside the abandoned red
fire engine with her foot, then guided Louise over to one of
the loveseats and sat down beside her.

"I'll call the police, the FBI, hell, I'll call the goddamned
President if that's what it takes to find these suckers." Louise
was trembling with indignation and fear now, and her eyes
began to fill.

Annabel fought to keep calm despite her own growing anxiety. It wouldn't help for both of them to become unhinged by their fears. "Look, Louise," she said, "Jason's your son and it's your decision. But the caller made it very, very clear—if the police get involved, they're going to kill him. Do you really want to take chances with Jason's life?"

"Of course not!" Louise snapped at her. "He's my son! I don't want any of this—" She ground her knuckles into her eye sockets. "I—I can't even think straight. *How the hell could this happen?*"

Annabel sighed deeply. "It's because of us," she admitted, contrite. "Whoever these people are, they thought they were snatching Nicky. I don't understand what's going on, either, but it has something to do with Dylan and his secret past."

"I've got it!" Louise said, wiping away a tear. "Tomorrow, when you take that phone call, tell them they took the wrong boy. They'll probably be watching you, and if you take Nicky along, they'll know you're not lying, right?" She shifted nervously in her seat. "Or, better yet—we can call that TV reporter who interviewed you before, get him to do a story for tonight's news. His interview will show everybody you've still got Nicky right here with you. Hell, Annabel, Nicky's the one they want, not Jason. Jason's no good to them at all."

Annabel reached over and laid her hand on Louise's arm. "Think about what you just said, Louise— *Jason's no good to them.*"

Louise nodded, her eyebrows knotted in confusion.

"Look, anybody who kidnaps a child in broad daylight and holds him for ransom isn't just going to bring him back and say, 'Oops, sorry, got the wrong kid.' *Think* a minute. If the kidnappers realize they haven't got Nicky Nettleton, they'll simply kill Jason, dump his body somewhere, and figure out some other way to get the money." They might do that anyway, Annabel realized, but Louise certainly didn't need to hear that.

Louise jerked her arm away from Annabel's touch. "God, I wish I'd—" She caught herself in mid-sentence, but physically shrank away from Annabel, a clear look of horror and revulsion on her face.

"I know," Annabel said. "You wish you'd never met me. Right now I must seem like pure venom to you, and I can't blame you for feeling that way. I've brought you nothing but bad luck and heartache and I—I can't begin to tell you how sorry I am. *Damn,* that sounds so inadequate!"

Her heart overflowing with sorrow and regret, Annabel trembled with suppressed emotion. "If—if I'd had any idea what I was getting into, I'd never have gotten you involved, Louise. Hell, I'd never have married Dylan in the first place. Then you and I never would've met, and you'd be far better off."

"Not a helluva lot we can do about that now, is there?" Louise was clearly, understandably, bitter. "Your husband's been murdered, mine is in China, and my baby's gone…maybe forever. Shoot! I can't even reach Sid to tell him what's happened. Not unless maybe I contact the State Department. When he goes to China, I never know where he's staying until he calls home."

Annabel shook her head. "You can't notify the State Department, Louise, not without getting the police involved," she warned, adding, "I want you to know I'll do whatever it takes to get Jason back. Not one thing less than I'd do to rescue Nicky."

Louise's chin quivered, but she fought against dissolving into tears. Her rage of a few minutes ago seemed to have played itself out and she suddenly went limp. "So—so let's try to figure this out logically," she said, slumping back against the love-seat's cushions. "Explain to me about this money they want."

"They claim Dylan stole twenty million dollars from—"

*"Twenty million dollars!"* Louise's rigid posture returned instantaneously.

"That's what the guy—the person—on the phone said."

"But how could somebody steal that much money? It must—it has to be illegal drug money, right?"

"Don't think I haven't been asking myself the same thing." Annabel related what Max had told her about the stock market account, worth about half of what Dylan had supposedly stolen, as well as the foreign bank account. "He thought there might be other accounts, too."

"Jesus."

"We can't assume it's drug money, though. There have to be other ways somebody could steal that much—fraud, maybe, or embezzlement, I don't know. Or maybe they were into counterfeiting or robbing banks or illegal arms sales. Crime isn't something I know a whole lot about, other than maybe spotting bogus airline tickets. Dylan obviously did *something* illegal, though, something really big. Otherwise he'd have no reason to hide all that money in the Cayman Islands."

"Or to keep moving around every few months. It's completely obvious he was running away from something or somebody." Louise gazed at Annabel with sharp, accusing eyes. "How in the hell could you have lived with Dylan all that time and *not know?*"

Annabel felt the sting of her friend's charge and recoiled. Yet she knew she had no real excuses. "Guess I didn't want to know," she admitted. "Truth is, I was living in a fantasy world while my husband was—I don't know—doing whatever it was he did. Maybe he was actively stealing money, or maybe he'd stopped and was simply running away with the proceeds, investing them so he could make more money. Dylan never told me a thing about any of it. By the time I was ready to demand that our marriage change or I was getting out, all *this* happened and—and—it was just too damned late." She drew a deep breath. "I don't know what else to say, Louise."

Louise glanced around her posh living room with its matching silk loveseats, imported lamps, original artwork on the walls, and antique secretary in the corner, as though bewildered that something so horrible as a kidnapping could possibly have happened here—in the safe, expensive cocoon she'd created for her second marriage. "How are you going to come up with all that money?" she asked.

"I'm not sure yet. Guess I can ask my lawyer's computer expert how to withdraw it from those foreign bank accounts. He can probably tell me."

"And just how do you plan to explain the deal so this computer guy doesn't turn you in to the cops?"

"I—I don't know. Guess it *does* look a bit suspicious."

"No lie."

Annabel thought for a moment. "Max," she said, finally. "Anything I tell my lawyer has to stay completely confidential. Certainly Max'll know how I can get my hands on that money without raising any red flags."

Louise looked skeptical. "You know what I think of lawyers—most of them are greedy crooks—and twenty million bucks is an awful lot of money. Can you really trust this guy?"

"I sure hope so."

Louise sighed. "Jesus, Annabel. *Hope so!* Hope so just doesn't cut it. My kid's life is at stake here! I mean, Jesus, get it together. It's not like you've got a great track record when it comes to judging men, and this one's a *lawyer,* for godsake."

Annabel bristled, tired of being attacked, no matter how justified Louise's anger might be. "You got a better idea?" she snapped.

Louise closed her eyes and pressed her fingertips against

her throbbing temples. "Guess not," she admitted after a moment's thought. "Just don't forget—this time, it's *my* son's life that depends on your so-called judgment."

MAX HAD JUST LEFT Harry's computer shop in downtown Monterey when he got Annabel's page with an emergency 9-1-1 added after the Zuckermans' phone number. He returned her call from his cell phone, only to have his client tell him she couldn't discuss her latest crisis on the telephone. He agreed to meet her at the Zuckermans' guest house as soon as possible.

Feeling a surge of adrenaline he never got from his usual cases, he called his secretary and asked her to cancel his afternoon appointments. Old Mrs. Joyner's will and the Schmidts' divorce settlement could wait another day.

As Max turned onto the freeway and headed south toward Carmel, he noticed it was time for the hourly news. He switched on the car radio and listened. A U.S. Senator was in San Francisco today, using his speech at a private university to criticize the President's economic plan, he heard, and both sides claimed progress toward settling an ongoing nurses' strike. It was the third item in the newscast that riveted Max's attention.

"An apparent homicide victim found in a rough Salinas neighborhood early this morning has been identified as an Illinois private investigator," the newscaster reported. "Jeffrey Link of Chicago was discovered by neighbors in the early morning hours. He'd been shot once in the chest, apparently robbed of all identification, and left in the parking lot of a small liquor store."

The report switched to an audio-taped statement by the Salinas Police Department's Public Information Officer. "The quick identification of the victim was made by a sharp-eyed police officer who was called to the scene," she announced. "Officer Jaime Gonzales remembered watching Jeffrey Link on a TV news report about the Dylan Nettleton murder investigation in Carmel. So we asked the Illinois Licensing Board to fax us Link's fingerprints and, shortly after they arrived, we were able to make a positive ID of the victim."

Max's knuckles whitened on the steering wheel. Was the murder of Jeffrey Link the reason Annabel had called him in an obvious panic? Maybe she'd heard about it on an earlier radio report. He recalled seeing that same TV interview of Link, a repeat of an earlier one about the PI having located the heir to the Oliver Nettleton fortune. On TV, Link had seemed a decent enough man, an average sort of guy who was genuinely pleased about bringing unexpected wealth to a long-lost heir.

Yet it now looked as though Link had been the catalyst in Dylan's murder...and maybe his own as well. Max figured there had to be a relationship between the two. First Dylan, and now the PI who'd found him, murdered—it couldn't possibly be a coincidence.

Yet the radio newscaster indicated otherwise. "At this time," he continued, "no connection has been made between Jeffrey Link's slaying in Salinas and that of Dylan Nettleton in Carmel earlier in the week. Link's rental car was found abandoned in downtown Monterey and his murder is being investigated as a car-jacking gone bad.

"It's not known what Link was doing in the Salinas neighborhood, which is notorious for its frequent gang warfare. He is the fourth man shot to death this year within a three-block area. All three of the other victims were known gang members."

As the anchorman segued to the weather forecast, Max switched off the radio, suddenly wondering whether his defending Annabel Nettleton was either smart or safe.

Maybe the cops were right and Link's death was a simple

car-jacking that had turned deadly. But the cops didn't know about Dylan's computer or the millions of dollars the young father had hidden away in foreign bank accounts. They didn't know about the Saturday night break-in at Annabel's Carmel cottage, either. And even if they did, they had a preconceived notion they were busily trying to prove—that Annabel had killed Dylan. Link's murder could threaten their efforts. Surely they couldn't believe Annabel also murdered the private investigator in Salinas sometime last night. And, if she didn't do that, then maybe she didn't kill her husband, either.

So the cops would look for another explanation for Link's murder—virtually any other explanation that didn't threaten their theory about Annabel's guilt.

To Max, however, this unexpected news boded something entirely different. It meant that Annabel was probably in danger from more than just from the police who wanted to put her on trial for murder. She also was in peril from whoever had killed Dylan and Link.

And, if Link had been killed because he knew too much, could Max himself also end up a victim?

He quickly pushed the thought away. If he wasn't willing to take a risk now and then, he told himself, his future would continue to consist of drawing up wills and negotiating divorce settlements until he died of boredom. That sort of work had been palatable when Betsy was still alive, and it had even been a godsend during the months when she was dying—he'd been able to do it almost by rote, allowing him to give most of his energy to her needs.

But in the past few months, he'd become famished for work that was more challenging, more meaningful.

Now that it had come to him unbidden, he couldn't throw it away simply because of a sharp stab of apprehension deep inside his gut.

# NINE

ONCE MORE, Nell drove the full length of Fremont Boulevard between its two intersections with Highway 1 without spotting the white van. She glanced at the clock on her dashboard. It was already well after noon and she realized she was famished.

She pulled into the Safeway's parking lot and drove up and down the lanes of parked cars. When she'd convinced herself the van wasn't here, she parked her Volvo and went into the grocery store to buy something to eat.

After returning to her car with the whole wheat crackers and wedge of brie she'd bought, she settled back into the driver's seat and rolled down the window for ventilation. The fog had burned off and it was growing warm here in Seaside, which was more sheltered from the Pacific's breezes than Carmel. She took a bite of brie, then a bite of cracker, and turned on the radio just in time for a local news update. Seeking reassurance that what she'd seen at the Zuckerman house wasn't some sort of LSD flashback, she hoped to hear a breaking news story about the kidnapping—if what she'd witnessed was, indeed, a kidnapping.

Instead, Nell heard the report of Jeffrey Link's murder.

"God!" she muttered. The cracker in her mouth turned to sawdust and she choked. Taking a long swig from her bottle of organic tangerine juice, she did her best to wash it down and clear her throat.

Nell's appetite quickly vanished as she contemplated the troubling news. The car-jacking story sounded highly unlikely to her. What were the odds? Probably the cops didn't even believe the story they'd put out to the media—maybe they wanted the murderers to think they'd gotten away with it, so they'd get sloppy and be easier to catch.

No, she figured the men who'd killed the little boy's father now had murdered that private eye she'd seen on CNN. Were they the same two now driving the white van?

The more she thought about it, the more Nell felt certain the body of Annabel's husband had to have been in that huge appliance box she saw being delivered while the young woman and her son were out of the house. The pair of deliverymen had arrived in a black pickup truck and Nell had been too far away to see their faces clearly as they unloaded the heavy-looking box and used a dolly to get it into the house. She couldn't say whether or not they were the same two men she saw today, but the black pickup truck could have been exchanged for the white van easily enough. For all she knew, both vehicles could have been stolen.

And, if the same guys who'd murdered twice now had snatched that poor child, what unspeakable things might they do to him? Would he, too, end up stuffed into a cardboard box like so much trash?

Nell shoved the crackers and cheese back into the white plastic Safeway bag. If that white van was anywhere in the area, she vowed, she would find it before the kidnappers had a chance to dump it—even if she had to drive up and down every one of the cross streets and through each store and motel parking lot until it got too dark to see.

She started her engine and pulled out of the parking lot, back into the continuous stream of Fremont Boulevard traffic.

WHEN HE ARRIVED at the Zuckermans' guest house, Max could tell Annabel had been crying. Her eyes were red and puffy and her mascara had run, giving her blue eyes a slightly raccoon-like appearance.

She hurriedly explained that she'd left her son at the main house so she'd have privacy to tell Max what had happened while they'd been lunching in Carmel. Her eyes filled from time to time, yet she managed to keep herself under control as she explained about Jason's kidnapping and the subsequent phone call she'd received.

Standing opposite Annabel in the middle of the tiny guest house, Max's heart went out to her and he was seized by a sudden desire to take this tall, strong, yet obviously emotionally vulnerable woman in his arms and comfort her. But he stopped himself. That would be completely inappropriate. After all, he reminded himself, he was merely her attorney, not her—Her *what?* he asked himself. His mind veered toward something more, but he forced the thoroughly unprofessional thought away and settled on "friend." If he didn't blow this case and he was lucky, he sincerely hoped, someday soon Annabel might begin to consider him her friend…perhaps even her very good friend.

"So that's why I've got to get hold of that money right away," she said somewhat breathlessly when she'd finished relating her story. Her pale brow was deeply furrowed with worry and she twisted a long strand of her blond hair around her index finger, yanking on it rhythmically in a self-punishing manner.

"I need to get Dylan's computer back and I need somebody to tell me how to use it to transfer the money and turn it into cash for Jason's ransom," Annabel added. "But the police can't find out what I'm doing. It all has to be completely secret. I thought about going to Harry myself, asking him to show me what to do. But I figured if you went instead, he might be, uh, he might be—"

"More inclined to be discreet?" Max suggested.

A faint, embarrassed smile flickered across Annabel's lips, then died. She sighed loudly. "Why beat around the bush?" she said. "I'm not ashamed to admit it—I'm scared to death Harry will go to the cops, I'll end up in jail, and Jason will die…because of me. Just when you think things can't possibly get worse…"

Max reached over and almost touched Annabel's trembling shoulder, then withdrew his hand as though he'd caught it acting of its own volition. What if she took the physical contact he meant to be reassuring the wrong way? When he'd touched her arm after the session at the police station, he'd felt her stiffen. And her embarrassment when Eileen Kopek had implied there might be an amorous reason for his being at Annabel's house on Sunday morning had been painfully obvious. He decided he'd better keep his hands to himself.

"Harry's pretty solid," he told her, hoping he was right. "You're smart not to go to him directly, though. We don't want him thinking you're sneaking behind your attorney's back, maybe planning to cash in all those millions and disappear."

"We can't tell him anything about Jason," Annabel warned as she turned away and began to pace the floor of the small guest house, her long fingers knotted together in front of her. "Not one word. I promised Louise I wouldn't do anything to endanger her son…nothing more than I already have, at least."

"*You* didn't put Jason in danger, Annabel. It was just bad—"

"Bad luck? Yeah, right. I've tried telling myself that, Max. But the truth is—" Annabel gestured toward the big house across the backyard. "The truth is that Jason would be home, playing happily with his mom and sister right now, if Nicky and I hadn't been staying here in the guest house, and if Louise hadn't been kind enough to offer to babysit for me. Then those horrible people might have *my* son instead of hers." She paused and took a breath, a tear now threatening to spill over onto her cheek. "Oh, hell, Max. This I *am* ashamed to admit— deep inside me, I'm *glad* they got Jason instead. No matter what terrible thing happens to him, I'm still grateful it's not Nicky."

Max nodded reluctantly. "Look, Annabel, I understand how you feel. I have a kid of my own and, if anything like this happened to Katie, I—well, I don't even know what I'd do. Don't up beat on yourself. What you're feeling is only human, what any parent would feel."

"Thanks for understanding, Max. But I still feel—I still *am*—responsible."

Max momentarily considered telling Annabel that Jeff Link had been found dead, but decided that news could wait. Link's murder probably had nothing to do with Jason's kidnapping, anyway. Annabel's caller had spoken of money Dylan had supposedly stolen, saying nothing about his expected inheritance. Telling her about Link's murder now would probably end up as just one more thing she'd feel guilty about—if the private eye hadn't been out here looking for Dylan, he wouldn't have been car-jacked, and so on and on…until she'd turned his death into something else she believed was her fault.

Instead, Max looked around at the small guest house. "Maybe it's time for you to leave here," he suggested, "both for your own safety and for Louise's." Surely he could help her find someplace else to stay…just in case.

Annabel shook her head vigorously. "No. I thought about that. My first reaction was to grab Nicky and run, to get out of here as fast as we could go, before anything could happen to him, too. But I'm stuck here. I can't leave town because of the police investigation, and I certainly can't show up anywhere else close by with Nicky. What if the kidnappers are watching me? They'll realize they took the wrong boy and— Anyway, as long as I'm staying here at Louise's, they can go right on thinking Nicky is Jason and Jason is Nicky, and both boys will be better off."

Max was impressed with the way his client had thought things through quite logically, even while under what had to be nearly unbearable stress. "So Nicky's going to be staying up at the big house?" he asked.

"Just during the day," Annabel explained. "Once it's dark outside, I'll sneak him back in here with me for the night. That should work out for tonight. Tomorrow, after I take that phone call, things may change. If I can give the kidnappers their money, we can get Jason back and then Nicky and I will find a motel room or a vacation rental or something."

Max thought for a moment. "Tell you what. I'll stop back over at Harry's shop and ask him to make me a backup copy of everything on that hard drive. I'll tell him I need it in case the cops confiscate the computer, give him a story about how I have to make sure my client can't be put at a disadvantage in court later on, if things ever get to that point. He'll buy it, I'm sure he will. Then Harry can keep the computer itself in his shop and Benny can fingerprint it this afternoon."

"I'm not sure I understand what that's going to do for us," Annabel protested.

Max did his best to explain his plan. "The backup diskette will include all of Dylan's passwords, his bank account locations—Harry found more than just the one—and the account numbers, the balances in each one, everything that's on his hard drive. Once we have that, we should be able to access those accounts from any computer, not just from Dylan's. But what I don't know yet is what it takes to actually transfer the funds to another bank here in the States and, frankly, I'm fairly positive we can't figure that out and manage to do everything by tomorrow morning."

Annabel abruptly halted her pacing and sank down onto one of the wooden chairs next to the small breakfast table. "But if I don't have the money ready for them by the time they call tomorrow, the kidnappers said they'd kill Jason." She looked lost.

"Look," Max said, sitting down across the table from her, "these guys don't want to kill a child. What they want is Dylan's money, and they're not stupid. When you take that phone call tomorrow, you'll have to make them understand that the money is in foreign bank accounts and it's going to take you a while to get it. If they really knew your husband, they shouldn't be at all surprised to hear he stashed his cash outside the country."

Annabel sprang back out of her seat and resumed her pacing. "How about this?" she said. "These are all numbered accounts with no name or Social Security number or anything like that attached to them, right?"

Max nodded. "From what Harry told me."

"Then how about I offer to give the kidnappers this backup diskette and they can transfer the money wherever they want it themselves?"

"That *might* work, assuming they're computer savvy. At the very least, it should delay things, which will give us a chance to figure out what to do next."

"Okay, then. That's what we'll do. I'll stop by and pick up the diskette from your office before I take that phone call tomorrow morning."

As soon as she'd made a decision, Max noticed, Annabel seemed calmer, resigned. He understood what that was like. Still, as her attorney, he knew he had to remind her of a difficult choice she was facing. "Sit down a minute, Annabel," he said. "There's one more thing we need to talk about." He waited to speak until she returned to the wooden chair and sat down across from him once more.

"You know these are really bad guys or they wouldn't have kidnapped Jason, right?"

"Of course, I know. But I have to do whatever I possibly can to save that child's life."

"I'm not suggesting otherwise. But I want you to understand something."

Annabel straightened up, as though bracing to receive a blow.

"If we get the police involved, tell them that Jason Zuckerman has been kidnapped in your boy's place—"

"No!" Annabel snapped. "I said *no cops!*"

"Just hear me out," Max pleaded. "What you need to understand, Annabel, is that these are very likely the same people who killed Dylan, probably because he wouldn't give them the money himself."

"I'm not stupid. I already figured that out."

"Of course. But have you considered this? By giving in to their demands and denying the police what could be a very good chance to catch Dylan's real killers, you may be costing yourself far more than the money. You could be losing your best defense against *your* being formally charged with murdering your husband."

Annabel closed her eyes and massaged her temples briefly. When she opened her eyes again, she shot Max a sad but resigned look. "That's a chance I'll have to take," she said softly. "I gave Louise my word and that's all there is to it."

As DUSK ARRIVED, Nell felt a surge of hope. She spotted a white van parked on Fremont near the Monterey entrance to Highway 1. She pulled into the curb a few spaces behind the van, looked around, got out of her Volvo and walked along the sidewalk, as though heading for the Chinese cafe on the corner. The pungent smells of garlic, ginger, and hot oil emanating from the restaurant made her mouth water.

As she walked past it, Nell saw that van seemed unoccupied. She glanced at the passenger side window, but could see nothing unusual and she didn't want to draw attention to herself by venturing too close. Discouraged, she realized she couldn't even be certain this was the same vehicle. And, even if it was, its being parked here on the street could indicate that the kidnappers had simply abandoned it.

"Damn!" she said aloud. She was tired and hungry and she'd accomplished nearly nothing today, except using up half a tank of gas she could ill afford. It was time to admit defeat, she decided, at least for the night. Soon it would be too dark to see anything, anyway. She told herself she could come back early in the morning and watch to see if anyone returned to the van.

In the meantime, Nell checked her dwindling cash before treating herself to an inexpensive takeout dinner of sweet and sour tofu with a side of rice at the Chinese restaurant. Bag in hand, she headed back to her car.

What if she'd jumped to a ridiculous conclusion this morning, she asked herself as she placed the warm bag of food on the passenger seat and braced it with her purse. What if there had been no kidnapping at all, and the two men had had a perfectly good reason for taking the boy? The child might be home right now and she'd feel like a complete ass for spending half the day chasing after them.

Nell headed back toward Carmel, planning to eat her dinner in the car after she got to the street where Annabel and her child were staying. After it became completely dark outside and there was a better chance no neighbors home from work would spot her, she could peek in the windows of the

Zuckerman house. With any luck at all, she'd be able to reassure herself that both toddlers were alive and well and safe at home with their mothers. Then she could abandon this crazy wild goose chase.

It was nearly eleven o'clock before the neighbors' lights went out and activity on the block settled down enough that Nell dared venture from the shelter of her parked car. Quietly, she dumped the remains of her dinner into a trash can three doors away from the Zuckermans' house, then crept along the sidewalk toward it.

But as she approached, she saw a tall, hooded figure carrying something heavy in one hand coming from the opposite direction. Shoot, she thought, it was probably another neighbor, somebody who might question her presence here at this late hour. She dropped back into the shadow of a cypress tree in the front yard of the house next door and silently waited for the tall figure to pass by.

But he turned into the Zuckermans' driveway, then disappeared around the side of the house. Holding her breath, Nell watched and waited, wondering why, if he belonged there, the dark-clothed man hadn't used the front door.

A few minutes later, the dark figure returned, sprinting back around the front of the house. The bulky object he carried now seemed much lighter, swinging freely in his hand as he jogged back in the direction from which he'd come.

"What the—" Nell muttered under her breath. Before the figure reached the corner and disappeared into the night, she saw a bright flash behind the Zuckermans' house, then smelled the unmistakable stench of smoke.

She ran toward the white house, but it looked sound enough. The smoke was coming from somewhere behind it.

Nell hurried around the side and into the backyard, just in time to see flames spread across the door of the guest house.

A PIERCING WAIL pulled Annabel slowly from the depths of sleep. She rolled over, wondering groggily why the teakettle was boiling at this hour. Had she sleepwalked into the kitchen and turned on the stove? Bone-weary, she pulled a pillow over her ear and tried to return to her dream, but the ear-splitting shriek persisted, refusing to let her slip back into slumber.

As she wakened fully, she took a breath and choked. The screeching noise wasn't a teakettle, she realized with a start; it was a smoke alarm!

She sat bolt upright in bed and gagged as she attempted to draw another breath of the acrid air. Her eyes stung and a thick haze billowed upward around her bed, limiting her visibility to no more than a foot or two.

Still, she could see that she was not in her familiar bedroom at home. Now it came back to her—she'd had to take Nicky and leave on a moment's notice. After the murder, the police had cordoned off her house and she'd had to move to Louise's.

*Nicky!* Her heart pounded and she broke into a cold sweat despite the rapidly rising temperature inside the small building. Where was he? Annabel stumbled out of bed, the rough carpeting warm beneath her bare feet.

"Help!" she tried to call, but she couldn't get her breath and the word came out as a croak. No one would hear her over the shrieking smoke alarm anyway.

Gasping for air, she dropped to her knees. She'd once read that in a fire you should stay low—smoke rises, so the air near the floor stays fresher. She began to crawl away from the bed and quickly became entangled in her old flannel nightgown. She yanked it up around her waist to free her knees and felt the harsh surface of the rough flooring scuff her tender skin. At least she could move now, but in which direction should she go?

Her eyes streamed with tears—both from the toxic fumes and from the terror that gripped her—and she could see nothing but billowing smoke. She would have to feel her way to the baby's crib—*thank God they were sleeping in the same room*—and then somehow manage to locate the door to the outside and safety.

Think! she ordered herself.

She was lost in the thick, choking haze and the air was running out fast. If her child was crying for her, she couldn't even hear him over the persistent wail of the alarm.

Remember the layout of the guest house and find your son!

As Annabel crawled away from her bed, a red-orange light flashed up the guest house wall ahead of her, fire consuming the drapes across the window that faced the main house. The flames illuminated a way out of the smoke-filled room, yet blocked it at the same time. But at least they showed her the path to the crib—the small bed stood between her and the fingers of fire that curled relentlessly upward toward the ceiling.

Fighting not to lose consciousness, she pushed herself along the floor until she felt the hard leg of the portable crib against her hand. She reached up and grasped one of the bed's safety bars, then a second, and slowly managed to pull herself to her feet. With the last of her strength, she reached over the top rail and picked up her son.

He was limp, twenty-five pounds of dead weight. She couldn't tell if he was still breathing.

*He couldn't be dead! There was no way she could survive losing another person she loved.*

The listless child clasped to her breast, Annabel fell to her knees, gasping and dizzy. Deprived of oxygen, her muscles had turned to jelly and her legs would no longer support her. Still holding her small son, she slumped to the floor and collapsed in a heap.

As she felt her child stir briefly in her arms and the flames began to spread across the floor toward her, she rolled into a ball, using her body to shield her son from the fire that threatened to consume everything it touched.

Then her world faded to black and she passed out.

# TEN

"FIRE!" NELL YELLED as loudly as she could. She banged on the front door of the Zuckermans' house. "Help! Fire! Call 9-1-1!"

When there seemed to be no immediate response to her shouts, she ran back to her car, cursing herself for not owning a cell phone. She grabbed the crowbar she kept for protection from underneath the passenger seat and ran back to the burning guest house.

Still she heard no rescue sirens approaching, but Nell could see that the side of the small guest house facing the main house was already burning briskly. A wall of flame engulfed the only doorway, preventing either entry or escape.

Her weapon gripped firmly in her hand, she skirted the burning building and tried approaching it from the ocean side. As she moved, a combination of oily black smoke and petroleum fumes burned her eyes, blurring her vision. Still, through streaming tears, she could tell that the large picture window facing the sea offered the only possible means of entrance to the guest house.

Gasping for air and feeling the blistering heat against her face, Nell swung her crowbar at the plate glass window with all the strength she could muster. She managed to punch a baseball-size hole in the glass. Cracks quickly spread outward from it, forming a spider-web pattern. She swung the crowbar again and again until most of the window was reduced to splinters of glass on the floor beneath its low wooden frame.

Using the crowbar as a scraper, Nell removed the remaining shards of glass from the windowsill. Then, tossing her weapon aside, she took a deep breath and, holding the edge of her sweater over her nose and mouth as a mask, climbed through the opening into the burning building.

Inside, the smoke was thick and the heat was quickly becoming unbearable. The shriek of a smoke alarm was suddenly silenced as the electrical wires leading to it burned through with a sharp crack and a shower of sparks. Even after the death of the smoke alarm, however, the hiss and crackle of burning fabrics and wood kept Nell from hearing any baby's cry or mother's plea for help.

Attempting to orient herself, she saw flames lick upward and rapidly consume the last of the draperies across the room. She stumbled forward in the murky, chemical-laden air, determined that another child was not going to die if she could possibly save him—even if this time she had to pay with her own life.

She tried waving her sweater in front of her face, but that did nothing to dissipate the smoke. With the glow of the flames to guide her, however, Nell's eyes began to adapt and she was able to make out a few shapes—the sofa, a table and chairs in the corner, the kitchen off to one side. And the small amount of fresher air entering through the window she'd demolished allowed her enough oxygen to remain on her feet for at least a few more minutes.

Suddenly she stumbled against something solid and pitched forward. Catching herself as she began to fall and managing to regain her balance, Nell looked down. She'd tripped over Annabel, lying unconscious and curled into a ball on the floor. Casting her sweater aside, she used both hands to yank on the younger woman's arm. She was probably thirty pounds lighter than Nell, but dead weight. Still, Nell managed to roll over the unconscious form. Underneath his mother, she found the little boy.

With heat searing her exposed face and hands, Nell scooped the child into her arms, carried him back outside through the broken window, and laid him on the lawn, away from the burning structure.

Now she thought she could finally hear a siren's scream in the distance, yet she knew Annabel couldn't possibly survive inside the burning guest house until the fire department arrived to rescue her. For all Nell knew, she might already be dead.

The child stirred slightly as the fresh, cold night air began to revive him. Nell looked down at his small shape and made a decision. The boy would live—she could see that.

But his mother still needed her help.

She screwed up her courage, took another deep breath, and headed back into the burning guest house.

AS SOON AS she'd realized what was happening and called 9-1-1, Louise threw a coat over her nightgown and ran out into the backyard.

"Annabel!" she screamed as she saw the guest house ablaze. "Annabel!" But she heard no answer.

She ran around the side of the building and was relieved to see Nicky lying on the grass, coughing weakly. "Where's your mama?" Louise asked him, terrified. She glanced at the burning building just in time to see a large, dark figure climb through the shattered picture window, then bend and strain to pull Annabel out through the smoky opening.

Louise rushed over to help the older woman lift the unconscious Annabel, then drag her limp body across the lawn to safety next to her son.

Dropping to her knees next to Annabel, Nell bent over at the waist, holding her chest and gasping frantically for air. She coughed until she spit up black phlegm. Finally, her hacking subsided into a constant wheeze.

"Incredible!" Louise exclaimed. "How on earth—?" She could see that the woman was completely exhausted, her face smudged with soot and her clothes and long graying brown hair singed. "Never mind, don't try to tell me now. Just stay here and rest. The paramedics are on their way." She helped the woman into a sitting position on the grass. "I'm Louise."

"I'm Nell," the woman gasped, then wheezed some more. Her eyes seemed to lose focus and she leaned back, supporting her weight with her right arm.

"It's okay," Louise said, realizing that Nell was having serious trouble breathing. It was no wonder. The woman was obviously not in great physical shape, and what she'd just managed to do would challenge a healthy young man, never mind an overweight middle-aged woman. "Just lie down, Nell. Help's on its way."

As the sirens grew louder, Missy came around the side of the blazing guest house, wrapped in a fuzzy pink blanket. "Mom!" she cried, hysteria clear in her voice. "Mommy! Where are you? I'm scared! What's going on?"

"Over here," Louise shouted, quickly showing her terrified daughter that nobody was left in the burning guest house. "Everybody's safe, and the fire department's coming. It's going to be okay."

Within less than three minutes, the fire fighters arrived and began to put out the fire before it could spread to the Zuckermans' main house. The paramedics began to administer oxygen to Annabel, Nell, and Nicky.

After determining that Nicky was stable, the younger paramedic, a husky Mexican-American, efficiently removed a large piece of glass from Nell's forearm. "That's going to need stitching up," he told her as he applied a pressure bandage over the wound. He held a stethoscope against her chest and listened. "Sounds like you inhaled plenty of smoke. Try to rest while we get a couple of gurneys. We'll take all three of you to the hospital, let the docs check you out."

Nell looked panicky. She yanked the oxygen mask off her face and protested, "No, no hospital! I'll be okay."

Louise picked up groggy little Nicky and cradled him in her arms. "No way," she insisted. "You're hurt, Nell. For godsake, you just saved two lives. I'm not letting you go like this."

Nell tried to get to her feet, but her knees were too weak to hold her and she slumped back onto the grass. "No insurance."

"Don't worry—it's okay. Just stay down. We're getting you a gurney," the paramedic told her.

"Guess I don't have much choice," Nell gasped.

Louise spotted a Channel Nine TV news crew arriving on the scene. *Damn!* The last thing they needed was some loose-lipped reporter telling the kidnappers that little Nicholas Nettleton was on his way to the hospital and not with them. If they found out they had the wrong child, they'd surely kill Jason.

Louise thought for a moment before speaking. "I want to ride along to the hospital with my son," she told the paramedics. "He'll be too scared without me." She shot Missy a warning look.

The girl nodded and kept her mouth shut.

"This little fellow is your boy?" the first paramedic asked.

"My son Jason," Louise lied. "And this is my friend, Annabel Nettleton. She was babysitting Jason in the guest house tonight. I got home late and they were both asleep, so I decided to leave him there till morning. And then *this*…" Louise gestured toward what had been the guest house. She'd been so proud of it and now it was little more than a pile of charred, wet timbers. Yet, with everything else that had happened, the loss of a mere building became completely meaningless.

"That'll be fine. We've called for a second ambulance." The paramedics lifted Annabel, who was now conscious but unable to talk with the oxygen mask clamped over her nose and mouth, onto a gurney and strapped her down. "We'll take the two women in the first and you and the boy can ride together in the second."

"Annabel," Louise said, doing her best to make sure her friend could hear her. "The baby's fine. I'm taking Jason to the hospital in the other ambulance, so you're not to worry about him." She hoped the look she saw in her friend's eyes indicated understanding of the ruse. Turning to the paramedics, she added, "My daughter's coming, too. I'm not going to leave her home alone."

The paramedic nodded.

As the TV photographer approached, Louise held Nicky's face against her coat and did her best to shield him from the camera's lens. She waved the cameraman away. "Not now! Can't you see people are hurt? We have to get them to the hospital."

Oblivious to her protest, the photographer aimed his camera and shot footage of the paramedics, each of the three women, Missy, and the little boy, then headed back toward the reporter, who was busily preparing for an interview with the chief firefighter.

Louise trudged behind the gurneys to the street, where her neighbors now were lined along the sidewalk, watching the excitement. Again, she kept Nicky's face shielded from view, hoping none of the neighbors would realize she was carrying Annabel's son and not her own and inadvertently blab to the TV news crew.

As soon as the second ambulance arrived, Louise and Missy climbed inside. It wasn't until the door closed against the prying eyes of the onlookers and journalists that Louise allowed herself a small sigh of relief.

ANNABEL LAY QUIETLY in the twin-bedded hospital room, feeling both lucky to be alive and totally confused. Her head throbbed, each breath she took irritated her raw windpipe, and the numerous scrapes and bruises on her body chafed painfully whenever she moved against the crisp white sheets.

Her foggy mind struggled to process the information she'd been given. As soon as the emergency room doctor had released her from intensive care, Louise explained in anxious whispers that Nicky was already upstairs in the children's ward, admitted under Jason's name. That much she could grasp—her son was safe, he'd survived the fire generally unharmed.

But the rest remained a puzzle.

Apparently the fire was no accident—the firefighters said somebody'd splashed gasoline all over the door of the guest house and lit a match. But who would want to kill her and Nicky? Had the kidnappers discovered they'd grabbed the wrong boy and decided to take revenge?

That scenario made no sense. It was far more likely the kidnappers would dispose of Jason, then come after Annabel and Nicky, finding some new diabolical way to force her to hand over Dylan's fortune. She could think of no motive for them to kill her before they got their hands on a single penny.

And who was the woman in the next bed? Louise had said her name was Nell Verducci, and she'd risked her own life to save them. But why? Annabel was virtually certain she'd never laid eyes on this woman before tonight.

She was startled out of her reverie by the low hum of a motor. She turned her head and saw that Nell was awake, adjusting the pitch of her hospital bed.

Perhaps she could try to solve at least one piece of the puzzle, Annabel thought. "I want to thank you, Ms. Verducci," she said, her voice hoarse. Painfully, she turned toward her new roommate. "Thank you very much for saving my life, and—and Jason's." She figured she'd better stick with the story Louise was telling, even in talking with the woman who'd rescued them.

Nell smiled through her exhaustion. "Call me Nell. And you're welcome. I'm glad it, uh, I'm glad everything worked out okay."

Annabel adjusted her own bed until she was at close to a sitting position. That made it a little easier to breathe and to talk. "I guess you already know I'm Annabel, Annabel Nettleton. I was just wondering how you came to be in the neighborhood. I mean, I'm incredibly grateful and—"

"You want to know what I was doing there."

Annabel blushed. "I'm just curious."

"If you have to know, I was getting ready to sleep in my car," Nell said.

How strange. Annabel had never noticed any homeless people in her neighborhood, and she'd been under the impression that the Carmel police did their best to usher the homeless out of town as soon as they arrived. But she chose not to comment on what had to be a difficult and embarrassing situation for Nell Verducci. Instead, she prompted her to finish her story. "So you saw the smoke from where your car was parked?"

"Not exactly. I went for a little walk along the street and saw this man coming toward me. He was carrying something heavy. When I saw him slip around the side of the house, I got curious, so I stayed in the neighbor's yard and waited. A few minutes later, the man came back. He was still carrying the same object, but it looked lot lighter now, and the next thing I knew, I spotted the smoke."

"Thank God." Annabel wheezed, then coughed. When she was able to breathe again, she thought of a way she might be able to repay Nell for what she'd one, at least in small part. "Sounds like you could use some cash," she said. "I've got a few thousand dol—"

"I don't want your money!" Nell snapped.

"Sorry. Didn't mean to insult you. I just thought—I mean, you certainly helped me. You risked your life for me. So if there's anything I can do for you, anything at all, I'm more than willing."

Nell's gaze wandered. "You don't owe me anything, Annabel. I did it for myself, if you want to know the truth. I—I just couldn't stand to let another kid die."

*Another* kid. "What do you mean?" Annabel asked, her guts clenching. "What other child died?" Could this woman have had something to do with Jason's disappearance? Was Louise's little boy already dead?

Nell shook her head as though to excise a tormenting thought.

"It was a long, long time ago," she said, finally. "I had a little boy once, but he died."

Annabel was relieved that Nell wasn't talking about poor little Jason Zuckerman. "I'm so sorry," she said. "I lost my parents, my husband, and my brother. Somehow I lived through it all." She told Nell about her futile attempt to donate one of her kidneys to save Erik. "My brother was my best friend. I thought then that losing him was the worst thing that could happen. But now I've got Nicky and, if anything ever happened to him, I honestly don't think I could survive. Losing your child is absolutely the worst thing I can imagine."

"It is...especially if..." Nell didn't finish her thought. "Anyway, don't waste your time worrying about me. You have your own losses to deal with. Your husband murdered and the police thinking you killed him, and now this fire."

*She knows who I am,* Annabel realized with a start. Nell

Verducci knows about Dylan and she knows about the police. Maybe she knows about Jason, too. She tried to ignore the increasingly spooky feeling she was getting. After all, this woman had just saved her life. "How did your little boy die?" she asked.

Nell's eyes filled and she took a breath before answering. "He got sick and he died, that's all. He just got sick and I—I…"

"Was it cancer?" Annabel's thoughts immediately rushed to what seemed the most brutal childhood disease. Even worse than the kidney disease that killed her brother Erik. She'd done her best, even given up part of her own body but she hadn't been able to save Erik, either.

Nell closed her eyes and leaned her head back against the sheets. "Look, Annabel, the subject is closed. I don't talk about my kid. *Ever.*"

"Sorry, didn't mean to pry." A tear of sympathy rolled down Annabel's cheek as she thought about what Nell must have felt when her child died, must still feel in the dark of night. She wiped it away. "But now you've saved my—I mean you saved another child's—Jason's—life. You must feel good about that."

Nell pushed the button to put the back of her bed back down again. When it was flat, she rolled onto her side, her broad back to Annabel. "What?" she asked bitterly. "You figure there's some big ledger up in the sky? That we get points for the good things we do and lose points for the bad?"

"It's possible," Annabel replied. She'd never been a particularly religious person, but she believed in good and evil, and tried to do the right thing whenever she could. "I have no idea one way or the other, really," she said, "but when I was a little girl, my grandmother always used to tell me that."

"Yeah, well, if there is, my score's probably so far in the minus column I'll never make it out."

"Don't sell yourself short, Nell. If somebody's keeping a ledger, I bet you're doing just fine, at least after tonight."

"Okay, believe that bull if you want." Nell pulled the sheet up over her ear. "But give me a break, okay? This is the first time I've been in a real bed in days. I'd like to get some sleep."

"Sorry, didn't mean to keep you up." Annabel wondered why she found it necessary to keep apologizing to this woman. Whatever she said, it seemed to rub Nell the wrong way. "I only wanted to thank you for everything you did for us."

"I'll consider myself thanked." Nell kept her face turned away so Annabel couldn't see the expression on her face. "And, Annabel, let's cut the bull, okay? I know it was your son, not Louise's, I carried out of that fire."

Annabel froze, unsure what to say.

"Don't worry about it," Nell added. "It's our secret. Now please shut up and get some sleep. We're both going to need it."

WARNER SLAMMED DOWN the telephone, his whole body trembling with frustration. Uncle Oliver was in a deep coma now, the nurse had told him, his lungs beginning to fill with fluid despite the oxygen she was continually pumping into them. And the only nutrition he was getting came through the IV stuck in his arm. The old man wouldn't last much longer, no matter what extraordinary measures they took.

Despite his issuing another threat to sue the nurses if they didn't somehow manage to keep Uncle Oliver from dying, Warner wasn't an unrealistic man. He knew there were limits to medical science's abilities and that they were quickly reaching them. Despite everything he'd done, all that he'd risked, his window of opportunity had shriveled to, at best, a day or two, and at worst, no more than a few hours.

Unless...

He switched on the hotel TV set and poured himself a cup of strong black coffee from the pot on the room service breakfast tray.

He became more and more irritated as a talk show hostess on the local channel's morning show bantered pointlessly with some local celebrity. "Come on, come on," he muttered to the set as he waited impatiently for the morning news cut-in to begin.

*Finally.* The story he wanted was at the top of the news, as he knew it would be in a small town like this. After all, this was a far cry from Chicago, where they had plenty of real news—government graft and corruption, gang wars, plane crashes, police chases, corporate takeovers, a hundred other big stories per day.

"Three people are hospitalized following a three-alarm guest house fire in Carmel last night…" the anchor began. Warner walked over to the TV and stared at the screen as the video switched to the on-scene reporter's account, related as a voice-over behind videotaped footage of the guest house fire.

His spirits sinking, Warner saw Annabel and another woman being carried into an ambulance on gurneys, then a shot of the neighbor carrying a blond child into a second ambulance, followed by her teenage daughter.

"The woman most seriously hurt is Annabel Nettleton, who suffered smoke inhalation," the reporter said. "She's been in the news several times lately. The first was when her husband, Dylan Nettleton, purported heir to the Nettleton steel fortune, disappeared. She came to public attention again when he was found dead in their rented Carmel cottage. That cottage is located next door to this guest house, where Annabel Nettleton had taken refuge following her husband's murder.

"The identity of the second injured woman is not yet known, but neighbors indicate she's not a local resident. However, the unidentified woman is being hailed as a heroine. Fire department sources say she spotted the fire and broke into the burning guest house by smashing a window with a crowbar. She managed to rescue both the unconscious Mrs. Nettleton and a small boy who's been identified as Jason Zuckerman, the year-old son of the guest house's owner."

Jason Zuckerman, Warner thought. Why was *he* in the guest house? And what about…

As the camera panned across the faces of the injured women, then to Louise Zuckerman, the cowering toddler in her arms, and her young daughter, Warner froze. His heart skipped a beat and the coffee cup fell from his hand onto the rug, staining it a dark, wet brown.

*No, it couldn't be…*

This was impossible, completely impossible. Obviously, his imagination was playing tricks on him. The strain was taking its toll, Warner told himself. He hadn't been sleeping. What was that slang phrase the teenagers used nowadays to describe what undoubtedly was happening to him?

*Losing it*—that was it.

Warner Schuman decided he obviously was losing it.


WHEN SHE AWOKE, Annabel found she could breathe much more easily than she had the night before. She squinted at the clock. It was already after nine. Her heart leapt as she remembered her morning appointment. What time was she supposed to be at that pay phone in Del Monte Center? Nine o'clock? Or was it ten? Was she already too late?

She swung her legs out of bed and shivered as her bare feet hit the chilly tile floor. She tried to stand up, but suddenly felt dizzy and sat back down on the bed, hard. *Damn!*

"Gotta get out of here," she said to Nell, who was propped up in the other bed, channel surfing on the television set, the volume turned down low.

"The doctor's supposed to stop by and check on us," Nell said. "Then maybe you can go. You were sleeping when they brought breakfast, but I told them not to wake you. Figured you needed your sleep more than a bowl of that wallpaper paste they served us."

"You don't understand. I've got to be somewhere. Where are my clothes?"

Nell rolled her eyes. "Maybe you got too *much* sleep, Annabel. You seemed a helluva lot more lucid last night. Your nightgown was a rag, all ripped and burned. I think the nurse threw it out. And whatever you had in that guest house is ashes. You leave here now, it's gonna be in your hospital gown, unless you can get somebody to bring you some new clothes. Besides, you're in no shape to go anywhere until the doctor checks you out. You almost died last night."

"But—"

"But nothing." Nell pushed another button on the TV remote. "We were on television," she said, changing the subject. "That news crew caught us on film." She sounded worried.

Annabel stiffened in fear. "What did they say about Nicky?"

"Not a word." Nell's voice quickly turned calm, reassuring. "Don't worry, nobody knows anything. The TV said the boy in the fire was Jason Zuckerman and that he's just fine."

Annabel sighed. "At least there's that."

The telephone rang.

"Gotta be for you," Nell said, pressing another button and muting the audio on a morning soap opera.

Annabel reached for the phone. "Hello."

"Annabel Nettleton?" a male voice asked.

"Speaking. Who's calling?"

"We had an appointment this morning."

Now Annabel recognized the voice. She cupped her hand over her mouth and the receiver, hoping Nell wouldn't overhear what she was saying. "How—how did you find me?"

"Lucky for you and your kid we watched TV this morning. Luckier for you we're feeling generous. Be there tomorrow. Same time, same place. And keep your damn mouth shut if you ever want to see your kid again."

"Is Nicky okay? Can I speak to him? He'll be so—"

The line went dead.

At least she had another day, Annabel told herself as she returned the receiver to its cradle. And Jason wasn't dead yet. He was going to be fine. She had to keep believing that.

She slumped back against the pillow with a sigh and turned her eyes to the television set just as Nell changed the channel once more and a familiar face flashed on the screen. "Turn up the volume, quick!" she said, sitting bolt upright.

Nell complied.

"…have turned up no further leads in the suspected car-jack slaying of the Chicago private investigator," the news anchor reported. "Police are searching the Salinas neighborhood where Link's body was found, as well as the Monterey area where the rental car was abandoned, for any clues to the slaying.

"Now this." The show cut to a commercial.

"What the hell is going on around here?" Annabel asked herself.

"You didn't know about what happened to that PI?" Nell asked.

Annabel stared at her roommate in surprise. "How could I possibly know?" Who was this strange woman, and how did she know so much about Annabel's life? "How did you know about him?" she asked, her eyes narrowing with suspicion.

"Hey, no big mystery," Nell said with a tolerant smile. "The story was all over the radio news yesterday."

Was that true? Annabel hadn't listened to the radio yesterday. With her police interrogation, Jason's kidnapping, and her subsequent panic over getting the ransom money, radio news was the last thing on her mind. Maybe Nell was telling the truth.

So Jeffrey Link was dead. Poor man, Annabel thought. She'd grown to like him. Was she somehow responsible for his death, too? And, if so, how? She lay back against the pillow and closed her eyes against the harsh morning light, thinking about where all this was likely to end and trying to retain a smidgen of optimism.

When she opened her eyes once more, Annabel saw Nell emerging from the bathroom, dressed in grimy clothes that reeked of smoke and were stained with blood on one sleeve.

"What are you doing?"

"My clothes weren't nearly as bad as yours," she said. "They didn't bother to throw them out."

Annabel wrinkled her nose. "Maybe they should have."

"So I'll change when I get back to my car."

"What about the doctor? You said the doctor was coming to check on us."

"He is. But I'm fine—all I did was inhale a little smoke—and I can't wait around. Got things to do."

"But you can't just—"

Nell walked through the door, her stride steady. "I just did," she called back over her shoulder.

After her odd roommate had gone, Annabel stared at the empty bed on the other side of the room, feeling a strange sense of abandonment.

MAX HURRIED ALONG the hospital corridor, gripping a bouquet of flowers in one hand and his briefcase in the other. He'd been worried when Annabel didn't show up at his office to get the diskette before her appointment at Del Monte Center, but discovered why as soon as the police called to let him know the coroner's report on Dylan had arrived.

"Too bad about what happened to your client last night," Sergeant Eileen Kopek had said over the telephone.

"What do you mean? What happened to her?" Max asked, nearly dropping the telephone. If Annabel had been killed, too, he'd never forgive himself. He'd been relieved to hear she was merely in the hospital, not the morgue. Still, it was obvious to him that somebody was trying to kill her, just as they had her husband, and he was shocked to learn that the police weren't even guarding her hospital room. He told Sergeant Kopek as much.

"You know we're a small department, Max," Eileen said. "We're already overburdened with Dylan Nettleton's murder and now this arson case to investigate. We don't have the manpower to do round-the-clock guard duty. We've asked the hospital staff to call us if anything odd happens. She'll be safe enough there."

"What about the child?"

"Jason Zuckerman? You think he was the real target of the arson?" Eileen asked. "I doubt it. And by the way, where's the Nettleton boy?"

Max quickly realized he'd come close to telling the police more than he wanted to, that his words could dig a pit for Annabel and Louise, one that might bury both of them, along with Jason. "Nicholas Nettleton is perfectly safe," he said without elaborating. "I'll pick up the coroner's report on my way to the hospital. If you people won't protect Annabel from whoever's trying to kill her, I guess I'll just have to do it myself."

The doctor had just left Annabel's room when Max arrived. He knocked lightly on the door, then pushed it open. As soon as he saw Annabel, he dropped his briefcase on the floor, shoved the flowers onto the bedside table, and sat down on the edge of her bed. "Annabel, thank God you're safe." He grasped her hand and looked into her deep blue eyes, feeling he might drown in their depths.

"I'm okay," she said, holding onto Max's hand like a life-line. "Thank God this wonderful, strange, incredibly brave woman saved our lives." She described the dramatic rescue. "Nell Verducci's her name and she's apparently homeless, living in her car."

Max took Annabel in his arms and held her tightly, burying his face in her thick hair that still bore a heart-breakingly strong odor of smoke. The poor woman must have been terrified out of her mind. "I'll always be grateful to Nell Verducci, whoever she is," he whispered.

Recognizing that he was losing his professional distance from his client once again, Max loosened his grip on her shoulders. But his heart leapt when he realized Annabel was hugging him as hard as he was hugging her.

A moment later, they both backed off. Max noticed that Annabel's complexion had reddened slightly, an effect he found quite charming. He covered his own mild embarrassment over displaying his emotions by averting his eyes while he reached for his briefcase.

"I just picked up the coroner's report," he told her, opening his briefcase and removing a legal document, "and it has quite an unexpected conclusion." He began to feel more in control of himself, now that the topic was shifting back to more typical lawyer-client business.

"Dylan wasn't killed in the cottage," Annabel guessed.

Max nodded. "Right, but we already figured that. The surprise is that he didn't die of a stab wound to the heart." He paused and watched Annabel's beautiful face. "Dylan was drowned."

*"Drowned?"* Her jaw dropped. "But how? And where? Did he end up in the water off Point Lobos after all?"

Max shook his head and referred to the report. "Dylan drowned in fresh—not salt—water. There were traces of tub and tile cleaner in his lungs, along with common chlorinated city water. The coroner's conclusion is that he probably was drowned in a bathtub."

Annabel looked at her hands, her expression unreadable. "Dylan was a big man," she said, finally. "I'm not exactly a small woman, but I hope the police are smart enough to realize I couldn't possibly drown my husband in a bathtub and then move him onto the bed. That would take two of me."

"I'll make them realize it, if they don't already," Max said as he shifted from the edge of the bed into a green tweed chair alongside it. "With a little luck, the police finally will start looking elsewhere for Dylan's murderer."

"It's about time." Annabel eyed the open doorway and lowered her voice to a whisper. "I got a call from the kidnappers this morning," she told Max. "They said they caught the story about the fire on TV, so they knew why I didn't show up at Del Monte Center on time."

"That's a piece of luck." Max still felt mortified that he'd obviously been last to know about the fire. "I brought the diskette with Dylan's offshore account information," he said, "so you'll have it whenever you need it. What did the doctor say about when you can leave the hospital?"

"Not only can I leave this afternoon, they're kicking me out," she replied. "Nicky—I mean Jason—too."

"Probably some insurance clerk decided you've had the allotted amount of coddling for one near-death experience," Max said with a smile, more of relief than jest. Surely Annabel wouldn't be released from the hospital if her health remained in danger and, without a police guard on duty, he felt she could be better protected from whoever was trying to kill her if she left here.

"Only trouble is, I haven't got any clothes. Louise said she'd bring me something. I just hope it's not one of her cast-offs. I wouldn't be able to get one leg into anything from that woman's wardrobe."

"Look, I want you and Nicky to come home with me," Max said, impulsively.

Annabel took a deep breath and Max thought he saw tears come to her eyes. She blinked quickly before speaking. "I— I'm touched, Max, but really, it wouldn't—"

"This is no time to worry about propriety," he told her. "You and Nicky can stay in the guest room. I just want—I *need* to know you're both safe."

"It's not that. I couldn't care less about what your neighbors think," Annabel told him. "But I absolutely refuse to put you and Katie in danger and, right now, let's face it—I'm dangerous."

"But—"

"Let me finish!" Annabel held up a palm. "I also have to worry about Jason and Nicky. Louise and I talked about it and we decided the safest thing for Nicky right now is to go home with her. He can continue to be Jason, as far as the public is concerned. I'll check into a motel in Carmel after I leave the hospital. That way, if the kidnappers are watching me, they'll see my son's not with me. Then, tomorrow, after I give them the diskette, I'll get Jason back and—and everything will be okay."

Max thought a moment and realized she probably was right about Nicky and, much as he longed to be a hero, he had no right to risk his daughter's life. If Annabel brought Nicky to the house with her, there was always a possibility the kidnappers would catch on, making Jason Zuckerman immediately expendable. He'd figure out a way to protect her at a motel instead.

"Okay," he said. "That makes sense. But I'll come back after lunch and check you out of here. I don't want you cornered by either the press or the police. We'll go someplace we can talk for a while without being overheard. Then I'll help you find a motel room where we can install a couple of guards to keep you safe until this thing is over."

Annabel nodded. Hoping he'd managed to lighten at least a little bit of her burden, Max thought he saw a flash of relief on her face. But he realized it could be wishful thinking.

"There's one more thing I need to ask you," he said, before leaving. "Do you know a man named Roy Pickett?"

Annabel shook her head. "Should I?"

"Possibly. Benny Everhardt, my PI, found his fingerprints on Dylan's computer."

Annabel wrinkled her brow. "This Roy Pickett, he doesn't work in Harry's computer shop?"

"No, it's nothing that simple," Max replied. "Harry's never even heard of the guy. Pickett's apparently some kind of criminal. Benny fingerprinted the entire computer rig, then excluded your prints and Harry's. The keyboard was an indecipherable mess—too many overlapping prints to get any clear ones—but he found three good clear prints on the side of the monitor. His FBI sources say they belong to Roy Pickett, whoever he is."

"Maybe he's the one who broke into the house that night," Annabel said with a shudder. "Maybe it wasn't Dylan after all."

"Maybe," Max agreed. But he thought it extremely odd that there hadn't been any other prints on the machine. Had Dylan wiped it clean on the night he and Annabel had their big fight, before he stalked out of the house? And, if so, why? Surely he couldn't have wiped the entire house clean of his prints. "Benny's collecting some information on Pickett for me," he told her. "He'll get it to me this afternoon. Maybe he'll find something that rings a bell with you."

"I'll search my memory, but I don't think I've ever heard the name."

"We can worry about that later. For now, just get some rest and I'll pick you up in a few hours," Max said, closing his briefcase. "Agreed?"

Annabel nodded. "Agreed. As long as Louise brings me something I can wear out of here. I'm not leaving in this hospital gown." Max was gratified to see her smile for the first time since he'd entered the room.

He decided not to burden her with the other piece of troubling information he held in his briefcase, not just yet. Annabel had no immediate need to know about what was missing from the coroner's report on her husband's death.

Surely she could wait until she'd left the hospital to learn that the coroner apparently hadn't bothered to run Dylan Nettleton's fingerprints through the FBI database.

Or if he had, the cops had altered the coroner's report to keep Dylan's background a secret from both the dead man's wife and her attorney.

# ELEVEN

As SHE CHECKED OUT of the hospital, Nell realized she'd left her purse in her car, back in Carmel. She had neither money nor transportation. Louise Zuckerman had guaranteed her hospital bill, so her lack of medical insurance was no problem, but Nell was forced to borrow bus fare from a sympathetic, gray-haired nurse who'd seen the TV news coverage of the fire and recognized her.

"Hey, hon, I'm honored to help," the nurse told her with a friendly smile. "Anybody who's got the guts to go into a burning building and rescue a couple of people shouldn't have to worry about a lousy couple of bucks." She pressed a five-dollar bill into Nell's hand.

"Thanks, I appreciate it. I'll pay you back after I get my purse out of my car."

"Forget it. Least I can do for a genuine hero."

Forcing a smile onto her face, Nell felt like a complete phony. Some hero she was—if the kindly nurse only knew.

She rode the bus back to Carmel, doing her best to ignore the curious stares of her fellow riders, including a woman who, sniffing audibly and making a sour face, moved to another seat as soon as Nell sat down.

Relieved when she finally reached her car and found it undisturbed, Nell quickly drove to a gas station and used the women's rest room to change into clean jeans and a sweatshirt. After gassing up her car, she headed back toward Seaside to resume her search.

Maybe she finally was having some luck, she thought as she spotted the white van, still parked down the block from the Chinese restaurant where she'd bought last night's dinner. This time, Nell parked her car in the restaurant's lot and approached the van directly, strolling back and forth on the sidewalk several times before she finally worked up the courage to examine the vehicle more closely.

Leaning against the van, she peeked in through the passenger-side window. The front compartment looked empty, except for a wrapper from a Snickers bar lying on the floor next to a Monterey Peninsula tourist map. There was some kind of paperwork tucked behind the visor on the passenger side, too, but she couldn't see it well enough to determine what it was.

Shielding her eyes from the glare of the bright morning sun, she tried to peer into the back of the van for any sign a child was now inside or earlier had been there, but without any windows in the back doors, it was too dark for her to tell. She tried the door handle and found the van locked.

This probably wasn't even the same van she'd seen at the Zuckerman house yesterday, Nell told herself as she took a last look inside. This probably was a complete waste of—

"Hey!"

Nell jumped as sharp fingers grabbed her shoulder, squeezing it painfully.

"What the hell you doing?" the man gripping her demanded. He was Asian, only slightly taller than she, but at least twenty years younger. Physically, Nell was no match for this guy.

Her heart pounding, she twisted her body and felt the fingers on her throbbing shoulder loosen slightly. "Just admiring the van," she gasped, terrified. With a lunge to the side, she managed to wrench her shoulder out of the man's grasp.

"Keep away from my wheels, bitch!"

Nell felt the man's spittle land on her face. She turned and ran back toward the Chinese restaurant as fast as she could, the angry confrontation spurring her on despite the laboring of her smoke-damaged lungs. When she reached her car, she looked back and saw that the young man was still standing beside the white van, staring after her. She felt a visceral stab of fear.

Relieved to reach the relative safety of her old Volvo, she drove through the restaurant's parking lot into the alley behind the building, where she pulled over next to a Dumpster to catch her breath and collect her thoughts.

The man who'd grabbed her looked a lot like the guy who'd snatched the Zuckerman boy. But was he the same one? Nell couldn't be sure. He might be just a guy who worked in the restaurant and believed she'd been trying to rip off his wheels.

Earlier, she'd been too far away to see the kidnapper's features clearly. This man was the same general size, though, and she remembered having a strong impression that the kidnapper was relatively young—in his twenties or maybe early thirties.

Nell put her car back in gear. She crept out of the alley and turned back toward Fremont on the first cross street she found. When she reached the stop sign, she glimpsed to her left and spotted the white van turning south off Fremont. She turned right onto Fremont, drove to the next stoplight, and executed a U-turn. Nervously, she approached the side street the van had taken.

This was probably another wild goose chase, she told herself.

Still, if this guy was the kidnapper and she could manage to find Jason in time, maybe she could earn another point or two in that big ledger book in the sky Annabel had talked about. If it really was a possible to accumulate enough positive deeds to make up for a lifetime of bad judgment and horrible mistakes, then maybe...

On the other hand, if she'd already spooked the kidnapper, not backing off while she still had the chance might mean both she and the little boy would end up dead. She made an instant decision that this was a chance she had to take.

Right now, doing something—anything—had to be a helluva lot better than staying stuck in the limbo she'd been in for the past three decades.

Screwing up her courage, Nell made the turn off Fremont and followed the route she'd seen the van take.

"MAMAMAMA!" Nicky screeched as Annabel and Max came through the front door of Louise's house. The little boy toddled across the floor on his short legs as his mother dropped to her knees and hugged him tightly. As far as she could tell, he was his usual energetic little self, displaying no lingering ill effects from last night's smoke.

"Oh, you feel so good!" Annabel said, burying her nose in his freshly shampooed, sweet-smelling hair.

She glanced up and felt a pang of guilt as she saw the look of agony on Louise's face—understandably, her friend was devastated that her son, too, was not part of this reunion. Giving Nicky a quick kiss, Annabel stood and went over to Louise. Hugging her slim frame, she said, "Thank you, Louise, for everything. I'll never forget what you've done for us. I'm going to get Jason back for you, if it's the last thing I do in this life. You have my solemn word."

"We shouldn't stay too long—they might be watching the house," Max warned. After Louise and Nicky had left the hospital by the front door and quickly were waylaid by a news crew, he'd sneaked Annabel, dressed in the clothes Louise had brought her, out the back way. As soon as they were sure they'd escaped the media, he'd driven her to Carmel to see her son. "Benny and his bodyguard will be waiting for us at the motel," he added, obviously anxious to go.

Reluctantly, Annabel said her good-byes, doing her best to explain to her small son why she was leaving without him. "Mama will be back to get you tomorrow," she promised, hoping with all her heart it was true. "You stay here and be a really good boy for Louise and Missy, okay?" It took every shred of emotional strength she could muster to turn and leave her clinging, whimpering child without breaking down, but somehow she managed.

Max drove them to the Seashore Motel, a place near the beach that he'd selected on Benny's recommendation. "We want her in a room with just one entrance," the private eye had said, "preferably something on the second floor. Enough space around the motel so nobody can enter from an adjacent building, but nothing out in the country." The Seashore seemed to fit the bill.

As he was parking the car, Max said, "Benny doesn't know about the off-shore bank accounts or the diskette. It's probably best to keep it that way."

"Why? Don't you trust him?"

"It's not a matter of trusting or not trusting him. It's a matter of need-to-know and so far Benny doesn't need to know."

Annabel, worried despite Max's assurance, nodded. When you were talking about millions of dollars, she supposed almost anybody could get greedy, no matter how ethical they'd been previously. Max was right. Why tempt fate?

As soon as she'd checked into the Seashore, Max introduced Annabel to Benny and Lester, the bodyguard. Benny was a tall, gaunt man in his early sixties with a thick shock of pure white hair, a carefully-trimmed mustache, and a rigid, military posture. He was impeccably dressed in a dark gray business suit, white shirt, maroon tie, and spit-polished shoes. Lester was equally tall, but closer to Annabel's age. He was built like a city bus and wore khaki pants, a denim shirt, and Nikes.

"Lester used to be a bouncer at a couple of the night spots on Cannery Row before he came to work for me," Benny said, with a clear note of pride in his voice. "He was an all-conference fullback in high school. He's an expert marksman, too. Lester will keep you good and safe here, ma'am, I guarantee it." The older man bowed almost imperceptibly in Annabel's direction.

Lester remained mute, his broad face expressionless and his meaty hands clasped behind his back

The two PIs were an odd couple, Annabel thought. Lester looked like a typical bouncer in a tough joint, or maybe a hit man in a cheap movie, while Benny seemed more suited to play the part of the cultured, accomplished butler in a Merchant-Ivory film. He reminded her of a taller, whiter-haired David Niven, and she couldn't help wondering how he'd come to be nicknamed Benny. With his stiff, formal demeanor, she'd have expected him to be known as Benjamin or, more likely, Mr. Everhardt. She found his air of self-confident competence reassuring.

The room was large for a Carmel motel, yet with three big men perched on the two chairs and the edge of the dresser while Annabel sat on one end of the small sofa, it felt cramped. She was exhausted, because of both the strain of the past several days and the fact that her lungs still ached from smoke inhalation. She was painfully aware of each rasping breath she took. Eyeing the bed with envy, she counted the minutes until she could lie down and sleep, if only for a few hours.

"Lester, check out the back of the motel, make sure we don't have any problems back there," Benny said.

Lester nodded and left without a word. Annabel began to wonder whether the huge man possessed the gift of speech.

After Lester had left, Benny pulled some papers from the inside pocket of his suit jacket. "I received the report you requested on Roy Pickett," he told Max.

Max walked over and sat down next to Annabel on the sofa, as though he wanted to be ready to protect her from what she might hear.

"Pickett's a garden variety bail-jumper," Benny reported, holding the papers in his hand, but reciting the facts of the case from memory. "He was arrested in Washington State, along with three cohorts, a few years ago. But he left the jurisdiction as soon as he posted bail. It was quite a sophisticated computer mortgage scam these young men were running—made millions stealing people's financial identities when the gullible applied for a home mortgage—"

"But how could…?" Annabel asked, her brow furrowed. She remained a novice when it came to computers.

Benny explained patiently. "People trying to buy a house would go on-line looking for the best mortgage offer they could find, and they'd end up at the bogus loan site these men set up. They advertised home loan deals at least a full percentage point, sometimes two, below what the legitimate banks were charging at the time." Benny shook his head and almost smiled. "Greed always seems to trump common sense, doesn't it?"

Annabel remained confused. "Did anybody actually get a mortgage this way?"

"Not a soul," Benny said, "but that wasn't the unfortunate part. Have you ever applied for a home loan?"

Annabel shook her head. She'd done nothing but move from rental to rental since her brother's escalating hospital bills had forced them to sell the Maine house they'd inherited from their parents. Maybe someday she and Nicky would be able to settle down in a home of their own, she thought wistfully. But for now…

Benny gestured with his hands as he explained. "Well, here's how that works, generally speaking. You fill out a stack of financial forms, disclosing all your basic economic information—your place of employment and how much you earn, your bank deposits, including account numbers, all your credit card numbers, where you're keeping the down payment cash for the house you intend to buy, your mother's maiden name, all kinds of personal and financial details. Usually, you do that paperwork at a bank, someplace reputable that you can trust, but these confidence men got people to do all this on the Internet.

"Once Roy Pickett and his partners got all that information on an applicant, they could clean out the poor man's finances within twenty-four hours. His down payment disappeared out of his bank and his credit cards were maxed out in an hour or two. Then they sold the rest of his financial data to a couple of underground outfits across the border in Canada, and the Canadians applied for new credit cards in the homebuyer's name. Within a couple of days, while the loan applicant was still waiting to hear if he was going to get his loan, the new cards were maxed out, too."

"And this scam actually generated millions of dollars?" Annabel asked, amazed.

"It certainly did. They conned literally thousands of gullible people. Some of these unfortunate folks are still trying to straighten out their credit ratings and climb out of the financial hole they ended up in, and it's been years. Theoretically, the Internet has better controls on this kind of thing today, but this was early in the game. All Roy Pickett and his friends had to do was change the location of their web site every few days and, by the time the police received a complaint on them, they'd already disappeared into cyberspace and reinvented themselves under a new name."

"Sounds like this scheme required a good deal of computer knowledge," Max said.

Benny nodded. "Those guys were intelligent, all right. For a while, anyway."

Max tented his fingers. "Sure, till they got caught."

"The irony is, if they hadn't been so greedy, if they had quit while they were ahead, they probably would have gotten away with it. But the con game becomes an addiction with some people. If five million dollars is good, ten million has to be better, so they'll risk what they've already stolen looking for more. It's like people who play the horses—they're never satisfied with the small win, never just take the money and run or quit the business while they're ahead." Benny shook his head, an expression of pity on his face. "Instead, they have to have more and more and more, until they finally trip themselves up.

"In the end, the Seattle police got their own computer expert to investigate the scam. They put in half a dozen phony loan applications, put a trap on the system, and managed to trace everything back to the source. They arrested four of the guys running the web site, although one of the officers told me there was talk there could have been one or two more involved."

"And this Roy Pickett, the man whose fingerprints you found on my husband's computer, was one of them?" Annabel asked, wondering if Pickett was the man who murdered Dylan, and if he was one of Jason's kidnappers as well. If so, he obviously was very formidable—both smart and completely ruthless.

"That's right, ma'am, Pickett was arrested. But the court, in its infinite wisdom—" Benny rolled his eyes "—figured this was only a white collar crime and set bail for the perpetrators. Pickett disappeared. The other three..." He referred to his notes for the first time. "Gilbert and Clifford Collier—they were brothers—and Peter Hoy, their bail was revoked as soon as Pickett disappeared, and they were given six-year sentences. Clifford Collier died in prison, stabbed to death by a gang member he supposedly had a disagreement with in the cafeteria, but the other two are out on parole."

"What happened to all the money they stole from the loan applicants?" Max asked.

Benny held his palms upward, displaying manicured fingernails. "In the wind," he said. "Nobody ever found it."

Annabel felt sure she and Max both knew where that money was, but she kept mum. As Max had said, Benny had no need to know. She now had a gut feeling that Dylan had been one of the con artists who'd somehow avoided being caught. If so, his constant moving around made sense—he'd been running from the authorities and probably from his partners in crime as well. No wonder he hadn't wanted the publicity that had to come with being Oliver Nettleton's long-lost heir. Maybe Dylan had promised to guard his partners' shares while they did prison time, to keep it safe for them in exchange for their keeping their mouths shut. But he'd obviously disappeared instead. If so, she could understand why this Pickett guy and the others would come after Dylan years later, as soon as that story about his pending inheritance hit the TV networks. They wanted their cut and probably, after doing prison time, they figured they were entitled to his share as well.

"Very good work, Benny," Max said. Benny nodded as though the praise was nothing exceptional. "Turn up anything else?"

"You mean on the dead—" He caught himself, eyeing Annabel guiltily. "Sorry, Mrs. Nettleton. You mean on Mr. Nettleton?"

Max nodded.

"There's no criminal record on him, at least nothing I could find. I did locate a California birth certificate documenting that he was born September twelfth, nineteen sixty-eight, in San Francisco."

"That's correct," Annabel confirmed.

"He has a current California driver's license, for which he traded in one from New Mexico," Benny continued. "His Social Security card was issued from Des Moines, Iowa. He owns two cars, a Honda and a BMW, both licensed in California. Other than that, nothing. No draft registration record, no businesses or real estate owned, no professional licenses. Nothing." He and Max exchanged a look.

"Okay, thanks," the attorney said. "I think Annabel here needs some dinner and a good night's sleep, which I trust Lester will make sure is also a safe night's sleep."

"You can count on it," Benny said, shaking Max's hand. "Don't you worry, ma'am. Nobody gets by my man Lester, ever. You won't be disturbed tonight."

"Thanks, Benny," Annabel said, feeling what little strength she had left quickly dissipating. Just the idea of sleep provoked her to yawn.

When Benny had left, Max took the diskette out of his briefcase and handed it to Annabel. "This has all the bank accounts and passwords on it," he told her. "I've got a duplicate in my office safe, just in case, but it'll be worthless the minute the accounts are liquidated."

Annabel took the diskette and held it for a moment. It looked so innocuous—a small square of gray plastic—yet it was worth far more money than she'd ever dreamed of. "I just hope the kidnappers will accept this," she said. She thought a moment. "I hope Benny was right about that loan scheme. If the kidnappers are the same guys who set up that Internet scam, getting the cash out of these accounts should be a piece of cake for them, right?"

Max shrugged. "It's still not too late to involve the police or the FBI," he reminded her.

"Absolutely not. We already talked about that."

"Just giving you a chance to change your mind if you want."

"Not my decision to make. Jason is Louise's child."

Max sighed deeply. "But it's your life on the line here, Annabel, and if anything happens to you, I don't—"

She placed a finger against his lips, silencing him. "Don't say it," she said. "I think I already know. But this is something I have to do. I promise I'll be as careful as humanly possible tomorrow morning."

Max sighed. "Guess I know when I've been beaten." He stroked her hair tentatively with one finger. "Order some dinner from room service and then try to get some sleep, okay?"

"Not going to bother with dinner," Annabel said, feeling herself fading fast. "Don't think I could stay awake long enough for it to get here."

Max planted a gentle kiss on her forehead and left the room.

As soon as he was gone, Annabel double-locked the door and set the alarm for seven the next morning. She slid the diskette under her pillow and lay down on the bed, still fully clothed, planning to rest for just a moment before showering and undressing for bed.

But she was sound asleep before Lester had completed his first rounds outside her room.

"YOU MOVE THE VAN back out on the street?" Gil asked, lounging on the sofa in the motel unit's small living room.

"Parked it in an alley this time," Peter said. He'd taken it to buy a few groceries and supplies, delivered them to the motel suite, then parked the van once more.

"Far enough from the motel?"

"Block and a half. No way anybody's gonna connect it to us. Figured it was better if it wasn't as visible this time—fat old bitch snooping around earlier was spooky."

"Probably just looking for something to rip off, way you figured." Gil reached into the refrigerator for the remainder of the six-pack of beer. He wrenched a can out of the plastic halter, popped the top, and took a long gulp. "Thought you said you scared the crap out of her."

Peter smiled at the memory. "Ran her off like a damn scared rabbit."

"So forget about it. Beer?" Gil yanked another can from the six-pack and held it out.

"Nah, gotta keep a clear head. Maybe you better lay off yourself. The kid wakes up again, I don't want you passed out like last night."

Gil slammed the refrigerator door shut and carried the remainder of the six-pack over to the sofa, where he plopped himself down. "Screw it. He ain't gonna wake up. Last time he did, I put one of those pills in some applesauce and fed it to him. Ate the whole thing."

"Jesus, Gil! That's Seconal. Give him a quarter pill, half at the most, the way I told you. Kid weighs what, maybe twenty-five, thirty pounds? Idea is to keep him quiet, not *kill* him."

The dark look on Gil's face sent a chill through Peter. "What?" he demanded.

"What do you mean, *what?* Where are your goddamn brains, Einstein?" Gil began to shout, his voice becoming louder as the effect of his fourth can of beer began to take effect.

"Keep your voice down."

Gil moderated his volume only slightly. "What's *your* bright idea—after we get the money, we just drive the kid back to his mama's house and hand him over? Way I figure, it don't matter whether the kid dies now or later. Either way, he's gonna be history the minute the grieving widow coughs up our cash."

It was times like this that made Peter wonder why he'd ever

teamed up with Gil after he left prison. His old cohort had been different before, in the good old days when they were living high, raking in the dough by using their brains...before Gil's brother was murdered. Now he seemed unable to differentiate between taking some sucker's money and taking a child's life.

"No reason we can't just drop off the kid somewhere after we get the money," Peter said. "McDonald's, maybe, or some supermarket around here. Somebody'll call the cops, report a lost kid, and his mom'll come get him."

"Jesus! Listen to yourself. McDonald's! I s'pose you think nobody's gonna notice two guys, one of them Asian for godsake, dumping a blond-haired kid at McDonald's and driving off. Nobody's gonna describe us to the cops, huh?"

Maybe Gil was right, Peter thought with a chill. Maybe they hadn't thought this thing through when they snatched the boy. Still... "Certainly the kid's not going to rat us out," he said. "Can't even talk yet. Our only problem is to find someplace we can leave him—someplace he'll be found quickly but where we won't be noticed. So maybe McDonald's is a dumb idea. Maybe we leave him in a gas station bathroom, something like that."

Gil drained his beer and reached for another. "Hey, Mr. Rocket Scientist, you're starting to worry me more than that kid. Fact is, it's a helluva lot easier to dump a body someplace than to get rid of a live kid and you know it. I've gone along with you so far, keeping him alive till we get our money. Even changed the little prick's stinking diaper, for godsake. But I am not gonna risk spending the rest of my life in stir so we can keep that son of a bitch thief's son alive a minute longer than we have to. No way, Peter! So figure it out—it's us or him and it ain't gonna be us."

"Screw it." In the past few days, Peter had learned he

couldn't discuss anything rationally with Gil when he was half in the bag, so why try? He stalked out of the living room and into the bedroom of the motel housekeeping suite they'd rented for the week. There, he stood at the edge of the bed and stared down at the motionless child, covered up to his neck by a blanket, his pale hair a vivid contrast with the maroon bedspread.

The boy's thumb was in his mouth and his eyes were closed. Was he already dead? Had Gil's feeding him that pill already murdered him?

As he looked down at the little child, Peter could detect no clear sign that he was breathing. He held his hand above the still figure for a moment, letting it hover while he considered whether to touch the boy's neck, to see if he had a pulse. And if he didn't find one, what then?

Peter noticed his hand was trembling and quickly stuffed it in the pocket of his pants.

With a quick shake of his head, he turned around, walked back into the living room, and grabbed the last can of beer off the coffee table.

# TWELVE

ANNABEL LAY IMMOBILE in the midst of the fire, the flames licking closer to her body as acrid smoke crept into her nose and mouth and choked off her breath. *This time you won't escape,* she heard a threatening voice say. *This time nobody will save you. You will burn in hell forever.*

"No! Please! I don't want to die!" Her nightgown exploded into crimson flames and she felt the searing heat branding her skin.

ANNABEL AWOKE in terror, her pulse racing and her parched throat tight and burning. She looked around, suddenly confused to find herself in a motel room that clearly was not ablaze. A stream of warm morning sunlight, rare in foggy Carmel, fell across the bed where she'd slept, still fully clothed.

As she tried to get her bearings, she could have sworn she heard thunder, but surely that was impossible on a sunny day. No, she finally realized, it wasn't thunder, it was a sharp banging sound—someone was banging on the door to the room.

"Mrs. Nettleton!" an unfamiliar male voice boomed. "Mrs. Nettleton! You all right in there?"

Had she called out in her nightmare? Annabel got out of bed on shaky legs, staggered to the door, and gazed through the peephole. So her huge bodyguard wasn't mute after all, she realized. Leaving the security chain on, she cracked open the door. "Sorry, Lester," she said. "Didn't mean to scare you. Guess I had a nightmare."

"Sure you're okay?"

The skin below the big man's bloodshot eyes sagged and he looked tired after staying up all night. Annabel wondered if he'd stood right outside her door all that time.

"I'm fine," she said. "Thanks for watching over me."

Lester nodded, wordless once more.

In the shower a few minutes later, Annabel reviewed what she could remember about her dream. The horror of the fire had been happening all over again, but this time there was no rescuer, no stranger—no Nell Verducci—to save her and Nicky. As hot water splashed against her body and she breathed in clean, refreshing steam, she felt her head finally begin to clear. Had there been a message in that dream, something she needed to heed? What came to mind first was a directive to find her rescuer.

Annabel turned off the water and stepped out of the shower, quickly drying herself with the luxuriously thick motel towel. She thought about Nell, the strange woman to whom she owed her life and her son's. Without Nell, they would both be dead now. She felt a rush of gratitude.

But Nell hadn't been completely forthcoming when they spoke at the hospital. She obviously hadn't told the whole story. There was something about the older woman rattling around in the back of Annabel's brain, some indication she wasn't simply an altruistic person who'd happened by the fire and decided impulsively to risk her own life to save others.

Of course! Now Annabel remembered clearly. Nell had said several things indicating she'd already known about Annabel's troubles—about Dylan's murder and that the police suspected her—*before the fire*. And Nell also knew Annabel and Louise had lied to the police and reporters, that they'd switched the identities of their sons. How did she know all that?

Obviously, Nell was no casual bystander. *But who was she? And did she know anything about the people who had stolen Jason?*

Annabel dressed quickly, noting that she still had an hour and a half before she had to be at Del Monte Center to take that phone call, before she had to talk the kidnappers into accepting the computer diskette in lieu of the millions of dollars in cash they'd demanded for Jason's return. Maybe that was enough time to find Nell again…providing she was still hanging around Annabel's old house.

"Lester," Annabel asked after she'd opened the motel room door again. "You have a car?"

The big man nodded mutely.

"How about giving me a ride back to my old neighborhood?"

"I'd have to check with Benny."

"Hey, you're supposed to protect me, not imprison me, right? If you don't give me a ride, I'll just have to call a cab." Annabel reached for the telephone.

Benny shrugged his massive shoulders. "Uh—okay, I guess."

Annabel headed out the door.

WARNER TURNED ONTO the street where the Zuckerman and Nettleton houses were located, completely unsure of his next move. It was an eerily strange feeling for him—he'd always been a planner, sometimes even a plodder, and he'd always known precisely what his next step was going to be well ahead of taking it. Warner routinely prided himself on being a man with an intelligent contingency plan for every possible scenario…until now.

Now, everything he tried seemed to fail miserably, and there wasn't much time left. Old Oliver wasn't going to last much longer, that much was certain. At best, Warner probably had a few more hours before everything he'd worked so hard to achieve over all these years retreated permanently out of reach.

As he turned his rented black Cadillac onto the street, he saw a battered old Chevrolet pulling into the curb in front of the Zuckerman house. He slowed and watched as Annabel Nettleton had a lengthy discussion with the driver and then stepped out of the car…alone. She waved as the driver, a huge young man, his massive head nearly reaching the Chevy's ceiling, drove off.

Why was Dylan's wife here alone? Where was Dylan's little son? Warner felt a new sense of panic, worse than when he'd watched that TV news report, the one about the fire that failed to mention Nicholas Nettleton, Oliver's probable heir. If the boy was dead, if he'd died in the fire, why wasn't that fact on the news? And, if he wasn't dead, where in God's name was he?

Warner turned his face away as Annabel lingered on the sidewalk, obviously surveying the cars parked along the street. It wouldn't do to have her take special notice of him. He sped past and turned at the corner, then U-turned on a nearby street and parked down the block, where he could watch the house without being seen.

As he sat in his parked car, Warner looked over the collection of surveillance gadgets he'd taken from Jeff Link's room at the Pine Lodge. He picked up the parabolic microphone, aimed it at the front of the Zuckerman house, and switched it on, but all he heard through its earphones was the rustling of the bushes in the wind. Maybe he was too far away, he thought, or possibly this device required him to be in line-of-sight of his target. These were devices he knew little about, but when he'd found them stashed in Link's room, he thought he might be able to use them. Certainly the private eye wasn't going to need them.

Warner put the mike down and picked up a pair of high-powered binoculars, quickly focusing them on the Zuckermans' front door. As he peered through the lenses, it seemed as though he was sitting a few feet from the house, not nearly a block away. Yet he felt certain nobody inside the house could see him.

He would simply have to quiet his nervous pulse and wait, Warner decided. For the time being, he would have to remain here in his car and watch the house until the woman came out again, with or without the boy.

Once he figured out what she was up to and where the little heir was, he would decide what to do.

Then he would use his superior planning skills to plot a fresh course of action.

SHORTLY AFTER EIGHT-THIRTY, Annabel drove Louise's Mercedes out of the Zuckermans' garage. The keys to her own car were undoubtedly somewhere in the burned-out rubble of the guest house, along with her purse. She prayed she wouldn't be stopped by the cops and asked to produce her driver's license.

As she drove along the street, Annabel made one last survey of the parked cars, looking for Nell, but the woman was nowhere around. Damn! She felt certain Nell knew something important, something she could be enticed to tell, if only she understood what was at stake here. After all, she'd gone into a burning building to save two people, so she'd certainly do whatever she could to save a kidnapped child's life, wouldn't she? Unfortunately, Annabel had no idea where to find her and no time left to look.

She slipped her hand into the purse she'd borrowed from Louise and reassured herself that the precious computer diskette was still there. She would have to rely on it, not on whatever Nell Verducci might or might not know, to save Jason.

Her thoughts now on the anticipated phone call from the kidnappers, Annabel didn't notice the new black Cadillac that pulled away from the curb shortly after she'd passed it, or the tall, thin man driving it.

The shopping center's parking lot was nearly empty when she arrived in the lower level parking lot near Macy's. The stores didn't open until ten, so only a few employees' cars were in the lot at this hour. She checked her watch—it was five minutes before nine—got out of the car, and walked over to the bank of three pay phones where the kidnappers had instructed her to wait.

At precisely nine o'clock, one of the phones rang. Catching her breath, Annabel grabbed it before it could ring a second time.

"Mrs. Nettleton?"

"Yes."

"You have the money?"

"Let me talk to Nicky first. Is he all right? You haven't hurt him—"

The voice took on a harsher tone. *"Do you have the money?"*

"Of course, I have the money. I mean I—"

"Good. Now listen carefully. I'm only going to say this once. Get in your car and drive to Lovers Point Park in Pacific Grove. Wait by the public phone outside the restrooms. In exactly twenty minutes, we'll call you there with directions for handing over the cash. And come alone or you'll never see your boy alive again."

"I understand. Lovers Point Park in twenty minutes. Please, just let me talk to—"

The line went dead. Annabel glanced at her watch. The entire phone conversation had lasted less than thirty seconds. The kidnappers hadn't trusted her, she realized. They'd obviously been afraid she'd gone to the police after all, that the phone call was being traced.

Her heart sank. This nightmare still wasn't over, and she hadn't even had time to explain about the diskette. She didn't have the luxury of taking time to feel frustrated, however. She had less than twenty minutes to drive to Lovers Point Park.

She sprinted toward Louise's Mercedes.

THIS TIME WARNER had no trouble working the parabolic microphone from his parking spot within sight of the pay phone bank. His spirits soared as he listened to Annabel's side of the phone conversation. So *that's* what had happened to the child, *that's* why he hadn't been in the fire—he'd been kidnapped! Probably by some nutcase who'd read the newspapers and thought the boy already had his grandfather's fortune.

Elated by this fortuitous new chance, Warner quickly formulated a new plan. He put his car in gear and headed for Lovers Point Park, taking care to put enough distance between his Cadillac and the Mercedes so that the Nettleton woman wouldn't realize she was being followed.

ANNABEL MADE IT to Lovers Point with seven minutes to spare. There were only a few people in the bayside park at this hour, most of them either young joggers or elderly folks walking their dogs. Under any other circumstances, she would have been able to appreciate the incredible beauty of the place. Seagulls screeched, swooped over the tops of cypress trees bent and formed by the wind, and dove toward the rugged shoreline. Sea lions perched on huge rocks in the bay and barked like a pack of dogs. And the air was pungent with a mixture of sea salt and cooking odors from the Tinnery restaurant across the street.

As she walked toward the restrooms, Annabel's stomach

responded to the smell of onions frying, reminding her she hadn't eaten in nearly twenty-four hours. Almost instantly, her hunger turned to nausea. How could she even think about food at a time like this, when her slightest misstep could cost Jason his life?

She found the pay phone and paced back and forth in front of it, her eyes scanning the face of each person who passed near her. Did she have time to use the pay phone to call Louise and let her know what was happening? She considered it, but quickly decided not to. What if one of the joggers, or even one of the old men with a dog, or somebody watching from the restaurant window was one of the kidnappers? There was no sense in taking foolish chances this late in the game.

Instead, Annabel paced and waited for the phone to ring.

PETER SAT IN the white van and used a stolen cell phone to make the call. From his parking spot in front of the Tinnery he had a clear view of the tall blond woman waiting nervously in front of the pay phone. He watched as she answered on the first ring.

"Mrs. Nettleton."

"Yes."

"Here's what I want you to do with the cash. It should fit into—"

"Wait a minute! You have to listen to me—I tried to tell you before."

Peter heard a nervous tremor in the woman's voice and his grip tightened on the cell phone. "You said you had the money!" he shouted at her.

"I do! I do have the money. It's just that—that Dylan hid it all in all these foreign bank accounts, in the Cayman Islands and places like that, where all you have is a number on your account, not a name. I got all the information from his com-

puter transferred onto a diskette—the names of the banks, the
account numbers, Dylan's passwords, everything you need to
move the money anywhere you want. But I—I don't know
how to do all that by myself. I'm really stupid about computers. Even if I did know how, I wouldn't have any idea where
to transfer the money."

*Damn!* Peter'd had visions of loading up a couple of suitcases with greenbacks and taking off for someplace new and
different, somewhere he could get a fresh start. He'd give Gil
his half, of course, that was only fair, but then he'd cut him loose
in a heartbeat. Gil was getting too damn psycho these days, and
Peter sure as hell didn't need more trouble. But now—

"Are you still there?" The woman was beginning to sound
hysterical. "Please, please talk to me. I'm not trying to pull a
fast one, honest I'm not. There's even more money in these
bank accounts than you asked for, closer to thirty million. You
can have all of it. It's just…I can't get it to you in cash this
quickly."

"Shut up and let me think!" Peter ran the idea through his
mind. What the Nettleton woman was saying made sense. That
creep she'd married probably hadn't kept all that cash in safe
deposit boxes. That he would have it in numbered off-shore
bank accounts sounded logical. But could he and Gil trust her?
It all came down to how much she cared about her kid, and
whether she thought the cops were capable of getting him back
for her. Still, if she'd contacted the cops or the FBI, would they
try something like this diskette switch? Probably not, Peter figured. Instead, they'd undoubtedly put together enough cash to
lure him and Gil out into the open and then they'd pounce.

"Where's the diskette?" he asked.

"I've got it right here with me, in my purse."

"You're not getting your kid back until I check it out and
transfer the money. If you're lying, he's dead."

"I'm not—I'm *not* lying. Honest. I'd never lie about something like this."

The woman was starting to sniffle now and Peter could see her wipe her eyes with the back of her hand. If she completely lost it, people in the park might begin to notice.

"Okay," he said finally, deciding to take the chance. "Put the diskette into the pocket of your jacket. Then take off the jacket and put it in that wire trash can at the north edge of the triangular parking lot." Peter saw the woman's head swivel around as she realized he was watching her as they talked. "Quit looking around and do what I told you!"

"Okay, okay, I'm sorry." She took something he couldn't see from her purse and slid it into the right-hand pocket of her denim jacket, then slipped her arms out of the garment. "How will I know when you've got the money?" she asked. "Nicky's just a baby, and he's got to be scared half to death."

Peter felt a faint pang of guilt as he heard the obvious anguish in Annabel's voice. Still, his share of the millions that could be—*had to be*—in those foreign bank accounts could go a helluva long way toward pacifying any guilt he might feel later on. "Come back to this pay phone at the same time tomorrow," he told her. "If the diskette contains what you say it does, we'll have the cash transferred by then and we'll tell you where you can pick up your son." That should keep Annabel quiet for the next twenty-four hours. "Remember—if you're lying, he dies," Peter warned.

"I swear I'm not!"

"Go put your jacket in the trash can, like I told you. Then drive away from here and don't look back."

Peter watched as the lanky woman did precisely as he'd directed. She laid her jacket on top of the papers and food wrappers inside the trash can, then walked, shivering in the cool morning breeze, toward a new Mercedes parked about fifty feet away. Without a backward look, she drove off.

He waited for five minutes, watching to see if anyone else approached the trash receptacle. When no one did, he got out of the van, strolled casually toward the north end of the park, and reached into the trash can. Holding his breath, he slid his hand into the pocket of the discarded jacket. His fingers quickly closed around a slim, square piece of plastic. He pulled out the diskette, slid it into the pocket of his own jacket, and glanced around the park. When no one seemed to take any particular notice of him, he headed back to the van.

Before he returned to the motel in Seaside, Peter decided, he would stop at the cyber-café he'd noticed in New Monterey and check out the contents of the diskette. If it seemed legitimate, he could use the café's Internet connection and have the funds transferred to a new account in less than an hour.

As he pulled away from the curb, he used the cell phone once more, this time to call Gil and let him know what was happening.

FOR THE DOZENTH TIME that morning, Nell put her ear to the motel wall and tried to hear what was happening in the adjacent unit. But all she heard was silence. Little boys were almost never this quiet, not unless they were sound asleep or something was terribly wrong. If Nell had learned anything in her half century of life, it was that.

After her confrontation with the Asian man yesterday, she'd managed to follow his white van to the Safeway and watch him enter the store. Fearful that he'd spot her if she followed him too closely, she waited outside the store until he came out, carrying two small sacks of groceries. He tossed them into the van, then took off in a hurry.

Was this the same man she'd seen at the Zuckerman house?

Nell still wasn't sure. She wished she'd had the guts to follow him into the store. Maybe some purchase he made—baby food, disposable diapers, a toy for a small boy—would answer her question. But if she'd followed him inside and been caught…well, she didn't even want to think about what events that could set in motion.

Instead, she followed the van again and watched as it turned into a motel parking lot a block south of Fremont Boulevard. The driver got out, carried the groceries into unit eight, then quickly reemerged and drove the van to an alley, where he parked it.

When she saw the young man get out of the van and head back toward the motel on foot, Nell became certain something very fishy was going on here. There was no logical reason for him to keep his van parked more than a block away from his motel, not when there was a parking space available right in front of the unit. Not unless he didn't want the van to be connected to the resident of the motel. Of course, there could be reasons other than kidnapping for the subterfuge, she told herself. Maybe the guy was a drug runner or wanted by the police for some other crime. Or maybe the van was stolen.

Damn, this was hard. Hadn't she already done enough, saving Annabel and Nicholas from the fire? Nell told herself she should buy a tank of gas and head back to Arizona before she got into even more trouble. She'd been a stupid fool ever to leave there, to risk everything because of—what?—curiosity, guilt, anger, a whole cocktail of emotions she suddenly could no longer swallow.

Still, if Jason was in that motel unit and she did nothing… *Damn!* She felt it starting all over again.

After battling her self-protective better judgment, Nell checked into the same motel. She requested unit seven, which, like unit eight, had no vehicle parked in front of it. "My lucky number," she told the elderly, emaciated desk clerk. "Always try for my lucky number."

Unit seven was indeed available and the clerk didn't seem to think her request for it at all strange. Nell held her breath as he swiped her MasterCard through the groove in the cash register, exhaling only when he handed the slim plastic rectangle back to her. Apparently—miraculously—she hadn't yet exceeded her credit limit.

"Number seven," the clerk said, tossing the key on the counter with a bored look. "Dishes are in the unit. You break 'em, you pay for 'em."

"Thanks." Nell grabbed the key, stowed her suitcase and two microwave meals she'd bought in her suite, and moved the Volvo onto a side street to assure her motel neighbor wouldn't recognize it from their earlier encounter.

In the hours since she'd checked into the motel, Nell had taken her first long bath in days and eaten a palatable dinner. Yet she couldn't relax in what, compared to living in the Volvo, seemed like luxury. She couldn't help thinking of little Jason. Was he really right next door?

As she threw the remains of her dinner into the trash and considered how she might discover what was going in the next unit, Nell heard a murmur through the wall—the faint thunder of male voices raised in anger. So the Asian man wasn't all alone over there. She quickly discovered that, by standing inside her living room closet with her ear pressed against the adjoining wall, she could hear much of what was going on next door.

So it was standing inside the musty motel closet, the old sweater she'd hung up earlier tickling her face, that Nell overheard the angry words between Jason's abductors.

"…fat old bitch snooping around earlier…" Nell heard. A chill overtook her and she shivered—the man was talking about her! What if they found out she was here, right next door, eavesdropping on their argument? Whatever they were up to, whether it involved Jason or not, she knew her life wouldn't be worth two cents.

But as the conversation progressed, she became more and more certain her hunch about the kidnapping was right.

"…ain't gonna wake up…" she heard the deeper voice say. "…I put one of those pills in some applesauce and fed it to him."

When she heard the word Seconal, Nell's blood ran colder. She knew something about Seconal. Hell, there was a time she'd known about an entire pharmacy of drugs—uppers, downers, psychedelics, coke, hash, mood-altering substances of every kind. There was a time she'd experimented with all of them. Although her memories of those days were often fuzzy, she remembered enough to know you didn't give a full Seconal tablet to a baby—not without taking a terrible, completely unacceptable risk.

She spent the rest of the night wrestling with her conscience. She could call the police, tell them a kidnapped child was being held next door. But Annabel and Louise clearly had decided against involving the police. Why else would they have tried to pass off Nicholas as Jason?

If Jason was already dead, Nell told herself, nothing she did would matter anyway. She could simply head back to Arizona, resume the sorry excuse for a life she'd been living, and forget about this place. About Jason. About everything.

But if the child was still alive and she did nothing… Could she live with that decision?

She thought about people like Annabel, the strong, sturdy, generous kind of folks who were willing to give up a kidney to a brother without a second thought, the sort who would give everything they owned to save a friend's child.

There was a painful contrast with herself, Nell believed.

She'd been anything but brave and giving in her own life. Instead, she'd made mostly stupid, self-centered decisions with dire consequences.

She wanted to think she'd changed, that she was no longer the immature girl she'd been thirty years ago. But had she really? She knelt on the closet floor and wept.

Nell stayed in the closet all night, intermittently falling asleep on the floor and listening for a reassuring sound from next door—Jason's cry, any indication in the men's conversation that he was still alive, even the crash of the police breaking in to rescue the little tyke.

But she heard nothing more until morning, when one of the men shouted, "Going to get the money. Be ready to split by the time I get back."

Nell peeked through a crack in the drapes and saw the Asian man crossing the parking lot at a trot, heading in the direction of his parked van.

Now, an hour later, she was still trying to make a decision. Did "be ready to split" mean making certain the boy was dead, that his little body was ready to be dumped by some roadside or buried on some remote hillside with no one to mourn him? She knew she had to do something to save him, if that remained possible. Yet doing the right thing could cause her endless problems of her own.

Was she ready to trade her own freedom for Jason's? That was the question. Yet, maybe there still was a way...

Nell grabbed her sweater and her suitcase and headed out of unit seven. She would let someone else make this decision. Jason was Louise's son, not hers; it was only right that Louise decide.

Nell would go tell Louise—and Annabel, too, if she was there—what she knew. Then, it would be the young mothers' problem, not hers.

Once she'd revealed her information, she could fill the Volvo's gas tank and head back home to Arizona.

WARNER WATCHED as a young Asian man got out of a white van parked across the street and zigzagged over to the trash barrel where Annabel had discarded her jacket. After he'd heard her end of the conversation, he'd briefly considered picking up that diskette himself. If it was really worth thirty million, that would be almost enough to compensate him if he got cheated out of his rightful inheritance from Uncle Oliver. But it was also possible the diskette was worth nothing—that Dylan's widow was pulling some sort of scam on the kidnappers—or, even if it was valuable, that Warner wouldn't be able to transfer those funds she'd mentioned.

In the end, it was plain, garden-variety fear that stopped him from picking up that diskette. From Annabel's end of the conversation and her actions, he could tell that the man on the other end of her phone call was nearby, positioned where he could watch her. So, if Warner ventured out of his Cadillac and over to the trash barrel, that same person undoubtedly would be able to see him, too. Although he had a gun tucked under the seat of his car, the last thing he wanted to risk was a shootout at Lovers Point Park. Not when he might finally have gotten lucky.

So Warner sat tight, consoling himself by thinking about his larger goal. He shoved the parabolic mike into the backseat and watched to see who would pick up the diskette.

Once the younger man had the diskette in his pocket, Warner saw him look around at the other people in the park, then head straight back to the white van. He let the van get half a block away before he pulled out from the curb and followed it. Luckily, the speed limit in this part of Pacific Grove was only twenty-five miles per hour, and there was no such thing as a four-lane highway, so it was easy enough not to lose the van in traffic.

He followed it into New Monterey, where Lighthouse Avenue widened to four lanes and was lined with shops. When the van pulled into the curb a few blocks after Prescott Avenue, Warner kept going, then circled back. It was still parked. He circled the block a second time and pulled into the curb fifty feet behind the van. Was the child being kept in this neighborhood? It seemed unlikely—this street was completely commercial.

Confused, Warner surveyed the local businesses. This block offered a liquor store, a bar, an Italian restaurant, a used furniture outlet, a rare book shop, and something called Cyber-Age. This last had a sign in its window that read, "Connect to the Internet—Just $3 for 15 Minutes!"

So that was it. The van's driver was already checking out that diskette, maybe even transferring the money Annabel had promised he could access with it. Warner smiled to himself. All he had to do now was wait, then follow the white van to little Nicholas. If the kidnappers hadn't already killed him, he could finish the job himself and make sure they took the blame.

If only Oliver stayed alive long enough, this could turn out to be Warner's lucky day.

WHEN ANNABEL ARRIVED at the Zuckermans' home, an old Volvo was in the driveway, blocking the entrance to the garage, so she parked Louise's Mercedes on the street.

As she walked toward the house, she saw Louise and Nell run out of the front door toward the Volvo. Eagerly, Annabel rushed toward them.

Louise's face lit up when she saw Annabel. "We know where Jason is!" she shouted, fresh hope shining in her eyes. "We're going to get him back."

"That's great!" The kidnappers must have called here after checking out the diskette, Annabel figured. This was wonderful news—they wouldn't have to wait until tomorrow to get Jason back after all. "Where's Nicky?" she asked as the other two women climbed into Nell's car.

"In the house with Missy. Don't worry—he's fine." Louise reported. "I called Max and told him what we were doing. He said he'd meet us there."

"I'm coming with you," Annabel said, deciding instantly. She pulled open the back door of the old car and climbed inside, shoving aside a pile of Nell's discarded clothes to make room for herself.

"Fasten your seat belts," Nell warned as she gunned the car in reverse, then shifted gears and tore down the quiet street.

As they sped toward Seaside, Nell told Annabel the story she'd already related to Louise, all about her surveillance of the Asian man and his partner. The hairs on the back of Annabel's neck stood up as she realized her earlier assumption had been dead wrong—the kidnappers weren't turning over Jason earlier than promised at all, and getting the boy back by going to the motel wasn't going to be anywhere near as simple as picking him up someplace his abductors had left him.

"You heard these guys talking through the motel wall?" Annabel asked, feeling a strong wave of apprehension.

"Whenever they raised their voices, at least," Nell said. "I couldn't hear everything they said, but I'm positive they're the ones who kidnapped Jason. When I saw the Asian man with the white van on Fremont Boulevard yesterday, I was pretty sure he was the same one I'd seen carrying the child outside Louise's house, but I couldn't be positive. Then, after I heard him talking to the other guy, I didn't know what to do about it. Like I told Louise, I considered calling the cops, but I knew she'd decided against that—"

"You did all that by yourself?" Annabel shook her head in amazement. "Good lord, Nell, why didn't you ask for help? You could have gotten yourself killed." Not to mention Jason, she thought.

Nell shrugged off Annabel's comment as she steered off Highway 1 onto the Fremont Boulevard exit. A few minutes later, she turned onto the side street leading to the motel and parked on the street, behind a black Cadillac. "They might recognize my car from yesterday, so I don't want to pull into the parking lot," she explained, pulling her crowbar out from under the driver's seat.

"Now what do we do?" Annabel asked as the women spotted the white van parked in front of unit eight. After hearing Nell tell her story, she wasn't at all sure coming here was a good idea. It might be safer for Jason if they just waited to hear from the kidnappers. After all, she'd paid them the ransom. Still, this had to be Louise's decision.

"One of us should stay in front of the motel in case they come out," Nell suggested. "Louise, why don't you stay here? They still think they've got Annabel's son, so they won't be looking for you. Annabel and I can sneak around the back and try to see into the bedroom. I'm pretty sure that's where they've been keeping your son."

Pale and obviously terrified now that they'd actually reached the place where her son was being held hostage, Louise nodded her agreement and ducked down behind one of the cars parked in the motel's lot. Annabel gave her friend's trembling shoulder a quick, reassuring pat, then followed Nell around the side of the low building.

They bent low, creeping around the rosemary bushes planted along the side of the motel, doing their best to stay out of sight of anyone who might question their presence.

The area behind the building was unkempt and weedy, lit-tered with broken bottles and discarded beer cans. Annabel caught the strong odor of decaying garbage from the over-flowing Dumpster parked in the rear corner.

"They're in the second unit from this end," Nell whispered as she rounded the corner. Annabel followed close behind, crouching down as she walked, her eyes flicking back and forth between the scrubby ground and Nell's ample backside.

Suddenly Nell shot bolt upright and stared straight ahead. Annabel's gaze followed Nell's and she saw a tall, thin man standing in the dirt, raising the window to unit eight. He held a gun in his right hand as he slid the window upward with his left. The window screen had already been removed and tossed aside.

"Warner!" Nell cried, her eyes wide and her voice thick with shock. "Warner Schuman!"

The man turned and stared at Nell, paling as though he'd seen a ghost. He quickly took aim, fired one shot in the women's direction, and disappeared through the window.

Grabbing her shoulder, Nell screamed in agony and dropped to the ground. The crowbar tumbled onto the dirt and she collapsed in a heap.

IN THE LIVING ROOM packing up their gear, Peter and Gil heard the gunshot.

"What the—?" Peter said, grabbing his gun. He threw open the door to the bedroom just in time to see a gray-faced man climbing through the window. "Who the hell—"

The man aimed and fired a second time, hitting Peter squarely in the chest. Red blossomed across his T-shirt as he jerked backward and fell to the floor.

But before the intruder could get off another shot, Gil appeared in the doorway, took aim, and fired his own weapon. Taking the .44 slug at close range, Warner whirled around and fell backward against the upper part of the window, his head smashing the glass. As he twisted from the bullet's impact, a shard of glass sliced through his jugular vein, impaling him on the window frame. Blood spurted across the room for the few seconds it took for his heart to stop beating.

GIL RUSHED OVER to the window, his gun cocked and ready. He tried to see whether there were any other cops out there—assuming this asshole intruder was a cop and not a freelance—but he didn't want to get too close to the dead man, who was hanging from the window frame like a rag doll. Using the corpse as a shield, Gil looked out, but could see nothing but an empty backyard and the six-foot wooden fence marking its end.

He bent over his fallen friend, but Peter's eyes were open and unfocused. Gil had seen that look before—it was the same one he'd seen on his brother's face after that greaser'd stabbed him to death in the prison cafeteria. Peter was beyond help.

Increasingly panicky, Gil figured he would need a shield to assure he got away from the motel. The kid would have to serve the purpose—he could dump his body in some farmer's field after he'd made a clean escape. Yanking the limp toddler off the bed, he hoisted him onto his left shoulder and carried him out of the room, skirting a wide path around Peter's dead body.

"Rest in peace, buddy," he whispered.

Gil rushed into the living room and placed his gun on the coffee table just long enough to grab the diskette and the computer printout Peter had made and slip them into the back pocket of his jeans. Hooking the keys to the van on a finger, he pressed the little boy's dead weight against his body with one hand and held the cocked gun in the other, then headed for the door.

As he shifted the gun to his left hand so he could unlock

and open the door, Gil heard the faint sound of a siren in the distance. It quickly grew louder. If the police weren't already out there, he now realized, they certainly were on their way.

Somebody had reported those shots.

"DON'T WORRY about me—I'll make it," Nell gasped, lying in the dirt and holding her injured shoulder, blood seeping between her fingers. "Take the crowbar and go find Louise. You've got to save Jason before it's too late."

Annabel hesitated only briefly. As she came back around the front of the building, she heard two more shots from inside the motel. What was going on in there? Good God, had the tall man—"Warner Schuman," whoever he was—shot Jason, too?

She gestured to Louise, who was already sprinting across the parking lot with a look of sheer panic on her face. Holding a finger to her lips, Annabel warned Louise to stay quiet.

Without words, she gestured to her friend to stand on the hinged side of the door to unit eight while she stood on the opposite side, the crowbar gripped tightly in both hands.

Her knuckles white against the raised crowbar, Annabel heard a siren in the distance, its sound rapidly growing louder. The police were coming, but somehow she didn't feel relieved. Would they make things better or worse for Jason?

Closer, Annabel heard a sharp click on the other side of the door as the deadbolt was unlocked. She shot Louise a warning glance, pressed her body hard against the building, and raised the crowbar.

The door opened slowly. In her peripheral vision, Annabel saw a swatch of Jason's red overalls, at eye level. There seemed to be no movement in the child's body.

A fraction of a second later, she saw a gun emerge from the doorway, followed by the man carrying Jason.

"Hey!" Louise yelled.

As the man swiveled toward the voice, Annabel swung the crowbar with all the force she could muster, connecting with the side of his head. His gun fired once, the bullet missing Louise's leg by mere inches and lodging in the grille of a parked car.

Louise lunged forward and grabbed her son as Gil's knees crumpled and he slumped to the pavement.

As soon as Louise had lifted Jason out of the way, Annabel swung the crowbar a second time. It connected with the gun like a golf club with a ball, sending the .44 skidding across the pavement a good ten feet and breaking two bones in the groggy Gil's hand.

Two Seaside squad cars skidded into the parking lot. Officers emerged with guns drawn as Max pulled up behind them.

"Drop the weapon!" one of the officers yelled, aiming his gun at Annabel.

It took her a moment to realize they were talking to her.

"Don't shoot!" Max shouted. "She's one of the good guys! Just put down the crowbar, Annabel!"

Annabel's shaky fingers loosened on the crowbar and she tossed it aside, well out of Gil's reach, then stepped away from the wounded man.

Louise gently shook Jason, trying to wake him, but he remained limp, his eyes firmly closed.

"Call an ambulance!" she shouted to the police. "Fast! There's something horribly wrong with my son!"

# THIRTEEN

ANNABEL WAS SITTING in the blue upholstered chair beside Nell's hospital bed when the older woman awoke from anesthesia following her second round of shoulder surgery in three days. The bullet had been removed shortly after Nell reached the hospital, but it had partially severed her rotator cuff, necessitating a second, more major trip to the operating room today.

"Annabel," Nell moaned as she came gradually awake. "What're you doing here?"

"Watching over you," Annabel told her, smiling. "Congratulations. It was a tricky operation, but the surgeon says you're going to be fine. As long as you complete your physical therapy, you'll get back the full use of your shoulder."

"Sure as hell don't *feel* fine," Nell moaned. "Lord, this hurts!" She lay on her back in the hospital bed, her left arm tethered to something that looked like a huge round bolster pillow.

"Want me to call the nurse?" Annabel asked. "She said she'd give you morphine for the pain if you need it."

Nell squeezed her eyes shut in agony, then opened them again. She took a deep breath. "In a few minutes. Want to stay sober at least until I can find out what's been going on around here." She'd been kept isolated from the others since the ambulance ride from the Seaside motel and kept in a separate part of the hospital while the police sorted out the events at the motel.

Annabel was pleased. She'd been hoping Nell would stay

alert long enough for them to exchange some information. "Jason's going to be okay, too," she reported. "It was really lucky you knew the kidnappers had drugged him with Seconal. The doctors gave him an antidote right away, and they're pretty sure he's going to recover without any permanent brain damage." She bit her lip and her eyes began to water. The past few days had been incredibly difficult ones—she felt like crying every time she thought about how close they'd all come to dying. "If—if it had taken much longer to get the poor little guy to the hospital, we might have lost him."

"Thank God."

"One of the kidnappers is dead," Annabel reported when she'd regained her composure, "the Asian man you followed around. His name was Peter Hoy. The other one, a guy named Gilbert Collier—the one I clubbed in the head with your crowbar—he's going back to prison, probably for the rest of his life." She couldn't help feeling a small swell of pride that she'd managed to fell Collier without getting anyone killed in the process.

"Good riddance."

"And Warner Schuman is dead, too. Apparently either Hoy or Collier shot him. Can't really be certain which one."

Nell winced again.

"Want me to get you that morphine now?"

"Not just yet." She glanced toward her bandaged shoulder and grimaced. "This really hurts, but I was thinking about Warner Schuman." She seemed to catch herself. "I mean all the dead people."

Annabel lowered her voice. "How did you know who he was?" she asked.

Nell kept her mouth closed, a guilty look on her face.

"I heard you call him Warner, right before he shot you."

"Should've realized you'd remember what I said." Nell

sighed wearily. "Guess I was so shocked to see him there, I just blurted it out."

"You don't have to tell me if you don't want to, Nell, but I've got to admit I'm dying of curiosity. Max—my lawyer, remember him?—Max did some research and found out Warner Schuman was the nephew of Oliver Nettleton's late wife. Oliver was my husband Dylan's grandfather." The rich old man had died only two days ago and things were still up in the air about the inheritance. Annabel still wasn't sure whether or not it might eventually come to Nicky—or even if she really wanted it to. There was so much bad luck attached to that money that it seemed jinxed.

"Turns out Schuman was in line to inherit all those millions if no blood heir was found," she added. "Max says the police now have proof it was Schuman who started the fire that almost killed Nicky and me—it would have, if you hadn't shown up. He still had the gas can he used in the trunk of his car and they were able to do some sort of chemical analysis on it. Plus, it was a bullet from the gun he used to shoot you that killed that private investigator, Jeffrey Link." Annabel detailed the police reconstruction of that murder. Schuman and Link had driven to Salinas together, where Schuman shot Link, robbed him of his identification, and hoped the private eye's death would be counted as yet another random gang shooting. Then Schuman drove to Monterey and ditched the rental car. "The cops found a cab driver who remembers driving him from the Doubletree Hotel in Monterey back to his hotel in Carmel on that night. Poor Jeff Link must have found out a whole lot more about Schuman's plans that he was supposed to," she said.

"Far as we can tell, it looks like Schuman thought he was climbing in that motel window to kill Nicky...probably figured he could get rid of the last blood heir, blame his death on the kidnappers, and inherit the Nettleton money himself. And he was within seconds of getting away with it all when we showed up. Except, of course, that he would have killed the wrong boy."

Annabel shifted in her chair and looked Nell straight in the eye. "So, Nell, I don't think anybody's going to mourn the death of Warner Schuman all that much. I'll ask you again. How did you know who Schuman was?"

Nell leaned back against the pillow and closed her eyes. "He—he was my cousin. I'm Eleanor Nettleton, Dylan Nettleton's mother," she said softly.

Annabel head jerked backward as though she'd been slapped in the face. She'd been expecting to hear that Nell was simply an old acquaintance of Schuman's, or perhaps that she'd once worked in the Nettleton household, but certainly not *this*. "You can't be!" she cried. "Dylan's mother is dead! He told me so himself, and so did Mr. Link. He—he said Oliver Nettleton got a letter years ago, telling him his daughter'd died of a drug overdose, that she'd been cremated and her ashes scattered at sea."

"I know," Nell said, wearily. "I wrote that letter."

"But I don't—"

"I'm Eleanor Nettleton—my friends always called me Nell. I'm Oliver's daughter," Nell said, "and I'm not dead, but I sure as hell spent a lot of years wishing I was. Didn't want to have to deal with my father, ever again. He'd always acted so damned disappointed in me, criticized everything I did, ever since I was a little girl, and I didn't want to have to explain to him how— But that's another story. Let's just say there were things I didn't want to explain to anybody, *especially* my father.

"Tried to kill myself a couple of times, but I wasn't even any good at that. So I did the next best thing—wrote Daddy a letter, pretended it was from a close friend, another hippie type he'd never want to know…and I told him I was dead. Figured that's what he'd expected would happen to me when I ran away from home, anyway. Far as he knew, I'd simply fulfilled the low expectations he had for me—I'd become a drugged-up hippie and burned out fast. Once Daddy thought I was dead and gone, I was pretty damned sure he'd never send anybody looking for me. Far as I know, he didn't even bother doing that when he thought I was still alive."

"But what about Dylan? If you're really Eleanor, how could you abandon your son, your own flesh and blood?" As a mother, Annabel couldn't imagine anyone doing such a thing. "Dylan believed you were dead, too, Nell. How…?"

Suddenly tears began to gush down Nell's face and she dissolved into choking sobs.

Her face registering confusion tinged with disgust, Annabel forced herself to pat the older woman's free hand as she waited for her crying jag to end. She wanted an answer to her question, for Nicky's sake if nothing else. Could this woman really be Nicky's grandmother? That would certainly explain why she'd risked her life to save him. Maybe she regretted dumping her son in foster care, letting him think she was dead, and later tried to make up for it by saving her grandson's life.

Eventually, Nell yanked her hand away and wiped at her eyes. "You're right," she admitted. "I did abandon my son…but not the way you think. I abandoned Dylan when he was four. He got the measles from one of the other kids at this commune where we lived down in Big Sur. I thought, no big deal, it's just measles, all kids get measles—or at least I told myself that close to thirty years ago. And I—I was smoking pot, dropping LSD, magic mushrooms…anything you can name. I was a self-indulgent little bitch at the time, to be honest, having myself a high old time. Having such a rollicking good time, I let my son die."

Annabel jerked out of her chair and stood over Nell. "*Die?* What do you mean, *die?* Dylan—"

"My son, Dylan Baez Nettleton, died when he was four years old," Nell said, her voice filled with anguish and self-loathing. "I buried him myself, me and my so-called friends, on the hill above our commune. Poor kid didn't even get a decent burial because those goddamned hippie friends of mine didn't want the cops to come sniffing around our pot farm. So we—we just dumped Dylan in a hole in the ground, like he was a dead dog or something." She dissolved into tears once more.

Annabel paced the room, her head reeling. Was Nell delusional? What she was saying was completely impossible, wasn't it? Dylan hadn't died at age four, he'd died at *thirty-four,* murdered by Peter Hoy and Gilbert Collier in that Seaside motel. Max had told her himself—the police found evidence in that motel room, evidence that cleared her of any suspicion in her husband's death. Hoy and Collier had killed Dylan there and then brought him back home, laid him out on the bed and stabbed him with Annabel's knife. If they'd been trying to get her attention, to issue some sort of bizarre threat that she shouldn't try to mess with them, they'd certainly accomplished their goal.

Nell blew her nose and got herself under control once more. "I know what you're thinking," she said, "that I'm nothing but a crazy old broad. It'd be easier for you if I were, but 'fraid not. Sit down and listen to me, Annabel. This is going to be difficult for you to hear, but you're going to have to."

Annabel obeyed, dropping back into the chair beside Nell's bed.

"Your husband was *not* my son, Dylan," Nell said firmly.

"My son has been dead since nineteen seventy-two. Your husband lied to you. He was not Dylan Nettleton, he was Roy Pickett."

"Roy Pickett?" Annabel had heard that name before. Of course! The fingerprints found on Dylan's computer. They'd matched a man named Roy Pickett. Pickett had been a partner-in-crime with Hoy and Collier, the guy who'd jumped bail while the others went to prison.

"Roy was one of the kids at the Big Sur commune," Nell said. "I remember him because he always was such a needy little boy. Always asking for hugs or hanging on somebody's leg. He wanted a daddy so bad it broke your heart. Used to go up to every man there, even if it was a transient who only stayed a couple of days. I can still see him, this look of desperate longing on his little face, asking some stoned, dirty old hippie, 'Are you my daddy?' His mother used to think it was cute…when she wasn't too high to notice what her kid was doing. Hell, half the time all of us were too high to know what any of our kids was doing." Her voice was filled with bitter self-loathing.

"I wasn't sure who this imposter—the guy who was claiming to be my son—was at first but, when I saw that photo in the newspaper after your husband was killed, the one that was supposed to be Dylan, I recognized the resemblance to little Roy Pickett right away."

"I—I need time to think this through," Annabel said, cradling her face in her hands. She felt like her world had been blown apart for the dozenth time in a week. Maybe Nell wasn't delusional after all, she began to think, as pieces of a terrible puzzle started to fall into place. Maybe Nell really *was* Eleanor Nettleton and, as she'd just said, it wasn't Eleanor who'd died all those years ago but her son, Dylan. Annabel had to admit it certainly was possible that, years later, when he'd jumped bail in Seattle, Roy Pickett stole Dylan's identity—literally *became* Dylan—because he'd remembered him as a child in Big Sur, a dead child who obviously wouldn't be using his own identity. Given the fingerprint match, maybe it was a lot more than just *possible*.

Annabel had read about fugitives from the law doing that sort of thing—finding a child who'd died before generating any public records, except for a birth certificate, then stealing that child's identity. Once you had a birth certificate, supposedly you could get a Social Security number, a driver's license, whatever you needed to "become" that person.

And, if what Nell was telling her was true, there wasn't even a death certificate on file anywhere for little Dylan Baez Nettleton. It would be a perfect setup for someone like Roy Pickett, someone who was trying to disappear.

Annabel stared at her lap, feeling uprooted and shaken to the core. If all this was true, she didn't even know what her own married name was! Or her son's legal name. Had she even been legitimately married? It seemed too much to take in all at once. "You say this all happened nearly thirty years ago, Nell. If—if that's true, I don't understand why you came here now, why you tracked us down." She looked up and saw that Nell's tired, lined face registered pain. Was it physical or emotional or both?

"I was watching TV back in Phoenix, where I've been living the last few years," Nell explained. "CNN, I think. A story about the disappearance of somebody named Dylan Nettleton came on. It claimed he was the long-lost heir to the Oliver Nettleton steel fortune, so I knew the name couldn't be just a weird coincidence. What would you do if you knew this so-called heir who'd supposedly disappeared was a fraud? And that Oliver Nettleton's real grandson, your only child, had been dead for close to three decades?"

"I—I guess I'd wonder what was going on."

"Damn right you would! I knew I wasn't crazy, Annabel—I certainly hadn't *imagined* my son's death, even if I did do a lot of drugs. I helped buried him, for God's sake. *I shoveled dirt on top of him.* So I had to find out what was going on, who was stirring up the life I thought I'd left behind, and—and I couldn't just call the cops, or my father, or—"

"Why on earth not? I mean, if what you're telling me is true, you must have thought my husband was trying to steal your rightful inheritance. Millions and millions of dollars were at stake."

"Jesus Christ! You still don't get it, do you? What I did was a *crime,* Annabel. I was such a lousy mother that I let my son die, and then I buried him. I didn't take him to a doctor when he was sick, and after he died, I didn't call the police, I didn't call the coroner, I did absolutely *nothing!* You can go to prison for that. And I sure as hell didn't want to go to prison. It took me all these years of trying to drug myself into forgetting what I'd done, two rotten marriages down the drain, suicide attempts, you name it. But I finally stopped using, and I stopped sleeping with anything in pants, and I actually had a job—a really crappy job, but it was honest work. And—and I guess—I guess I didn't want to risk losing what little I had, not after all this time."

"So you tried to find out for yourself what was going on."

Nell nodded. "I pretended to be a homeless woman—nobody even notices them nowadays. Hell, the homeless are part of the scenery to most people. Nobody even looks at them." She shook her head. "Guess I really *was* a homeless woman, basically. Certainly couldn't afford the motel rates around here. Anyway, I parked on the street, lived in my car, and watched your house. Figured you were in on the scam with your husband."

"I wasn't! Never!"

"Don't split a blood vessel! I know that now. I know you were a victim in this thing. Roy was, too, I guess, in an odd sort of way. He sure didn't want all that publicity, did he? I mean, all he really wanted from Dylan was a fake identity so he could hide from the cops."

"And from his partners, those guys who went to prison while he made off with all the money."

"Ironic, when you think about it, isn't it? It was greed that caused Roy to steal Dylan's identity in the first place. But the possibility that he could inherit millions more by being Dylan Nettleton ended up getting him killed." A strand of graying hair fell forward into her eyes and she tucked it back behind her ear.

Annabel couldn't help feeling sympathy for this woman who'd been so hard on herself for so long. No matter what she'd done years ago, she had saved Annabel's life, and Nicky's. That fact would never change. "How old were you when your son died?" she asked.

"Twenty-two," Nell answered. "Plenty old enough to know better."

"Look, Nell, you've punished yourself for thirty years over this. Don't you think that's long enough?"

"Maybe." She thought for a moment. "You know that thing you told me after the fire, that idea about God or whoever keeping a big ledger book, recording all our good deeds and all our bad deeds?"

Annabel wrinkled her brow. Had she said such a thing? "Maybe..." she admitted, trying to remember.

"Well, I was way, way in the hole before I came here. Now—now I think—I hope—maybe I'm a little better off."

"I should certainly think so. You saved at least three lives, Nell—mine, Nicky's, and Jason's—and you risked your own to do it, over and over again. You got shot. And you were injured in the fire, too, all trying to save other people. If God is keeping some kind of ledger, I'd say you've got to be looking pretty darned good right now."

Nell nodded. "I hope so," she agreed. "I'm no hero, you know. The truth is, I just couldn't do it again—stand there and let a little boy die while I did nothing, I mean. But that's probably not going to hold much water with the police."

"What have the police got to do with it?"

"Wake up, woman—haven't you been listening?" Nell shook her head. "I just told you I let my son *die*. I buried him without telling the authorities. I probably used every drug you ever heard of. I helped grow pot. Need I go on with my list of personal sins?"

Annabel reached for Nell's hand and squeezed it. "Listen to me, Nell. You've got to stop beating yourself up. I'll ask Max to be sure, but I bet there's a statute of limitations on all those things. I mean, we're not talking murder here, right?"

Nell shook her head. "Hell, no. At least I never murdered anybody."

"Then what are we talking? Maybe child neglect at the worst, illegal burial of a body, a bunch of old drug stuff from the sixties and seventies. I doubt the police are going to care about any of that anymore."

"Please don't tell Max what I said," Nell begged, stiffening noticeably and twisting in the bed. "Geez, this shoulder hurts!"

"Why not? I'll get Max to represent you. He can see to it that all this goes away, and then you won't have to worry about the police anymore."

Nell made a sour face. "You know Max can't represent me, Annabel."

"Why not? If you're worried about his fees, I'll—"

"It's not about money, silly, it's because he's representing *you*. Don't the words *conflict of interest* mean anything to you?"

"You and I don't have any conflict of interest, Nell. You mean about the inheritance? If Nicholas isn't really related to Oliver Nettleton, I'm certainly not going to try to pass him off as his grandson and heir. I don't care how many millions are involved. If you're Oliver's daughter, it's your money. Max can help you prove you're entitled to it. And, besides," she added, "he isn't representing me anymore."

"Why not?"

"First, because the police no longer suspect me of killing Dylan—I mean, my husband." She simply couldn't think of her husband as Roy Pickett—she'd never even heard of Roy Pickett until a few days ago. "And second, because Max fired me."

"Max *fired* you? Why in hell would he do that?"

Annabel blushed. "Because he says it's unethical for an attorney to date one of his clients."

Nell raised an eyebrow. "You don't say!" She broke into a grin, but it quickly turned into a grimace of pain. "Think I could use that morphine now," she said.

Annabel pushed the bell to summon the nurse, who promptly gave Nell an injection.

"Hey, this is good stuff," Nell said, as she leaned back against her pillow a few minutes later and began to drift off. "If I didn't know better, I might think I was right back in the seventies."

"WHAT'S COOKING?" Max said, creeping up behind Annabel as she stood over his kitchen stove and circling his arms around her waist. "Smells great." Although she and Nicky were now living in a new vacation rental house—she hadn't been able to make herself move back into the one where she'd found her husband's body—they were spending the evening at Max's place, and she'd promised to cook dinner for everyone.

She twisted around to face Max and kissed him lightly on the lips. "Real gourmet stuff," she told him, "genuine Spaghetti-O's for Katie and Nicky." The children were playing together in Katie's bedroom, sharing the new picture book about an orphaned baby otter's life that Annabel had bought for Max's daughter.

"What, the adults don't get to eat tonight?"

"Later," she said with a smile. "I know it'll be a major sacrifice to pass up the Spaghetti-O's, but I've got some local salmon for the grill, a fresh green salad, and a wild rice casserole in the oven. Just thought we'd let the kids have their supper and get settled in for the night first. You and I can have a glass of wine while they're eating."

"Sounds good. And, if we can get them both to go to sleep at a reasonable hour, I can think of something I'd really love for dessert," Max said, sliding his hand downward from Annabel's waist and cupping her fanny.

"Can't imagine what you've got in mind, counselor," she said, giving him her best imitation of a leer.

"Bet you can manage to figure it out."

She gave him another quick peck on the lips. "Call the kids, will you? I'll dish up their supper."

After everyone had eaten and the children were asleep, Katie in her own room and Nicky in a portable crib in the guest bedroom, Annabel and Max relaxed in the living room, sharing a glass of port before they washed the dishes. "Find out anymore about what's happening with those foreign accounts?" she asked him. It had been nearly a month since the shootout at the motel. Although the police had catalogued the diskette and printout found in Gil Collier's pocket after his arrest, they'd had no idea it represented millions in stolen money until Max and Annabel told them.

"The Seattle cops say they're working out some sort of deal with the FBI," Max reported.

"So the people who got cheated will get their money back?"

"That's the goal, and it probably will happen eventually, but it's going to take months, at least, to figure out who all the victims are and to locate them. It's possible some of them never filed police complaints and others may have died or moved away. There probably will be dozens of complications, and there won't be any pay-outs until the FBI guys are sure they've got a complete list of everyone who lost money in the scam."

"But they are going to try?" The subject had been weighing heavily on Annabel's mind.

Max nodded. "I talked with a friend of mine who writes for the *San Francisco Chronicle* and he's eager to do a story on this. It's the kind of thing that's perfect for the wire services—millions of dollars in Internet fraud proceeds recovered, victims to be repaid in full, that sort of thing. Should get national attention. Soon as it does, I guarantee we'll have claimants crawling out of the woodwork. Then the big problem will be sorting out the real victims from the phonies."

"I really appreciate your help on this, Max," Annabel said, setting down her glass on the coffee table and snuggling up next to him on the sofa. There was something about this man that made her feel safe whenever she was around him, something manly and protective, but her attraction to him was even more than that. She felt a strong sense of security in knowing she'd never have to doubt Max's honesty or wonder if he really was who he claimed to be. Max Garrity was the polar opposite of Annabel's late husband.

"Hey, no problem," Max said, giving her a squeeze. "I'm as glad to see those people get their money back as you are."

"For me, it's a lot more than doing a good deed, though," she said. "It—it's bad enough that someday Nicky's going to know his father was a con man and a thief." The coroner finally had run the fingerprints taken from her husband's corpse through the system. When they matched those of fugitive Roy Pickett, her last doubt was erased and she'd had to accept the truth, as much as it tore her apart and made her doubt her basic instincts about people. "I just want to be able to tell my son we did the right thing and gave back every penny his father stole."

"It's going to be okay, Annabel," Max said, tilting her chin upward and kissing her lips gently, "really it is. Besides, by the time Nicky's old enough to understand, if I have my way, he's going to have a new dad to help take care of him. You know I'll be the happiest man in the world the day you marry me and let me adopt Nicholas as my son."

Annabel's brow furrowed as she fought against an impulse to shout, Yes, yes, yes, I'll marry you! Instead, she told him, "I still need time, Max. I made a terrible mistake once because I didn't think things through well enough. This whole thing has made me wonder if I'll ever be able to trust my impulses again. If—when—I ever get married a second time, I'm going to have to be a thousand percent sure it's right."

"I understand. You can have all the time you need—I'm not going anywhere. Just remember, I'm not Roy or Dylan or your parents or anybody else who's ever disappointed you. I'm just plain, old, boringly faithful Max, the guy who loves Annabel with all his heart."

"You're anything but plain or old or boring," Annabel said, her chin beginning to quiver. What had she done to deserve a man like Max, to make him actually love her? She blinked back tears of joy, then changed the subject before she gave in to an impulse she feared she might regret tomorrow.

"I got a call from Nell today," she said. "She told me the DNA test you ordered came back, that it proves her identity conclusively." A tissue sample had been taken from Oliver Nettleton's corpse for comparison to Nell's and sent off to a DNA lab. "Sounds like she's in line for that inheritance."

Max grinned broadly. "I'm delighted Nell told you herself," he said. "As her attorney, you know I can't talk about a client's case…much as I might like to share her fantastic news."

"She told me that, if she does get her father's millions, she plans to open a residential drug treatment center for street kids."

Max nodded.

"She also told me a few other things," Annabel said, suddenly feeling sad.

Sensing her shift in mood, Max stroked her hand. "What's that?"

"We talked a little about—about Nicky's father—" Annabel still had trouble calling her husband Roy instead of Dylan, so most of the time she simply referred to him as Nicky's father. "Nell says she remembers that his mother was a real tramp, a woman who had no idea who her son's father was and didn't much care. She used to be high most of the time, and she'd bring home guys and have sex with them right in the same room where her son was sleeping. The woman OD'd a year or so after Nell's boy died. After that, Nicky's daddy— Roy—ended up in foster care, and that's the last time Nell heard anything about him until she came to Carmel. At least one thing he told me was actually true—his mother did die of an overdose and he lived most of his boyhood in foster care."

"I know," Max said, squeezing Annabel's hand. "I've been doing some research of my own, just in case you felt you needed to know more about him."

"Well, don't keep me in suspense."

"Sure you can handle this?"

"Absolutely. He's my son's father. I have to know everything."

"Okay. Here's what I found out. Roy Pickett lived here in California until he went to college up at the University of Washington—got himself a full scholarship. That's where he met the Collier brothers and Hoy and they hatched their computer fraud plan. But before that, from the time his mother died until he was eighteen, Roy lived in thirty-three different foster homes."

*"Thirty-three?"* Annabel gasped. "How could that be? I thought maybe four or five…"

Max sighed. "Wish I could say his situation was unique, but I'm afraid it's not. Some foster homes are abusive and the kids get yanked out. Others decide they can't handle a foster child after all, or they don't like the one they've been given, and they send him back to Social Services. Foster parents can get sick, or decide their biological kids need more care. Or the money dries up. There are a million reasons kids in foster care get shifted around from home to home. But the bottom line is—"

"That poor Roy probably was lucky he even *survived* that kind of life, never mind ended up smart and motivated enough to get into college on a scholarship."

"Roy was undoubtedly intellectually brilliant," Max said. "He had no lack of brains. What he lacked was a strong moral center and, knowing the way he was brought up, it's not hard to see why."

Annabel twisted a strand of hair and sighed. "His son is going grow up with a strong moral center," she promised, "if it's the last thing I do."

"With you as his mother, he can't miss," Max said, pulling her closer to him and kissing the top of her head. "I'd bet my life on that."

Annabel gazed up at Max, saw the raw longing in his eyes, and felt herself melt. Could she really ask for a better father for her son, or a better husband for herself? She didn't think so, yet she knew she had to give herself time to be absolutely certain before risking another lifetime commitment. And in her soul, she really believed Max would still be there, that he would keep his promise to wait until she was a thousand percent sure.

Her lips found his mouth and kissed him deeply. "The dishes can wait," she whispered when they came up for air. "Before one of the kids wakes up, let's go get some of that dessert."

# HARLEQUIN®
# INTRIGUE®

## WE'LL LEAVE YOU BREATHLESS!

If you've been looking for thrilling tales of
contemporary passion and sensuous love stories
with taut, edge-of-the-seat suspense—then
you'll love Harlequin Intrigue!

Every month, you'll meet six new heroes
who are guaranteed to make your spine tingle
and your pulse pound. With them you'll enter
into the exciting world of Harlequin Intrigue—
where your life is on the line
and so is your heart!

## THAT'S INTRIGUE—
## ROMANTIC SUSPENSE
## AT ITS BEST!

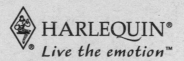

HARLEQUIN®
*Live the emotion*™

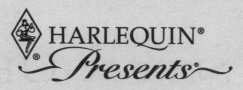

# HARLEQUIN®
## *Presents*

**The world's bestselling romance series...**
**The series that brings you your favorite authors,**
**month after month:**

Helen Bianchin...Emma Darcy
Lynne Graham...Penny Jordan
Miranda Lee...Sandra Marton
Anne Mather...Carole Mortimer
Susan Napier...Michelle Reid

**and many more uniquely talented authors!**

Wealthy, powerful, gorgeous men...
Women who have feelings just like your own...
The stories you love, set in exotic, glamorous locations...

**Seduction and Passion Guaranteed!**

HPDIR104

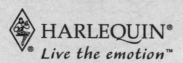

## Harlequin Historicals®
### Historical Romantic Adventure!

*From rugged lawmen and
valiant knights to defiant heiresses
and spirited frontierswomen,
Harlequin Historicals will
capture your imagination with
their dramatic scope, passion
and adventure.*

*Harlequin Historicals . . .
they're too good to miss!*

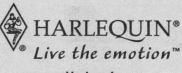

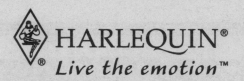
HARLEQUIN®
*Live the emotion*™

Upbeat,
All-American Romances

flipside
Romantic Comedy

Harlequin Historicals®
Historical,
Romantic Adventure

INTRIGUE
Romantic Suspense

HARLEQUIN ROMANCE®
The essence of
modern romance

HARLEQUIN®
*Presents*
Seduction and passion
guaranteed

HARLEQUIN *Super* ROMANCE®
Emotional,
Exciting, Unexpected

*Temptation*
Sassy, Sexy, Seductive!